# Cavalier Queen

## FIONA MOUNTAIN

preface

Published by Preface 2011

10 9 8 7 6 5 4 3 2 1

First published in Great Britain in 2011 by Preface Publishing

20 Vauxhall Bridge Road
London, SW1V 2SA

An imprint of The Random House Group Limited

www.randomhouse.co.uk
www.prefacepublishing.co.uk

Addresses for companies within The Random House Group Limited
can be found at www.randomhouse.co.uk

The Random House Group Limited Reg. No. 954009

A CIP catalogue record for this book is available from the British Library

ISBN 978 1 84809 167 2

The Random House Group Limited supports the Forest Stewardship Council® (FSC®), the leading international forest certification organisation. All our titles that are printed on Greenpeace approved FSC® certified paper carry the FSC® logo. Our paper procurement policy can be found at www.randomhouse.co.uk/environment

Typeset in Fournier MT by Palimpsest Book Production Limited, Falkirk, Stirlingshire

Printed and bound in Great Britain by Clays Ltd, St Ives plc

# CAVALIER QUEEN

Fiona Mou  was a press officer at BBC Radio 1 for ten years and is the aut  our novels. She lives in the Cotswolds with her family.

Also by Fiona Mountain

*Isabella*
*Pale as the Dead*
*Bloodline*
*Lady of the Butterflies / Rebel Heiress*

Paul,

This is for you

x F

*'Jermyn, in whom united doth remain*
*All that kind mothers' wishes can contain*
*In whom wit, judgement, valour, goodness join*
*All these through a comely body shine*
*A soul composed of the eagle and the dove*
*Which all men must admire and all men love'* —

'The Civil War', Abraham Cowley (1618–67)

# Part 1

# *1660*

Henrietta was not ready to die. But she had lived with the threat of death often enough to have thought much about it, and she knew exactly what she wanted inscribed upon her tombstone.

*Here lies Henrietta Maria de Bourbon. Daughter of France. Queen of England. Widow of the martyred King Charles I of England and Scotland. Mother of the restored King Charles II.*

That was the sum of her life. Who she was. All that she was.

Rather . . . it was how she wished to be remembered.

But would it be?

A hundred years from now, two hundred, three hundred . . . what would the history books say about her then? Would it all be forgotten, this gossip-mongering and speculation that had gone on now for nearly half a century? Or was it repeated so loudly and so often, even now, that it had already become accepted fact?

That she was Harry Jermyn's whore and her sons his bastards – not princes at all. That theirs was a shameful attachment that had led to the downfall of the English monarchy and the death of the King of England. That his blood was on their hands.

People like to gossip, they love a scandal. More than that, it seemed to Henrietta, they always need someone to hate. For a long time, for the people of England, that someone had been her, and still she didn't understand why.

And so she wondered . . . when she and those she had known and loved were all dead and buried, would anyone honestly believe those rumours, even if they were written down and recorded somewhere? Did people truly believe them now?

Should they believe?

# 1624

Princess Henrietta Maria gave an impatient and dramatic little sigh as she stared out of one of the windows of the Palais du Louvre for what felt to her like the hundredth time that morning. It was still the same familiar view: the moat and the palace guards and the pointed slate-roofed towers and pavilions.

Oh, how much longer until the Englishmen arrived? She had been waiting for hours. Well, one hour at least. Henrietta hated waiting. It felt more like ten hours to her. She had been counting down the minutes.

Abruptly turning her back on the offending window since it did not offer the sight she wanted, and making sure her spaniel pup was paying proper attention, she threw the ball down the long gallery again, ignoring the scornful gazes of the dead Kings and Queens of France who watched from the gilt-framed portraits lining the long panelled walls of the gallery which linked the Louvre to the Palais des Tuileries.

'Well, go on, Mitte,' she commanded. 'Fetch it.'

The dog just sat there, looking up at her mistress with eyes every bit as black and doleful as those of Henritta's royal ancestors, as if the girl were not to be taken at all seriously. The sides of Mitte's brown-and-white furry body pumped in an out like a bellows and her pink tongue was lolling, despite the fact that the thick stone of the walls behind the wainscoting and the Palace's proximity to the Seine made it so icy cold in the gallery that the leaded glass in the windows was frosted on the inside as well as out. Mitte was weary of this game now and she was not the only one.

Henrietta scooped the dog into her arms, passionately kissing the furrowed, velvety head. Mitte was not yet fully grown but her claws were sharp and they dug into the pale silk sleeve of Henrietta's gown as she received an equally exuberant lick on her cheek.

Henrietta giggled and wiped her wet face with her palm. 'I suppose I'll have to get it then, won't I?'

As she picked up the half-chewed ball she glanced again towards the window and what she saw now made her heart thump with excitement against the tight bones of her corset. Excitement . . . and more than a little trepidation. They were here! At last! The ambassador and his gentlemen attendants from England. Quickly setting the dog down, Henrietta ran across to the glass, bouncing up on tiptoes the better to see.

The view was often obscured by the swirling mists that rose from the River Seine, but not today. Today she could see very clearly the bright cavalcade of horses drawing the crested coach as it passed beneath the tall avenue of cypress trees and came clattering towards the frosty drawbridge. The Swiss Guards in their white-feathered hats snapped to attention and there was a fanfare of trumpets. But the importance of these foreign visitors needed no proclaiming, at least not to Henrietta. She knew very well who these gentlemen were, and why they had come with their instructions all the way from London. The ambassador's name was Henry Rich, Lord Kensington, and the purpose of his semi-informal visit was to discuss Henrietta's betrothal, to the English Prince of Wales.

Henrietta was fourteen years old now, a child no longer, but a woman of marriageable age, and she had been preparing for this day since she was born. She had been raised with the single purpose of becoming consort to a king. To be a queen, according to her mother, who had been Queen of France, was for a girl like Henrietta the summit of all earthly ambition.

She was the youngest of three princesses. Her eldest sister, Elizabeth, had been wedded to King Philip of Spain at the age of thirteen, and it had been the plan for the girls' other sister, Christine, to marry King James of England's firstborn son, Henry, who was said to have been extremely handsome and athletic. But, tragically, the prince had died of typhoid when he was sixteen. So Christine was married to the Prince of Piedmont instead and had gone off to live with him in Turin.

Now it was Henrietta's turn.

She had always known, of course, that as a princess of France, her betrothal, when it was arranged, would be of far greater importance than just the union of two people under God. Her marriage would mark the strategic military alliance between two nations; it would be used for the advancement and protection of France against the power of its long-time enemies, the Spaniards, and for the benefit of the Catholic faith. Which was all very well . . . just so long as the Prince of Wales was as handsome as his brother had supposedly been. Henrietta hugged Mitte tighter, lifted the little dog up close to her face and pressed her cheek against the soft head as she whispered fervently into one floppy ear, 'Let him be handsome.'

The prince's name was Charles and one day, when his father King James died, he would be crowned King Charles I of England, Scotland and Ireland. This much at least she did know. He was reputed to be one of the finest princes in all of Europe and was said to be deeply religious and scrupulous in his daily prayers, which was of course imperative. But even if he were not so fine and good, it was Henrietta's duty to love whomsoever was chosen to be her husband. And if that were to be Prince Charles, then it was Prince Charles whom she would love. But, oh, she so wanted to know what he looked like.

She had in fact glimpsed him once, about a year ago, from a distance, but she had had no idea who he was at the time and so had taken absolutely no notice. Unbeknown to her, he had watched her dance. He and his companion, the Duke of Buckingham, had arrived in Paris in disguise, wearing bushy wigs and going by the names of John and Tom Smith. But they hadn't been very interested in Henrietta either then. They were on their way to Madrid, on a dashingly daring adventure to win the hand of the Spanish Infanta for Charles. They had simply stopped off at the Louvre en route, where they had been admitted to the vast, dimly lit hall to join the spectators at the rehearsal for a masque. Next morning they had been recognised by a maid who had once been a linen-seller in London and the news of their secret arrival soon spread around the entire court.

Henrietta had been captivated by the drama and the romance of the story, which had appealed to her vivid imagination, fed as it had been since infancy on the troubadour poems and tales of chivalry that had inspired the whole idea of courtly love still very popular in the French court. She had chattered excitedly about Prince Charles with her brother's wife, Queen Anne, sister to the Spanish Infanta whom the Prince of England had been so determined to marry. Henrietta had laughed to hear of it, saying what a pity it was that he had gone so far as Spain to seek a wife when he might have found one much nearer.

Now he was doing just that. The trip to Madrid had proved fruitless and negotiations with the Spanish had broken down for religious reasons, the Catholic Spanish king declaring he would rather send his daughter to a nunnery than let her marry an infidel, a Protestant heretic. Henrietta's family had no such objections, so long as her marriage might be advantageous to Catholics. So when Charles had failed to find his queen in Spain, he had turned instead to France. And Henrietta.

These past few days she had done little else but think about him and daydream about him and try to imagine what he might be like. Her tutor, Monsieur de Brevis, had once made her trace in her copybook a Latin text composed by her brother Louis, listing the virtues of various kings, namely truthfulness, courage, temperance and grace. Henrietta prayed that the would-be king she was to marry would be blessed with all these qualities and more. That he would be everything that a future king should be. Tall and strong and brave, obviously. With a happy, smiling disposition and a good sense of humour, since Henrietta was inclined to gaiety herself. Her brother Gaston, Duc d'Orléans, swore she had laughed up at him from her cradle on the very day she was born. She liked people who laughed a lot, and who made her laugh back. She wanted to marry a merry man just like her father, King Henri IV, had been. She wanted to marry a good, wise man, who would make a good and wise king, respected and beloved by all his subjects. A man to whom she could devote her whole life and whole heart, as any wife should.

She hoped also, if it were not too much to ask, that he might share her passion for music and theatre.

As soon as she could walk, Henrietta had eagerly joined in the little ballets and comedies that were staged by the troupe of her father's legitimate and illegitimate children, who all grew up together at the Château of St Germain-en-Laye, a few miles from the centre of Paris.

She had always loved to dress up, to sing and to dance. More than anything in the world she loved the great court masques – the music and the poetry, the drama and the make-believe of them. And their fantastical settings. Like seascapes and pyramids and gilded chariots drawn by enormous swans, carrying children dressed as gods of love; or angels and demons with burning sceptres who duelled while lightning flashed around them in the pretend sky. The guards always had to hold back the crowds who besieged every doorway for a glimpse of the theatricals; still more watched from tiered scaffolding stands around the walls. Henrietta enjoyed every second of every minute, even the long hours of rehearsing and costume fittings. They must have such masques and theatricals at the English court surely? And dancing? Life in England could not be so very different from life in Paris.

Henrietta remembered how her sister Elizabeth had sobbed and clung to her mother and the other little princesses when the time came for her to kiss them all goodbye before she left for Spain. She still wrote such sorrowful letters home, describing how she cried nearly every day because her husband was short and fat and kept leaving her on her own. It would be even harder for Henrietta. She would be exiled to England, which her godfather Pope Urban had said was as good as delivering her to hell and the devil, it being full of heretics who despised and persecuted all followers of Rome.

Henrietta touched the smooth rosary beads at her waist and fought down her fear. Never in her life had she sought to avoid a thing because she was frightened, and she was not about to begin now. She was, after all, a Bourbon, with the blood of the powerful Medicis running through her veins also. She was Henrietta Maria, named for both her parents. King Henri IV of France, who had earned the title of Henri le Grand – Henry the Great – because of the immense courage he had displayed in military engagements, and Marie de' Medici, who was known throughout the whole of Europe to be utterly indomitable. Henrietta was regularly accused of taking after her mother in that, which Marie told her she should regard as a compliment since obstinacy, or determination as Marie preferred to term it, would serve her well in life.

Besides which, Henrietta could not really believe that bad things would ever happen to her. She had spent her childhood in enchanted surroundings: gilded palaces filled with the finest Italian art, and ornamental gardens fragrant with lemon trees, lilies and roses. She wore bejewelled silks and danced in cloth of silver. As Madame of France, the senior remaining royal daughter, she had her own grand suite of rooms in the Louvre and even her own small throne. She slept in a state bed hung with silks and velvets and embroidered in gold thread; she travelled in velvet-upholstered coaches, was serenaded by orchestras of violas and flutes; ate feasts which ended with desserts of spun sugar and candied almonds. She had never known any different sort of life and so could not imagine herself in any different setting.

She curled her fingers around the cool smoothness of the small ivory crucifix hanging from the rosary. In any case, God would grant her the strength and courage she needed to face whatever trials life might have in store for her. Her future was in His hands. Or rather in the hands of her mother. In truth, it was Marie de' Medici rather than King Louis XIII, Henrietta's brother, who had extended this invitation to the English Ambassador.

Whose coach was even now rattling into the courtyard!

There were so many questions Henrietta was burning to ask, about the man who would be her husband and the country that would be her home.

She quickly set Mitte down and, lifting her skirts, turned and ran the length of the gallery. Mitte's paws skittered as she chased behind, and the tap-tap of Henrietta's silk-slippered footsteps echoed on the polished wooden floor. At the foot of the wide, curved marble staircase, she nearly crashed headlong into Mamie St George. Mamie's mother was Madame Montglat, or Mamangat as Henrietta and her brothers and sisters affection-ately called their governess. Mamie was not really called Mamie either. Her real name was Jeanne, but the children all called her *Mon Amie*, or Mamie for short. Mamie had been Henrietta's nurse since she was a baby and was now her maid-of-honour.

Of a similar age to Henrietta's eldest sister, Mamie was Henrietta's most favoured companion besides her brother Gaston, even if she did take liber-ties sometimes. She was overly fond of ordering people about as if she were a governess, just like her mother, but she was always serene and elegant with sharp features and sharper eyes. Now they came to rest disap-provingly on the ball in Henrietta's hand. Balls were not allowed inside, nor running for that matter, for dogs or for princesses.

'I was just coming to find you, Madame,' Mamie said. 'You are wanted immediately by the queen your mother.'

'To greet the gentlemen from England?'

Mamie smiled. She knew how desperately Henrietta had been longing for them to arrive. 'They have gone directly to the apartments of the Duc de Chevreuse, who is a friend of the ambassador's apparently. Your mother and Queen Anne are waiting for you in the Grand Salle, so that they may escort you there.'

'Now?'

'Yes, now.' Mamie picked up Mitte to stop her from trying to follow Henrietta, as the pup was wont to do. 'Well?' she asked, shooing Henrietta. 'What are you waiting for? It's not like you willingly to wait for anything.'

This was quite true. Henrietta had a reputation for doing everything, from talking to walking, in a tearing hurry. But now she hesitated. 'How do I look?'

'Like a princess.'

'There are some ugly princesses,' Henrietta pointed out.

'Well, you are a very pretty one.'

'Thank you, Mamie.' But Henrietta still looked doubtful. She was accustomed to flattery and never tired of it, vanity being another sin of which she was sometimes accused – unfairly she felt. It was true that she had a great liking for pretty dresses, but so did any girl her age unless she was very strange! Henrietta didn't have a vast number of dresses to choose from, considering that she was a princess, and secretly preferred plainer styles to the gem encrusted silks and brocades that both her mother and her brother's wife Queen Anne tended to favour. In anticipation of the ambassador's arrival today, she had on her absolute favourite. It was of white silk with a tight bodice closed in front with bows of cherry-pink satin ribbon and finished at the waist with large richly embroidered tabs. The sleeves were full, with flounces of lace ruffles at the elbows. She wore a string of pearls around her neck, and a cherry-coloured ribbon twisted with more pearls in her hair.

She knew the dress was very flattering and on good days was more than ready to believe people when they told her that she was exceptionally pretty. But that did not mean she did not sometimes suffer from the crushing insecurities typical of most young girls. Now not even Mamie's reassurance was quite enough.

There was a large gilded looking-glass hanging on the wall nearby and Henrietta went over to it, trying to see herself through strangers' eyes – strangers who had come here expressly to judge if she was fit to be their future queen. She had scrutinised her reflection often enough recently to nurse some hopes that Lord Kensington, in his report back to the prince and the king in England, might describe her as pleasing.

In fact, she was more than that. Her complexion was pale and clear, delicately flushed now with excitement, and in her small face her eyes appeared very large and very dark. The Comte de Soissons, who had professed undying love for her for at least six months, had told her they were black as ebony but sparkled as bright as stars, and she was willing to take his word for it. Her hair was long and thick and black too, and she wore it curled in to intricate ringlets around her temples and cheeks, with a single lock left to tumble beguilingly over her left shoulder, in the fashion that was currently very popular in Paris.

Henrietta was eternally thankful that she did not have what in her family was called the 'Austrian lip', the slightly protruding jaw which her brother Louis had had the misfortune to inherit from their mother. She did think her own mouth a little too wide, though the beautiful Duchesse de Chevreuse had assured her, with a saucy smile on her perfectly painted face, that most gentlemen would see that as an asset. Henrietta had not understood why this caused some of the ladies to titter behind their hands but she guessed it had something to do with what went on between men and women in their bedchambers, since that was the glamorous Duchesse's favourite topic of conversation, as indeed it was the whole court's.

Nobody, though, would ever convince Henrietta that any man would think it a good thing she was so small. At less than five foot tall, she was doll-like and appeared as delicate as china. She looked much younger than her fourteen years, more child than woman still. There were, in fact, little girls of no more than ten years who were considerably larger than she. Henrietta wished every day that she were taller. But she could be very pragmatic when she needed to be, deciding now that since she could not suddenly grow five inches or gain five and twenty pounds, there was no use worrying over it.

She spun back to face Mamie, making her skirts twirl. 'Wish me luck then.'

Mamie gave the princess a quick tight hug. '*Bonne chance*, Madame. They will all love you, I know it.'

'Mamie, I do hope you're right. For all our sakes.'

\* \* \*

11

As her portraits clearly showed, Marie de' Medici, Henrietta's mother, had been a strikingly attractive girl with bright gold hair, a perfect oval face, flawless skin and heavy-lidded almond eyes. But she had grown exceedingly plump since the death of her husband King Henri, when Henrietta was just a baby, and now Marie had at least three chins. She dressed always in black with a great veil of crêpe and around her neck a huge cross, encrusted with diamonds. Queen Anne was wearing a gown of dark green satin embroidered with silver and gold and studded with gemstones and diamond buttons, looking every inch the Queen of France. She was Spanish, fair and curvaceous, and was said to have the whitest, most beautiful hands in all of Europe.

Henrietta felt rather insignificant as she left the grandeur of the Grand Salle to follow in the wake of these two supremely majestic queens, with a train of ladies to accompany them. The tall double doors of the Duc de Chevreuse's apartments were flung open and, regally, they all swept through.

The ambassador's visit was unofficial and exploratory, which was why he was not being received in full state. But this informal reception was more than usually informal. The Duc and Duchesse de Chevreuse were in the process of dressing for the masquerade that was to be performed after supper so their salon was in disarray, with leather masks and high-heeled dancing slippers and feathered plumes scattered here, there and everywhere. Elaborate costumes were draped over oak coffers and chairs and tables, colourful as the fine tapestries which hung upon the walls.

Lord Kensington and his attendants were equally gorgeously attired, in bright silk slashed doublets, with capes swinging from their shoulders. They were all standing around, talking and laughing loudly, faces still flushed from the cold February air outside, or else from the heat of the sweet-scented juniper logs blazing in the hearth and the plentiful cups of warm Hippocras wine they had been served. English footmen in tan livery, pages and valets, musicians and costumiers, were milling around them and there was a general air of anticipation.

But a hush descended as the royal party entered and the English gentlemen turned and bowed low with a sweep of their plumed hats. They looked not to the two queens but the little princess, since she was the sole reason they were here at all. Realising this, Henrietta's cheeks flushed far pinker than theirs beneath the appraising gazes. She was struck with a desperate urge to run away and hide, except that there was nowhere to go.

She so wanted to make a good impression, not to let her mother and brother down, but any confidence she'd previously felt utterly deserted her now, leaving her feeling acutely self-conscious and exposed, as if every facet of her character were on display along with her pretty face. There flashed through her mind all the taunts and teasing she had endured from her brothers and sisters over the years, as well as all the loving but some-times exasperated criticisms and complaints of her governesses, tutors and confessors. Of which there were several.

Besides, having no natural patience, Henrietta suffered from a quick temper. Since she was a baby she had liked having her own way. She was also frequently criticised for being giddy.

But she had many admirable qualities, including a wit that was just as quick as her temper, and impeccable manners. Sister Madeleine, the Carmelite nun who was in charge of her religious instruction, commended her for having the kindest, warmest heart. In addition to that she sang and danced exceptionally well. Not that she could demonstrate that right now, much as she liked to sing and dance at every suitable opportunity.

Lord Kensington stepped forward and bowed low. He had shoulder-length brown hair that was very tightly curled, a pointed chin emphasised by a pointed beard, and the most neat and elegantly arched eyebrows Henrietta had ever seen on a man. 'I am charmed to meet Your Majesties,' he said to the two queens in smooth and very precise French. 'And the little Madame,' he added, addressing Henrietta.

Her cheeks burned hotter still. She wished she had some command of English so that she could welcome him with a word of it but, being a poor linguist, she did not, so quietly bade him good day in her own tongue.

There followed the expected polite exchange, in French again, about their crossing, which had been rough apparently. As Henrietta had never been on board a sailing ship or even so much as seen the sea, she was unable to contribute. Lord Kensington then informed her mother that he had brought a miniature portrait of the Prince of Wales with him.

'Oh, how thrilling!' Anne exclaimed. 'Where is it?'

'Right here.' He patted his upper chest. 'I am wearing it around my neck.'

'Do please show it to us right away, sir,' the Duchesse de Chevreuse urged, giving Lord Kensington her most captivating smile.

Henrietta's heart was beating frantically, but entirely pointlessly, since she knew that etiquette forbade her from being shown the prince's likeness until he had formally requested her hand. She didn't even bother to ask if she might see it too, but when the Duc and Duchesse, her mother and Anne and the ladies all hurried off with the ambassador to the closet, laughing and chattering away, leaving Henrietta behind. Her patience was tested almost beyond endurance. She felt so consumed with curiosity she feared she might burst.

She also felt a little lost, stranded amongst all these unfamiliar foreign faces. But since she was their hostess and they were here to appraise her, she knew that she must try to make polite conversation. She turned to the portly, greying English envoy who stood nearest to her, rocking back slightly on his heels with his hands linked behind his back. 'How do you find Paris, sir?' she asked him shyly, but keen to know. 'Is it very like London?'

The only answer Henrietta received was a blank smile. '*Pardon*, Madame?' He spoke in such an appallingly bad accent that it was evident he could understand about as much French as Henrietta could English. Which was to say, barely a word. At a loss, she turned to another gentleman, who appeared equally uncomprehending.

'I think there can be nowhere in the world so magnificent as Paris.'

The words were spoken in a deep, velvety voice, and had come from the far side of the room. Henrietta saw that it was one of the ambassador's young gentlemen attendants who had spoken, though in French so perfect that he might have been born here at the Louvre. Relief flooded through her and she felt almost ridiculously grateful. She smiled at him and he smiled back, the most warm and friendly smile.

She was thrown into utter confusion.

It was if her eyes were playing tricks on her, or else she was caught up in a wonderful dream. The Prince of Wales was supposed to be hundreds of miles away, across the sea, in England. Only his portrait had been brought here to France. This gentleman was not he. He was not dressed in princely robes, nor had he courtiers hovering around to attend to his every whim. Nobody had bowed to him, or announced his presence. And yet . . . despite all that, he so closely resembled the image of a tall, elegant, golden prince that Henrietta had come to nurture and cherish in her heart, that for one disorienting moment she was certain that the English were playing some great and clever trick upon them all and the prince himself had returned, incognito, to win *her* hand this time, just as he had once journeyed in disguise to Spain in search of a bride.

Henrietta felt such a rush of happiness, such a powerful sense of connection, that she had mentally to pinch herself, hard and sharp, to remind herself that this could not be the man she was destined to love, and with whom she was to share the rest of her life. That he was but a lowly ambassador's attendant.

Even so, how had she not noticed him before . . . the instant she had come into the apartment, in fact? He was stylishly but unostentatiously dressed in black silk, his doublet slashed at the sleeves to reveal the creamy satin shirt underneath. There were high white buckskin boots setting off his long legs. But what made him so striking was that he was very tall, easily over six foot, and broad with it, with shoulders like a Trojan hero. Despite his imposing stature, however and the mature timbre of his voice, he was clearly no more than a few years older than Henrietta herself; could not yet be twenty. He had a fresh face and bright blue eyes. His hair, worn much longer than the ambassador's, was golden-brown flecked with red and copper, loosely curling and thick. He had a strong, square jaw with a dimple right in the middle of his chin, partially concealed by a short beard.

He walked over to Henrietta with all the easy grace and bearing of a prince, and yet with a deference and humility that was the opposite of regal conceit, so that she understood immediately how it was he had escaped her earlier observation. He was the perfect servant, with an uncanny ability to blend into the background, remaining out of sight until the instant his services were required.

Close to, he seemed taller still, towering above her so that she had to lift her face to look at him. He in turn looked down, silently, into her eyes. It was almost as if he were feeling as shy and disoriented and confused as she.

Here was the perfect opportunity to ask all those questions she had been so keen to pose. Only now, for some strange reason, her mind had gone completely blank and she couldn't recall a single one. Similarly, he was behaving as if he'd suddenly lost his tongue.

'It is my first time in your country, Madame,' he said eventually. 'I sincerely hope it is not the last.'

He had such a deep melodious voice that it was as if she were listening to her language being spoken for the first time. She had never realised it could sound so beautiful. 'You speak such excellent French, sir,' she told him quietly. 'I assumed you must have been here many times.'

'It is very kind of you to say so.' He seemed delighted by her compliment. 'I am told I had a talent for languages from a very young age. I could count up to ten in French almost before I could do it in English. It is what secured me my position here at the embassy.'

How could she resist such an opening? 'What?' she asked, quick as a spark. 'Being able to count to ten?'

He laughed the merriest laugh. It was very infectious and Henrietta giggled up at him, liking the fact that she had amused him so much. She glanced round at their straight-faced companions. None of them had been able to understand the joke; indeed had no notion of what the pair of them were talking about. It made it feel almost as if they were alone. 'Who are you, by the way?' Henrietta asked. 'What is your name?'

'It was very remiss of me not to have introduced myself. Please forgive me.' He gave a courteous bow and said, just as courteously, 'I am Henry Jermyn. My friends call me Harry.'

Henrietta's big black eyes widened in surprise. 'Really?'

'You think I would deceive you, Madame? I assure you, I would never do such a terrible thing.'

She had not meant that at all. 'It's just such a coincidence.'

'That you are Princess Henrietta and I am Henry?'

She giggled again, shaking her head. 'That your name is Jermyn.'

'I'm sorry, I don't quite understand . . .'

'Jermyn,' she repeated. 'As in . . . ?'

'It derives from St Germain, I believe.'

'I was raised at the Château of St-Germain-en-Laye. It is my favourite place in the whole world.'

He looked a little stunned, as if the revelation of this link between his name and that of the château where Henrietta had spent the majority of her childhood was somehow significant. She felt it too, in a way. It was almost as if they had just discovered they were related, that a bond had been forged between the two of them long before they had ever met.

'For what reason do you so favour St Germain?' he said. 'If I might ask?'

'The hanging gardens mostly. They are like a wonderland, with so many lovely things it's impossible to describe.'

'Will you not at least try?' He smiled. 'For my sake.'

Actually, Henrietta was only too glad to, having inherited a great passion for gardens as well as for architecture from her mother. 'There's a summer-house on a wooded hill,' she began enthusiastically. 'It looks right out over the River Seine. And there are steps leading down from the terraces, and underneath them there is a little grotto, with a fountain in the middle, made of seashells and coral. The water from the jet hits the roof with such force that that it falls again like heavy rain.' She broke off to draw breath. She had always had a tendency to speak too quickly, and because she was still nervous was aware that she was practically babbling now. In French. To an Englishman. Though Henry Jermyn was not looking at her with any lack of understanding, but as if he had followed every word with ease and was genuinely interested in everything she had to say. 'No matter where you stand,' she finished more slowly, 'you get very wet. It is most refreshing on a hot day.'

'I'm sure it must be.'

'There are marble and shellwork figures in alcoves in the walls that also spout water,' she added. 'Many of them move.'

'They move?'

'Yes.' Henrietta giggled again, wondering why she kept doing that and thinking she must stop herself or he would think her giddy like everyone else did. Why she cared so much what he thought, she really didn't know. But care she did. 'There's a mechanical blacksmith who strikes an anvil. And nightingales which sing and flap their wings and . . .' She was about to tell him how, in the middle of the grotto, there was also an automaton of Neptune with his trident, who came out of the pool riding a chariot, but was prevented by her mother and Anne and their ladies who, annoyingly, chose that moment to come flurrying back into the room with Lord Kensington. Henrietta realised only then that she had missed her chance.

She had not asked one single question about the Prince of Wales or about England. She didn't care. Though she'd have liked very much to go on talking to this Englishman about anything. Everything.

'I should like you to know, sir,' her mother was saying to Lord Kensington, 'the king my son is very much in favour of this marriage, and now I have seen the prince, I myself cannot commend him more highly.'

Henrietta thought that if only he turned out to be like Henry Jermyn, even just a little, then she too would be very happy. What was it he had said his friends called him . . . Harry? 'Arri,' she tried softly, to herself.

Following the two queens as they swept out of the apartment, she could not resist a last glance over her shoulder at him and it made her heart skip to see that his face was turned in her direction, that he was watching her.

'Well, Henrietta?' her mother inquired. 'Are you not dying of impatience to hear all about your prince? Knowing you, I'd have thought you'd be begging me to tell you every tiny detail the instant we were out of the room.'

'Of course I want to know,' she said, as the ladies crowded round her in the passageway, eager to share their own opinions of the portrait. 'Is he . . . very tall?'

Anne laughed at her. 'My dear, what a thing to ask! How on earth are we supposed to fathom his height from a portrait of just his face?'

Henrietta flushed as if she had been caught out somehow. 'Is it a pleasing face?' she amended quickly.

'Most pleasing. If a little thin perhaps.'

'What colour are his eyes?' Blue, she secretly willed. Let them be blue.

'Brown,' Anne said.

'Rather serious,' added Henrietta's mother.

'Solemn would perhaps be a better word,' Anne decided.

Behind the closed door, where the ambassador and his gentlemen had no doubt resumed their drinking, Henrietta heard Harry Jermyn's distinctively merry laughter and felt more confused than ever.

That night there was a grand banquet in honour of the English visitors, to be followed by the ballet performed by Anne, Henrietta and a host of courtiers.

On the top table sat King Louis, Henrietta's brother, whose long face and big brown eyes were in part concealed by his mane of wavy black hair. Louis might sit upon a gilded throne under a red embroidered canopy but he never looked particularly comfortable there, playing the king. He far preferred to be out with his dogs or falcons, or working with his hands at his forge, or printing press, or carpenter's bench. He could make a pair of shoes as well as any cobbler. He loved to cook, too, and made the most delicious marchpane.

Queen Anne was seated beside him, wearing a gown of grey satin with a light upstanding ruff of delicate lace. But it was Henrietta and Louis's mother who dominated the table with the combination of her formidable presence and the vast expanse of black silk that was needed to cover her stout bosom and belly. She was deep in conversation with the English Ambassador, no doubt holding forth just as she did with Louis, trying to tell him how to rule his kingdom. She had done so relentlessly since taking on the regency when he had become the boy-king, except for a brief period after his advisors had seized power in a bloody coup and had his domineering, interfering mother sent under arrest to the Castle of Blois, a hundred miles south of Paris.

The Englishmen had all been honoured with prestigious places tonight. It was with pleasure Henrietta found that, despite his relatively lowly status, Harry Jermyn was seated right beside her.

'*Bonsoir*, Madame,' he said, then went on to explain respectfully in French: 'Since few others in our party can speak your language, my Lord Kensington suggested I sit here with you, or else you'd have nobody to talk to.'

'Thank you, sir,' Henrietta replied, feeling shy with him again. 'That is very considerate.'

'Shrewd of me too.' He smiled. 'Since I expect we'll be served the finest cuts.'

'We will,' she confirmed. 'In time.'

The scents of candle-grease and wood smoke and ill-washed bodies which usually pervaded the palace had been replaced tonight by the mouth-watering aromas of cooking, but the wait for the liveried pages to parade in with the first course always seemed interminable to Henrietta. The Bourbons all had healthy appetites, even when they were ill.

Harry seemed quite content, though, taking in the pale carved classical columns and statues, the richly painted ceilings and bright tapestries, the paintings and frescoes on the walls, the gleaming black-and-white marble floor, and the enormous ornate candelabra and silver sconces in which burned over a thousand candles, making the room as bright as day.

Glad to see that he seemed suitably impressed, Henrietta was minded to ask him about the palaces in England. But the grand prior finally arrived, leading the parade of liveried footmen who brought in the steaming salvers and chargers of food, and soon the multitude of dishes covered the entire table, so many that the platters all overlapped at the edges. There were salads, fricassées, roast and baked meats, carbonados. There was chicken roasted in fried breadcrumbs, quails, eggs, cocks' combs, salmon and pâtés and cheeses, and all manner of other delicacies.

There was another wait while the priest blessed the food, making the sign of the cross above the lavish spread, before at last everyone took up their knife, the butlers uncorked the stoneware bottles and the Gascony wine started flowing freely into silver goblets. The sound of tinkling tableware added to the general hum of conversation, laughter, and music from the orchestra playing in the corner.

Harry helped himself to a generous portion of duck pâté that he spread thickly on his bread.

'Do you eat much pâté in England, sir?' Henrietta asked him.

He had just taken a large bite and had his mouth full, so could only shake his head. She couldn't help thinking that those bright blue eyes of his could on no account be described as solemn. She noted also that there was enough food on his plate to keep her fed for an entire week. Tall and broad as he was, there was no fat on him, so it was hard to imagine where it would all go. She supposed, though, that being so tall he needed to eat more than other people. Or else, perhaps, besides a shortage of pâté there was no good food in England at all and he was hungry. Which was worrying.

'What do you usually have with your bread then?'

'Cheese mostly. Albeit not half so fine as yours.' He reached for his cup, raising it to her in a toast then putting it to his lips, tasting.

She copied him and took a long swig, hoping it might help her to relax.

'Your wine is excellent too,' he pronounced.

There was a soothing quality to his voice and it struck her that they were opposites in every way, he and she. He spoke as calmly as she did quickly, just as he was tall and she was tiny.

The fine French wine he had so praised, or more precisely the speed with which she had drained a whole cup of it, together with the excitement of the occasion, was making Henrietta feel unusually bold. She might be shy and blush in front of complete strangers, but she did know how to flirt. Everyone at court knew how to flirt. It was practically the only way that the gentlemen and ladies of their circle communicated with one another; it was almost instinctive to them. Henrietta had had fun practising and testing out her skills on the sons of nobles and lords and on pageboys, but somehow this was different. It didn't feel like practising at all. She tilted her head slightly to one side and looked up at Harry from beneath her silky black lashes. 'Do you find everything in France to your liking, sir?'

His eyes flickered over her face, made her heart flutter and race in the most extraordinary way. For a moment she thought he wasn't going to answer. '*Oui*, Madame,' he said softly, faultlessly gracious. 'Very much so.'

The ballet after the banquet involved all the queen's ladies and relations. Anne, draped in a costume of white silk embroidered with gold thread, and wearing a white-and-gold mask, took the lead part of Juno, Queen of the Gods and wife of Jupiter, a lady of majestic bearing and imposing beauty, a role that might have been made especially for her. Wearing white tulle and lace, Henrietta played the character of Iris, the fleur-de-lys, flower of France.

Rehearsals had taken place in the Grand Salle every day for a whole month so that everyone could learn the intricate steps and turns. There were various complicated geometric figures; interlacing squares and chains, circles and lozenges and triangles, and dancers also had to remember to maintain the correct position and distance between each other. Henrietta knew she was a talented dancer and she loved performing, loved applause, but even so she had been nervous about appearing before such an important and judgmental audience. Her nerves left her, though, as soon as the music started and the rhythms and cadences of the violins and lutes and oboes took hold. She let them lift and direct her until her legs no longer felt shaky but supple and strong. When she danced her smallness felt like a bonus rather than a disadvantage, making her agile and dainty, and tonight she felt so totally and unaccountably happy that she might have been dancing on air. No longer self-conscious and shy, she soon completely forgot where she was, who she was even, or that she had any audience at all.

Until she had to sing her solo. Her mother was well known for her vocal gifts and Henrietta had inherited that talent from her, but though she liked to sing almost as much as she liked to dance, it was again intimidating, knowing she was on her own now, being listened to and watched so closely. She began quietly but very sweetly. The song was addressed to her mother, and told her she had the same colouring as the sun that shone perpetually on her. Marie looked delighted by it and even from a distance Henrietta could see that Lord Kensington's lips had curved to in an appreciative smile. Which made her end her performance on an inward sigh of great relief.

Then came the thrilling moment when the masked dancers invited the audience on to the floor, which immediately became thronged with swirling silks and satins and glittering pearls and jewels. Henrietta partnered the king her brother for the sarabande, then danced the galliard with Lord Kensington, who handed her to the Duc de Chevreuse as soon as he saw the Duchesse whirl by, her hips swinging provocatively. Marie de Rohan, Duchesse de Chevreuse, was considered to be one of the most beautiful and desirable ladies at court, and if the gossip was to be believed, Lord Kensington most certainly thought her so. The pair of them had been inseparable all afternoon, after falling instantly in love with each other. Just as it was supposed to happen. Just like in the medieval romances and the poems of the troubadours. In those verses and stories of lords and ladies and their gallant knights, love was always, always at first sight, its arrows entering by the eyes and travelling straight to the heart.

How wonderful it would be if that happened when first she met the Prince of Wales. Henrietta tried hard to concentrate on contemplating that happy occasion while she danced the branle with Harry Jermyn, but was distracted by the warmth of his hand. The way it covered hers entirely because it was so much larger, the way the top of her head came no higher than the middle of his broad chest. She couldn't help thinking how, if only he would hold her more tightly, her head would rest right against his heart. But despite the natural strength of someone of his height and build, he held her with great tenderness, as if she really were a lily, a delicate little flower of France, that he did not wish to risk crushing.

'You've already won at least one English admirer, my lady,' Mamie whispered knowingly in Henrietta's ear when the dancing was over and they were being served the traditional preserved cherries, candied violets, and comfits spiced with nutmeg and cinnamon.

Henrietta gave her friend an innocent look. 'Who?'

'Him.' Mamie tipped her head not so discreetly towards Harry, who was laughing easily with some of the French nobles, another cup of wine in his hand. 'The tall, good-looking one.'

At which point Harry glanced across at them, almost as if he sensed he was being discussed.

'See.' Mamie popped another candied violet into her mouth. 'He can hardly take his eyes off you.'

Henrietta sneaked a glance at him from beneath her lashes. 'Don't be silly.'

'I'm not. He was gazing at you the entire time you were dancing, and when you sang it was as if he were spellbound. I don't think he blinked once.'

Henrietta looked down at her fingers which were dusted with sugar. She brushed it off. 'It's only so he can help Lord Kensington make a proper report back to England about me, I'm sure.'

Mamie looked doubtful.

'Why else?'

'Why is any man interested in a pretty girl?'

'I am not a pretty girl.'

'You are extremely pretty, my lady.' Mamie grinned. 'As I keep telling you.'

'I mean, I am a princess,' Henrietta said. 'And he is . . . he is . . .' It did not matter what he was, but rather what he was not. Namely a prince, an heir to a throne, a duke even, or some other noble. 'He is amusing company,' she conceded, unable to stop herself from glancing back at him just one more time. 'And very gentle-mannered.' She wagged her finger at Mamie. 'Now no naughty thoughts,' she warned, aping her brother's reprimand when courtiers were being too flirtatious or risqué for his modest tastes. For instance, when the Duchesse de Chevreuse had commented very pointedly earlier, before dancing with Lord Kensington, that a man must satisfy his wife in bed in order to keep her from straying.

Now Mamie promptly pretended to pull a non-existent hat brim over her eyes, just as Louis did to show his disapproval of low revealing necklines, and both girls collapsed in fits of uncontrollable giggles.

\* \* \*

The wrangling over marriage portions and contracts, and the composition of Henrietta's proposed English household, had begun; it was clear to all that it was going to be some time before it was finished. Meanwhile, Lord Kensington took to visiting Henrietta, her mother and Anne every day, either in the queen's audience chamber after morning mass, or else joining them in the fields where they took the air in the evenings before vespers. Sometimes they all went for afternoon walks in the gardens of the Tuileries, which was a place Henrietta loved almost as much as St Germain.

Created by Marie's distant cousin Catherine de' Medici to remind her of her native Florence, the garden was divided by long allées into rectangular sections planted with lawns, bright ordered flowerbeds, and small wildernesses of trees, intermingled with arbours, trellises and rows of mulberry bushes. It was the largest garden in Paris, enclosed by the rue Saint-Honoré on the north, the Louvre on the east, the Seine on the south, and the city walls and moat on the west.

It was spring now and the sun glittered so strongly on the water it almost hurt to look at it. Lately it had seemed to be shining particularly brightly above the Cathedral of Notre-Dame across the river. Henrietta, as alert for signs and portents as anyone, read this as a positive indication, since if all went well that was where she would be married before too long.

She had talked eloquently to Lord Kensington about art and architecture, had charmed him by telling him how much she enjoyed riding – an activity unusual in France but common in England so he informed her, but still she had not asked him half the questions she longed to ask. He was so grand and important that Henrietta was afraid of saying something that might make her look foolish. So it was on the pretext of resuming the conversation she'd begun with Harry Jermyn at that first banquet that she excused herself one afternoon, leaving Lord Kensington with the Duchesse de Chevreuse and Marie, and went to catch up with the young Englishman.

Mitte frisked along at Henreitta's heels as if she could smell the hint of spring in the air. Even though it was unseasonably mild, the party had dressed in fur-lined cloaks and beaver hats, expecting it still to be wintry outside, so everyone was more inclined to stroll than to stride out. Harry's legs were so long compared with Henrietta's that she had the perfect excuse to forget all about trying to be ladylike and walk instead at her usual rapid pace. She had to take two steps to his one, just to keep up with what for him was merely a leisurely amble. Seeing this, however, he considerately slowed his pace still further.

He barely glanced at her, though, seeming to be more interested in the pale stone pavilions and wings of the Louvre and the gallery which stretched for three-quarters of a mile along the river, starting from the medieval fortress with its arrow-slit windows. Henrietta's mother did not like the Louvre, considering it to be vastly inferior to the *palazzi* of Florence where she had grown up. Henrietta herself had never been to Florence. France was the only home she had ever known, the only land she had ever seen, and now, faced with the prospect of having to leave it soon, she felt she had never loved it so much. The Louvre was immensely impressive to her eyes, particularly the gallery her father had built and the colonnade, though that had been left unfinished and was little more than a grand façade.

'I trust English palaces at least are as splendid as French ones, sir?' Henrietta said. 'Even if your wine and cheese fall short of ours.'

Harry gave her a sideways smile, then seeing that she genuinely wanted to know, turned his attention back to the buildings on their right. 'There are certainly some similarities.'

'Such as?'

'King James's principal residence is the Palace of Whitehall and is made up of a complex of galleries and privy gardens strung out alongside the river, just as they are here. But the buildings themselves are entirely different.'

'In what way?'

He pondered before replying, as if he'd not really considered this before. 'Whitehall is . . . more of a muddle.'

Henrietta giggled at his choice of words, wondering if his French were not so impeccable after all and he had made a mistake. 'A muddle?'

'Yes.' He smiled. 'A muddle.' He sought to explain. 'Instead of carved columns and statues such as appear everywhere in Paris, the buildings of Whitehall are of red brick ornamented with black and white chequerwork. And whereas here you appear to strive for uniformity and clean lines, Whitehall is a hotchpotch of turrets and battlements and pinnacles, all crowned with heraldic beasts, lions and unicorns and suchlike, holding gilded flags and vanes.'

'That sounds wonderfully medieval.'

'Well, yes. I suppose it is.'

Architecture being a subject close to Henrietta's heart, she could not resist this opportunity to demonstrate her knowledge. Though why she should feel such a constant need to impress the ambassador's attendant even more than the ambassador himself, she was still not entirely sure. 'So whereas the builders here have aimed to recreate a classical world . . . Paris was founded by the Trojans, you know, and named after Helen's lover . . . in England you still live in the age of chivalry?'

Henry looked slightly dumbfounded.

'My mother has taught me to have a deep understanding and appreciation of architecture,' Henrietta explained, smiling proudly. 'And of art.'

'You will have much in common with our Prince of Wales then,' Harry said quietly, eyes fixed on the ground. 'Following his late brother's example, he has become a great collector.'

'You have met him?' Henrietta asked eagerly.

'I have had that privilege.'

'What's he like?'

She realised instantly that she should not have asked, had put him in an awkward position. She was not just any girl inquiring about a potential suitor. She was a princess of France and the man after whom she inquired was heir to the throne of England. Harry Jermyn would be aware that the balance of power in Europe could be critically altered by this proposed union and that what he said now was of the greatest diplomatic sensitivity. Yet he was not really a diplomat, not an ambassador, nor even an envoy. It was not his place to impart this kind of information and it was unfair of her to expect him to do so. But she could see that he did not want to disappoint her by refusing, and she could not resist taking advantage of that.

'Is he as tall as you?' she pressed.

'Nobody is as tall as me,' Harry replied with a smile in his voice and a grasp of diplomacy that would surely have impressed his master.

'Do you think the prince will mind that I am so small for my age?'

'Whyever should he mind?' Harry said simply. 'When your wisdom and conversation are infinitely beyond your stature?'

This may be his first visit to France but he clearly learned fast. He'd evidently moved in French aristocratic circles long enough to perfect his skill in the art of flattery. He had spoken with the perfect hyperbole of a true French courtier. And yet . . . Accustomed as she was to being flattered, Henrietta was touched by what he had said. It sounded unusually genuine. So many of the compliments other people paid her did not. Much as she liked to hear them and was quite ready to believe them, she had to admit that often they did not ring true. She did not quite know how to respond to Harry's sincerity, so instead gave her customary reply to any compliment. 'You are most kind, sir.'

'Merely honest.'

The irises were out in all their glory and instantly deflected Henrietta's attention. She stopped to admire them, bending down and drawing one of the purple blooms to her nose to inhale its elusive fragrance. The scent of snow and of sadness, she thought.

'You like flowers, Madame?' Harry asked her.

Henrietta picked up Mitte who was jumping about around her skirts, wanting to be carried. 'I love them,' she said.

He smiled at her unrestrained enthusiasm. 'Before you ask then, let me assure you that we have irises in England too. And the new tulips and lots of other blooms besides. Growing by the roadsides we have hawthorn, buttercups, primroses.' He reached out and stroked Mitte's ears. 'Dog roses even.'

Henrietta giggled. 'Strange name for a flower.'

Harry let Mitte lick his fingers, around his rings. 'They are almost as pretty as your little friend here.'

'London in springtime is as beautiful as in Paris then?' Henrietta asked, hopefully.

His lips parted as if to answer, but he seemed to think better of it, letting his hand fall to his side. 'Listen,' he said. 'I have been thinking.'

'Thinking, sir? About what?'

'About how I might help you.'

'Help me?'

Harry glanced over his shoulder to make sure there was nobody within hearing, and lowered his voice in any case. The look he gave her then was rather mischievous. 'The serving girl who attends us at our lodgings was once one of your maids, I believe.'

'She was,' Henrietta confirmed, puzzled, wondering why he should sound so pleased about this. Why it should even concern him.

'If you were to ask her to inquire of my Lord Kensington if she might borrow the portrait of the prince that you might look upon it, I am certain he would not refuse you.'

'But . . .' Henrietta drew back, gaping at him.

'But what?'

'I can't possibly do that! I could get into the most terrible trouble. You too, if anyone found out you had suggested it. It could jeopardise negotiations. Everything. I daresay you could lose your position.'

'It is kind of you to be so concerned for me,' he said. 'But I would not be suggesting this if there were any risk for either of us. I have made enquiries. Trust me. It is all in hand. There will be no problem.'

He sounded so confident that she could not for a minute doubt his judgement. She would trust him willingly. But Mamie was entirely wrong about him, evidently, Henrietta thought, with a stab of something that felt surprisingly like disappointment. If he liked her in the way Mamie believed he did, he'd not be in such a hurry for her to see the prince's portrait, now would he? Unless he believed she'd find it disagreeable, of course.

'Why would you go to such trouble for me, sir?'

'It just seems to me unfair,' he said very gently, 'that everyone else has seen the portrait but you, the person whom it most concerns.'

In the privacy of her apartment, overlooking the Jardin de l'Infante, Henrietta told Mamie of Harry's plan, keen to see what the older girl would make of it.

'Well, he's obviously so hopelessly devoted to you already that he would put your own interests before his own,' Mamie decided instantly. She had relieved Henrietta of her ermine-trimmed cloak and was still holding on to it somewhat covetously, looped tightly over her arm, absently stroking the fine fur as lovingly as Henrietta stroked Mitte. 'He wants to prove to you that his primary concern is to serve you.'

'Not at the risk of his own reputation, surely? You will tell Louise to be discreet, won't you?' Henrietta fretted. 'And you will tell her to bring the portrait directly here?'

'Of course.' Mamie put the cloak away in the coffer and turned to go.

Henrietta could not have felt more nervous or excited if she was about to meet the prince in person. She could scarce believe that she was about to see his likeness at last, and waited in a fever of anticipation for Louise to return.

At last the girl came into the closet holding a small gold case in her hands, the silky blue ribbon tied to it trailing from her work-roughened fingers. Her young, slightly pock-marked face was alight with the thrill of romantic adventure as she held out the gold case to Henrietta. 'Here you are, Madame,' she said proudly.

The door securely shut behind them, with Mamie standing guard over it, Henrietta took the case with trembling fingers and went to sit in a chair by the hearth. Blushing a little at her own audacity, she opened it and looked at it in the firelight.

The first thing that struck her was that Anne had been entirely right about the prince's eyes. They were indeed sorrowful, unspeakably so. Large and slightly protuberant and sorrowful as Henrietta's beloved spaniel's. The saddest eyes she had ever seen in her entire life. His whole face was sad, positively tragic. She wondered at the cause of his sorrow. Whatever it was, it made her feel sad too, just to look at him.

But there was also much to admire. His face was almost as delicate as her own, with fine high cheekbones, and he had thick, wavy brown hair which fell down to his shoulders from a centre parting, a perfectly trimmed moustache and a short pointed beard like a Spaniard's. His nose was long and straight, a noble nose, and his mouth was full with a firm set to it, which spoke of inner strength. The general impression was of a thoughtful, sensitive and reserved, if rather fragile, man, who nonetheless knew his own mind.

Henrietta's kind and passionate heart overflowed with a tender love for him. What this unhappy prince badly needed was a wife who liked to dance and sing and be merry. Someone who could perhaps teach him to be a little giddy even, now and again. She would do all in her power to banish that sadness from his eyes, if only he would let her.

So what did it matter that he did not measure up to her vague but treasured ideal of a strong, golden, smiling prince? It had been pure fantasy, and this face she saw before her now was real, a real prince, a real man who needed a wife's love and care.

'Only let me come to you soon,' she whispered, touching the little image of his face with her fingertips. Seeing it at last made her long to be married more than ever.

\*   \*   \*

Though there were banquets almost every evening Henrietta did not sit beside Harry at table after that first occasion, so it was not until the following afternoon that she had a proper opportunity to thank him.

He was very popular, one of those people everyone seemed to want to know and to be near, so as usual he was at the centre of things. The Englishmen had congregated in the apartment of Henrietta's mother where they were sitting around at small tables playing dice and Lansquenet with some of the French courtiers, gambling being an occupation that transcended language barriers and which Harry seemed particularly to relish. She watched him for a moment, absently stroking his beard, contemplating a move. But seeing that she was lingering nearby obviously wanting to speak to him, he immediately excused himself and abandoned his game. As he rose from his chair to join her, Henrietta was struck again by his long-limbed height and the languidly powerful grace of his walk.

'I cannot adequately express my gratitude to you, sir,' she said quietly. 'For what you did for me yesterday.'

'You are very welcome. And you need not worry,' he added when he caught her glancing apprehensively at the ambassador. 'My Lord Kensington will not breathe a word. Our little secret is entirely safe.'

Henrietta turned her face up to his. 'How can you be so sure?'

'Lord Kensington told me so.'

'What did he tell you?'

'That he would rather die a thousand deaths than betray the trust of a young lady who is as beautiful and good as any angel.'

He made the words sound so heartfelt that Henrietta felt a little dizzy, and once again was at a loss as to how to reply.

Harry looked down at his right hand, long fingers slightly curled, inspecting his neat, oval nails, as if he felt more awkward than she. 'I trust you liked what you saw?' he said.

It took her a second to realise he was talking about the prince's portrait and to drag her mind back to that. 'I did,' she told him. 'Very much. Though Queen Anne was right about the prince's eyes. She said they were very solemn, and they are. Or at least they are in that portrait. Does he really look so terribly sad?'

'It is fair to say that, he does. With good reason, I believe.'

'What reason is that?' She hardly dared to imagine and Harry looked as if he hardly dared to tell her, already regretting having spoken so candidly.

'With respect, sir, you can't just make a comment like that and then leave me in suspense. I promise you, I shall not love him any the less for it, whatever it is.'

'No,' he said thoughtfully. 'I don't believe you would.'

'So tell me what you meant?'

He directed her to a small table, decorated with gold-leaf, which stood by the window where they could talk in more privacy. They sat opposite one another and he gathered up a scattered deck of cards, beginning shuffle to them distractedly but with expertise, as if it helped him to think. 'Prince Charles has not had an easy time of it.'

'Hasn't he?'

'My father was a courtier. Just a minor one, but it means I have some knowledge of the prince's early life.' He paused for a moment, as if deciding how best to begin. 'He suffered from much sickness as a child and was not expected to live long, let alone become heir to the throne. He lived very much under his brother Prince Henry's shadow, and a very gilded shadow that boy did have. England's golden hope and promise he was, the perfect prince destined to be the perfect warrior king.' But there was distinct disapproval in Harry's tone, which was completely at odds with his words.

'My sister Christine was supposed to marry Prince Henry.'

'It was as well for her that she did not.'

'Why?'

Harry set down the cards in a neat pile. 'He was a bully, I am afraid. Prince Charles idolised him, loved to ride with him in the joust, and copied his passion for fencing and shooting with crossbows and muskets. In return Prince Henry tormented his little brother and upset him terribly by telling him that he'd have to make him archbishop, since the robes would hide his legs.'

'What's wrong with Prince Charles's legs?' Henrietta asked, much alarmed.

'Oh, nothing at all now,' Harry corrected himself quickly. 'But for a long time his illness gave him a weakness in his joints, in his ankles and knees and hips, that made it difficult for him to stand or walk. He has shown tremendous courage and determination in overcoming the weakness through hard exercise.' Harry's voice now was full of unfeigned admiration and sympathy. 'He runs in the park every morning without fail, and he practises longer and harder than anyone at his riding. He has become an excellent horseman as a result. He's still very shy and reserved, though. He was so afraid of his father's temper that he cultivated a way of moving round the court like a planet in its own sphere, so naturally and quietly that nobody noticed him. Becoming heir to the throne seems to have given him not more confidence but less.' Harry broke off, still looking at Henrietta, then picked up two dice and gave a little chuckle as he shook them in his hand. 'A fine diplomat I shall make! As attendant to the wooing ambassador, I am sure I should not have told you any of that.'

'The what?' Henrietta laughed loud enough to cause people to look round, leaned in a little closer to Harry, lowered her voice and repeated, 'The . . . wooing ambassador?'

'That is what he calls himself, did you not know?' Harry's grin relaxed into a broad smile. 'My Lord Kensington sees himself as Cupid, come to win your heart for the prince and his for you. And here am I, undermining all his good work by telling you the prince is shy and had weak legs. Except . . .'

'Except?'

He looked quite pleased with himself now. 'I don't think I have done him a disservice at all.'

'Have you not?'

He shook his head. 'On the contrary, I rather think I have advanced his cause.'

'How so?'

His eyes softened. 'Because you are such a generous and warm-hearted person, Madame. And I see nothing but compassion in you.'

She did feel compassion for the prince. Of course she did. Who could not? Oh, she would accept him and love him just as he was, for himself, with all his shortcomings and faults. But what if it was not reciprocated and the testimonies he was receiving about her were not all complimentary? What about her own shortcomings . . . literally? Harry had assured her already that her small stature would not be a problem, but she still feared the prince's reaction to it. No doubt he had been dreaming of taking a statuesque and voluptuously elegant beauty for his bride. Someone like Marie de Rohan. Someone at least half a foot taller than Henrietta.

She took a deep breath, forced herself to ask, 'What has the prince been told of me, sir? Do you know?' She was sure Harry must have been privy to the communications with England, since she had heard that he assisted the ambassador with his correspondence, being particularly good at letter-writing.

'What could my Lord Kensington say, Madame?' Harry mused gently. 'What could any man say about you? But that you dance as well as anyone, and your voice when you sing is beyond all imagining. That you are a girl of as much loveliness and sweetness as any under heaven, and that none deserves the prince's undying affection as much as do you.'

It was extraordinary, these things he kept saying to her. It was lovely hearing such things, of course, from someone so charming and popular and handsome, but it was a little overwhelming and for a moment left Henrietta dumbfounded.

Harry's face immediately broke into a disarming smile. 'My lord is the wooing ambassador after all,' he reminded her, instantly making light of all he had just said, as if to spare them both any further embarrassment. Or as if he regretted having laid open his heart and revealed his true feelings. 'You understand that it is his job to promote favourable opinions by emphasising Your Highness's finer qualities?'

'Oh. Yes.' Henrietta nodded vigorously, playing along. 'But of course.'

It was at Henrietta's suggestion that a small royal party, comprising her, her brother the king and the two queens, took Lord Kensington and his entourage on a coach ride to see some of the sights of Paris. 'If you think the Louvre is splendid, sir,' she said to Harry, 'just wait until you see the Place Royale. And the new palace my mother is having built.'

That was where they began: the Palais de Luxembourg. It was Marie de' Medici's great project. The Medicis were a dynasty of builders and Marie had had it designed in the style of the family's vast and luxurious Italian palace. This French version was extraordinarily elegant, too, with a three-sided entrance courtyard and ornate central block flanked by protruding wings. The General of Waters and Fountains had been instructed to create a park around it in the style Marie had known as a child, and two thousand elms had already been planted.

'The foundation stones were laid when Princess Henrietta was three years old,' Marie proudly told the little party as they stood in the wide courtyard.

It would be several years more before the interiors were finally compete, but Marie had her gilded study now and Peter Paul Rubens's vast sequence of allegorical paintings representing her life had been completed and installed. Henrietta experienced a sudden swooping sense of loss to realise that, in all likelihood, she would be leaving France just as Marie and Louis abandoned the Louvre and finally took up residence in this magnificent palace that had been under construction for as long as she could remember. Her mother would move into the grand apartments on one side and Louis into the matching suite on the other. But she, Henrietta, might never get to live there after all. No matter, she told herself. She would be Queen of England, with a dozen palaces and castles of her own, just as stylish and elegant as this one.

Henrietta noticed that Henry was gazing up at the building with a rapt admiration that pleased her. She would have liked to talk to him about his impressions but Marie hurried them on. 'To the Pont Neuf,' she commanded, and turned to waddle her way back to the state carriage, which stood awaiting them at the edge of the courtyard.

Preceded by six running footmen and drawn by six chestnut horses with red plumes on their heads, the carriage headed for the wide, decorative bridge that had been built by Henrietta's father. He had been an even more enthusiastic builder than was her mother. The bridge, its stone arches linking the Île de la Cité to both banks of the Seine, was the first to have no overhanging houses on it, which made for a windy crossing. It was also the first to have pavements on each side which, along with the roadway itself, were crowded as usual with carriages and horses and a proliferation of street-traders. There were book-sellers and flower-sellers, as well as assorted pickpockets and acrobats and a whole host of quacks who claimed to be able to do everything from smoothing wrinkles to pulling bad teeth to replacing lost ones.

Henrietta especially wanted their visitors to see the bronze life-sized statue of her father on horseback, mounted on a pedestal listing his famous military victories, which had been erected on the tip of the Île de la Cité. Her mother was keen to show off the promenade of the Cours La Reine, with its triple avenues of stately elms, which she had had built between Chaillot and the Bois de Boulogne.

Lastly they came to the vast paved square of the Place Royale where they all disembarked, the better to appreciate the immense symmetry of the elegant square and the three-storey white stone and red-brick pavilions and nobles' houses ranged all around it.

This had been Henri le Grand's greatest dream and vision. Now, in the brilliant spring sunshine, the glittering fountain at its centre refracted a pale, broken rainbow. Again Henrietta experienced a pang of regret as reality struck home, the realisation that soon she might be leaving this city and her homeland for good. Come next spring, it was most probable she would not be here. She tried to take it all in, the splendour and the painstakingly crafted detail, to fix it in her mind. She shut her eyes for a second or two to see if she could picture it still. Perhaps, if she tried hard enough, she'd be able to capture it like a painting she could take with her to England.

She caught Harry watching her and he quickly looked away, turning his attention back to the great buildings surrounding them. Henrietta saw that he appreciated them as she had done, even before she knew anything much about them. That he was as moved by their beauty and artistry as by a stirring piece of music or a great artwork, and she was delighted to find that he instinctively cared for what interested her so passionately.

'I have to tell you,' he said, anticipating her inevitable question, 'that unfortunately England has no buildings that quite compare to this.'

Somehow, deep down, she had known that already, but it still pained her to hear it.

'You could build some,' he said, seeing her disappointment and trying to alleviate it. 'You are, after all, the daughter of two great builders.' He cast a winning smile at Marie de' Medici. 'Why not build French houses in England, just as your mother has built Italian houses in France?'

Henrietta was so excited by this idea, which she thought the most perfect one she'd ever heard, that she brightened instantly and, to her mother's evident approval, pointed out some of the finer details to Harry. True appreciation for a building came from knowing how to read and analyse it, so she quickly ran through the crucial principles of classical architecture for his benefit: how it was all about balance and regularity, proportion and grandeur. 'My father wanted to make Paris ordered as well as beautiful,' she said. 'People still remember how during his reign they saw nothing but builders at work. He banned timber-framed buildings and his notion was to replace all the narrow medieval streets with royal squares, modelled on the *piazze* of Rome.'

It delighted her to see Harry's appreciation enhanced by the greater understanding her explanation had given him. 'He obviously loved this city as much as you do,' he observed.

'More than you know,' Henrietta's mother interposed tartly. 'He converted to Catholicism with the words, "Paris is worth a mass." Let us pray the Prince of Wales is of the opinion that a Parisian princess is worth a mass too.'

Henrietta noticed Harry exchange a look with Lord Kensington, a deeply anxious look, which suddenly took away her enjoyment of their jaunt and made her want only to get back in the carriage and drive straight home.

Henrietta did not worry for long about why her mother mentioning the word 'mass' and the Prince of Wales in the same breath should have caused the ambassador and Harry Jermyn to look so troubled. She was too busy trying to be patient while they all remained locked away for hours on end with her brother and the commissioners, in the protracted discussions which were held day and night around the long oak council table. It was not easy when the long days stretched into longer weeks.

At least there were continual banquets and dancing to keep everyone entertained, as well as Harry's amusing company and conversation. As the weather warmed, small afternoon meals were taken outside beneath the trees and there were more leisurely walks in the gardens of the Tuileries. The allées of orange trees were laden with the most beautiful scented blossom which drifted down upon their hair and clothes, and then the roses came out on the trellises – red roses, pink and white and orange, rambling over the wooden arches. The terraces were lined with a double row of white mulberry trees, part of an orchard of thousands grown to feed silkworms.

To Henrietta it was paradise. But James Hay, Earl of Carlisle, who arrived in May, declared himself indifferent to anything France had to offer. A foppish Scotsman in an ostentatious square standing ruff, he had a good figure but a face like a camel's, and Henrietta took an instant dislike to him. He described England as the real paradise on earth, the wealthiest and most splendid country in all the world. Rather than making Henrietta more impatient than ever to see it for herself, this had the opposite effect. She felt such pride and love for her own country, especially while on the brink of being exiled from it, that she took any slight to it very personally. She was a daughter of France. A French princess. And anyone who slighted France slighted her.

Nevertheless she was glad the earl had come. He had brought with him two more envoys to assist in the dealings with the French commissioners, and far more importantly he also brought a letter from Prince Charles, addressed personally to Henrietta.

Her first love letter.

The Scotsman presented it to Henrietta in her Grand Salon, where she sat upon her own little throne. Three paces before it the earl stopped and bowed deeply, going down on one knee. Henrietta stood. With a careful curtsey, she took the letter from him and formally thanked the absent Prince of Wales for this testimony he gave her of his affection.

She longed to jump down from the dais and run to her chamber or to the gardens, to sit on her bed or by the river, and read it slowly, alone, so that she might savour every word. But she knew she'd never be permitted to do that. There was nothing for it but to sit back down upon her throne, break the red crested royal seal and open it where she was, with everyone eagerly watching. The wording was stiff and formal as the expensive parchment upon which it was written, but nonetheless she read with joyful tears in her eyes.

'Well? What does he say?' her mother inquired, all but snatching the letter out of Henrietta's hands to read for herself.

Henrietta clutched it tighter, not wanting to let go even for a second, but she knew there was no use in saying it was private. Nothing about this courtship was. 'He says that since he cannot have the happiness of beholding me in person, he keeps my portrait in his cabinet and often gazes upon it.'

'I should hope so too. Anything else?'

She folded the letter carefully. 'I hope only that I can merit the place I have in His Highness's good grace,' she said, her voice trembling with emotion.

She slipped the letter inside the bodice of her dress where it rested close to her heart, and there she carried it about all day. When she undressed and went to bed, she tucked it under her pillow and went to sleep dreaming of becoming Princess of Wales.

Negotiations looked to be progressing smoothly, if slowly. But as summer moved towards autumn, they began to unravel. There was one problem after another, and it seemed that at the root of most of the trouble was one man: George Villiers, Duke of Buckingham, the man who had accompanied Prince Charles on his romantic Spanish adventure.

'How dare he consider us so dishonourable?' Henrietta's mother railed at Lord Kensington from her gold-tasselled throne. Her podgy hands clenched the ornate gilded arms; her face flamed above her black silk dress.

And she accuses *me* of having a hot temper, Henrietta thought to herself. She loved her mother and was not frightened of her the way other people were. Well, not very. But she didn't dare interrupt to ask what was wrong, had to wait along with everyone else and let Marie explain in her own good time.

'How dare he presume to think that my son would sell his own sister,' Marie ranted on, 'on condition that we will make an alliance with England against Spain?'

Henrietta left her mother and slipped through the crowds of courtiers who constantly surrounded her brother, vying for his attention. 'Who is the Duke of Buckingham?' she asked Louis quietly, going to sit on a little stool by his feet. 'I mean, why is he so important?'

'He is King James's Lord High Admiral and Master of the Horse,' Louis explained, leaning towards her and speaking slowly, so as to avoid the stutter which had plagued him since he was a little boy. 'More importantly, he is the king's favourite. Some say he is the most powerful man in England, because the king loves him so much he will do anything the duke asks of him.'

'What does Prince Charles think of him?'

'Overly much it seems. Apparently he and the duke are close as brothers.'

Remembering how unkind his real brother had been to him, Henrietta felt glad in her heart that the prince had such a friend. It was just a pity that this duke was making things difficult for her.

But by and by it was agreed to keep the issue of a warring alliance entirely separate from the marriage contract.

'So the treaty can be signed now?' Henrietta had intended it more as a statement than a question, but her brother did not take it that way.

'It is not as simple as that.'

'What now?' She could feel her temper rising, knew that she was in real danger of losing it. She was beginning to realise she should not have taken it for granted that this marriage was a foregone conclusion, bar the last-minute haggling over the minutiae of the contract. 'Is it the Duke of Buckingham's fault again?'

'It is not a case of fault,' Louis said evenly. 'I am merely taking advice from my first minister.'

'Cardinal Richelieu's fault then?' Henrietta had seen the cardinal leaving the audience chamber earlier that morning in his flowing scarlet robes. He had a grey beard like a goat's, a large, beaky nose, a soft, silent tread and an iron will. Her brother was very dependent on him, wrote to him every night describing the day's events and asking his advice. This he generally heeded so unquestioningly that Henrietta's mother complained it was unclear which of them was the master of whom. Richelieu wielded as much power with the King of France as, seemingly, the Duke of Buckingham did with the King of England. And both of them were real nuisances. 'Does the cardinal not want to see France allied to England?' Henrietta argued, furious now. 'Because he is going the right way about making sure . . .'

'King James promised to write a letter pledging to cease persecuting his Catholic subjects,' Louis cut in. 'The cardinal now feels that is not sufficient. We should demand a clause guaranteeing complete freedom of worship for them, and stipulate that all the laws penalising them should be repealed by the English Parliament.'

'You are not very good at waiting, Madame, are you?' Harry commented mildly, having seen Henrietta storm out of her brother's audience chamber, unable to control her anger one minute longer.

She had gone directly to find Mitte and was now sitting on a window seat with the dog in her lap, brushing the soft white and brown fur in an effort to calm herself. Harry must have come specifically to find her, wanting to help, but she was in no mood to respond to his teasing, however gentle and well meaning. There now seemed every likelihood that negotiations would break down entirely. And where would that leave her? Without a husband or a future or any promise of one. Rather that, in a way, than this intolerable waiting and uncertainty, this not knowing when or if. At mass there were regular prayers for the souls of children who had died before they were baptised and were left in limbo. Henrietta felt as if she were trapped there too.

'Is your king going to agree to these new demands?'

Harry sat himself down beside her, folded his arms across his chest. 'That I can't say, but I am certain at least that he will listen.'

'Are you always so annoyingly optimistic?' Henrietta stopped combing, let Mitte jump down. 'What does Prince Charles say to all this anyway?'

Harry grinned to himself, which Henrietta found so irritating she wanted to punch him on the nose. 'I'm glad you find it so amusing.'

'Sorry,' he said, totally unruffled.

'So what does the prince say?'

'Words not fit for a lady's ears.'

'I have two brothers. I am quite sure I have heard far worse.'

His grin broadened still further, as if he found her temper thoroughly entertaining. No doubt it was. She knew she was over-reacting but she couldn't help it.

Seeing her lingering scowl, Harry cleared his throat. 'The prince says . . . well, he says . . .'

'What? Out with it,' she snapped impatiently, sounding exactly like her mother even to her own ears.

'The Prince says the French monsieurs have played him so scurvy a trick that if it were not for the great respect he has for you, he would not care a fart for their friendship.'

Henrietta looked at him for a moment and then she burst out laughing. Either the prince had an excellent sense of humour and one that was as irreverent as hers, or else he had a temper as fiery. Either way, she liked him all the more for it and somehow felt reassured that all would turn out well in the end. Though she realised that, in truth, it was Harry's sense of humour which had cheered her rather than the Prince of Wales's. 'Thank you,' she said.

Harry pushed his palms against his thighs and rose to go. 'Any time.'

At the height of summer there was an evening concert on the river, whereupon the entire court took to the water in gilded gondolas lit by lanterns and serenaded by violins. It reminded Henrietta that there was one question she had not yet asked about England, one very big and important question – or at least it was very big and important to her. She could have raised it with the ambassador in their regular conversations but she hadn't quite been able to bring herself to do it. The answer mattered to her too much somehow. But now seemed the perfect time to broach it. She left the royal barge's sheltered awning and went to sit on the velvet cushioned bench beside Harry in the front of the barge. 'Tell me, sir,' she began, her heart in her mouth, 'I have long been meaning to ask. Is there much music and dancing in England?'

'Indeed. Prince Charles loves music and theatre almost as much as he does art.'

Something in Harry's manner marred the happiness she'd otherwise have felt at hearing this welcome information. Henrietta had watched him earlier, listening to the music with a faraway look on his strong, handsome face. It had intrigued her because she'd taken him for a straight-forward, jovial fellow who was only really interested in drinking and gambling and joking around with his friends, but she wondered now if perhaps she'd been wrong about him. If he had hidden depths. Perhaps he wished to listen properly to the music and resented her interruption. Whatever the reason, it sounded as if he did not want her there. It was almost as if her presence distrubed him in some way and he would rather she leave him be.

She would have done precisely that and gone off to find someone else to talk to, had he not immediately detained her by elaborating, as if he did not really want her to go at all. 'Amateur theatricals were a favourite pastime of the prince's mother, Anne of Denmark,' he explained. 'When Prince Charles was nine he appeared in one of her productions, in a green satin tunic sewn with gold flowers. That said, members of the English royal family usually content themselves with walk-on parts. It is not considered at all appropriate in England for women to sing and perform on stage in public.'

Henrietta was astounded and indignant. 'Not appropriate?'

He gave a slow shake of his head, an amused smile. 'I am afraid not,' he said, sounding more like his usual self. 'Not that there's any reason why that cannot change.'

'See, you're doing it again.'

'What am I doing?'

'You say something disappointing and immediately follow it up with something more positive and hopeful. Did someone teach you to do that, or is it just how you are?'

Henrietta's mother leaned forward and prodded her on the shoulder with one fat finger. 'Henrietta, you really must not keep pestering that poor gentleman,' she instructed strictly. 'Or Monsieur Jermyn will rue the day he learned to speak French.'

'Not at all.' He twisted round to face Marie. 'It was worth the hours of studying just for the pleasure of talking to your daughter. And to Your Majesty.'

'You have a very silken tongue, Monsieur Jermyn,' Marie simpered. 'You would make as fine a courtier as you would an ambassador. I predict that you will go far.'

Henrietta did not feel able to probe him any more about England after her mother's reprimand, so she asked him instead about himself, finding that actually, she wanted very much to know more about his life. 'So when I was growing up at the château that is named after your family, where were you? Where was home for you when you were a little boy?'

'Rushbrook Hall,' he replied. 'Near a town called Bury St Edmunds, in the county of Suffolk. My family have lived there for generations.'

'That's where you learned to speak French?'

'It is.'

'Were you very studious?'

'I have never been afraid of hard work.' He looked out over the sparkling blackness of the river, towards the barge where the violins were playing, the beautiful music drifting out into the warm city night. 'So long as I can enjoy myself afterwards.'

'And how do you most like to enjoy yourself?' Henrietta asked playfully, glancing at his near-empty cup. 'Besides drinking our fine French wines and feasting on French cheeses and pâtés, that is?'

'The same ways as every other young man, I expect,' he replied quietly.

He looked at her and his eyes connected with hers, held them, as if he were trying to read her thoughts or else wanted her to read his, to impart some message that he was unable to put into words.

Somewhere high above their heads a rocket shot into the night sky, exploding with a bang into a sparkling flower, a bloom of red and green stars. There was a corresponding sensation low in Henrietta's belly that flashed down her thighs, a drag and fizz and burst of heat, exciting, disconcerting, that she had never before experienced.

Harry turned his head away from her abruptly, seeming to shake himself, and Henrietta blushed at the sudden conviction that he must have been thinking of the secret, mysterious pleasures that preoccupied all young men. Girls too, from what she could gather, given the ardent whispers that she regularly overheard amongst the maids and the ladies alike. Pleasures that were entirely forbidden to her until she married. Which, at this rate, she might never be.

She knew she should have felt offended to realise that he was thinking such naughty thoughts about her, as if she were one of the maids whose derrière he might see fit to pinch sneakily. But she wasn't offended at all. In fact, she liked it. More than she could say.

The river party was over and Henrietta lay in her great state bed with its silk and velvet hangings. The noise of continued roistering amongst the bargemen and the musicians added to the occasional barking of dogs and the wailing of the city cats was keeping her awake.

She was filled with a restless hunger. She feared nothing would ever happen to her. She was nearly fifteen and it felt as if life were passing her by. Her sister had been married for two whole years by the time she was fourteen and Henrietta had never even been kissed. She longed to be kissed, sometimes so desperately it made her want to cry. She tried to imagine what it would be like to have the Prince of Wales kiss her and caress her and whisper sweet words to her. But it was Harry Jermyn's beautiful deep voice she heard in her head, that merry laugh of his. She found it hard to imagine what the prince's English voice might sound like, and from the portrait she had seen of him it was even more difficult to imagine him even smiling, let alone laughing.

Things had finally quietened a little, and with the reassuring lump of Mitte curled up at her feet as usual, she drifted off to sleep, only to be woken again by a raucous burst of male laughter from somewhere outside. 'Bad luck, Jermyn,' bellowed one of Henrietta's countrymen in French. 'Not your night, is it? '

Instantly wide awake again, eyes open in the darkness, Henrietta turned over on to her back, listening.

'Not anyone's night any longer,' said another voice. 'It's practically morning. If you were hoping to sneak back to your rooms under cover of darkness, Jermyn my friend, I'm afraid you've left it rather too late.'

'Walk tall and proud and give the maids an eyeful, eh?' someone else called, an unpleasant snigger in his voice.

'Walk tall! The man can barely stand.'

'He's not that incapacitated. Still, ought we not to help him?'

'I say leave him there. He has the little Madame's favour. Let that keep him warm. Let that shield him from shame.'

More harsh laughter. Then retreating footsteps. Silence.

Henrietta knew that 'the little Madame' was the Englishmen's name for her, and was dismayed to hear herself spoken of in such a way; to realise that her friendship with Harry Jermyn was evidently noted and commented on, was the subject of some gossip, jealousy even. If it should get back to King James and Prince Charles . . . but she had done nothing wrong. She could not imagine what it meant, though: *Let that keep him warm. Let that shield him from shame.*

She pushed back the covers and climbed out of bed. Mitte stirred and Henrietta stroked her until she settled again, curled in a tight ball in the folds of the blankets.

She opened a gap in the curtains. The garden was lit with the first blue light of dawn but was quite still. The voices, though, had seemed to come not from just beneath her window but further away, around the other side of the building. Still intrigued, she ventured out into the passageway, crossing over to a vacant room that looked out over the courtyard. One of the kitchen boys was scurrying from the direction of the bakery with a basket of fresh loaves and pastries. She was about to go back to bed when, from the corner of her eye, she caught a slight movement over by the entrance to the porter's lodge, a pale shape huddled in the doorway.

She didn't know if it was more out of curiosity or concern that she decided to go and investigate, but whatever it was, she was glad that she had a single-piece gown she could put on relatively quickly by herself, without the need for assistance. It was still too warm to warrant taking a cloak, so she pushed her feet into her silk shoes and went back out into the passage. Her heart beating hard as a drum, she walked down the dimly lit stone stairs, down another corridor and then the steps that led outside.

As she came to within a few feet of the lodge she could see that the shape crouched in the doorway was that of a man, except that he seemed not to be wearing . . .

'Don't come any closer!'

Henrietta would have recognised his low sonorous voice anywhere, slightly slurred though it was. 'Monsieur Jermyn?'

'Leave me alone, Madame, I beg you.'

She walked tentatively nearer, trying to get a better look at him. 'Are you all right, sir?'

'Perfectly well. Thank you.'

But, patently, he was not. Not only was he evidently rather drunk, but she saw now that he was also stark naked, not even wearing a smock. Her hands shot up to shield her eyes at the same time as he rose unsteadily to his feet and covered himself with his hands.

'I lost them,' he said, before she had even asked.

'You lost your clothes?' she replied, incredulous.

'I did.'

Henrietta made a gap in her fingers to peek at him, caught between acute embarrassment, a desire to giggle, utter fascination and the most powerful kind of excitement. She had never seen a man naked before and was totally entranced by the curly fair hairs on his bare chest and around his navel. It was with the most enormous effort that she stopped her eyes from drifting lower, but just allowing her mind to imagine what might be concealed behind his cupped hands made her heart pound frantically and set off again that feeling, low and deep inside her, like a flint being struck. 'How did you come to lose them?'

'Gambling. Now if you'll kindly be on your way, I'll be on mine.'

'If you don't mind my saying, sir, you have a long way to walk, with no clothes on.'

'Fortunately it is a mild morning.'

She could see that he was shivering nonetheless. She shivered too, though she was not at all cold. She scanned the adjacent buildings. There was already a fair amount of movement over by the stables, and the kitchens and dairy too as more servants started about their daily chores. 'What if someone sees you?'

'It will not go at all well for me. But if I am caught talking to you like this, I'll be in much worse a case, believe me.' He sounded genuinely frightened. 'Please go, for both our sakes.'

She knew very well that her indisputable maidenly virtue was something the Prince of Wales, or any future husband, would value even above her royal French blood; that it would not be at all helpful to her marriage prospects for her to be caught talking to a naked man at dawn, to put it mildly. But she couldn't just leave Harry like this.

'Wait!' she said. And with that she turned and ran, as fast as she could, back to her chamber, whereupon she snatched her cloak out from the chest and ran all the way back to the porter's lodge. She held the cloak out to Harry. 'Here,' she said breathlessly. 'Put this on.'

He made no move at all towards it and it took a moment for Henrietta to realise that he couldn't, not without moving his hands and exposing himself.

There was nothing else for it but to do the job herself. She stepped nearer to him but as she did so he shrank back against the door, regarding her almost warily. He was considerably taller and stronger than she, but there was something about his nakedness, the sheer helplessness of his current predicament, that made him seem touchingly vulnerable. She was so close to him she could see the throb of his heart as it beat, hard and fast, in his chest. As hard and as fast as her own.

'Perhaps if you turn a little?' she suggested.

He bowed slightly too. Between them they manoeuvred it so that Henrietta was able, just about, to reach up and around him with both arms, draping the cloak over his broad shoulders. Her fingers brushed his skin. It was surprisingly soft but cold as marble. His breath was warm, though, and she caught the smell of rum on it, which was strong but not at all unpleasant. Full-length on her, the cloak hung to just below his knees.

He raised his chin a fraction like a little boy, so that she could fasten the clasp for him. It wouldn't quite reach, however.

'My hair,' he said, diffidently.

The problem, she saw, was that it was trapped under the collar and was so thick that it was preventing the clasp from meeting. Managing somehow to hold the two edges of the cloak closed with one hand, with the other she reached back and under his curls. Feeling increasingly self-conscious, she gathered them up and lifted them free.

She tried the fastening again, the intimacy of what she doing and the sheer strangeness of the whole situation dawning on her and causing her to fumble now. He raised his own hands to help her, making her realise that he must have uncovered himself to do so, so that she then became entirely preoccupied with trying to stop her eyes from straying downwards.

Before she knew what she was doing or had time to stop herself, she leaned forward and kissed him, on his lips, a fleeting kiss but one that lasted long enough for her to taste him, gave him just enough time to respond, to shape his mouth to hers before she sprang back, leaving him looking perhaps even more stunned than she felt.

She touched her fingers to her lips. He swallowed hard. They stared at each other. Then she turned and ran, all the way back to her chamber, her face burning and her heart hammering and her mind spinning with the enormity and danger and the sheer wonderfulness of what she had just done. In that one moment she felt as if she had left her childhood behind, had become a young woman. The worst of it was, she could never, ever breathe one word of it to anyone, not even to Mamie.

Next morning she discovered that despite having been the worse for wear from drink the night before, Harry had gone out early, hawking with Louis. The king's passion for falconry being even greater than his love for shoe-making and cookery, he spent hours out in the fields hunting wild duck and quail and rabbits with his beloved peregrine and sparrow hawk. So it was not until much later that day, loitering near the cobbled mews, that Henrietta saw Harry returning, looking extraordinarily elegant astride a grey stallion with a gerfalcon perched on his gauntleted wrist.

As he dismounted, he offered Henreitta nothing beyond the usual courtesies. She tried to tell herself that he must be very embarrassed and ashamed by what had occurred, but that did not mean she was not sorely hurt and confused by his apparent indifference, a little angry also. It was in such stark contrast to what had passed between them just a few hours before. Not that she did not feel shy with him too, painfully so. As usual he was wearing black silk breeches and a shirt with a wide lace collar that was like a mantle over his shoulders, but it made Henrietta's cheeks flame and her belly quiver to think that she had seen all but the one most fascinating part of the body now concealed beneath those clothes. She had seen him naked as the day he was born, and, shamefully, she could not banish the picture of him from her mind. All through matins that morning and vespers later that evening, eyes open, eyes closed, she could not make it go away, and when she retired to bed and lay in the sultry summer darkness with only Mitte for a companion, the image filled her head, was all that she could think about, all that she wanted to think about. That and the feel of his kiss which sent a shudder through her whole body, so delicious and devastating that she wondered how men and women kissed each other and then just went about their daily lives as normal. She wanted to see him naked again, wanted another, longer kiss from him so badly she felt she might die if she could not have it.

When she had retired for the night she'd discovered her cloak, neatly draped over the foot of her bed, where she could still see it now. She didn't think he'd have risked giving it to someone else to return, which would have meant him having to find an explanation for how he came to have it in the first place. But if he had not given it to anyone else, it meant he had brought it back himself, had been here, in her chamber. She wished he were here still. Doing . . . what? Her fevered imagination stretched not much beyond kissing and cuddling yet it was as if something powerful were stirring and awakening in her body, as if she were on the brink of some thrilling discovery. As she lay there in bed, her thoughts lingered again on the captivating vision of Harry's bare shoulders, the curly dark-gold hairs on his chest, the smooth jut of his hipbones, the cup of his hands over his loins. Just thinking about that made the hot, heavy, throbbing ache intensify in her own, a sweet kind of itch, which might drive her mad if she could not relieve it.

Given that men had no compunction about making water in public there had been several occasions when she'd seen them doing it against one of the palace walls, holding something in their hands. She'd heard tell how the more brazen amongst them sometimes turned and showed themselves to girls, but they'd never dare do that to the king's sister. Worse luck, she often thought. She'd listened often enough to the ladies, though, discussing the part of a man which hung between their legs, to know that just seeing one could make a girl flush. It was this which gave pleasure to a woman, this which was in itself an object of great desire.

Was it desire she was feeling now?

Curious, she slipped her hand under her nightshift, touched herself there. It felt bad and at the same time too good to stop. Until she realised she'd be honour bound to tell all to her confessor.

If only they would all just hurry up and sort everything out. She was sure that just as soon as she was with Prince Charles, she would stop thinking about Harry Jermyn. All the time. To the exclusion of all else. Finding any excuse just to be near him, to talk to him. Though she felt so shy now that she was barely able to be in the same room or to say a word to him without blushing. And when he spoke to her or smiled at her it made her insides feel as if they'd turned to water.

Time dragged slowly on into autumn. The cypress trees retained their dark green scaly leaves but the gardens were otherwise colourless, dead. The streets around the palace which had not been subject to Henri le Grand's improvements turned to viscous mud, and mist hung so low and thick over the river that the roofs of Notre-Dame was almost completely obscured. Henrietta refused to read this as ominous, but there were times when she felt as melancholy as the weather. Her mother did too. People had begun to talk of the marriage being broken off and Marie was in such a state about it that she wept whenever her daughter's name was mentioned. Why, oh, why, was there no news from England of terms for an agreement?

Henrietta found some consolation in the little love letters that Prince Charles continued to send to her. He professed that he was eternally hers, that he thought of nothing else but of hastening the day on which he would have the honour of kissing her hands, that he would happily hazard his life to do her service. He sent her pendants and brooches of diamonds and sapphires of remarkable beauty, and told her they were unworthy of her. In reply she told him how much she cherished his love and friendship, and sent him a ribbon from one of her dresses to wear at a tournament.

She was expected to love Prince Charles, was ready to love him, did love him, as much as she could love a person she had never even met.

It could not be love that she felt for Harry Jermyn. But if she was honest with herself, she was not only depressed about the possible failure of all her hopes of marriage. She was also very afraid that if negotiations were terminated, the English Ambassador and his retinue would leave the Louvre and she would not see Harry any more. If the marriage did go ahead, however, it seemed inevitable that he would travel with her entourage to London.

'A compromise will be reached between our two countries, you'll see,' he said to her kindly one day, finding her returning from the chapel where she had gone to spend a quiet hour or two alone, pleading on her knees with the Holy Mother for precisely that.

Henrietta smiled up at him and felt her legs go weak as they did every time he spoke to her or smiled at her, when she saw him walking towards her or even when she just heard his voice in another room. They never mentioned what had occurred at the porter's lodge but she was sure somehow that he thought about it too, perhaps not as often as she did, but often enough. It was there, underlying every conversation, every glance, adding a sweet tension to all that passed between them.

She knew him well enough by now to know that his faith in the power of the diplomatic process was as unshakable as her faith in God, but instinctively she trusted him and took just as much comfort from his calm confidence that an agreement would be reached with the English as she had taken from her prayers.

Then it transpired that there was yet another obstacle, and that God Himself was the problem.

The court had just watched a marionette show featuring puppet Chinamen, and Henrietta, Louis, Gaston and their mother had sat down to a simple supper of kidney soup and preserved fruit, when Marie mentioned that the dispensation needed from Henrietta's godfather, the Pope, in order for her to marry a heretic, had not been forthcoming.

Henrietta set down her soup spoon with an exasperated clang. 'When shall we have it? Next week? Next month? Next year? When I am old and grey and . . .'

'Who can say?'

'Enough,' her mother commanded. She brought her own spoon to her lips, sipped from it and swallowed with a calmness that drove Henrietta mad. Nothing put Marie de' Medici off her food. 'If you must know, I think the Holy Father is trying to delay matters long enough to frustrate the signing of the treaty altogether.'

At this Henrietta sprang to her feet as if propelled out of her chair by the sheer force of her anger. She found it impossible to sit still when she was cross. 'Why would he do that?'

When Marie did not answer, Henrietta turned to Louis. 'Well, my lord?'

'I bid you be silent,' their mother instructed him.

Which was the one way to guarantee that Louis would be anything but. 'Henrietta has a right to know her godfather's reservations,' he replied, quietly defiant, before turning to address his sister. 'The Pope is of the opinion that this union will bring you only great unhappiness, Henrietta. More than that, it will place you in grave danger.'

'How? What do you mean?'

He clicked his fingers and his page, waiting dutifully at the side of the room for just such a request, handed him a letter which Louis in turn held out to his sister. 'Here,' he said. 'I knew you'd want to read it for yourself.'

As Henrietta sat back down and took in the Pope's words, irritation was replaced by a stealthy dread which stole into her heart as if it were creeping up through her fingers from the fine vellum itself. The Holy Father had an insight into the attitudes of the English from his priests who had travelled to that country on conversion missions, and he feared that if the King of England relaxed the bloody penal laws against Roman Catholics, it would enrage his Protestant populace, who would blame Henrietta and vent their anger on her.

She could not forget, try as she always did not to dwell on it, that her own father had been assassinated by a religious fanatic, a man who had disapproved of his tolerance towards Protestants so vehemently that he had ambushed him in his carriage and driven a knife into his heart. Henrietta had been told often enough how her first public appearance as a baby had been at her mother's coronation at St Denis, and how she had been taken back there in her nurse's arms less than two weeks later to attend her father's funeral. She was far too young to remember it, but had heard others tell of their memories so often that they felt like her own. There were times she was quite certain she could still hear the citizens of Paris, insensible with grief at the loss of their beloved king, throwing themselves on the ground in their uncontrolled weeping and wailing.

Henrietta did not want to die as her father had died. But she did want to be loved as he had been loved. She had been quietly confident that even if the English despised Catholics, they would make an exception for her and love her. She had known nothing but love all her life and therefore had a deep-rooted belief that love was all she would ever know. She was the baby of the French royal family, the king and queen's last-born child, the prettiest and smallest princess who had grown up petted and pampered by her parents, sisters, brothers and servants, by the whole court. It was beyond her really to imagine that she would not be equally adored in England. She decided that for once the Holy Father must be wrong. But she was curious. 'What do the English do to Catholics, exactly?'

'They repress and punish them in every way,' announced Cardinal Richelieu, who had just entered the room in his scarlet robes. As Henrietta turned to him he stepped forward with a courteous bow. 'May I explain?' he asked her mother, in a way that brooked no objection.

'By all means.'

He took a deep breath. 'Queen Elizabeth of England introduced a series of vile and wicked laws devised to suppress the practising of the Catholic faith through the loss of freedom of worship . . . of estates and property . . . of life itself,' he began. 'Just to hear mass in England renders offenders subject to severe fines, and anyone found to have an allegiance to Rome, or refusing to attend Anglican services, faces imprisonment or the penalties for high treason. Over a hundred and fifty English Catholic martyrs died on the scaffold under a law that made it high treason for any Jesuit or priest even to be in England, and a felony for anyone to harbour or help them.

'King James added even more oppressive and savage measures to the statute book. The cruellest of all prohibits recusants from remaining within ten miles of the City of London, or to move more than five miles from their place of residence till they have obtained licence to do so from four magistrates and the bishop of the diocese or lieutenant of the county. They are forbidden from practising as lawyers, physicians or apothecaries; from holding office in any court or corporation; from commissions in the army or navy; and from discharging the duties of executors, administrators, or guardians. Any married woman who has not received the sacrament in the

Anglican church for a year before her husband's death forfeits her dower and jointure and is debarred from claiming any part of her husband's goods. Husbands and wives, if married otherwise than by a Protestant minister in a Protestant church, are each deprived of all interest in the lands or property of the other. They are fined one hundred pounds for omitting to have each of their children baptised by a Protestant minister within a month of birth. Houses of suspected recusants are liable to be searched at any time, arms and ammunition seized, and any books or furniture destroyed at will. Does that answer your question?'

'That is why your marriage is so very important,' Marie explained. 'The agreement we make with England will call for all these evil laws to be repealed and so will ease the troubles of Catholics throughout that blighted kingdom. You will be as a blessing to them. And when you are queen, you can do even more to help them.'

'*If* she is given the chance to become queen,' Louis said solemnly.

'We have not yet given up,' Marie said determinedly. 'A way will be found.'

It had been three months since Henrietta's last confession. She entered the quiet candlelit sanctity of the royal chapel, the scent of incense hanging in the air making her feel instantly closer to God; to want to be a better person. As she went to sit on the stool by the screen, she felt the usual mixed emotions: relief at being about to unburden herself and be forgiven, combined with the inevitable nervousness that accompanied confessing anything to anyone.

She trusted her confessor, Father Pierre de Berulle, implicitly, though, and knew him to be relatively unshockable as well as compassionate and fair. He was a fervent and eloquent statesman with a reputation for saintliness and great theological knowledge and wisdom; had been Father Confessor to Marie de' Medici herself before he became Henrietta's confessor. Since she had never really known the man who sired her, Father de Berulle was the closest to a real father that Henrietta had. Though the advantage of him being a priest rather than a parent was that she could tell him things she'd never tell a member of her family, all kinds of things, knowing he would never betray her confidences and could absolve her of her sins at the same time.

'I've been vain and impatient,' she said. 'And I lost my temper.'

The priest gave an affectionate sigh. The princess's confessions varied little from month to month. 'How many times, Your Majesty?'

'Too many. I lost count.'

'Say ten Hail Marys and . . .'

'I've been having sinful thoughts too,' she blurted.

'About what?'

Her cheeks burned and she said more quietly, 'About a person, Father.'

There was a creak as the priest sat up straight on his chair behind the screen. If he were a dog his ears would be pricked by now. 'Which person?'

'A man.'

The priest was silent for a moment. Henrietta knew he would ask for no name if she did not volunteer one, which she was not about to do. 'Did these thoughts lead to anything?'

Henrietta paused, could not bring herself to say it.

'Go on, child.'

She took a deep breath. 'When I think about him I touch myself and it . . .'

'No need to go into details,' he cut in, but gently. 'You know that is wrong?'

'Yes, Father,' she said. And then: 'Is it worse than losing my temper and disrespecting my mother and being vain?'

'No, Madame,' he said kindly. 'It is a sin that all normal, healthy young people commit. Old ones too, for that matter. The important thing is to know where to stop.'

'I kissed him.'

'You kissed him? Or he kissed you?'

'I kissed him.' She nearly confessed that he had been naked at the time but realised that would be misconstrued and decided it had no bearing. 'Only a small kiss. And then I ran away.'

'I am glad to hear it. Ten more Hail Marys,' the priest said. 'And let us both pray very hard that you are soon married!'

Their prayers were answered. Either that or Harry Jermyn was right. God or the diplomatic process had prevailed, and a resolution was reached at the beginning of December.

'The final agreement is very pleasing,' Louis told Henrietta with a satisfied smile when they were out riding together though the bare wintry fields near St Germain, the earth hard as iron beneath the horses' hoofs and the air crisp with frost. 'You are to be given every latitude to continue to practise your religion in England. Mass is to be freely celebrated according to Roman rite, with the sacraments administered in properly ornamented chapels. You are to have an establishment of priests, headed by a bishop, and your household is to consist entirely of French Catholics. The children of your marriage are to be brought up by you until the age of twelve. The penal laws against Catholics in England are to be relaxed, just as we had hoped. The clauses which guarantee this are to be kept secret but clauses there are. It is an excellent start.'

The treaty was sanctioned at the beginning of December, and while it was quickly taken to be countersigned at Newmarket, where King James and Prince Charles had gone for the horseracing, a fleet was being made ready to take the French princess to England.

Henrietta's mother found her standing before a portrait of the late King. Even in his fifties, King Henri had had a lively twinkle in his eyes.

'Do you think I will make a good queen?' she asked, without taking her eyes off her father's face.

'Who are you asking? Me or him?' Marie came to stand behind Henrietta, enveloping her in the cloyingly sweet perfume that was made in the palace perfumeries, a scent that was redolent of Henrietta's childhood. Marie looked over her daughter's head at the picture of her husband. 'There is no doubt that you have your father's nobility and courage, his wish to alleviate the sorrows of this world.'

'Thank you, Mam.' Henrietta was not at all convinced she had those qualities, but hoped she might find them hidden away somewhere, when the time came.

'He was one of the most popular kings France has ever known,' Marie continued. 'Beloved by the people for his bravery, and for ending thirty years of religious civil wars and giving France unity, religious tolerance and prosperity. He has been dead for over ten years, but he will always be knows as Henri the Great. As far as the people of France are concerned, at least.'

Henrietta wished she remembered more about him. Christine and Louis had told her how he'd visited St Germain often and had kissed and hugged them all the time, let them sit on his lap at the table and drink wine from his cup and laughed when they sprayed him with water from the fountain.

'You are his name-child,' Marie said to Henrietta now. 'Rightly so. Since you resemble him, in features and in character, more than any other member of this family.'

'Do I?' Henrietta struggled to find a physical resemblance in herself to that strong soldier's face with its short grey beard and slightly hooked nose. He looked more like a general than a king, and Henrietta was sure she'd make a hopeless general, thrilling as it must be to serve as one. Apart from being female, she was impatient and quick-tempered, vain and giddy, which were hardly the ideal qualities. Though she liked to think she could be brave if she needed to be, she had never really been put to the test. 'We both have eyes that are big and black,' she conceded.

'And roving,' her mother said in a harsher tone. Henrietta turned round and Marie looked hard at her. 'You may not even know your own nature yet but I can see it in you. You are your father's daughter through and through. In every respect. And your father had appetites that made him need a different lover for every day of the week.'

This was no news to Henrietta. He might have died when she was just a baby, but she knew several of his many paramours all the same. No secret was made of them. There was flirty Jacqueline, and fifteen-year-old Charlotte whom Henri had met in the year of Henrietta's birth. And beautiful Gabrielle d'Estrées, whom he had always claimed was the great love of his life. He had eight illegitimate offspring, of whom more than half had been brought up with Henrietta and her legitimate brothers and sisters at St Germain.

'You are your father's daughter,' her mother repeated more critically, 'and given that it is widely accepted women have more powerful desires than men, and far less control over those desires . . . Mother of God help you, is all I can say! It is evident already that you enjoy the company of beautiful young men every bit as much as your father enjoyed the company of beautiful young women. Though, in your case, it is one beautiful young man in particular, yes?'

Henrietta's cheeks flushed scarlet. This was not a conversation she wanted to have with anyone, least of all her mother.

'Surely you did not think it had escaped my notice?'

'He has done nothing,' Henrietta said, rushing to defend Harry even before herself. 'His behaviour towards me has always been entirely respectful and correct and . . .'

'It it hadn't, believe me, he'd be long gone. As I am sure he is wholly aware. But his sudden absence would cause eyebrows to be raised even more than having him remain. Besides, I have never been unduly concerned. As well as being utterly charming, Jermyn has impeccable judgement, is intelligent, shrewd and undoubtedly ambitious. As I said to him, he will go far. So long as he exercises proper control over himself, where you are concerned.'

'Mam, please,' Henrietta begged, squirming. 'Can we not speak of this any more?'

'Just be warned. It may be acceptable for kings to take lovers, but it is an entirely different matter for their queens. Looseness in women causes excessive slipperiness of the womb,' Marie qualified, at her most excruciatingly frank. 'Which interferes with a woman's principal duty to reproduce. And, in your case, the political, economic and social stability of England and the future of the crown itself is entirely dependent upon your ability in that quarter. The legitimacy of your offspring is of paramount importance.'

There was a celebratory ball that night at the Louvre, more fires and fireworks. Henrietta stood on the terrace watching the blazes all across Paris, trying to put her mother's uncomfortable conversation from her mind as she listened to the different sounds of gunpowder, the booming of the mighty guns in the arsenal and the thud, pop and crackle as multicoloured stars rocketed and flashed and shimmered, lighting up the night sky.

She had made a point of going nowhere near Harry but he sought her out instead, so what was she to do?

'You look happy, ma'am,' he said.

'I am,' she said, overly bright, surreptitiously checking to see that her mother was not watching. 'It is the happiest day of my life.' The words sounded hollow even to her own ears. After all the waiting there was a great sense of anti-climax. Nothing to do with her impending marriage felt real. All that did feel real right now, very real, was that Harry was standing so close to her that she could feel the warmth from his body. She had such a strong urge just to reach out her hand and touch him that she almost feared she might do it involuntarily. She clasped her hands together, to give them something to do. She wondered how he'd feel if he knew what she was thinking. But when he turned his face to hers and she looked into his eyes she was sure that what she wanted he wanted too, just as much.

I must stop this, she told herself sternly. I must. I must. I am marrying the Prince of Wales.

She made herself ask Harry an appropriate question. 'So will there be celebrations in your own country tonight, sir?'

'There will undoubtedly be bonfires and bells.'

'People will be happy that I am marrying your prince?'

'Good Englishmen will be pleased,' he said, with something that she had come to recognise in him: a diplomat's tactful evasiveness.

'And bad Englishmen?'

'Those who call themselves Puritan will not be quite so pleased.' His tone now sounded more disparaging than diplomatic.

'What is . . . Puritan?' she asked, her tongue having trouble with the unfamiliar vowels.

'Those who reject worldly pleasure and sensual delights, who call for stricter religious and moral discipline and simpler acts of worship.'

'Are you a Puritan?'

His smile looked a little sad. 'Surely you know me well enough by now to realise that I am not a man to reject worldly pleasure and sensual delights.'

What was he talking about? Cheese and wine again? Or those other pleasures and delights he had hinted at before, which she did not dare to think about now? Which she could not help but think about every time she saw him . . . and even when she did not. 'You are not Catholic though, are you?'

'Anglican,' he stated. 'From *Angleterre*.'

'Then your soul is in peril, sir,' she told him imperiously, suddenly very afraid for him. 'When you die, you will not go to heaven.'

She sensed him resist further comment, which annoyed her. 'You do not wish to discuss your faith with me?'

'Only because I sense that any discussion would be futile. That you are immovable on this subject and therefore it can lead only to disagreement between us. And I do not want to disagree with you. Especially over something that I know matters to you so much. Especially not tonight. Everyone is entitled to their own beliefs,' he added evenly. 'I respect yours and ask you to respect mine.'

She did, or she liked to think she did. And yet . . . She didn't want him to die and go to hell, or to live his whole life under a misapprehension. 'Just what *are* your beliefs?' she demanded, turning to face him fully. 'I should like to know.'

He gave a small smile that was more like a silent sigh of resignation, accepting that there was going to be no easy escape from this inquisition. 'Let me begin by telling you what I don't believe. I'm sorry to say it, but I think it's nonsensical to believe that bread can magically be transformed into flesh and wine to blood. And you show me any mention of Purgatory in the Bible and I'll be more inclined to listen to your Pope.'

Henrietta's eyes flashed with a mixture of anger and dismay. That he could be so misguided, so simply wrong. She had thought his judgement so sound, until now. 'Do a great many other people in England think Catholicism . . . nonsensical?'

'Unfortunately there are those who see it as rather more than that. Who see it as evil and dangerous.'

'Yes, so I have heard. Let me guess. The Puritans?' she tried again.

'Very good,' Harry said, referring to her pronunciation.

'It's a bad word though, *oui*?'

'It is a word you will encounter often, I fear.' He took a deep breath. 'Perhaps I should teach you some others? More pleasant ones.'

She shook her head, turned away again. 'Not now. I am not in the mood.'

'May I speak candidly, Madame?'

'You generally do.'

'I have to confess I find it astonishing that, despite this lengthy preparation for your betrothal and the extensive trousseau you are to take with you, nobody has seen fit to equip you with even a few words of English. It's not too late, of course.'

Henrietta frowned. 'But the king speaks French, doesn't he?'

'He does. However, the vast majority of his subjects do not.'

'I am not very good at languages,' she admitted. 'As far as my mother was concerned, it was not important for me to learn such things. All that mattered was that I should be brought up a good Catholic. But at least I know what a Puritan is now.'

'Would that I had taught you any word but that.'

She looked out over the familiar firelit city and when she drew in her breath the icy air, smelling strongly of gunpowder and smoke, was sharp as a knife at her throat, so that she felt suddenly afraid of leaving the only world she had ever known for one so strange and hostile. She drew her cloak more tightly about her shoulders. 'You will be coming with me, sir, won't you? To England?'

'If you wish me to.'

'Of course I wish it.'

'Then know that I will gladly follow you to the ends of the earth in order to serve you.'

'Would you?' she asked, looking up at him coquettishly from beneath her eyelashes. 'Why?'

'Because . . .'

'Because?'

'Because I want to see you become the great queen I know you will be.'

His answer should have pleased Henrietta. She wanted very much to be a great queen. But it seemed so far in the future, another life yet to be led, and for now she was just a young princess, a girl, and she had wanted him to say something else. After the way he had looked at her, she had been so sure he was going to say something else. To give some other reason altogether why he wanted to stay with her.

# *1625*

Just as the marriage arrangements had been conducted and finalised without Henrietta having set eyes on Prince Charles, so now she was to go the whole way and be betrothed and wedded to him *in absentia*. As if he were a phantom prince, the engagement and wedding ceremony were to take place in Paris without him. A proxy wedding, with a substitute bridegroom.

'Who will act the part of husband right up to the point of getting into the bed with you,' Mamie giggled. It was her task to entertain Henrietta while she sat through the long, daily process of having her hair fashioned with the heated curling irons. But Henrietta did not share Mamie's amusement this time.

Given all she had heard about the Duke of Buckingham and the great trouble he had caused, she was dismayed to hear that it was he who was to travel to France to represent Prince Charles before escorting her, as Princess of Wales, back to England. Much as her husband-to-be was reputed to love the duke, she did not like the idea of having to stand at the altar beside him, of all people. But then word reached France that he would not be coming after all. King James was suffering from a severe fainting fever and the duke would not leave his bedside until his health was sufficiently improved.

It never did. Three days later, Henrietta's mother called her daughter to her audience chamber and, before the English Ambassador and his attendants, broke it to her that King James had died of the bloody flux and that his last wish was for his son's marriage to proceed as intended.

Henrietta's first thought was for Prince Charles who had just lost his father. She imagined his tragic eyes looking more tragic than ever.

'Your prince is a prince no longer.' Marie reached out almost reverently to rearrange one of Henrietta's glossy black ringlets. 'He is King Charles of England, Ireland and Scotland. Which means that you, my daughter, will enter England as its queen.'

Lord Kensington led the cheers. 'Long live the King! And the Queen!' When the applause had died down he muttered aside to the Earl of Carlisle, 'And rid us of Buckingham. His position has remained unchanged, I take it? He continues without rival?'

'The new king cherishes him no less than did the old,' agreed the other man. 'He has already appointed him gentleman of the bedchamber. They are constantly in each other's company.'

Henrietta had understood most of what the two men had just said. She was surprised how much English she had picked up just by being in the company of English people for so many months. She could not speak the language, did not dare even attempt a phrase, but she could understand more than a little now.

'Apparently nothing is done at court without the duke's sanction,' the Earl of Carlisle continued.

'Well, this wedding will be,' Marie pronounced decisively, silencing the conversation as was her way. 'It will go ahead next month as planned, but the duke cannot now stand in for the new king, since he must be present at King James's funeral which will not be held for weeks. The Duc de Chevreuse will stand as proxy bridegroom instead.'

Excellent, thought Henrietta. She liked the Duc de Chevreuse.

At the end of April a suave, dark-haired, moustachioed English courtier named George Goring arrived, armed with the necessary documentation. Tailors, dressmakers, embroiderers and jewellers set to work, and almost before Henrietta knew it, it was May, the month in which she was to be married.

At the beginning of the month there was a formal betrothal ceremony in the king's audience chamber at which Henrietta wore a sable-trimmed cloak. But on the day before her wedding she exchanged her usual elaborate gown for a plain wool dress and retreated to the tiny, bare, white-walled cell of the Carmelite Convent of the Inception at Faubourg on the edge of Paris.

She had spent many peaceful hours there during her childhood, having always found great solace in its tranquillity and simplicity and in Sister

Madeleine's advice and compassion. None of Henrietta's childhood troubles had ever been too trivial for her to listen to, and she had treated the loss of a milk tooth or a sisterly squabble over a ribbon as if it were a matter of the greatest consequence. When Henrietta's pet dog, the first Mitte, had died, Henrietta had sobbed for hours in Sister Madeleine's arms, and together they had buried the spaniel in the convent garden, lit candles and held a little funeral mass.

Sister Madeleine never seemed to age like other people, and just as she had always seemed as wise as an ancient person, her face, encircled by its starched white wimple, had remained unchanged over the years, still perfectly unlined and serene. Henrietta wished she could be more like her but knew that her character was even less suited to being a nun than an army general. She did not possess many or indeed any of the virtues required for that role either, such as infinite patience and tranquillity, though she did try very hard every day to be good and pious.

After she had served the nuns in the refectory with her own hands and later joined them for vespers, she knelt by her narrow truckle bed before the icon of the Virgin Mary and the wooden crucifix, her hands clasped together. Sister Madeleine came to join her.

'Shall I pray with you?' the nun suggested softly, kneeling by Henrietta's side and bowing her head. 'Not that it makes the prayers more likely to be heard if they are spoken by two voices rather than one. Our Lady hears and sees all, of course. But if I know what is in your heart, I can continue to pray for you when you leave.'

Henrietta closed her eyes. 'I pray that King Charles will love me very much and I him,' she said ardently. 'That we will be blessed by many children, daughters as well as sons. I pray that the king's subjects, the people of England, will also take me to their hearts. And that I may further assist my fellow Catholics in that country.'

Sister Madeleine added her own prayer. 'I pray that your holy marriage will bring relief to the poor English Catholics greatly oppressed for their religion, and that you succeed in bringing the king back to the faith of his ancestors, and all of England safely back into the arms of Rome.'

Henrietta knew this was what everyone at court was most sincerely hoping for, what everyone in France was hoping for. They believed it to be her destiny, and a glorious destiny. To Henrietta it felt like a heavy responsibility to place on her frail shoulders and she was not sure she was equal to it. But it was such a worthwhile aim that she would not be daunted, would do her very best not to disappoint. She had been brought up to believe that, with God's blessing, everything and anything was achievable.

'Amen,' she softly said.

Henrietta's wedding day, the eighth day of May in France, was the first day of May in England, according to that country's calendar. May Day. But a less spring-like day there could not have been.

It dawned cold, dismal and wet, but the splendour of Henrietta's robe more than compensated for the dullness of the weather. It was made of cloth-of-silver and gold, patterned all over with the lilies of France and ornamented with cascades of diamonds and coloured jewels, with hanging sleeves that reached to the ground. The long train was of pale blue velvet and more cloth-of-gold, and was so heavy that Mamie and Mademoiselle de Bourbon, who were to carry it, had to beg assistance of an equerry to help them take some of the weight. Upon Henrietta's head was set a crown encrusted with diamonds and pearls, also so heavy that it felt as if her neck might snap beneath it.

She felt as if she were dressed for a masquerade, that this wedding was nothing more than another glittering court entertainment. The sense of unreality had only increased. It was as if it was all happening to someone else. She was just playing a part. And not very well at that. She could not feel any real emotion, no swell of joy or apprehension, such as she'd always imagined she'd experience on her wedding day. She was deprived even of the carefree delight she'd taken in real theatricals. Though she could not help but be swept along by the grandeur and sense of occasion as, late in the afternoon, the procession prepared to make its way from the archbishop's palace, where Henrietta had gone that morning to dress.

The scene, as Henrietta could not help but view it, was spectacular. They were to walk along a long and lofty temporary gallery, which was supported on pillars draped in violet and gold satin and decorated with gold fleur-de-lys.

Among those waiting to join the parade was Lord Kensington, who had recently been made the Earl of Holland in recognition of his achievements in negotiating the marriage. The ambassador and his attendants had all temporarily cast off the mourning clothes they had been wearing for King James, and were so magnificently dressed that Henrietta was reminded of her initial confusion, when she had all but taken Harry for a prince. In a black velvet suit slashed now with silver, he looked so handsome that her heart jolted at the sight of him. She wondered if she should feel guilty for that, this being her wedding day, but decided she need not. It was not as if she were wishing she could marry him instead. That was impossible, of course it was. She was a royal and he was a nobody. A nobody who was her friend. A nobody who was the first man she had seen naked and had kissed, and whom she secretly longed in her heart to see naked again, to kiss again.

She tried to catch his eye, needing a smile from him, but at first he would not look at her at all. And then he did, his gaze travelling over the richness of her gown, up to her small, pale face, to her enormous dancing black eyes and the great crown set on top of the cascade of long glossy black ringlets. She felt the distance between them yawn wider, and realised suddenly that it might be a very lonely business, this being a queen.

For now at least she had her brothers to support her. On her right along the arcade walked King Louis, all in gold like a sun king, and on her left was Gaston, who was not much taller than his little sister, and whose impossibly bushy black eyebrows always reminded Henrietta of two fat beetles. They were preceded by a hundred of the king's Swiss Guard, drums beating and standards unfurled, followed by royal trumpeters, oboes and more drums, the master of ceremonies and Knights of the Order of the Holy Ghost.

Then came counts, dukes, marshals, chevaliers and all the peers of France, their robes studded with diamonds. Marie de' Medici, who had chosen not to forego her customary black, walked a few paces behind, with Anne, in rose pink satin embroidered with silver.

Henrietta was amazed to see the great crowds of people who had gathered despite the incessant rain, so many that side streets had been barricaded and patrols were needed to keep order. Stands that had been specially erected were crammed and the cathedral square was thronged with horses, grand coaches, and hundreds upon hundreds of people, all cheering and craning their necks for a better view.

'It's you they've all come to see, Henrietta,' Gaston whispered, giving her arm a squeeze where it was linked through his. 'They've been waiting all night and all day, most of them, despite the wet weather.'

It was an extraordinary feeling to be surrounded by so many well-wishers. Despite the clouds and the rain, it made Henrietta feel warm and sunny inside, this proof that she was so loved by the people of France. How she loved them all back, each and every one. How she was going to miss them all. She wished they could come with her to England. All of them. But it served to convince her that the people of England would welcome her with as much warmth and would grow to love her just as much.

Because she was marrying a heretic, Rome had decreed that the wedding could not take place inside the church but must be performed outside the west door of the cathedral where a temporary dais and a canopy of gold had been erected. A stage, if ever there was one. As the bridal party came in sight of it they were greeted by a great fanfare from the king's drums, trumpets and oboes.

Almost miraculously the clouds cleared and the sun came out as the Duc de Chevreuse, in black velvet slashed with gold and a scarf bedecked with gold roses, took his place beside Henrietta. The short ceremony, led by Cardinal de la Rochefoucauld, called on her to renounce all rights to the French throne, and this she did with sorrow, as if she were renouncing France itself, along with her status as its princess and daughter.

When it also called for the English Ambassador to vow to honour and serve her with respect and reverence, the Earl of Holland knelt at her feet along with his envoys. But Henrietta immediately looked beyond them, for Harry. In the mass of people arrayed behind he was easy to find, towering head and shoulders above everyone else.

She received her smile then, just a small one but it was enough. She knew beyond a doubt that though he was not quite an ambassador yet, though he need make no public vow to her, Harry had made one in his heart, would continue to honour and serve her just as he had privately promised to do, just as he had done from the moment they had first met. In a way that made her feel more queenly than all the rest of the pomp and ceremony had done. It made her think of the knights in romances who had pledged to honour, with their every deed, the highborn ladies they had loved.

With the sign of the cross, Henrietta and her proxy bridegroom were proclaimed man and wife according to Catholic rite. As soon as the Duc de Chevreuse had slipped the heavy, jewel-encrusted ring on to Henrietta's small white finger, George Goring departed the busy cathedral square, vowing to ride all night in order to reach Boulogne as soon as was possible, to rush back across the sea to England with the news that at last the new king had a new wife.

Henrietta moved into the candlelit dimness of the cathedral for the nuptial mass. The bare stone walls of Notre-Dame had been decorated with tapestries and shimmering tissues of cloth-of-gold, silk and silver. In the chancel, pieces of silver tinkled down from high up in the scaffolding, thrown by the heralds, each coin engraved with the heads of Charles and Henrietta on one side and of Cupid on the reverse. Mass was observed from an elaborately covered dais built in the centre of the choir stalls and everyone then went back to the archbishop's palace for the wedding banquet. The tables were covered with silk carpets beneath two layers of linen tablecloths, and the best royal dinner service had been laid out.

'I am graced by three queens now,' Louis said sweetly, smiling at his wife and his mother and then at his sister. Henrietta was accorded the privilege of taking the place at his left, as Queen Consort of England.

At least Henrietta had the chance to dine at her mother's new Luxembourg Palace even if she was never to live in it. The feasting continued in its high-ceilinged gilded state dining rooms for several days, accompanied by yet more fireworks that were sent up from a boat in the middle of the Seine as well as from almost every street in Paris. Fifty cannons had been positioned all along the quay below the gallery and the firing of these added to the ongoing din.

Henrietta had been given to understand by the Earl of Holland that King Charles would be crossing the Channel imminently, but though she passed each day in a mounting and almost unbearable fever of impatience and excitement, still he did not come to her.

Instead it was the Duke of Buckingham who arrived, with a vast army of attendants including two and twenty watermen, all clad in sky blue outfits embroidered with silver anchors. Even without them, he would have made an extremely grand entrance. His sword and hatband were encrusted with flashing diamonds and he wore an extravagant suit and cloak of deep purple satin, embroidered all over with rich oriental pearls which seemed to have been attached with such showy but surely intentional carelessness that dozens cascaded off like a shower of raindrops as he moved. A page scurried in his wake, hastily sweeping them up, but when he handed them back, the duke did not deign to take them.

His arrival was celebrated with a week of processions and fireworks, rejoicings and feastings. The whole of Parisian high society gathered in the Palais de Luxembourg for a magnificent banquet of sweetmeats where all kinds of music played and there were fireworks in the garden, the most imaginative display seen in Paris for a long time, with flowers and wheels and dancing fountains of lights. Though nothing could outshine the Duke of Buckingham.

'Do you not think him the best-made man in the world?' Anne sighed, after he had danced, to great applause, and flirted outrageously with her nearly all evening.

Most of the ladies of the court clearly agreed with her, dithering and fluttering and preening whenever he came near, while their husbands, including Louis, looked on and scowled with jealousy.

Anne's rapturous expression made Henrietta furious. She did not think her sister-in-law loved Louis well enough and she'd heard the gossip that this was the reason they had no children, why France still had no heir. 'I do not find the duke better made than the king my brother,' she said to Anne tartly.

Determined not to like George Villiers though Henrietta had been, she had to admit that his riot of black ringlets, curled moustache, strange dark eyes and pointed Spanish beard did make for a very attractive man, just as his tall and lithe physique made for an impressively agile and athletic dancer, attributes which she would normally have found appealing. But he moved with a languid insolence and there was a cruel curl to his sensuous lips that made her recoil from him, putting her instantly on her guard whenever he came near.

'My purpose in coming to France is to hasten your departure, madam,' he told her silkily. 'The king is dying with impatience and love for you.'

'And I for him,' Henrietta said warily.

But a few moments later she overheard the duke whisper to the ambassador, words that chilled her heart. 'Whatever you do, don't let on to the little queen that our king's ardour is driven purely by financial necessity. The vaults are so depleted that calling Parliament is a matter of urgency, but His Majesty must postpone it until the queen's arrival. That is the only reason he is in such a rush to have her come to him.'

Henrietta refused to believe that her husband, as she must now think of this man she had not yet met, could be as callous as his friend. It also worried her to think that the English court was so poor.

But no matter the reason for the king's keenness to have her there, it seemed that he was going to have to go on waiting. The entire royal household was to journey to the coast to see Henrietta off, and getting them all on the road was no easy feat, not to mention marshalling the four hundred French courtiers who were accompanying her to England.

Her new retinue included counts and countesses, cooks and kitchen staff, including a specialist patissier and baker. There were chambermaids, linen maids, laundresses and dressers. A clockmaker, a jeweller, physician, apothecary, secretary and master of the horse. Plus musicians, gentlemen ushers, pages, grooms and coachmen, all of whom were to be fitted out in new crimson tunics and plumed hats. In charge of them all was her grand chamberlain, Comte Tanneguy Le Veneur de Tillières, accompanied by his wife. The queen's ladies were headed by Mamie while Father de Berulle led an ecclesiastical entourage, which included a bishop who was a young aristocrat with connections to Cardinal Richelieu, a grand almoner, two abbots, chaplains, clerks and twelve priests.

Then there was the extensive trousseau to be prepared, consisting of a dozen lovely new dresses, one fantastically worked with gold and silver embroidery on a background of black, another in grey satin, and another in white with a long train. Henrietta also had a new royal robe in violet velvet embroidered with fleur-de-lys and edged in tiny arabesques. Plus four dozen nightdresses, a dozen nightcaps, and five dozen handkerchiefs.

Household goods included Turkey carpets, a dressing table, a large silver mirror, vinegar jars, solid gold tableware, sugar basins and perfume pans. Henrietta was also taking with her forty horses as well as carriages, some heavily built for country roads and others swathed in velvet for the city, plus litters for grand processions and mules to carry the litters. There were bridles, saddles, decorative coats and plumes of feathers for them. There was a great bed with yards of red velvet curtains embroidered with silver and topped with white ostrich feathers. Mamie was taking silk-embroidered bed furnishings and the priests serge, along with wooden tables and chairs and pewter plates for their cells. Four sets of plate were to be sent for celebrating mass, with crucifix, chasubles and stoles.

The palace was in uproar as all was carefully packed into trunks before being loaded on to carts and wagon. The dismantled bed frame had a whole wagon to itself, with another just for the linen and hangings.

Henrietta was not allowed to help with the preparations but noticed that that there was one person who was quietly at the centre of things, Harry, displaying his impressive talent for organisation, smoothing out problems along with ruffled feathers and generally getting things done. He had appointed himself unofficial assistant to the Comte de Tillières and seemed to be working by far the harder of the two. In so doing he was serving Henrietta just as he had promised to do. Only it meant he was kept so busy he barely had a second to spare to talk to her any more. She missed their conversations and his company more than she had imagined possible, and was cross with him for ignoring her, even though she knew that was unjustified. But he appeared to relish being so fully occupied, throwing himself into the work as if he welcomed the distraction, as if his very life depended upon it.

At least Henrietta had Mitte, who was so afraid of being left behind, or else trampled underfoot, that she stuck close by her mistress and followed her around all day while she wandered the familiar rooms, saying sad goodbyes to the portraits and statues and embroidered figures in the tapestries that were like old friends to her. There were also plenty of real people to say goodbye to: footmen, guards, gardeners and kitchen maids; as well as a menagerie of animals such as Louis's gerfalcon, horses and hounds, to which Henrietta suddenly developed the most powerful sentimental attachment now that she had to leave them all behind.

Further delay was caused by Louis himself who succumbed to a feverish cold, but eventually he recovered sufficiently for them to be on their way. As the train left Paris in full state, trundling in bright sunshine down the avenues of walnut trees past fine country houses, Henrietta kept her eyes fixed firmly ahead, fighting back tears. She so wanted to turn round for one last look at what she must now think of as her former home, but she knew she must be strong and brave and not look backwards but only forward, to a wonderful, happy new life as beloved queen of a beloved king of a beautiful country. She'd not have been able to see anything much if she did look back, besides carts and wagons. She was travelling at the head of the great baggage train, in a litter with curtains and cushions of velvet embroidered in gold, drawn by two mules in scarlet housings. With her were travelling not only the French royal family and all their courts but the entourages of the Earls of Carlisle and Holland and of the Duke of Buckingham, as well as the new French Ambassador to England, the Duc de Chevreuse. The huge cavalcade overran the road like ants on an anthill.

There was much to occupy Henrietta and stop her thinking sad thoughts. Throngs of people lined the route so that she was greeted with tumultuous shouts of applause the whole way. They were escorted as far as St Denis by the city archers, the militia, crafts guilds and trumpeters, and the jolting journey was constantly slowed by colourful pageants, with children dressed as angels and flowers and dancing donkeys.

Louis came only as far as Compiègne in Picardie, on the banks of the River Oise. At the edge of the forest he swung himself down from his horse. Henrietta clambered out of her litter and hugged him. There were tears streaming down her face and her throat was so painful and tight with emotion that she couldn't actually say goodbye.

He presented her with a pretty engraved silver box and when she opened it she saw that it was filled with marchpane, painstakingly shaped into a fleur-de-lys. 'I made it for you myself,' he said.

That made her hug him harder, want to cry harder too. 'That's so kind of you,' she sobbed.

'Don't eat it all at once now.'

'I won't. I'll save some until I reach England. And I'll think of you every time I taste it.'

'Only then?'

Henrietta flung her arms around her brother and hugged him again. 'Every hour of every day and every minute of every hour,' she cried passionately.

Promising to write to him constantly and tell him everything, she watched him swing back into his saddle before she returned to the litter. The ache in her throat made it hard for her to swallow, let alone eat, so she just clutched the little box of marchpane to her as hot, salty tears continued to stream down her cheeks.

Upon reaching Amiens, they were again delayed by illness when Henrietta's mother caught Louis's cold and was forced to take to bed in the convent that stood in the shadow of the town's soaring gothic cathedral. Her physicians told her she would need a full month to recover properly.

Meanwhile the papal legate arrived, a balding, dignified man with gentle eyes. Henrietta met him from his coach in person, going out to the court-yard to greet him and conduct him to the room that was serving as her presence chamber. Together with a letter from Pope Urban, he presented her with the gift of the Golden Rose, an exquisite ornament of finely wrought precious metal. Henrietta thought it the most beautiful object she had ever laid eyes on.

'The Golden Rose is of great holy significance,' the legate told her sombrely. 'It is blessed by the Holy Father himself and given away only occasionally to the greatest and most devout notables of our church. It is presented to you as a mark of the fact that you have been called to England for a great and glorious purpose. The eyes of the spiritual world will be upon you now, madam.'

The Pope reiterated that rousing message in his letter. He urged Henrietta to be as a guardian angel to the English Catholics, to join the most holy queens. To be like Esther, wife of the King of Persia, who employed her husband's love for her to save the Jews from massacre. Like Bertha who paved the way for the Christian conversion of England. The letter empha-sised what Henrietta already knew. That it was her prime duty to lead King Charles towards the one true church.

'I will pray daily for His Majesty's conversion,' she told the legate as he held her hand in his before climbing back into his carriage. 'I swear that I will do all that I can for the poor Catholics of England.'

She stood and watched the coach pull away.

'The first thing you should do as queen is learn to behave in a proper manner,' said the Duke of Buckingham, who had come up unobserved behind her.

She faced him. 'I beg your pardon, sir?'

He nodded towards the legate's departing coach. 'You have servants to greet your guests and bring them to you. It is not fitting for you to do it yourself.'

'On the contrary,' Henrietta retorted. She could not understand why the duke had taken such an obvious dislike to her or why he had set himself against her from the start. 'There is nothing wrong in treating with respect the representative of the head of my religion.'

The duke ingored that. 'I have a message for you from the king your husband.'

Displaying impatience akin to Henrietta's, King Charles had begun sending messages to the English Ambassador and the duke, insisting that his wife, should come to him quickly. This was another such message. Henrietta thought his urgency endearing, until Buckingham spoiled it for her yet again.

'His Majesty is growing impatient merely as a result of the English people and Parliament complaining about these delays. The Puritans are putting about a claim that the Pope has ordered Your Majesty to suffer fifteen days' penance as punishment for marrying a heretic.'

When Marie de' Medici heard what lies the English were peddling, she ordered Henrietta to continue without her.

'But we can't just leave you,' she cried, setting aside her book and clutching at her mother's plump, clammy hand. Marie lay huddled beneath a great mound of blankets and fur rugs that increased her bulk, and Henrietta was sitting on a little stool at her bedside, where she had been reading aloud to her from the psalms. 'I don't care what they think of me in England.' She had so far managed not to contemplate their imminent separation but now it was suddenly an inescapable reality, she wanted to defer it for as long as possible.

But Marie would brook no more delays. 'Anne will stay with me and look after me,' she said, her voice croaky but resolute. 'You will have Mamie and all your ladies. And Gaston will see you safely on board ship.' She gave Henrietta's hand a brisk pat. 'Now we must say farewell quickly, for fear of tears.'

Too late. There seemed to be a rock in Henrietta's throat and tears were already coursing down her cheeks again, but she hastily dashed them away. If her mother was not going to cry, then she must not either. She leaned towards her mother to kiss her but Marie held out her hand to prevent it.

'You really should not even be in the same room as me,' she said. 'It won't do to greet your husband with a sniffle and a red nose on your first night together, now will it? I am already praying that you will be writing to me within a few months to tell that you have honoured your wifely obligations and are with child.'

Such talk made Henrietta want to cling to her mother's hand all the tighter. Much as she had longed for kisses and caresses, for love and marriage and children, she wished now that she could remain a child herself. She wished she could stay here in France. She had such a yearning to go back to the château at St Germain, to stand under the fountain in the grotto and run laughing down the terraces in the sunshine with Gaston and Christine and Elizabeth and all her father's illegitimate children. For nothing ever to change.

Her fears showed in her face, which her mother reached out to stroke. 'Come now. You have listened to the chatter of the court ladies long enough to know what to expect in your marriage bed. The first suffering will be momentary and then you will experience joy like no other.' She looked Henrietta in the eye. 'Or I sincerely hope you will, since conception is impossible without real pleasure. Just as real pleasure is impossible without conception.' She reached beneath her pillow and pressed into her daughter's hand a letter. 'Let it speak to you when I am no longer with you to speak for myself.'

'I shall keep it with me always,' Henrietta promised, recognising her mother's hand. 'And read it often, so that you may continue to give me counsel.'

Marie gave a sniff. 'Well, I hope you heed my advice more readily than does your brother.'

'I will. I swear I will.'

Henrietta knelt for her mother's farewell blessing.

'You are my daughter only so long as you remain the daughter of Jesus Christ,' Marie said with emphasis. 'If you change your religion, or fail to change that of your husband, I give you curses not blessings.' Henrietta was used to her mother's zealotry and so did not find her words as harsh as she might otherwise have done. The advancement of Catholicism had always been the ultimate driving force of her life, far more dear and important to her than her family, her country or life itself, which ended only in death, and an eternity in heaven or hell. All she was doing was trying to impress upon Henrietta the vital role she was to play in saving England, saving souls. 'Now go,' Marie said more gently. 'And may God go with you.'

With the poignant almond sweetness of Louis's marchpane in her mouth, Henrietta read her mother's letter as the convoy trundled on towards Calais. The words were so vivid that Marie might have been right there beside her.

*I say to you here, sincerely, all I should say to you in the last hour of my existence if you should be near me then. Love and respect your husband and do nothing that could displease him even a little. Give thanks each day to God that he has made you a Catholic, a faith you must maintain more dearly than your life. God has sent you into England for those who have suffered for so many years. The king's conversion must be your most ardent desire on earth.*

*You have only God for a father and can never lose him. It is he who sustains your existence. It is he who has given you a great king and placed a crown on your head, and is sending you to England where he requires your service. Offer your soul and your life to him who has created you.*

*I would rather see you die than to live so as to offend God. Be firm and zealous for the Roman Catholic religion. Honour the holy virgin whose name you bear, the mother of our Lord and Saviour. I bid you adieu.*

Her mother, Sister Madeleine, the Pope, God himself . . . They were all expecting so much of her.

The party left Amiens to a loud artillery of salutes and reached Boulogne at five o'clock in the afternoon. Henrietta's very first sight of the sea. Like an excited child, she leaped from the litter almost before it had drawn to a halt and ran down on to the sandy beach.

The sky was grey and the sea matched its colour almost exactly. She had imagined it bluer and so much smaller. Nothing had prepared her for such vastness. It was almost impossible to believe that anything at all could lie beyond the wide and distant horizon, that the world was such a large place and France such a tiny part of it. She had assumed that she would actually be able to see England across the sea, that likewise once in England she'd be able to look back and see France; that the Channel was just a wider version of the Seine. It had once been called the Narrow Sea, after all. It did not look at all narrow from where she was standing.

Seagulls wheeled overhead, screaming. There was a bracing breeze coming off the water and she breathed deep of it, filling her lungs. The salty, fishy tang was nothing like the often rather putrid smell that emanated from the Seine. The river didn't have waves either – ripples, yes, but the advancing crests of water totally fascinated Henrietta. It was mesmerising, watching them rolling in, breaking, with their white frills like lace, their roar and crash and subtle retreating hiss. In fact, they held her so rapt that she failed to notice when one swept higher up the sand. She dodged back, laughing, but was not quite quick enough.

Gaston thought this hilarious. 'Ha-ha! It caught you.'

She lifted the damp hem of her gown and looked down at her wet, sandy silk slippers, not caring that her toes were cold.

Gaston took her arm and they headed towards the wide harbour where a great warship named *The Prince* lay at anchor, its tall masts pricking the low clouds, its gilding and the tiny square panes of its myriad windows glittering in the last rays of the sinking sun.

It was a glorious sight and Henrietta's spirits lifted with the promise of adventure. 'When do we sail?' she asked

'First fine morning.'

'Oh, but I can't wait even until tomorrow morning.'

'Well, there is a surprise,' Gaston laughed.

She saw that there was a fleet of little craft bobbing in the lee of the ship. 'Let's go out now in a rowing boat.' She gripped her brother's arm and danced round to face him. 'Oh, please, Gaston, please say that we can!'

'I'm not sure.'

'I am a queen now, I'll have you remember.' She let go of him and struck a regal pose. 'I wish to go upon the sea and I command you to take me.'

'Very well then.' He swept an exaggerated bow. 'Your Majesty.'

It was all arranged. Gaston handed her into the tiny rocking boat, and took up the oars. Henrietta was accustomed to being in a state barge on the river but this was very different. It was one thing being able to see land clearly on either side, quite another to be so far adrift that even the one visible shore soon seemed unreachable. She had the sense that the sea was far deeper than the river too. The waves, which had looked small enough on the beach, tossed the little vessel to and fro. They seemed perilously close as they slapped high against the sides, spraying Henrietta's face and hands.

'My lips taste salty,' she said, licking them with the tip of her tongue.

Gaston smiled. 'You carry some steel about you, I'll say that for you. I know no one else who would put themselves at first sight on an element as dangerous as the sea for mere pastime. But we should head back,' he added. 'It'll be dark in no time.'

The windows of some of the inns and cottages huddled near the harbour were already glowing palely with candlelight but Henrietta was so enjoying this time alone with her brother she did not want it to end. How she was going to miss him . . . both her brothers. How she was going to miss everyone and everything.

She had needed less courage to go out upon the sea than to meet the English dignitaries who had crossed over to welcome her. Or perhaps to take a good look at her. They all seemed to be relations of the Duke of Buckingham. There was his mother, Lady Mary Villiers, and his sister Susan Feilding, Countess of Denbigh. She and his niece Eleanor Villiers were tall, dark and slender, and looked just like him. His wife and duchess, Kate Villiers, on the other hand, was not like him at all, had a sweet nature, and was surprisingly plain with frizzy hair and a long nose with a bump on the ridge of it. Their infant daughter, Mary, petnamed Mall, was a precocious little girl with a mop of chestnut curls beneath her lace cap. Dressed in a miniature corseted gown of peach satin and brocade, she delighted in showing everyone how high she could kick her legs then demonstrating how fast she could twirl, making her skirts spin out around her.

'I told you English people like to dance,' Harry smiled at Henrietta.

At which point Mall performed such a rapid pirouette that she promptly toppled over. Harry gallantly offered her his hand to help her to her feet. She slipped her small fingers into his and gripped tight on to them, then gave him a pert smile and a pretty curtsey and pranced and danced along beside him as they proceeded on board ship to dine.

The cannons were fired and Henrietta imagined, romantically, that even if he could not actually see France, King Charles, who was surely waiting for her on the English coast, would hear that distant booming sound and think of her. She imagined again, for the thousandth time, their first meeting. She expected that he'd make a similarly grand entrance to the Duke of Buckingham, in glittering robes and with a train of nobles, and she rehearsed again in her head all that she would say to him, had been so longing to say to him.

At dinner she was seated at the table in the great cabin between Lady Mary Villiers and the Duchess of Buckingham and tried to hide her nerves, keen to please these important English ladies. There was a whey-faced young boy named Toby Matthews in attendance to interpret, but having to wait for him to repeat in English what Henrietta had first said in French, and then waiting again for him to translate into French what the duchess or Lady Mary Villiers said to her, made the conversation stilted and awkward and hugely frustrating for someone like Henrietta, who was naturally very talkative, not to mention lacking in patience. For the most part they talked about people and places she did not know and it all made her feel horribly homesick for France even before she had left it. She would have far preferred to have Harry translate for her, but Eleanor Villiers had seated herself beside him and kept him engaged in conversation for the entire duration of the meal.

She came to Henrietta's side as they made their way off the ship. 'I think Mr Jermyn is a little in love with you, madam.' She made it sound like an accusation.

'Is he?' Henrietta asked, not meeting the girl's eyes. 'What makes you say that?'

'He cannot stop talking about you . . . about how full of wit you are and with such a lovely manner of expressing it. How you have a face which opens a window into your heart where a man might see such goodness. He predicts that you will be extraordinarily loved by our nation, and deserve to be so.'

Henrietta did not dare even glance at him, though the urge to do so was strong. 'That is very generous of him.'

'We shall have to wait and see if he is right, won't we?'

Even though they had only just met, Henrietta had the sense that Eleanor Villiers did not like her any more than did her uncle the duke. How horrid they were, both of them.

The ships could not sail due to a summer storm blowing in the Channel and, scandalously, the duke took advantage of the delay to gallop back to Amiens to continue his flirtation with Anne there – as if further to prove Henrietta's low opinion of him.

When the sea calmed and there was a southerly breeze the duke returned and Henrietta was rowed out in an English longboat to *The Prince*. It lay low in the water, its hold laden with the vast array of goods she was taking with her to England for her household as well as the sixty thousand gold coins that made up her dowry.

As the flagship was escorted out of the harbour by a flotilla of little boats and cannon firing a salute, Henrietta stood at the stern. Mitte was clinging to her skirts, trembling violently at the unfamiliar rolling motion of the ship, her ears twitching frantically at the creaking of the timbers and the crack of the great white sails which bellied overhead. There was a strong wind filling them, driving the ship on at such a pace that it left spumes of spray in its wake, stretching back to the diminishing shore. Henrietta watched the coastline of France recede; the harbour and cottages grew hazy and were soon reduced to tiny specks. For once something was happening much faster than she wanted it to.

'It's not really so far, you know,' Harry said, coming to stand beside her. He leaned with his forearms on the wooden rail, one booted foot up on a coil of rope as the wind blew the long fair curls from his face.

'That is easy for you to say, sir. You are going home.'

'France has come to feel like home to me these past months. Your Majesty will return there. As will I, I trust. One day.'

'I'm still not used to being called Your Majesty. I keep thinking it must mean someone else. My mother or Anne.' She felt a pang of sadness just to speak their names, to picture their faces, not knowing when she should see them again. That one day Harry spoke of could be a long time coming.

'Well, Your Majesty shouldn't stay out here too long.' He smiled, standing straight and drawing his cloak about him against the strengthening wind. He glanced up at the darkening sky. 'It's turning stormy.'

The rain came on minutes after he had spoken and the sea grew quickly choppier with waves that reared high as houses, terrifying walls of water that toppled down, dousing the decks and perilously tossing the ship. Determined as Henrietta had been to stay at the rail until she could see

France no more, when Harry came to take her arm and lead her below, she knew she could not argue. Staggering like drunkards, gripping on to whatever was to hand and getting soaked through, they made their way down to the cramped, low cabins. Mamie and Father de Berulle were already there. Mamie looked petrified. The pitching of the ship as it rode the crests of the waves and sank into the troughs seemed even more violent below decks than above and soon gave Henrietta the most terrible seasickness to add to her homesickness. Mamie suffered just as badly, so the pair of them lay curled up in their wildly swinging hammocks, moaning about how ill they felt and listening to the Duchess of Buckingham and some of the other ladies who were already vomiting noisily into pails, the sound and the reek of it making Henrietta feel sicker than ever. The candle flames that provided the only light flickered wildly with the pitching of the ship and kept going out. Her stomach churned and she desperately swallowed down the saliva that kept filling her mouth, trying not to retch. How awful it would be to have to greet the king her husband smelling of vomit! But she soon stopped caring about anything but reaching dry land, half fearing that they never would.

'Where are the priests?' Maimie whimpered. 'I would confess my sins while there is still time.'

Henrietta could not make out her friend's whispered confession but was aware that one by one others started calling out for the priests so that they might do the same as Mamie. But the priests were as ill as everyone else and were unable to be everywhere at once, so believing death to be imminent, people started shouting out their declarations of guilt, the depth of their fear and the pressing need for absolution removing all restraint.

In the midst of this mass confession, Harry came to Henrietta's hammock bearing a cup of ale. 'I have had it warmed for you, ma'am,' he said kindly, raising his voice to make himself heard above the noise of the screeching wind and lashing waves. 'It will help settle your stomach.'

She sat up and drank gratefully, taking small sips to avoid spilling it as the vessel continued to pitch and toss. Harry watched over her, bracing himself against the post from which her hammock hung as they both listened to the catalogues of misdeeds, greed and lies and lustful thoughts, cried out over the roaring of the storm. It was close to the way Henrietta imagined hell would be. Fetid, dark, subterranean, with wildly flickering flames, the howling of the wind like the howling of the hell hounds, and all around the groans and moans of the sick and suffering and fearful, wretched people calling out their sins and begging for forgiveness.

Harry gripped the post tighter as the ship took a violent plunge. 'I tell you, they are all going to live to regret this.'

'I like your use of the word live.' Henrietta smiled at him. 'Do you really think we will? Live, I mean?' She knew even as she asked that he was no better equipped to predict the outcome of this voyage than she or anyone else. But she had come to depend upon his judgement, no matter what.

'No Queen of England has ever drowned,' he declared.

'Is that really so?'

'To my knowledge, it is.'

'You always make me feel so much better.' She saw that he, however, did not look well at all. 'Are you sick too?'

'As a dog,' he admitted.

She offered him her cup which was still half full. 'You have the rest then.' He shook his head so she thrust it at him more firmly. 'Please. Share it with me.'

He took it from her, dipping his head almost shyly before he drank. 'Thank you, ma'am.'

She could not help but wonder what would happen if she confessed her sins along with everyone else; if she admitted right now, in Harry's hearing, to having troubling daydreams about seeing him naked again and kissing him. What would his reaction be?

How tempting it was to say it, to find out! Yet she could feel no contrition. If she were to die now, how glad she was that she had at least kissed a man, just once.

Twelve hours later it was still drizzling but the storm had blown itself out. Though her legs felt shaky and her stomach still delicate, Henrietta ventured up on deck again, to stand at the bow of the ship this time for her very first sight of England. Towering white cliffs reared up in front of her and her unsettled stomach swooped again, this time with anticipation and apprehension. Her new home, and waiting for her here, finally, would be her new husband, whose land this was.

They entered Dover in the early evening, the ships sailing towards shingle banks and anchoring in the harbour protected by its stone jetty. There were rows of cottages all along the harbourside, in the pale shadow of the cliffs surmounted by a castle. The rain had come on heavily again and Henrietta stepped from the boat on to the little bridge which the king had considerately had constructed to aid disembarcation. But he was not there to meet her after all. She could not believe it. Disappointment pierced her and she struggled to hold back tears of hurt and anger and frustration. Was he not longing to meet her as much as she longed to meet him? Why had he not come, even now? Hardly anyone had. Though the fleet did fire guns in salute, there was only a small crowd of bedraggled country people to cheer her arrival.

'It would not be done like this in France,' Mamie grumbled.

'It most certainly would not,' the Duchesse de Chevreuse seconded.

Henrietta heartily agreed with them both.

An elderly man had come forward to receive her. Unsteady on his feet and with rheumy eyes, he bore the title of earl marshall and informed her that the king and his court were waiting for her at a place called Canterbury. Henrietta had no idea where that was, how far away or how close.

'It is only consideration for you that keeps His Majesty away,' the Duke of Buckingham said smoothly, speaking in affected French. 'He did not wish to introduce himself to Your Majesty while you are travel-weary. I believe it was your own mother who begged him to allow you a night alone in which to recover from your passage.'

Henrietta did not know whether to believe him or not. She wanted to and tried to, while, chilled and miserable, with the wind hurling sharp arrows of rain in her face, she picked her way up the steep, forbidding ascent to the grim castle above the harbour. It was more of a fortress in truth. In construction it resembled many a French castle, built around a towering square keep, but it was nothing like the pretty French châteaux where Henrietta had spent her childhood. This place was dank and depressing, with a twisted black newel staircase and thick dark walls. The rooms smelled fusty and were very poorly furnished.

'Shabby,' the Comte de Tillières, her lord chamberlain, asserted, inspecting the chamber that had been prepared for England's new queen. He tapped the relatively simple and somewhat rickety oak frame of the bed, the wood grown almost black with age. It was ornamented with a carved crown, but otherwise did not at all resemble furniture intended for royalty. 'This is a disgrace. In France this bed would not be seen as fit for a servant,' he protested.

Henrietta agreed with him, just as she had agreed with her disgruntled ladies, but did not have the strength to be angry. 'It doesn't matter,' she sighed, perching wearily on the edge of the bed. It was so high that her feet did not quite touch the ground. 'At least it's not rocking.'

Messengers had been sent to tell the king that his wife had arrived. The next morning, when Henrietta was breaking her fast on an English meal of ale, ham and a round loaf of white bread, a page informed her that His Majesty had ridden into the castle.

'About time too,' the Duchesse de Chevreuse muttered, her tone as disparaging as it had been the previous day.

Henrietta forgot all about her earlier disappointment. She was told that the king would willingly wait below until she was done eating, but could not force one more morsel down her throat now that he was here at last. She rose from the table instantly, her legs trembling and her heart as agitated as a caged bird.

There was more disappointment awaiting her, though. She had been expecting elaborate robes and a lavish entourage, but soon saw that the King of England, Scotland, and Ireland had few companions and did not look much like a king at all. He was dressed very modestly and soberly in dark blue velvet and a black cloak, adorned only with the embroidered silver star of the Order of the Garter. The only touch of colour he wore was a sky blue ribbon around his neck, from which hung the oval pendant of the garter order, depicting the figure of St George slaying a dragon carved from onyx and surrounded with diamonds. A single pearl drop earring hung from his left ear, a rather feminine-looking affectation considering the rest of his appearance. What shocked Henrietta more than anything was that he was so very short. She had been so concerned that he would find her lacking in height, she had never once considered it might be the other way round: that he would be small himself. A taller wife would have towered over him. When Henrietta stood before him, tiny as she was, she came all the way up to his shoulder. He walked oddly too, as if his legs were stiff and bandy, for all that Harry had said there was nothing wrong with them now.

But Henrietta recognised the slightly protuberant, sad eyes of the pensive young man in the little portrait she had held in her hands and gazed at for so long, the man she had so yearned to meet and was still ready to love. She fell to her knees and started to make a little speech, which she had practised in French and which was recommended to all royal brides. 'Sir, I am come into Your Majesty's kingdom to be made use of and commanded by you . . .' She wanted to say and do the right thing, to please him, but could not tell if she was going about it the right way. It was all too much for her. She completely forgot what she was supposed to say next and burst into tears.

She would have taken hold of his hand and kissed the back of it had he not raised her to her feet, wrapped her in his arms and kissed her with many kisses. 'I shall go on . . . k-kissing you until you are done c-crying,' he said, quietly and kindly and with a stammer so like her brother Louis's that she felt a rush of fondness for him.

When Charles released her, Henrietta saw that he was looking down at the hem of her gown. She wondered if perhaps she appeared taller than he had been led to believe, and he was wondering if she was cheating by wearing stack-heeled slippers. Feeling more at ease now, she swept aside her skirts and showed him her shoes, assuring him that she stood upon her own two feet. 'This is how high am I.' She smiled, risking a little joke. 'I have no help.'

Disconcertingly, however, he did not respond at all to her humour but looked very earnest as he took her arm and led her to a small side room where they could be alone.

'You have not fallen into the hands of s-strangers, you know,' he said stiltedly, stuttering again. 'But into the wise disposal of G-God, who would have you leave your family and cleave to your husband.'

'I know that, your Majesty.' There was something else that she had rehearsed in her head, which came out now sounding equally as stilted. 'But coming to a strange country where I am ignorant of the customs, I will make many errors. I am young and inexperienced and you must not be angry with me for my faults, but tell me when I do anything amiss so that I can avoid repeating the mistake.'

'I grant your request and thank you for it,' Charles said stiffly. 'And d-desire you treat me as you ask to be treated.'

When they went back out Henrietta presented all her servants by name to him, taking care to introduce them in order of rank, thinking, from what she had seen of him already, that Charles was the type of man who would appreciate and expect that level of formality.

Meanwhile Mitte was introducing herself to one of the king's hounds. The two dogs were sniffing at each other inquisitively.

'Rogue, come here!' the king ordered.

'They seem to be making friends.' Henrietta smiled, stroking Rogue who gave her hand a good sniff too, followed by a lick.

Mitte gave a jealous little growl. Rogue sprang back and someone muttered sarcastically that they hoped the queen didn't snarl like her pet dog.

When the whole party sat down to dine the Duc de Chevreuse resumed criticising the English. 'His Majesty arrives a day late, ill dressed and poorly attended,' he muttered to his duchess in Henrietta's hearing. 'I only hope the food is not equally poor.'

'I could forgive much if he would only smile,' the Duchesse de Chevreuse commented, casting a sly glance at the king.

Henrietta was trying not to listen to them but she could not help but hear Father de Berulle who was standing close behind her chair and leaned forward to whisper in her ear, 'May I remind you that it is the eve of St John the Baptist, ma'am? A fast day.'

Henrietta looked down at her plate. The king himself had carved for her generous portions of venison and pheasant. If she refused to eat she would undoubtedly cause deep offence, to him and to his entourage, besides which the sea air had made her ravenous and the smell was delicious. So hoping God would forgive her, just this once, she ignored her confessor and ate heartily. English food on the whole seemed plainer than French, with fewer sauces, but was tasty enough.

As preparations were underway to leave for Canterbury imminently, Mamie followed Henrietta into her carriage, sitting down beside her mistress as she always did as maid-of-honour.

'You are not to sit there, madam,' the king instructed her in English. 'My Lord the Duke of Buckingham's relations are to have the honour of travelling with the queen.'

Henrietta did not understand what he had said, but his expression and the tone of his voice were enough to alarm Mamie.

The king corrected himself and repeated the command in French. 'You are not to sit there.'

Mamie looked doubtfully from the king to the queen and then to the ambassadors. She did not budge.

'I ordered you to remove yourself,' Charles repeated, even more severely.

'Please, my lord,' Henrietta intervened, 'Mamie always travels with me.'

'Not this time she doesn't. I have promised the Duke of Buckingham that his duchess and Lady Mary Villiers may have the honour of riding with you.'

Henrietta felt a surge of panic, not knowing what to do. The French Ambassador would be furious if Mamie were ejected in favour of the Buckingham ladies. Not only would it show a great lack of respect for her countrywoman, it was also a gross violation of etiquette since Mamie's appointed place was by her side. But Henrietta did not wish to offend the king any more than she wanted to cause trouble with her French retinue. What hurt her most was that his primary or only concern was seemingly for the Duke of Buckingham's family, rather than for her. Tears pricked Henrietta's eyes but the king stood firm, this time completely unmoved by her weeping.

At a word from someone who might well have been Harry, the English Ambassador intervened. 'With respect, sire, Her Majesty is very young to find herself all alone amongst people whose language and customs are unfamiliar to her. It is only natural she should cling to her friend.'

'Very well,' Charles relented, with a scowl at Mamie.

Mamie scowled back. 'So His Majesty would listen to his ambassadors above his own wife and queen,' she complained sourly to Henrietta once she was seated next to her again. 'I am not here because you said you wished me to stay, but because the ambassador said that I should be.'

Henrietta felt even more dispirited. She could hardly believe that she had had her first disagreement with her husband within hours of meeting him. It did not seem to bode at all well for their future. But what she feared more than that she could not bring herself to say. She had taken it for granted that King Charles would love her as his letters had indicated, and as she was ready to love him back. But it seemed that he loved the Duke of Buckingham far more passionately. She had discovered at dinner that he even had an indulgent pet name for him, calling him Steenie for 'Saint

Stephen', who in the Bible was said to have had the face of an angel. Though the duke was the opposite of angelic, in Henrietta's opinion.

They were to travel to a place named Barnham Down and the first miles of the journey proceeded to the cheers of assembled onlookers. Church bells rang, the roads were strewn with green rushes, roses and flowers, and the trees bowed under the weight of people who had climbed them to gain a better view, throwing their hats into the air as the party passed by beneath, which greatly raised Henrietta's spirits. English, as these commoners spoke it, sounded very different from the language of the nobles and courtiers she had met and she couldn't understand any of the words that were called out to her. But she did not need to. The smiles said all that needed to be said, welcoming, friendly smiles on friendly English faces that looked absolutely no different from French ones.

The Kent countryside was not so very different from France either, gentle and quite flat, with wattle-and-daub cottages, gothic churches, and gentry houses with clusters of tall chimneys and diamond-paned casements. Between the deer parks and country towns stretched tracts of moor and heath, marshland and pasture, dotted with sheep and cattle. Nearer to the villages the fields were divided by well-kept hedges. There were cherry orchards and village greens, duck ponds and gravel paths by the riversides, in the little towns they passed through. Harry had previously assured her of the abundance of English flowers in the fields and hedgerows, and indeed there were blue cornflowers and bright red poppies visible everywhere.

At Barnham Down they were met by local dignitaries and their wives who escorted them to a palace that had once been the Abbey of St Augustine and was now the home of Lord Wotton. There was a bowling green and a number of country ladies had assembled there in two neat rows. As Henrietta waited to be led between their ranks she realised she knew very little of English etiquette, which was evidently different from the French procedure. 'What should I do?' she whispered quietly to the king.

'Let them curtsey and kiss your hand.'

The ladies all made three low curtseys from a distance, and when they approached Henrietta she held out her hand for them to touch it to their lips. She was unable to utter one word of English in acceptance of their warm greetings and remembered then how Harry had offered to teach her some. She wished she had let him.

A state banquet was held in a grand house outside the city walls and then Henrietta and the Duchesse de Chevreuse retired to bed early in the gatehouse. It was an improvement on the rooms in Dover Castle but the duchess did not think it was much of one. She seemed determined to find fault, as did Henrietta's entire retinue.

'I fear we have been as much deceived in His Majesty's attributes as we have been concerning his country's riches,' the Duchesse commented disapprovingly.

Henrietta had wanted to think well of England and of its king and was still trying to do so, but being only fifteen years old she could not help but be swayed by the opinions of her older and more worldly-wise friends. Once again her spirits plummeted to utter despondency, leaving her wondering if she had made the most terrible mistake.

On the evening of Monday, 13 June, in the candlelit vaulted Great Hall of what had been the Benedictine abbey, Henrietta and Charles were married again. The wedding music was performed on a great organ with burnished and gilded ranks of pipes that reached almost as high as the roof, the musician's feet and hands working the keyboard and pedalboards and stops to create a mighty swell of sound. But the ancient stone hall was icy cold and echoing, the ceremony not nearly so magnificent as the one at Notre-Dame. It should have been more memorable and special for all that, for the simple reason that this time Charles was actually present. But he was still so frosty with Henrietta, and even more so with Mamie and her other French servants whose very presence he seemed to begrudge, that it proved to be far from the joyous event Henrietta had dreamed it would be. As she took her place by her bridegroom at the altar, he stood stiffly and barely acknowledged her, making it seem as if he wished the whole business could be speedily over and done with.

She couldn't fail to notice Harry standing towards the back of the congregation, his hands clasped in front of him. She had once thought his blue eyes could never be solemn, but they were now.

'He looks wretched, poor man,' Mamie whispered as they made their way out. 'He must be aching with jealousy, thinking of you going to the king's bed.'

'Why? It's not as if he could conceive of ever taking me to *his*, is it?' Henrietta snapped.

'Stranger things have happened,' Mamie quipped, glowering at Charles's set face as if he were now her sworn enemy. 'Kings sleep with commoners all the time. Why not queens?'

Like the wedding ceremony that had preceded it, dinner was a relatively simple affair with only a dozen or so dishes, many of which consisted of wild birds: lark and partridge and pheasant. Much claret was consumed, though not by the king, who sipped abstemiously from his cup, dabbled his fingers in a small silver bowl with great fastidiousness, then waited for a page to pat them dry them for him before he rose from his chair and held out his hand to Henrietta. She stood up as he did so, feeling terrified as well as embarrassed.

'Here we go,' George Goring sniggered, rising also, along with almost everyone else. 'Gentlemen . . . ladies . . . time we all went up to bed. To the king and queen's bed that is!'

Henrietta saw the king's cheeks turn pink and the Duchesse de Chevreuse gave a low, derisive chuckle. 'Lord help us,' she whispered into Henrietta's ear. 'His Majesty blushes like a maid.'

Henrietta giggled, thanking God for her friends though she was able to see the amusing side of the situation without their help. 'Like an *English* maid, you mean?' she corrected. 'Since when do French maids blush?'

'Very true.'

'Bring on the posset and the bridecake,' James Hay chanted.

'There will be no posset or bridecake,' the king rebuffed. 'I have no taste for either. Nor for throwing stockings and the rest of the abhorrent ribaldry that generally accompanies these occasion. My wife and I shall retire to bed alone.'

Not quite alone, though. The company plonked themselves back down upon the chairs and benches set at the long tables, muttering their discontent. All, that is, save for the Duke of Buckingham, who with his customary supreme confidence remained standing by the king's side. Seeing this, the Duchesse de Chevreuse promptly stood up again beside Henrietta. 'If he's going with the king then I shall attend Your Majesty,' she said under her breath. 'Perhaps I should give His Majesty some instruction about what to do in bed while I am about it,' she added throatily.

The four of them made their way out of the hall, far more sedately than most brides and grooms on their way to a bedding. Up a grand oak staircase they went, along a twisting passage, through a series of guarded doors, into the inner sanctum of the royal apartment: the bedchamber. A fire had been lit together with slender wax tapers; a jug of wine, two goblets and a bowl of fruit were set out on a low table. The room was dominated by a great state bed, ornately hung with silk, its four-poster frame carved with cherubs and acanthus leaves, corners adorned with ostrich plumes.

Henrietta averted her eyes so as not to have to contemplate what she'd be expected to do in that bed very soon.

In silence, and with great care and attention, the duke began the process of unfastening the hooks and laces of the king's doublet. The duchess followed suit with Henrietta's corset. Stockings, garters and slippers were silently, almost ceremoniously, removed and set neatly aside. Head still bowed to the task of undressing the king, the duke glanced sideways to watch as the duchess helped Henrietta out of her petticoats. The look he cast her was not at all lascivious but superior, as if he considered her far beneath him, utterly insignificant, or else was determined to make her feel that way.

Henrietta turned aside so that she at least did not have to see him.

When both she and the king stood in just their smocks, the duke bowed low to his master, then cursorily in Henrietta's direction, and made to leave. The duchess did likewise, with a backward glance designed to instil courage in Henrietta but which had the opposite effect, making the young queen want to run right after her sophisticated friend. To Henrietta's surprise, Charles did follow them, not at a run, but with his rather ungainly, stiff-legged walk.

She peered round the door to see where he was going, what on earth he was doing. As soon as he had seen the duchess and the duke out, he moved methodically back through all the outer rooms, bolting the doors, one by one, with his own hands. There were seven of them. Seven doors and seven bolts. It seemed to take forever. The almost brutal sound of each bolt being shot made Henrietta flinch, served to increase her mounting sense of panic. She realised that he was determined that they should have some privacy and that the bolts were to keep the carousing courtiers out. But it felt instead more as if he were locking her in, trapping her here alone with him, so that he could do to her whatever he wanted.

She poured the wine, her hands shaking so much that she spilled some on the table, and held out a cup to Charles when he had finally finished with the locks. 'Your Majesty.'

He took the proffered cup, looking not at it but at her.

She wrapped her arms around herself, not that she was cold but because she had never been undressed in front of a man before and wanted to cover herself. They were both enveloped from neck to knee by their smocks, but to be clad only thus was considered to be as good as naked. It certainly felt that way to Henrietta. Though, by the same token, the King of England in his undergarments was a world away from Harry Jermyn in Paris at dawn, when he had gambled away every stitch of his clothing. The sight had a totally different effect on her too. Instead of the heart-pounding excitement and fascination she had experienced that other time, now Henrietta felt nothing but apprehension and a wish to be left alone. She had no urge whatsoever to discover what was concealed beneath the king's smock in the way that she still burned to see what Harry had hidden behind his hands. She had no desire to kiss him. Perhaps if they'd not had that argument about the Duke of Buckingham's relatives riding in her coach then things would have been different. Perhaps then Charles wouldn't have seemed so cold and distant.

Though he was making a concerted effort to be less so. Ensuring their privacy, drinking with her, looking upon her with his sad but kindly eyes. 'I have never known a woman,' he announced quietly, setting his cup down carefully on the table. 'So we are both novices.'

She was surprised that he had waited until he was married. Men usually didn't. Or at least not the men Henrietta had known in Paris. She was grateful to him for admitting it to her, for not trying to pretend he was more experienced than he was, when she obviously lacked the experience to tell the difference. It was thoughtful of him, to try to reassure her. Though, in a way, she'd rather have had him know what he was doing. Then again, it was good that it was to be the first time for both of them. He looked so unsure of himself suddenly that she utterly forgave him for their earlier misunderstanding and tried to think of some words of encouragement to offer in return for those he had given her. But all that came into her head was her mother's advice about fulfilling her queenly obligation, how the sole purpose of copulation was to beget an heir, and commenting on that at this precise moment felt wrong.

It was too late for talking anyway. Charles seemed keen just to get on with things now and went round to one side of the great bed.

Henrietta went to the other.

He turned back the sheets and they both climbed in.

Henrietta lay very still on her back as he shifted closer to her, making the starched linen and deep feather mattress creak like first footsteps in deep, fresh-fallen snow. Charles leaned over, rather clumsily put his arm around Henrietta's shoulders and pressed his mouth to hers. Their noses got in the way, almost knocked, and there was an absurd moment where they both adjusted their heads and went a little cross-eyed in the process. Henrietta stifled the urge to giggle, tried closing her eyes instead. Charles's lips were dry and his moustache felt scratchy. It wasn't a proper kiss at all, which she knew was supposed to involve tongues – or at least that was how it was done in France – and no sooner had they started than he drew away again.

Then he put his hand up her smock, between her legs, and stuck his finger up inside her. Her whole body went rigid with the shock of it and she gave a little gasp. She wanted nothing so much as to push him off, but with heroic self-restraint she submitted to this brutal examination because she knew that she must. It felt like the most horrible kind of intrusion, a violation, but at the same time she was not unduly surprised, had heard that it was a common enough thing for a man to do, was perfectly reasonable really, for a new husband, especially one who was a king, to want to confirm that his wife was still a virgin before he deflowered her.

No sooner had he withdrawn his finger than he lifted his own smock a little and Henrietta finally saw what it is that a man has between his legs.

He seemed to invite her to look at it and she was driven to do so anyway, out of pure curiosity. She was amazed by the shape and the size of it. It was thick, and half as long again, hard and stiff as a marshal's baton and sturdy enough to stand up on its own.

The mere sight of an erect penis was considered to be more than sufficient to inflame a girl, but it was having no such effect on Henrietta. Certainly she had no desire to touch it or hold it, as girls generally liked to do, and the idea of having it inside her was quite terrifying.

Charles seemed to think he had done enough to prepare her, however, and all of a sudden climbed on top of her. He seemed not to know quite where to put it and she felt his knuckles dig against the inside of her thighs as he used his hand to guide himself before he thrust inside her. He felt bigger than he had looked and it hurt, far more than his finger had done. She was sure he must split her open. He pushed again and she felt the tear and sting. She bit down on her lip, knew she must at least lie there and put up with it, even if she could not respond. On no account must she burst into tears now, and so she made herself think of gardens, of how a husband is the tiller and sower of the ground. How she was the patient ground being tilled as his spade dug into her. Again and again. He made a sound in the back of his throat that was halfway between a grunt and a sigh and, mercifully, it ended quite quickly, with a flood of slippery warmth and wetness that she realised must be the spill of seed, the fluid of extraordinary powers and properties which was supposed to bring women to a state of ecstasy.

He rolled off her and she turned away from him on to her side, pushing her smock between her legs to dry herself. She drew up her knees against the soreness, fighting tears. She'd have given anything to be back in her chamber at the Louvre, in her own bed, with Mitte curled at her feet.

Charles, on the other hand, seemed quite pleased with the way it had all gone. He fell into a deep, contented sleep, arising next morning at what was a late hour for him in a jocund mood. He was considerably more talkative than he had been so far and Henrietta heard him laugh for the very first time, joking with his household about how he had outsmarted them with all those bolts. Which somehow made it so much worse.

Sitting off to the side in a high-backed chair, quietly stroking Mitte who had come scampering to Henrietta the instant she had entered the hall for breakfast, she felt Harry's eyes resting on her and looked up to meet them. He was the only other person, besides her, who was not laughing along with Charles. Henrietta could not understand that. If he had been jealous, thinking of her lying with the king, then he'd surely be glad to see that it had been a disaster for her. But he didn't appear glad at all. He looked as miserable as she felt.

It made for a very colourful procession, the liveried footmen, coachmen and postillions of the English and French court riding together out of Canterbury with standards unfurled. Henrietta tried hard to put the night's events behind her as they left via the old north gate. They spent the following night at Cobham. When she pretended to be asleep as the king came to her bed, he was considerate enough not to try and wake her. Next day they boarded the gilded royal barge at Gravesend for the last stage of their journey, up the wide River Thames to Whitehall.

There was no sun but it was stiflingly hot and humid. Henrietta and Charles were both wearing green velvet and beads of sweat trickled down Henrietta's spine, inside her tight and heavy gown. She was standing on deck with the king so that people could see them. The barge was towed by a vessel propelled by twelve liveried oarsmen who were all sweating profusely, with dark wet patches at their armpits. There was hardly any breeze, and the golden lions of the royal standard hung limply above their heads.

The air and the flag were practically all that was still, though. They were surrounded by hundreds of beautiful painted and gilded barges and ornamental vessels belonging to the nobility and merchants, and by the time they reached London Bridge they had been joined by a wonderful gay floating pageant of small craft, some of the boats containing trumpeters and drummers who made the most extraordinary noise, albeit a very joyful one.

It was a show to rival Henrietta's wedding day in France and it warmed her heart once again to see this further evidence that the people of England were so friendly. That they had turned out to welcome her in such large numbers more than made up for the half-hearted reception she had received at Dover and even for her disagreement with the king. Maybe this wasn't such a dour country after all, maybe Charles would turn out not to be so solemn once she got to know him better.

Two hundred decorated warships of the navy were lying at anchor along both shores. They saluted their king and queen with a volley of great shot which grew louder the nearer they drew to London. As they passed the immense, square, white stone keep of the Tower of London, its guns discharged a royal salute – such a deafening peal as Henrietta had never heard before and quite terrifying in its volume.

The heat was oppressive enough for a summer storm. The tide was surging beneath the pillars of the bridge so fiercely that when the barge shot through on its current the tossing and pitching beneath her feet reminded Henrietta of her perilous voyage from France. Only it did not last long enough for her to feel sick again and she was not at all frightened as some of her ladies looked to be, gripping the edge of their seat with white knuckles or clinging on to each other's arms. Henrietta was too excited to be afraid, too busy enjoying her first sights and experiences of London.

As they passed St Paul's Cathedral and the Strand and the noblemen's houses with their formal gardens lining the northern bank, the wind got up, giving instant life to the festive pennants and flags and standards. The rain came on then, sudden and heavy. Henrietta and Charles moved inside the barge to avoid getting wet but she insisted the windows should be left open so that she could put out her hand and wave to the infinite number of spectators lining the riverbanks, hanging out of windows or crushed on to wherries and ships. They were getting terribly wet. Some more so than others. One of the craft, upon which stood easily a hundred people, all crowded upon the nearest side, overbalanced and turned turtle, sending all those aboard tumbling into the murky, rain-stippled water of the Thames.

Henrietta gripped Charles's arm. 'We should do something,' she cried anxiously, worried that they were all going to drown.

Fortunately there were so many lighters darting to and fro that everyone was quickly rescued, having suffered no more than an ignominious ducking. The cheers and shouts grew louder than ever. Occasionally she caught a cry of what sounded a little like 'Henrietta', but not quite.

'No one knows what to call you,' Charles mused. 'We must decide what it shall be.'

She frowned at him. 'How about Henrietta Maria, Your Majesty? Since that is my name?'

He shook his head. 'Far too fanciful for this country's tastes, I am afraid. Too much of a mouthful. No, we must make you sound more English.'

'But I am not English.' She was more than happy to be Queen of England but she would always be a princess of France underneath. Nothing could change that.

Charles ignored her protest. 'When prayers were said for you in my chapel the other day, they called you Queen Henry.'

'Queen Henry!' Henrietta instantly looked round for Harry, wanting to see his reaction, to share the joke with him. He met her eyes, his shoulders shaking slightly as he struggled to suppress a laugh.

'Henry is a good name,' she said softly, smiling at the person who bore it. 'Only . . . I am not sure it suits me. Or anyone in petticoats and skirts for that matter.'

'You are right,' Charles agreed, deadly serious. 'Henry was my brother's name. It won't do for you. Mary then,' he settled. 'You shall be Queen Mary.'

The holiest of names, a version of her second name, Maria. That she could live with.

But all trace of amusement had vanished from Harry's face, to be replaced by a look of near horror.

'You don't like Mary, sir?' Henrietta asked him, puzzled and surprised.

Charles looked over at him too. Looked beyond him, around him, as if he didn't think his wife and queen could possibly be seeking the opinion of an ambassador's assistant, if indeed he even knew Harry's role in their entourage.

'Speak, sir,' Charles ordered, sounding half bemused and half put out. 'If my wife so values your judgement, then let us hear what it is.'

'Your Majesty,' Harry complied in his most deferential tone, not seeming at all nervous to be so thrust to the fore, 'I fear the people may find unfortunate associations with the name Mary.'

'It is the blessed name of Our Lady,' Henrietta pointed out to him lightly. 'How could anyone possibly object to that?'

He was not quite able to meet her eyes. 'The only previous English queen to bear the name was Mary Tudor, ma'am,' he informed her respectfully, as if that should mean something to her.

Which it didn't. 'So?'

He looked down, then back at her, and she thought it was just because he was reluctant to show up her obvious lack of knowledge.

The Duke of Buckingham was not nearly so reticent or tactful. Henrietta hadn't even realised he had been eavesdropping on their conversation until he made an unpleasant scoffing noise. 'Otherwise known as Bloody Mary,' he threw in glibly. 'Because, in her attempt to return England to Roman Catholicism, she had over three hundred innocent Protestants burned at the stake.'

Henrietta instantly recognised Whitehall Palace from Harry's vivid description of it. Rambling red-brick Tudor buildings with small square windows sprawled along the riverbank beneath a chaos of different rooflines and elaborate chimneys. Despite their being decorated with flags and glittering weathervanes, Whitehall looked more like a collection of little houses than a proper palace. It bore no comparison with the vast and stately Parisian palaces Henrietta had left behind.

The party disembarked at the slippery, moss-covered stairs that led up from the water to the privy gardens, a grid of gravel pathways lined with low box hedges and enclosed by a high wall. Ranged around this garden to the south and east was a rambling labyrinth of halls and houses, chapels, galleries and courtyards. A public highway, King Street, ran right through the middle of the grounds from Charing Cross to Westminster, accessed by two great stone gateways. It was thronged with a constant stream of carts and carriages and hawkers on foot. To the west of this road was a mass of recreational buildings grouped around a large octagonal cockpit. There were tennis courts, bowling alleys, a tiltyard for jousting. To the east were kitchens, pantries and stables, and the residences of the courtiers. To the north were the state apartments, one set for Charles and a smaller set for Henrietta.

Given the jumbled nature of the exterior of Whitehall Palace, Henrietta was pleased to find the interior very elegantly furnished. Bright Turkey carpets were flung artfully over couches and tables as well as floors; the panelled walls were hung with tapestries and paintings and she instantly recognised the work of her mother's favourite, Peter Paul Rubens, as well as the familiar styles of Titian and Caravaggio. There were impressive displays of classical busts, ivories, porcelain and crystal.

The queen's own suite of rooms had wainscoted walls and low, leaded windows hung with red velvet, which looked out over the busy river.

'Not unlike the view from the Louvre,' Father de Berulle commented. 'So how do you like your new quarters, ma'am?'

'As soon as the walls are hung with French hangings and the portraits of my family that we've brought with us, it should start to feel like home,' Henrietta replied. 'At least a little.'

The new queen's arrival at Whitehall was marked by a series of celebrations.

The first took place in the Banqueting House, a building very different from the rest of the palace. Constructed of smooth silvery-grey stone in the classic Italianate style, it rose incongruously above all the red brick, looking totally out of place. It resembled something Henrietta's parents might have had built in France, though she had never expected to see such a place in England. Harry had not been strictly correct when he'd said London had nothing to compare to Paris. It had this.

As she rode towards it, dressed in her new black gown embroidered with silver and gold beneath a purple velvet cloak, Henrietta pressed Charles for details of its history and construction. She learned that his father, the late King James, had submitted designs for a stupendous new palace to be built in the Italian style. The new Banqueting House had been urgently needed to replace a wooden one destroyed by fire, but the rest of his plans had been abandoned. Perhaps it was that which lent that beautiful but solitary building an almost ominous quality. It was a place designed for public enjoyment, though, and Henrietta's interest in it grew when she also found out that it was here the court entertainments were held.

Inside the beautiful high white walls she and Charles sat side by side on their thrones under the canopy of state and Henrietta was proclaimed queen. The articles of the marriage treaty were read aloud in English and French by the ambassadors before the whole court, and it was also confirmed, embarrassingly for Henrietta, that the marriage had been consummated. An Anglican bishop gave his blessing after which Charles rose to kiss his wife's hand. A banquet and dancing followed and went on long into the morning.

The bed Henrietta had brought over from France had been erected in her chamber, but after Mamie had helped her to undress and brushed out her hair, Charles sent for Henrietta to come to his. She slipped on a gown over her shift and was led to the king's bedchamber by one of his gentlemen, bearing a candle to light the way along the narrow winding gallery that connected their two apartments. The shutters had not yet been closed and Charles stood with a goblet of wine by the window overlooking the moonlit privy gardens. Alone with him, Henrietta felt as if they were strangers still. Worse than strangers, enemies almost.

'I hope you will be happy here,' he said in a sombre tone.

'I am sure that I shall,' Henrietta replied, sounding uncertain.

But when he closed the shutters and moved towards her and kissed her, it was not unpleasant. His breath was fresh and his mouth gentle upon hers.

There was an advantage to his shortness. It meant he had to bend his head only a little way to meet her lips. When he penetrated her this time there was only minimal pain. But she did not like the feeling of being invaded by him, and his vigorous probing and jerking back and forth seemed to her vaguely absurd. There was certainly not even a hint of the ecstatic joy her mother had spoken of. Henrietta wished she knew what she was doing wrong. She was sure it must be her fault, because if this were all there was to lovemaking then women wouldn't like to do it half so much as they seemed to. From his grunts and moans she could not tell if Charles was enjoying it or found it a great effort. But if what everyone said was true, that conception did not occur without pleasure, but neither did real pleasure occur without conception, then there was no way she was ever going to be able to make a baby. Maybe things would improve for her with more practice as her mother had also suggested, but it seemed unlikely.

Afterwards Charles sat up, reaching for a calfskin-bound book which lay on the table beside his bed, alongside his Bible. He opened it seemingly at random and read in the candlelight as closely as if he were studying the scriptures. When he caught Henrietta trying to read the title he reverentially closed the covers and, read it a loud for her: *'His Majesty's Instructions to his Dearest Son, Henry the Prince.'*

'Your father wrote it for your brother?'

'For his heir. Who turned out to be me.' Charles rested his fingers on the cover of the book, which was tooled in gold. 'He intended it to act as a fair and impartial counsellor.'

'When I left France to come here, my mother gave me a letter to serve the same purpose.' Henrietta was delighted to have found some common ground. 'Just a little letter, though. Not a whole book. She told me to keep it with me always and I have it beside my bed too.'

'My father meant, by giving his advice, to guide his son and successor on the path to becoming a good king,' Charles explained. 'That's what I want to be. Not a great king, but a good one.'

In the candlelight Henrietta saw the honesty in his dark eyes, along with the sadness and uncertainty. It made her want to reach out and put her hand over his, but she did not quite dare. That seemed, oddly, as if it would have been far more intimate than the closeness they had just shared.

'My father was a great king,' Charles said. 'The first ever monarch of a united England, Scotland and Ireland, which he called Great Britain. By marrying his sons to the Hapsburgs of Spain or the Bourbons of France, he wished to demonstrate to the world the true greatness of his new realm, to reunite Protestant and Catholic Europe and create peace throughout Christendom.' He reflected for a moment. 'I, though, have no wish to be known as Charles le Grand. I shall be content merely to be remembered as Charles le Bon.'

'What is the difference?' asked Henrietta with genuine interest. She was thinking of her father who had been Henri le Grand and also sensing that this might be an opportunity to gain a better understanding of the reserved stranger whom she had married. 'How does your father advise a king to go about being good?'

'By being as a natural father to his people,' he said. 'True glory lies in striving always to serve the public good. And by cultivating the four cardinal virtues of wisdom, temperance, fortitude and justice.'

To hear him speak those words gave Henrietta a strange feeling of having come full circle. She had once written those very words, or very similar ones, in her copybook, had dreamed of marrying a king who possessed those very qualities. It was as if by writing them she had made her wish come true, had conjured him. It gave her hope that, despite their initial differences, they might get along together very well.

Her warm and pretty smile encouraged Charles to continue. 'My father writes in depth about a king's duty and responsibility, how important it is for him to establish just laws. How it is even more important to set a shining personal example, which provides a pattern of godliness and virtuousness. In that regard you must help me to become a good king.'

Henrietta was enjoying their conversation, feeling heartened by the things he was telling her and the very fact that he wanted to confide in her. Just as when they had first met and he had stemmed her tears with his kisses, she glimpsed the sensitive, gentle man she had seen in his miniature portrait, the man she had been so ready to admire, to like, even to love. She would willingly help him be a good king, or a great king, whatever he wanted to be. 'Tell me how I might assist you, Your Majesty? I should like to.'

'A king is placed on his throne by God and therefore owes God his duty of service. The key to fulfilling this duty is the determination to strive to conquer one's own passions. Temperance is the most crucial virtue . . .

demonstrated by moderation and restraint in language, dress and manners. A man cannot be thought worthy to rule and command others if he cannot rule his own affections and appetites.' Charles paused for a moment as if to impress upon her the importance of what he said. 'A good king must establish his own household and family as models of harmony and decorum. That is what I mean to do. Do you understand me?'

She saw again a dogmatism in him that frightened her a little. 'Yes, Your Majesty,' she said. 'I understand.'

Next morning Charles was awake and out of bed long before Henrietta, had attended prayers with his chaplain and completed his riding exercises before she had even stirred.

When she was woken at last by the brightness of the sun streaming into the room, she threw on a wrap and went through to the king's privy chamber. She was startled to find the Duke of Buckingham already there, lounging in a chair, his shirt undone, feet up on the table, eating a sugared plum. He was wearing his feathered hat even though he was in the king's presence. And the king did not seem to mind at all.

When the duke saw Henrietta, he tossed the half-eaten plum into the fireplace and gave her his insolent smile. He swung his long booted legs to the floor and swept off the hat in an exaggerated bow. 'I will leave you to your lovely wife,' he said to Charles.

Decorum must have a very different meaning in England than it did in France she thought! Temperance too. The festivities continued that night with a banquet at York House, the duke's magnificent residence on the Strand. It was an extravagant feast designed to demonstrate his considerable riches and power, and it rivalled any held in France. One dish comprised a sturgeon that was a staggering six foot long and had, a few hours before, obligingly leaped from the Thames into a sculler's boat just downstream of the privy steps, as if to prove that the great duke had not only the King of England, but all the country's fish and fowl at this command also.

The duke, dazzling in bejewelled white silk, assumed the seat of honour beside Henrietta and, with his usual audacity, took that opportunity to criticise her openly. For the way that, as he phrased it, she allowed her confessor to wander in and out of her apartments whenever he chose.

'Nobody is permitted to enter His Majesty's private apartment unless specifically invited,' he informed her.

Except for you, Henrietta silently seethed. And half-dressed and in your hat too.

'Even noblemen must take their place in the antechamber and wait their turn according to their rank,' the duke emphasised. 'His Majesty has asked me to instruct that the same order be observed in your household as in his. It is his belief that a queen, like a king, should be approached at all times with respect and reverence.'

Henrietta did not know whether she was more taken aback by the nature of this grievance and the sheer hypocrisy of it, or by the fact that it was the duke who had made it instead of her husband. Hurt and angry, she glanced at Charles, but he turned aside and struck up a timely conversation with the Earl of Arundel. 'Why does His Majesty not talk to me about this matter himself?' she inquired, her voice a little unsteady.

'Because I offered to speak to you on his behalf.'

'Then tell His Majesty this on *my* behalf.' She set down her knife beside the half-picked fishbones. 'I had hoped that I would be given leave to order my household as I pleased.'

'I am sure you know full well that your duty is not to please yourself but the king,' the duke countered slickly.

'I am not accustomed to such strict protocol. Nor are my priests. It was not thus observed in France.'

'You are not in France now, madam. Or had you forgotten?'

With hindsight, Henrietta wondered if she should have refused to enter into any such discussion with the duke. Not that it would have changed anything. It seemed that whatever she did was wrong.

'You asked me to point out your mistakes,' Charles said to her harshly when they were in his bed that night. 'I cannot believe, having done that, you would then insult me so publicly.'

It was like being in a labyrinth, trapped at every turn, in a place where regular rules did not apply. 'What was I supposed to have done? I only said what I did say in public because you chose not to discuss this with me in private. And whatever you have heard to the contrary from Buckingham, sire, I assure you that I did not insult you at all.'

'I am afraid that I see things rather differently.'

Charles was lying very definitely on his side of the bed and Henrietta on hers. No parts of their bodies were even close to touching, and she suspected it would remain that way even in sleep. Not a toe would stray across the dividing line, as if there were a great invisible bolster thrust between them, battle lines now drawn within their marriage bed.

She did not want Charles to touch her, hold her, and yet she did. Or for someone to. She had never felt so lonely and alone. And cold. It was so cold in England, even though it was supposed to be summer. It would have been lovely to cuddle up beside a warm body. Her thoughts immediately turned to Harry but she pushed him from her mind. Though he was part of her retinue, things were not how they had been in France. He never sought her out as he once had, or said flattering things to her, and she had come to the conclusion he did not like her so much any more. Maybe he was disappointed in her for failing to win English hearts, or even the heart of England's king. She must try harder. But she was so annoyed with Charles she couldn't allow things to rest, let alone try to make amends. She couldn't even grant him the last word. She had to hold on to her pride at least.

'I must say, I fail to see how anyone could regard spending time with one's confessor as a mistake,' she closed, and before he had chance to reply had turned over with her back to him, curled up and tried to sleep.

But she could not. Tears trickled out of the corners of her eyes on to the pillow. She turned her face into its cool muffling softness and bit her lip, not wanting Charles to know that she was crying. It did not make sense to her. When he was safely asleep, she pushed back the bedcovers and, taking a candle, crept quietly from his chamber to her own. She picked up the looking glass and stared at her face by candlelight, then touched it lightly. She had black eyes which sparkled bright as stars, and curls as glossy as a raven's wing. She had been told this all her life but was not sure she could see these things now. She could dance and sing as sweetly as anyone. Couldn't she? She had a warm heart and a quick wit and . . .

Why did her husband not love her?

The king's coldness towards her and his rejection of her, the English court's failure to love her, made Henrietta feel undesirable and unlovable. No matter that the looking glass showed her otherwise, for the first time in her life she felt ugly, and as if she would remain alone and unloved for the rest of her life.

\* \* \*

Not for the first time, she woke to find Charles gone.

She quickly learned that he was a man of strict regularity and routine. He had set aside days for listening to requests from petitioners, and he divided each and every day into sections devoted to different activities. He rose promptly at six every morning and did nothing before he had attended prayers with his chaplain. Then he exercised by either running or riding in the nearby parkland named after St James. After he had broken his fast, several hours were given over to attending to business with his privy councillors, Lords Northampton and Percy amongst others. This inner circle was distinguished by the wearing of the same insignia of the Order of the Garter as was worn at all times by the king: medals of St George slaying the dragon, which hung on blue ribbons around their necks, and the large silver rayed star embroidered in silk thread emblazoned on the left of their riding cloaks. Following his meetings with these councillors, the rest of the king's time was apportioned between more prayers, discussing acquisitions for his art collection with Lord Arundel and his agents, dealers and advisors, reading and eating.

Despite the duke's and the king's criticism, Henrietta's household retained the more informal and relaxed atmosphere that she had been used to in France and far preferred. She liked to spend her days surrounded by her friends and priests, by a profusion of pet monkeys, birds and lapdogs, by laughter and chatter and music. Harry was often to be found in her rooms, usually in the company of the Earl of Holland and a group of English gentlemen, but she had stopped waiting for him to smile at her or talk to her, never looked up to find his eyes resting on her as they once had.

She didn't have much to do with English people at all, even less with English ladies than English gentlemen. The Duke of Buckingham's relations were never far away from the centre of the court, the centre of power, but seemed to spend most of the time busy with their embroidery needles, an occupation Henrietta's mother had never encouraged, preferring to leave it to professionals. Henrietta had already instructed her chief embroiderer to pattern the king's blood-red velvet riding saddle with a leaf and stem design in gold galloon as a surprise for him, hoping still to mend relations between them.

Meanwhile she filled the mornings and afternoons as she had in France: playing cards, writing letters to her sister in Piedmont, taking part in amateur theatricals and concerts with her household. As in France, such activities were punctuated by regular attendance at mass, vespers and compline. But the first masses Henrietta had attended in England had proved very unsatisfactory. The marriage contract had stipulated that Catholic chapels be provided for her at all the palaces, but none as yet had been built. The only available space was Henrietta's closet, where she had set up a little private altar with candles and images of Mary and the saints.

One morning she was making her way there with a veil upon her head, accompanied by her lord chamberlain and followed by six of her ladies and her priests in their flowing clerical habits, when they met Toby Matthews, the boy who had been sent to translate on board *The Prince*. But the moment he saw Henrietta's party he scurried away, head down, as if the mere sight of them might damn him to hell.

Father de Berulle found him afterwards and asked him why he had behaved in such a way, and he confessed, shame-faced, that the king had ordered that no Englishman or woman was to go near the French when they were about their Popery, as he called it. It made Henrietta suspect that the construction of her chapels was not as high on her husband's list of priorities as it should be.

'It is to be expected,' Father de Berulle sighed. 'It sickens me to hear, as I do every day, how Catholics in this country live in perpetual fear of prison or the hangman. Unable to seek God but while trembling.'

'I do not feel at liberty yet to talk to the king about putting an end to Catholic persecution,' Henrietta sighed. She could not help but take her confessor's comments as a direct personal criticism, a sign that he too was disappointed in her, and they stung. She was disappointed in herself, knowing that Charles would never listen to her, or only to scold or dismiss her. 'I will of course speak to him as soon as the time is right,' she added quietly, wondering when and if that time would ever come. 'In the meantime, I shall insist we are at least provided with a proper chapel,' she determined.

She was expected to hold court later that day, which entailed all and sundry coming to watch her eat dinner in her chamber. Despite the lack of ceremony upon Henrietta's arrival at Dover, she had soon found that the English court was far more ceremonious even than the French, with the most formal rules for dining etiquette.

The table had been covered with white linen over an oriental carpet. A large salt cellar and platter of new baked bread were placed in the centre. To the side stood ewers for the washing of royal hands; a cupbearer with glasses and decanters was ready to present wine on bended knee after mouths had been wiped on napkins. None were seated but the royal couple, with an array of ladies and gentlemen standing in semi-circles behind their two thrones. After grace was said in Latin, a procession of gentlemen wearing swords entered bearing platters of meat and fish. At the head of the table the server set down every dish for the carver to cut a portion from each. The courtiers who had carried them in first tasted small pieces and it was expected that the king and queen would also sample a portion of every dish.

The room was so overheated, with its roaring fire and the sheer number of people who were packed inside, the ladies with their wide skirts crushed and crumpled against each other's, that everyone was slightly irritable, Henrietta included. She realised that it was therefore not the best time for her to raise such a delicate issue as the proper provision of chapels, but not being one to put off for a minute what could be done immediately, raise it she did. 'When are my chapels likely to be finished, Your Majesty?' she asked Charles, politely enough.

'What's wrong with your closet?'

'What's wrong with it!' Henrietta set down her spoon, trying to keep calm. 'For a start, there's not nearly enough room.'

'Use the great chamber then,' Charles suggested in an offhand way. 'And if the great chamber is not large enough, then there is always the garden, and if the garden does not serve you, perhaps the park is the fittest place.'

For someone so set on maintaining a harmonious household, he was going a strange way about it. Henrietta forgot all about staying calm and not arguing. Her blood was boiling, and it had nothing to do with the temperature of the room. How could he be so unkind, so rude to her in public? She refused to cry any more. Instead she lifted her chin, her black eyes flashing. 'If that is your attitude, sir, then I shall . . . I shall grow rapidly weary of England and . . . and wish myself home again.'

'There are a good f-few English people who are wishing you h-home already,' he snapped tersely, stuttering badly in the heat of the moment. 'It is a great expense to feed all these f-foreigners. Popish, overdressed and arrogant f-foreigners at that.'

Henrietta pushed her plate away, scowling round at the assembled English people as she did so. If they thought her arrogant already, she may as well not disappoint. And if they begrudged feeding her friends, why should she entertain them by eating in front of them? She was in no mood now to be gawked at anyway.

They obviously got the message because within a few moments most had turned tail and gone.

Henrietta felt guilty for her behaviour later, when she returned to the palace after taking the air with her ladies and dogs and saw something that made her suspect there might be a valid reason for Charles's earlier tetchiness.

The lack of provision of a chapel was not the only clause in the marriage contract that had not been fulfilled. So far Henrietta had not received a penny from the king. She'd had to borrow money from Mamie in order to pay her servants and even to buy some ribbons to match her new black gown, as Mamie reminded her when they were out walking in the privy gardens. Determined to press for a resolution to this matter as well as a proper answer to her earlier question, Henrietta left her maid-of-honour to round up the animals and marched directly to the king's rooms.

She halted when she saw him pacing up and down his dimly lit withdrawing room. He was alone except for his dog Rogue, who lay curled up asleep by the fire. Charles had a sheet of parchment in his hand from which he was quietly reading aloud to himself as he strode back and forth, with a look of such dogged concentration on his face that it invited no interruption. There was an air of intense privacy about him, and a fierce pride too, that warned Henrietta he'd not want to be caught by her, so she ducked into a window embrasure to spare him. Rather than quietly slipping away, though, she stayed to watch. Not in order to pry, but because his behaviour reminded her so much of her brother, the French king.

Charles was speaking in English, using many unfamiliar words. She didn't understand half of what he was saying, but she instantly grasped what it was he was doing. Louis did exactly the same thing. Whenever Charles stammered over a particular word he would rush over to his desk, grab his pen and scratch out a line on the paper, quickly scribbling in something else.

There were certain letters of the alphabet that Louis had always particularly struggled with and stumbled over, and when he was preparing a speech he took great pains to find ways of avoiding having to say any words that began with those letters – to find in advance substitutes without the sounds he found most troublesome. Henrietta used to help him sometimes. Just by sitting with him, being his audience and letting him practise on her for as long as he needed to, or offering suggestions for alternative words and phrases that would be less likely to trip him up all the time. And by reminding him to breathe and relax.

She longed to set all their past differences aside and go to Charles and help in the same way. But how could she help him, really? Besides having no true comprehension even of what he was trying to say in the first place, she did not know him well enough. Did not know him at all. She might deeply offend him with her offer. He could be so formal and pompous that she sensed he might well be mortified just to know that she had witnessed this problem of his.

There was at least one small thing she could do for him, though, understand what he was saying. She strained her ears to pick out a few of the half-recognised words, repeated them in her head to make them stick, determined to check their exact meaning, just to be sure she had it right.

'Money. War. Spain. Money. War. Spain.' She kept muttering the words to herself as she went to find Harry.

He was precisely where she had expected to find him, doing precisely what she had expected to find him doing. Gambling again. He had struck up a firm friendship with her lord chamberlain and the pair of them were sitting at a table by the fire in the great hall with the Earl of Holland, teaching some of the younger courtiers to play cards. As she made her way over she saw Harry glance at the hand of one of the young gentlemen, Tom Killigrew, the king's page, and lean in towards him slightly, as if he were attempting to cheat. Instead, he tapped one of Tom's cards with his finger, saying in a rather loud whisper, 'Try that one, lad.'

The boy's face lit up in a beaming smile as Henrietta swept across the hall, her slippers pattering on the flags with her usual light but hurried steps.

'Money-war-Spain,' she exclaimed in English. Then in French, 'What does it mean?'

'Money is *argent*, ma'am. War, *guerre*. Spain, *Espagne*. His Majesty was obviously rehearsing his speech for his first opening of Parliament tomorrow,' Harry explained readily, with the total lack of condescension that had always made her feel able to ask him anything. 'His Majesty has never addressed the Lords and Commons before and does not have an easy task ahead of him. He needs to persuade them to grant him the means to continue the war with Spain that he, or should I say the Duke of Buckingham, began last year.'

'Oh. I see.' Harry seemed as well informed about affairs of state here as he had been in France. From the table she absently picked up one of the playing cards, which happened to have a queen on it, and tapped it against her chin. 'I know nothing of English politics. It's a pity you won't be there, too, so that you can enlighten me afterwards.'

'Ah, but I will be there, ma'am. On the benches of the Commons. I am now the Member for Bodmin.'

She was amazed. 'You are a Member of Parliament?'

'I have recently won a seat, yes.'

'Congratulations.' Her mother had said he would go far, but how far and how fast? 'I am pleased for you, truly. Only . . .' She slapped down the card, flicking her gaze upward to look back at him. 'I hope it doesn't mean I shall lose you. As my interpreter, I mean.'

'I shall not be going to live on Bodmin Moor, I can promise you that, nor spending every hour in Westminster.' He smiled. 'Your Majesty does not need an interpreter to make your own wishes plain, though.'

'What can you mean, sir?' she asked, thinking she knew full well.

'It was most impressive earlier, the way you drove away a whole crowd from your room with just one scowl.'

'Do you think I was too fierce?'

'What I think, madam, for what it's worth, is that however little you are in stature, you have the spirit of a giant.'

Henrietta beamed, feeling instantly as tall and strong as one. So he did still like her after all, even if he ignored her for most of the time now. 'Thank you, sir. And for the English lesson.'

'You are very welcome, ma'am.'

Before Charles went in procession to the Palace of Westminster to open Parliament in full state, the yeomen of the guard had to undertake a search of the cellars. So the Duke of Buckingham informed Henrietta with apparent relish.

'Why do they do that?' she asked innocently, attempting to be friendly. 'What are they looking for?'

'Gunpowder,' he replied with a cruel smirk. 'And Papists. Twenty years ago there was a failed plot by English Catholics to blow up Parliament and kill King James. We've been on our guard against those of the Roman faith ever since.'

When the search was completed, and no Catholics were found lurking beneath Westminster, the king donned his full regalia. It included a crown, even though he had not yet been officially crowned, a robe trimmed with ermine and a golden sceptre. But for all the trappings of majesty, he looked nervous.

Henrietta felt nervous for him. If only he were taller and stronger-looking. If only she were too. She'd heard whispers that people were already speculating she was much too petite and delicate ever to carry a baby. Taller people commanded more respect, that was the truth of it. The fierceness Harry had noted in her was her way of compensating, of making sure she was heard and seen and taken notice of despite being so small. It occurred to her that perhaps Charles's uncompromising strictness was his way of doing the same, a means of self-defence.

The plan had been for Henrietta to watch the state procession from the windows of the Duchess of Buckingham's apartments in Wallingford House, one of the duke's less imposing mansions, situated at the corner of the Whitehall tiltyard which looked out over the route to Westminster. She had dressed in her new grey silk French gown 'specially for the occasion and Mamie had spent hours with the curling tongs, taking particular care that each tiny intricate ringlet coiled perfectly around a thread of pearls.

Just as they set out to walk across the privy gardens, though, it began to spit with rain. Henrietta slowed her pace and looked up at the blanket of charcoal cloud which threatened a heavier downpour. Their dresses and hair would be completely ruined by the time they reached Wallingford House.

'Let's not go,' she decided. 'We may just as well watch from my rooms.'

No sooner had they made themselves comfortable, on a row of silk upholstered chairs drawn up to the windows, than the Duke of Buckingham appeared. He told Henrietta that she had offended her husband by not going to Wallingford House as arranged.

'Surely the king has far more important concerns than which window I sit at?' she replied.

'He sees his wife's obedience as being of prime importance.'

'It is raining. I don't wish to get wet.'

'Perhaps for the sake of avoiding further argument you should go, ma'am,' the Duc de Chevreuse advised her quietly. 'It is only a drizzle and looks to be easing off now.'

Not wanting to be accused of vanity again, Henrietta rose from her chair, but resentfully. 'Very well,' she sighed. 'I will do as you say.'

Celebrations were in full swing in the duchess's rooms by the time she arrived, claret flowing and musicians playing, everybody chattering and exicited amidst a great air of celebration and anticipation. Henrietta was glad she had come after all. But just as she had removed her cloak, been handed a cup of wine and started chatting to the duchess, the duke reappeared.

'His Majesty is more angry than ever with you, ma'am,' he said with a pout. 'Since you obeyed a Frenchman rather than him. The King wishes you to leave here immediately.'

'What?' He could not be serious. 'This is ridiculous. I came here expressly to please His Majesty and now he wishes me to go again?'

'Your Majesty preferred to watch from your rooms anyway.'

'That was before. I am enjoying myself now. I want to stay.'

'His Majesty says that you must not.'

'Please tell him I wish to. Ask him to give me permission.'

The duke departed again, appeared for a third time. Rather than speak discreetly to Henrietta, he delivered the king's refusal of her request in front of all the assembled courtiers. 'His Majesty orders Your Majesty to leave at once by absolute command. If you do not, he will postpone the opening of Parliament.'

Henrietta was embarassed, astounded and angry. She did not know whether to laugh or scream and stamp her feet. She glanced at the silent faces gathered around her, many of which wore expressions of discomfiture or surprise, but saw no sympathy. She wished that Harry were there.

Instinctively, it was him she wanted and turned to when most in need of help and support, or just for someone to explain what was going on, what she should do in response. Not that anyone could contradict the king's order.

'If it is His Majesty's absolute command then of course I will obey,' she said tersely. It was the king's God-given right to make demands, even if they were ludicrous ones. Along with absolute devotion to the Catholic faith, Henrietta's mother had instructed her in the absolute power of kings. That kings were answerable only to God, not to men. They were appointed by God to be as a god on earth and must be obeyed, just as God in heaven must be obeyed. Which was what she had been trying to do all along!

'It seems that in England obedience is a crime,' Henrietta remarked as Mamie helped her back into her cloak. 'I cannot believe that all this trouble has been caused just by my saying the weather was bad and that I wished to remain inside!'

Just when she had been trying to have kinder thoughts about Charles and excuse him for his uncompromising behaviour, too. Nonetheless, Henrietta's mother, in her letter of instruction, had ordered her daughter not to displease her husband. She knew that she should apologise. Even if she did not quite know why or how she had displeased him, she had evidently managed to do so. Again. But before she went to see the king, she wanted to know in what mood she was likely to find him. That would depend upon how his debut speech to the Houses of Commons and Lords was received. She sent for Harry as soon as he had returned from Westminster.

'Did all go well today?' she asked as he took a chair opposite her in her privy chamber.

'It rather depends on one's definition of the word "well", ma'am.'

How was it he could always make her smile? 'By your definition of it, sir?'

He stretched out his legs, leaned back in the chair and took a deep breath that made his chest expand and rise in a way that seemed to her strangely powerful. 'To be honest, it did not go well by any definition,' he said. 'His Majesty failed to win Parliament's support. His speech was very short. But even so, they did not let him finish before they began shouting him down.'

'Why?'

'His tone. It was terse to the point of being aggressive. I am sure he did not mean to convey that impression at all. It is merely that he finds face-to-face confrontation difficult, I think. He is not a natural public speaker. I expect he is very aware of his failings and frustrated by them, which is why he over emphasises sometimes and digs in his heels when he feels his wishes are not being honoured.'

'You heard what happened earlier, at Wallingford House?'

'I did,' said Harry gently, filling those two short words with more understanding and sympathy than had been shown by the rest of the Wallingford House crowd put together. 'It is the king's own awkwardness and shyness that prevent him from being able to make people listen to him; that prevent him from commanding the deference and respect that he knows are his due. Which only serves to make him more belligerent, and determined to be obeyed at all costs.'

'You are very perceptive and wise, I think.'

'I don't know about that. But after the way he ordered you about today, can you see why he did not win Parliament's support but instead alienated many of its members?'

'They would not listen to him?'

'His Majesty could barely make himself heard.'

'What did he do?'

'He left.'

'*Il était vexé?*'

Harry smiled. 'In a huff, yes.'

Her own annoyance with Charles did not stop Henrietta from feeling indignant on his behalf. 'He has the divine right to demand respect and obedience.'

'But he would make life so much easier for himself and for everyone else if he learned how to make a demand at least sound like a request.'

'Spoken like a true diplomat,' she said with admiration.

A king needed to be a diplomat too, though. And yet this king was not. Another crack in her dream. She had wanted to be loved by a king, and she was not. She had wanted to marry a king who was well loved . . . and seemingly that was not the case either.

Charles was alone in his privy chamber reading a book with Rogue at his feet. Where his ministers had failed to put themselves, Henrietta thought.

Outside his window church bells were tolling. The plague was back, the dead waited for burial. It was the same every summer in Paris too.

'Did King James leave any advice about how to manage a difficult government?' she inquired gently, taking a chair opposite him.

Charles reached down and fondled the dog's ears. 'My father believed in Parliament,' he said. 'He believed that kingship should mean governing in complete partnership with Parliament. That abiding by existing laws and refraining from excessive taxation would bring the rewards of loving subjects who may live in security and wealth and justly praise their king for their good fortune. I believed that once too. But today . . . I know I am not good at public speaking,' he admitted with a frankness that touched her. 'I lack the words, the arguments and the powers of persuasion. What it takes to command respect, loyalty and obedience. They would not have dared act thus with my father.'

Henrietta sensed his bitter disappointment in himself for not measuring up to his father's example and his own expectations of himself. She knew exactly how that felt. 'Your Parliament didn't grant you what you wanted?'

'They were more keen to debate religion,' he answered flatly.

'Religion?'

'Throughout England, our marriage was opposed most passionately by people who fear Catholic oppression and the French in particular. The Puritans don't want you here.'

Henrietta flinched. He was blaming her for what had happened today? *Was* she to blame? It came as a great shock to hear that it was her faith, her very presence, that had caused such ill feeling. That though the king's subjects may welcome her, his Parliament did not. That it was not their new king they had turned against, but his new queen. She knew the Duke of Buckingham did not like her, nor did most of his family. But the whole government too? These Puritan people she kept hearing about? She felt confused, disoriented almost, as if she'd not so much arrived in a different country as an entirely different world. The bells were still tolling, tolling, the ominous announcement of death. So different from the peals of rejoicing that had greeted her entry to the city. The sound seemed full of foreboding. She wished it would stop. 'Does anyone want me here?' she asked quietly. 'Beside my fellow Catholics, I mean?'

She wanted only for Charles to say that he wanted her. He did not. 'My father's advice was to steer a middle course between the pride and error of Popery and the extremism of the Puritans, and after much searching I have myself concluded that the Church of England is the best in the world. But Parliament suspects that I'll make too many concessions to the Catholic community as a result of taking a Catholic queen. They want to see the strictest enforcement of the existing penal laws.'

'Our marriage treaty prohibits that.'

'I do not need reminding,' Charles replied.

He did, though, since he had not abided by its terms as yet. Maybe he regretted marrying her. Maybe that was the real reason he had seemed so determined to find fault with her earlier.

'I am sorry your Parliament finds me so offensive but I would have you know that I would rather die than offend you,' Henrietta said. 'I beg you not to treat me again in the manner you did today, scolding me before the whole court. People will think . . . they will think that you do not love me.'

Charles regarded her in silence for a moment and then rose from his chair. He crossed to the door and held it open, inviting her to leave. 'If that is how you feel, madam, please torment me with your visits no longer and I will not torment you with mine.'

Next morning the Duke of Buckingam informed Henrietta that the king would visit her bedchamber no more, nor admit her to his, until she had begged his pardon with due humility. 'If you do not do so within two days, His Majesty will treat you as a person unworthy to be his wife and expel your household.'

'I did as I was told. I can hardly beg the king's pardon for that, can I?' Beneath her skirt, she stamped her foot in exasperation. 'I do not wish to discuss this with you.'

'There is no discussion to be had. All the king requires is your humble apology.'

But what was she to apologise for now? Whatever it was, it seemed that she must do it. In order to do so she had to wait in the presence chamber along with various gentlemen until the king had finished his business with his lord chancellor, the Earl of Pembroke.

'Sir, if I have upset you I am truly sorry,' Henrietta said, when her turn came. 'Please tell me how I may avoid making the same mistake again. What did I do that was so wrong?'

'You assured me that it was raining when I told you it was not.'

Henrietta had to bite her lip to stop herself laughing out loud at the sheer ridiculousness of it. 'I would never have thought that an offence, sir,' she said with as much diffidence as she could muster. 'But if you believe that it is, I will try not to commit it again. I beg you to think of it no longer.'

Seemingly that was enough. He embraced her brusquely. 'I shall try not to.'

Soon plague was killing thousands a week, the contagion spreading west from the city so rapidly that the king ordered Parliament to be adjourned. Henrietta's household was moved away from the city to Hampton Court. Given that he was not strictly part of that household, though he had been living in it for over eighteen months, Harry was not going with them.

'You'll like Hampton Court, I think, ma'am,' he said. They had been walking with some of Henrietta's ladies in St James's Park, past the aviary of bright-coloured birds and the pens that contained the crocodiles and elephant that Charles's father had introduced. They paused to sit on a bench near the physic gardens. 'King Henry VIII was a great builder and gardener and was determined that the gardens he laid out there would outshine even your King Francis's palace garden at Fontainebleau.'

The air was scented with rosemary and thyme, but for once Henrietta felt little interest in talk of planting schemes and palaces. In the absence of any crumb of affection from her husband, she needed a sure sign that Harry still cared about her. She needed to know that he was even half as reluctant to part from her as she was from him. Some tangible evidence, something definite to take with her and hold on to.

Did his eyes linger for just a second on the scarlet ribbon that tied the long lock of her black hair, as if he wanted something tangible too, wanted to reach out and touch it, wanted her to untie it perhaps and give to him for a keepsake? Or was that just wishful thinking on her part?

'It's red,' he said.

'I'm sorry? What is?'

His eyes travelled to hers. 'The palace at Hampton Court. Reddish-pink anyhow.'

'Oh. That.' She felt a crushing disappointment which she knew was ridiculous and that she must conceal at all costs. 'It sounds splendid.'

'*Merveilleux* and *magnifique*.' He smiled.

Oh, how she was going to miss him, his sense of humour, just having him to talk to, just knowing he was there. 'Why does the Duke of Buckingham hate me so?' she asked suddenly. 'You promised me when we first met that you would never lie to me,' she appended quickly. 'Please do not try to shield me from the truth. Whatever the reason, it's better that I know.'

Everything about him seemed to say, no, it is not. 'It is nothing personal,' he said carefully. 'I mean, it is not Your Majesty personally that the duke has issue with. How could it possibly be?'

'What then?'

'Look, ma'am . . .' He pinched the bridge of his nose.

'I am looking. And I see that I've done it again, haven't I? I've asked you a question you'd rather not be called upon to answer. I am sorry, truly. But I have nobody else to consult.'

He looked slightly taken aback, but pleased. 'You flatter me, I think.'

'Not at all. That would be the wrong way around entirely, wouldn't it? Flattery is for courtiers, not queens.' She steered him back to the matter in hand. 'My husband seems especially susceptible to the duke's flattery.'

She knew Henry well enough to realise that he was pondering the most tactful, diplomatic way of explaining – selecting words that would help not harm. He gave his beard a thoughtful stroke. 'George Villiers's power at court has depended on his remaining always first in the king's affections,' he said eventually. 'First with King James and now King Charles. Despite their kinship they are very different kings, very different men. James was not . . . how can I put it? His wife would never have been a threat,' he rephrased. 'In the way that you might be.'

She didn't tell him that it all made sense now, because it didn't at all. He could speak in such a roundabout fashion sometimes that it was quite maddening. Endearing too, though, as was so much about him. She waited while he went round again.

'The duke is afraid of the king loving you more than him, of losing his foremost position to you. Of thereby losing his influence. He has striven to make the king dependent on him, devoted to him, to ensure he retains his favoured place, and is afraid of His Majesty becoming dependent upon and devoted to his lovely and spirited wife instead.' Harry let out a breath. 'That's it. In a nutshell.'

'I see.'

'Best thing to do when he tries to make mischief is not to retaliate.'

'I'll try.' What else was there to say? She wanted to prolong the conversation, just to keep him there for a few seconds longer, but couldn't think of a valid reason. 'Well, I shall tell you if I think King Henry succeeded in his goal to outshine Fontainebleau. Next time we meet.'

'I shall look forward to that.' Harry said it with such feeling that it made her pulse quicken in that way he so often and so easily made it do.

'I too.'

It was as if neither of them wanted to be the first to look away, or to move, so they just stood there, saying nothing, yet saying everything, and it was the most extraordinary moment, like silent music, or poetry with no words.

When Henrietta gave him her hand to kiss, the touch of his fingers was enough to ignite sparks inside her, like the glitter of sunlight flashing on the ripples of the Seine, and she knew also that there was nothing wrong with her after all.

Except that she was evidently soft in the head. Fool that she was, more like a sentimental little maid than a queen of fifteen years, when it came time to use the ewer later, she did not want to wash the place where his lips had brushed her skin.

The gardens at Hampton Court most definitely did not outshine Fontainebleau, in Henrietta's opinion. But they did come close enough to raise her spirits as the royal barge approached the landing stage. The steps led to a water gallery, with square plots of grass decorated with posts topped by the lions, dragons and other painted heraldic beasts that the English seemed so keen on and which Henrietta liked too. If they'd come by road instead of river, they'd have entered through the equally magnificent castellated gatehouse with its astronomical clock. Despite all she had taught him about architecture, Harry had not thought to mention that, nor the magnificent clocktower adorned with reliefs of Roman emperors that were set into the warm rose-tinted brickwork.

To top it all, the state rooms and royal apartments were more sumptuous than any at Whitehall, with the most beautiful ornamental plaster ceilings. But the king announced that he had no intention of sharing those rooms with Henrietta: he was leaving immediately for a place called Oatlands, to spend some days hunting. The duke was to remain at Hampton Court and wasted no time in stirring up more trouble.

'It is no wonder His Majesty prefers to go to Oatlands,' he commented almost as soon as the king had departed and Henrietta had sat down to eat in her private dining hall. 'I must warn you that he will not long put up with your coldness towards him.'

*Her* coldness? Henrietta remembered Harry's advice, took a deep breath and bit her tongue.

'If you continue in this way, you will be the unhappiest woman in the world.'

The vague but dark threat, so blatantly uttered and so totally unprovoked, was like the rumble of cannon fire. It sent a tremor of fear through her, gave her a sense of just how devious and dangerous the Duke of Buckingham could be. It was doubly disturbing somehow, such offensiveness issuing from the mouth of such a beautiful man. Beauty and charm were all the king saw, all the duke let him see, and she knew that even if Charles had been there he would not have defended her.

'I was not aware that I had given my husband any cause for complaint,' said Henrietta, trying to be proud and conciliatory at the same time. 'And I cannot believe he would deliberately set about making me unhappy. As for you, sir, I know that you do not like me, but I am prepared to live on civil terms with you, if you will do the same with me.'

She thought that Harry would have been proud of her for that little speech.

As was Mamie. 'Well said, ma'am,' she applauded when the duke had gone.

It didn't do much good. Next morning, after mass, Henrietta went to explore the flowerbeds and arbours, the tree-lined walks and ornamental lakes and ponds of the gardens and grounds. The sun was hot, with a cooling breeze rustling the treetops and rippling the water where ducks and swans were swimming. She stopped to admire the tender wall shrubs growing on the south-facing walls of the tiltyard and the exotics along the privy garden terrace. The rose garden was stunning and everywhere was bright with flowers. When she reached the elaborate summer house that stood on the south side between the palace and river, the duke came to join her.

'My wife, sister and nieces have expressed a wish to become ladies of Your Majesty's bedchamber.'

'I am perfectly satisfied with the ladies I have brought with me from France.'

'I don't wonder, since their company enables you to carry on as if you are still there.' The duke tossed his hair over his shoulder like a girl, but his smile was not at all girlish, laced as it was with devious purpose, underhand and triumphant. 'It turns out that cases of plague have already been reported in this neighbourhood,' he informed her casually. 'The king has given orders that you are to move to Windsor. You are to travel there with my niece Eleanor.'

Henrietta made an effort to show no resentment, but Mamie had no such restraint. 'It is an outrage to go on denying me my right of entry to the royal coach!'

'I know it is. But what can I do, Mamie?'

There was plague in Windsor too. Which meant Henrietta had to endure the company of Eleanor Villiers, a dark, lissom female version of the duke not only in her beauty but also in her bitter tongue, for further long hours as they hastily moved to the Palace of Nonsuch. It seemed to Henrietta that all they did in England was travel, travel, travel. Though she was glad they had come to Nonsuch. The layout of the palace was simple, comprising fortified gatehouses and courtyards, but the inner courts were ornamented with breathtaking stucco panels. The southern face was decorated with ornate Italianate decoration, with tall octagonal towers at each end topped with onion-shaped cupolas. The gardens were equally lovely, with fountains and grottos that resembled those at St Germain and in the Tuileries.

Henrietta encourged Mamie and the rest of her French ladies to play about with her in the pools in the warm summer sunshine.

'I feel like a child again,' she giggled.

'You may be married, but Your Majesty is not yet sixteen.' Mamie smiled at her indulgently. 'Don't you go forgetting that.'

It was such a relief to be here after the starchy etiquette of Whitehall, and during the following days they had a wonderful time putting on dances and theatricals, dressed up in their most exotic gowns and hats and jewels, dancing with crowns of flowers in their hair, posing for imaginary painters, and generally giggling and cavorting around. On one occasion they paraded through the hall pretending they were at the court of Marguerite de Valois, Queen Consort of Navarre, whose passion for culture and the arts would have made her very at home in such an extraordinary place as Nonsuch. They had several pet monkeys between them, as well as hounds and spaniels like Mitte and pretty fluffy lapdogs, and they dressed them all up in ribbons and necklaces of pearls which suited the lapdogs in particular and which they actually seemed to like very well.

'Vain little *chien*, aren't you?' Henrietta cooed, kissing one of the little dogs. She had not realised how much she had missed the luxury and warmth and gaiety of home, feeling for the first time that she might find it again in England. 'Life's not so bad,' she sighed contentedly to Mamie, when they were sitting in the lemony sunshine with their petticoats frothed up round their calves and their toes in the sparkling fountain. 'I mustn't complain.'

'When people say that, it generally means they are about to.'

Henrietta laughed. Whatever would she do without Mamie and the rest of her friends? 'At least the king has no vices and, unlike my father, he keeps no mistresses.'

'He has the duke,' Mamie said. 'He's like a mistress.'

Henrietta rolled over on to her stomach, started plucking petals off a daisy. 'Very true.'

'You know what they say about George Villliers, don't you?' Mamie said, her voice tinged with the thrill of salacious gossip about to be shared. 'That he's got where he has solely on the strength of his pretty face and long legs. They say that he and King James kissed in public and . . . well . . . the duke was King James's gentleman of the bedchamber and slept in his chamber at night, so . . . you know . . .'

Henrietta twisted her head round to stare at her. 'No,' she said categorically, sitting up again. 'Absolutely not. I shan't believe it.'

'Your prerogative, but it's common knowledge. "Your Majesty's humble slave and dog". That's how the duke used to sign his letters to the late king. And you know the manner that dogs and other beasts . . .'

Henrietta clapped her hands over her ears. 'Ugh! Hush, will you? I don't want to think about it.' Which was not strictly true. It was such an appallingly wicked image that it was strangely fascinating. And it explained a lot. Charles too loved the duke, but not in *that* way, surely? Not in a physical way? In which case, it all made sense. Why the duke was so perturbed when his new king took a wife to his bed. Why he was so determined to create friction between them. No wonder Harry had dissembled when she had asked him about the duke. But being the lover of King James! She flung herself back on the grass and looked up at the glazed blue sky. One of the little lapdogs came to lick her face with a wet tongue, the pink bow on her topknot drifting loose. Henrietta gently pushed her away. 'And English people say it's we French who are perverted.'

'Do they?' Mamie asked.

Henrietta stretched luxuriously on the warm grass and Harry's face came into her mind, along with other parts of him. She bit her lip, remembering the taste of him. 'Have you not heard of French tricks?' She smiled to herself. 'We are supposed to be wholly depraved and wanton.'

Charles was now residing at Woking but separation did not improve relations between the king and queen. It was evident that Buckingham was telling tales, manufactured, trivial tales, that were nevertheless clearly guaranteed to raise Charles's hackles, so that when he did come to Nonsuch to see Henrietta, or to sleep with her, all he did was complain. About her so-called frivolous behaviour or what he called her 'exotic' French fashions and hairstyle.

'I reminded His Majesty that Your Majesty is only just sixteen,' Father de Berulle told Henrietta on the way back from mass. 'I told him that he finds fault with your dress and other innocent little pleasures and pastimes it is only natural you would enjoy at your age.'

'What did his majesty say to that?'

That he would not mind you enjoying yourself so much if you at least did it in English. He says you waste your days in idle silliness rather than bothering to learn his language. That marriage has not changed you one whit and you have remained thoroughly French in your sentiments and habits.'

'Perhaps that is because I *am* French. This is the duke's doing, you do realise?'

'Both the duke and the king behave towards you with great insolence. I have told them so.'

Henrietta stopped walking. 'Have you?' she asked, delighted that he had been so outspoken. 'Have you really?'

'I have. I told them also that you are passionate and young. I tell you that you are perhaps too obstinate . . .'

'I am not!'

'It might improve relations between you if Your Majesty did learn a little English. The king is already hampered by his stutter, and it would be easier for him if in addition to that he did not also have to converse with you in a foreign tongue.'

'I think it best that my husband and I do not converse at all,' she declared hotly.

In July they moved yet again, this time to a palace called Blenheim in a village called Woodstock. The spread of the plague meant that Henrietta was learning the names of lots of English royal residences and towns at least.

Blenheim was situated on a low hill within a great walled park with lawns and a lake. But most pleasing of all to Henrietta was a stately chapel with a wonderfully wrought roof and eight arches with little windows set above them. The perfect place for her to celebrate mass. But within days her household was ordered by the king to leave Blenheim and travel to Lord Southampton's mansion at Titchfield Abbey, near to the New Forest where Charles was again hunting.

On the first night both households dined together in what had once been the refectory but was now the great hall, and this time it was not the Duke of Buckingham or Charles or Henrietta who caused friction but the king's Protestant chaplain and Father de Berulle, who ended up having a shouting match.

Assuming it was his privilege, the king's chaplain, John Hackett, had started to say grace. But Father de Berulle, on seeing Henrietta's annoyance at this assumption, valiantly began saying his own Catholic grace at the same time, raising his voice to drown out the Protestant Englishman. Hackett gave him a shove with his elbow and raised his own voice another notch. Father de Berulle moved to stand by Henrietta and, taking further encouragement from her amused approval, spoke louder still. So it went on, until both men were nearly screaming grace as each attempted to drown out the other. Henrietta tried not to laugh. It was a juvenile game, but very comical. She suddenly wished that Harry were there, certain somehow that he would find it as amusing as she did.

Charles was not amused, however, but disgusted. Before the two clerics had finished bellowing their blessings, he rose from the table and took firm hold of Henrietta's hand to lead her away. 'I'll not stay and listen to this,' he said.

'But they're nearly done,' she protested, looking back over her shoulder, her black eyes still sparkling with mischief and suppressed laughter. 'They've nearly reached amen.'

'I'll not partake of food that has been blessed in such a blasphemous fashion.'

'Not eat, Your Majesty? Surely you would not . . .'

'I hope you are not hungry.'

Henrietta was always hungry and hated the idea of missing dinner, which had included roast duck brought from the lake at Blenheim. 'Not at all, your Majesty,' she said through gritted teeth.

They had not lain together in some weeks and Charles practically leaped on her as soon as the chamber door was closed, pulling her into his arms, not roughly but not gently either, peremptorily enough to alarm her. He made to kiss her and she turned her head away, wrenching herself free. She tugged her bodice straight and ran a hand distractedly over her curls to smooth them. Charles was breathing heavily and looked peeved. Henrietta put what distance between them she could by going to sit on the carved chair by the hearth, though the evening was too warm to warrant a fire and the grate was empty except for a few ashes and half-charred logs.

'What's the matter?' he said irritably, not having moved from where he stood by the door.

'I'm sorry,' Henrietta said in a whisper. She looked down at her hands, neatly folded in her lap. 'All that shouting earlier . . . It's given me a headache.'

'Everything gives you a headache,' he snapped. 'When you do not have a headache, you avoid my company for some feigned reason of piety. You deny me the principal comfort of marriage. I tell you, other men would not stand for it! My courtiers tell me that if it were their wife, they'd exercise their rights far more often than I do. I ask little of you and even that you make difficult.'

She knew he was right and that his anger was well justified. But she could not seem to help the aversion she felt to physical intimacy with him. She did not want him to touch her. It was as simple as that.

She knew it had not gone unnoticed, knew what everyone was saying about her. The speculation throughout the court was that what she dressed up as modesty and piety was just an unnatural distaste for lovemaking; that she was forever having her priests take confession only she had nothing whatsoever to confess.

It did not help matters when it became evident next day that the king felt perfectly at liberty to discuss this most private of matters with the Duke of Buckingham, who in turn felt perfectly at liberty to discuss it with Henrietta, finding her in the hall once more, where her assorted ladies and courtiers were assembling with their various animals, prior to going for a walk in the old abbey orchard.

'I hear Your Majesty takes direction from your priests as to how to behave behind the bed curtains,' the duke said. His tone was quietly conversational but the women stopped their chattering to listen. 'I hear that under the pretence of confession, these bawdy knaves interrogate you as to how often a night the king kisses you. They have such influence over you that I understand you always obey them when they tell you it is the feast day of such and such a saint, and that you must not let the king so much as touch you.'

Even the dogs had stopped yapping, at least those inside. Outside the hunt was preparing to depart. Henrietta could hear the packs of buckhounds barking and baying. She felt a sudden pang of sympathy for all hunted animals. She had never really hated anyone before in her life but she hated this man. The only dignified response was turn and walk away with head held high, so that was what she did, calling over her shoulder for her ladies to follow her with their menagerie of dogs and monkeys.

'I'm sure the duke and His Majesty are so ignorant of our ways that you could invent saints if you wanted to,' Mamie said supportively. 'Saint Swithin. Saint Saturday. They'd not know the difference.'

Henrietta laughed, not because she found what Mamie said very funny, but to show that she did not care what the duke had said.

'How can he accuse you of being too French in your ways with one breath and then in the next of not being passionate enough? It's a contradiction in terms. The man is an idiot.'

Henrietta laughed at that too. She was still so angry that when they entered the hall where a Protestant service was taking place, attended by the duke's two nieces and others of his relations, she did not divert her path or even slow down, but inspired by the mischievousness that had taken hold of Father de Berulle at dinner the previous day, carried on parading through the hall, laughing and talking louder than ever, encouraging her ladies to do the same and causing the preacher to halt his sermon and the worshippers to look round in dismay at the noisy disruption.

Henrietta found such delight in this simple act of revenge that one promenade was not enough. When she and her entourage had reached the other side of the hall, she spun on her heel to face the way she had come, waited just long enough for the preacher to resume his lesson and the worshippers to focus on him once more, then strode boldly back across the floor with her ladies, dogs and monkeys all obediently following, giggling at the thrill of such open rebellion.

The congregation and priest all scowled now, tutted and turned to each other in outraged astonishment. Henrietta didn't care. She'd not had such fun in a long time, and when she arrived back where she'd started she and Mamie fell about laughing. Her anger was forgotten for now, along with the earlier shame.

# 1626

Amid flurries of snow and days of thick frost and ice, the Christmas festivities were followed, just over a month later, by another even larger celebration, the king's coronation, which was set to take place on 2 February: Candlemas.

Henrietta should have been crowned with Charles but could not be because the ceremony was to be conducted in Westminster Abbey, a Protestant church, with the Protestant Bishop William Laud officiating. By way of a solution, the Bishop of Mende offered to crown her himself, but the Archbishop of Canterbury would have none of that. The Bishop of Mende's alternative suggestion was that the ceremony should take place outside the church, but the English prohibited that also. Charles suggested Henrietta sit segregated from everyone else in a latticed box, but this time it was the Bishop of Mende who put his foot down and would not sanction such a compromise.

It was a diplomatic quagmire and there were no diplomats around who were skilful enough to haul everyone out of it. The Earl of Holland had temporarily returned to France, along with his attendants including Harry. There were other ambassadors, including the Duc de Chevreuse, but the problem seemed too thorny for them to tackle.

'The English are being perverse,' the duke stated to Henrietta. 'Insisting on holding the coronation on Candlemas, when they know full well it is a day of high festival for the Roman church.'

'So what are we to do?'

'We have two options,' the Bishop of Mende interjected. 'Your Highness's coronation must either be postponed or else abandoned. Either way, if that heretical ceremony goes ahead, you must not be present, ma'am. It will offend the Holy Father to see you on your knees before a

Protestant bishop, and insult the English Catholics who have invested so much hope in you.'

'I can't just stay away.'

'You can do no other. You could watch from the window of the gate-house near King Street, if you must. That way you'll see all the comings and goings.'

'No matter,' Mamie comforted her. 'It's Candlemas after all. We'll have our own festivities. We know how to celebrate better than priggish English Protestants anyway.'

But when the day came and Henrietta took up her place in the gatehouse as the bishop had suggested, she was in no mood for celebrating. She did not want to do anything to spoil her friends' pleasure, but she could not bring herself to join in as they gleefully went about lighting dozens of candles and blessing them and putting them in the windows where the flames flickered in the wintry draughts.

Mamie grabbed Henrietta's hand and tried to drag her into their dancing circle but Henrietta shook her head and let them carry on without her, swirling and twirling wildly with their silk skirts swishing in the flickering shadows, as if Candlemas was no Christian ceremony commemorating the ritual purification of Mary forty days after the birth of the Lord Jesus, but the ancient pagan festival of light that had once marked the mid-point between the winter solstice and the spring equinox.

Henrietta wanted no part in the equally heathen ceremony going on in the abbey, of course. That would have been wrong, for all the reasons put forward by her bishop. But this felt just as wrong. The king being crowned without his queen.

The people clearly thought so too. When the thousands flocking to the Abbey happened to look up at the gatehouse and saw the queen standing solitary at the candlelit window, while her ladies frolicked about in the background, they did not wave or smile or bow. Some of them pointed up at her, all looked contemptuous, making Henrietta fear she had made a grave error of judgement in heeding the bishop's advice to her to stay away.

She watched the king ride to his coronation alone, mounted on a huge grey mare. The order of ceremony followed that of the crowning of medieval kings. Charles wore the vestments adopted since the time of Edward the Confessor. Instead of the customary royal purple, he was clad all in white. It was a bleak day, even for midwinter. The skies were overcast, heavy with grey cloud, and the light was dismal. The snow and ice and frost had all melted, leaving grey streets and grey stone. All that sparkled now was the king. In such dreary surroundings he appeared otherworldly, shining like a saint. Five hours later, after his shoulders, arms, hands and head had been anointed with sacramental oil, he rode out of the Abbey dressed in black velvet robes trimmed with ermine, the Confessor's crown upon his head.

When Henrietta joined him for the celebratory feast he made a little joke of the way he had spent the day, putting his two hands to the crown and lifting it a fraction, as if doffing a cap to her. But it only served to draw attention to the fact she wore no crown of her own.

The Duke of Buckingham had plenty to say on that matter.

'He believes the English will take my absence as a grave insult which they will never forgive,' Henrietta said to the Duchesse de Chevreuse later.

'Oh, ignore him.' Marie held up a little mirror and proceeded to check her perfectly painted face for non-existent flaws. 'What do you expect? He criticises every single thing Your Majesty does.'

'The duke has his own critics now.'

Henrietta looked up, not that she needed to in order to ascertain who it was who had stepped into her withdrawing room. That deep, rich voice and perfect French accent were enough to tell her, as was his uncanny knack of appearing out of the blue just when she most needed him.

Harry bowed, took one of Henrietta's hands warmly between both of his and kissed it.

'Monsieur Jermyn. You're back!'

'I believe so.' He smiled.

'How lovely it is to see you.'

'You too, ma'am.'

'You were saying, sir?' Mamie prompted, for once more impatient than Henrietta. 'About the duke?'

'I have come directly from Westminster,' he said, still addressing Henrietta. 'Parliament accuses Villiers of extreme vanity and dangerous recklessness, of squandering the king's treasury on extravagant feasts and clothes and unnecessary wars with Spain. They say that it is no wonder the country is facing penury. But the two Members who have called for his impeachment have been sent to the Tower and His Majesty has summarily dismissed Parliament.' It was said with a snap of finger and thumb. 'The Lords tried to make him see how hazardous it would be to the country for him to try and rule alone. They begged him to let them sit for a few more days. The king told them he would not let them sit for one more minute. His relations with Parliament were not exactly smooth before, but now he has made them much worse. He is determined to set about getting money by forced loans and other means. God knows what will become of us all now.'

But Harry's voice didn't reflect the gloominess of his words, which made Henrietta wonder if perhaps there was a chance that he was as happy to see her as she was to see him.

But no sooner had he arrived at Whitehall than it was Holy Week, when Henrietta and her ladies were to go into retreat at Somerset House. The long gallery had been divided and fitted up into simple cells and an oratory, and there they sang the hours and lived together in seclusion like nuns, Mamie acting as abbess. On days when they were not fasting they shared the long table at mealtimes, ate and drank from earthenware vessels, spent the rest of their time in perpetual prayer and went about barefoot.

On Holy Thursday Henrietta walked barefoot to Tyburn, a place that had haunted and disturbed her since she had learned of it. The triple gallows starker than the bare trees, its towering eighteen-foot-high triangular profile against the colourless winter sky was a ghastly sight. As she walked, Father de Berulle rode along slowly beside her in his coach. Upon reaching their destination, Henrietta knelt for a few moments at the centre of the triple tree where so many Catholic saints and martyrs had died the most agonising death. So many still suffered horribly in this land. But the king seemed determined not to fulfil the terms of their marriage treaty, and since they were on such bad terms themselves there was nothing she could do about it.

Overcome with a sense of the bravery and supreme self-sacrifice of the martyrs, Henrietta closed her eyes to whisper a prayer for their souls. 'God give me the grace to die for my religion if I have to, as they have done,' she whispered.

\* \* \*

It was the tradition in England that soon after Easter the whole court set out on its summer progress, journeying around the countryside, staying at various noble residences, remaining perhaps six weeks at one, two months at another, so that the whole kingdom had the benefit of seeing the king. It was a huge undertaking since everyone and everything went with them: monkeys, lapdogs and the chapel choir, which performed beautiful music wherever they stopped.

On May Day new carriages adorned with gold and silver fringes were ordered, together with braided uniforms for the coachmen and footmen and all the other attendants. For all this careful planning, things did not always go smoothly. Even splendid new equipages broke down, and wagons went astray. And so it was that Charles and Henrietta's households arrived at Hampton Court ahead of all their bedding.

Not that Henrietta minded sitting up drinking wine and talking instead of going to bed. When Charles visited her at night now, it was only for the sake of appearances and he scarce spoke to her except to scold. Besides which, she had a raging toothache that would prevent her from sleeping and wine was at least serving to dull the pain. A little.

It had been raining heavily all day, so when eventually the lost wagon did arrive, the bedding was damp and in need of drying by the fires. Presently this was achieved and all were able to retire. But the sheets could have done with an extra airing and Henrietta couldn't get warm. The pain in her tooth was throbbing a tattoo in time with her pulse. Lying down made it worse so she sat up, and when even that became unbearable she got out of bed again, threw on a robe and walked about.

She tried to distract herself by making a list of who she wanted to administer her dower lands. It wasn't a terribly taxing decision. These were profitable posts and two of them definitely had to go to Mamie and to Bishop Mende, to reward them for being such loyal friends to her.

She heard footsteps in the passage outside the door, an uneven tread she recognised as Charles's, and inwardly she groaned.

'What are you doing up?' he asked.

'My tooth aches.'

'Makes a change from your head.' But he regarded her with some sympathy as she stood before him in her long white smock, her small bare feet sticking out beneath it and her hand pressed hard against her sore cheek. 'Come here, let me see.' He took her over to where the candle stood on the nightstand and she tilted back her head, gingerly opening her mouth so he could peer inside. 'Which one?'

Henrietta indicated a tooth to the top left.

Charles took her chin in his hand, adjusted the angle of her face. 'I can't see anything wrong. There's no inflammation, no outward sign of an abscess.'

'Maybe it'll be gone by morning.'

He let go of her. 'Like your headaches?'

The tenderness was to be short-lived then. 'Please, let us not argue tonight.'

'Do you think that's possible?' He sounded so regretful then that Henrietta let him take her by the hand and lead her over to the bed, but in order to delay the inevitable, she placed in his other hand the list she had been making, and in so doing averted one argument by starting a whole new one.

They were both sitting up, backs against the ornately carved headboard. Charles set the list aside without a glance. 'I'll read it tomorrow. But if there are French names on it, I have to tell you now that it is impossible for them to serve you in these positions.'

'With respect, all have recommendations from my mother.'

'It is neither in your mother's power nor yours to name them without my leave.'

'Then take my lands back. You may as well, if I have no power to put in whom I choose.'

'Remember to whom you speak! You ought not to abuse me so.'

'Nor you me, Your Majesty. I am a daughter of France.'

'A daughter of France is no great thing.'

'If you think that, then why did you marry me? Why? I don't know why you wanted to when you treat me so unkindly. I wish you hadn't. I wish I'd never met you. Nothing I do is right. All we do is argue.' She was trying hard not to cry. 'I have never been so miserable, so totally miserable, in all my life.'

All Charles did was lie down and huddle up with his back to her, dragging all the blankets with him. 'This conversation is ended,' he said.

As was much else between them, it felt to Henrietta.

By morning her toothache was so bad that it was all she could do to stop herself from rolling around the bed in agony. Charles was utterly unsympathetic, returning from his jousting exercise to tell her not to make such a fuss. The apothecary was sent for and prescribed a salve of oil of cloves to be placed directly over the painful tooth, which did lessen the pain a little.

A couple of days later, when Henrietta developed a sore throat, cough and fever to add to her woes, Charles merely walked away. Once she was recovered he did return to her bed, not for love of her, he said, but for love of his people who needed an heir.

The court returned to London for the betrothal of little Mall Villiers to the Earl of Pembroke's heir. Mall was six years old now, pretty and precocious as ever, very spoiled by both her father and the king. Her saving grace was that she was an ingenious prankster. At the celebratory banquet, when she sneakily poured pepper into her father's ale while he was not looking, it made Henrietta laugh more than she'd done in a long time. Doting on his daughter as he did, the duke laughed too. When he had done choking.

The feasting and dancing went on for days and Henrietta's ladies were still in a merry mood when Charles appeared in her apartments at three o' clock in the afternoon, a time when he was usually reading. As usual, Mamie and the rest of Henrietta's companions were dancing about and chattering, playing their lutes and amusing themselves with the dogs and monkeys. Henrietta sat very quietly, waiting to hear what Charles had to say. She could tell by the look on his face that she was not going to like it at all. Not that she ever did like what he said to her these days. She had come to dread the sight of him in his star and garter medallion and cloak. Dreaded the sound of his stuttering voice. Sometimes she hated him. He had made her hate him. He and the hateful Duke of Buckingham.

'I wish you to retire with me so that I may s-speak to you alone,' Charles said.

'I would rather stay here, Your Majesty,' Henrietta replied, out of stubbornness but also because her tooth had started hurting again. She had applied more of the oil of cloves but did not want to have to move about, which seemed to aggravate it.

'Then do me the courtesy of dismissing your women.'

This she did, though reluctantly, and when they had all fluttered off, Charles locked the doors against them. As on her wedding night, she had the sense that he was locking her in as much as locking everyone else out. 'I must inform you,' he said, 'that for your own good and the good of this country, I am sending your people back to France forthwith.'

Henrietta went hot and cold at the same time and her legs started shaking as if she had suffered a relapse of the cold that had make her take to her bed a few weeks before. 'Not all of them?'

'Every one.'

She jumped to her feet. 'Not Mamie, please not . . .'

'I shall be especially glad to be rid of Madame St George,' Charles said, raising his voice to silence Henrietta. 'Ever since I refused to allow her to ride in the royal coach she has s-set you against me. You are surrounded by c-companions who give you bad counsel and have encouraged you to neglect the English tongue and this nation in general, as well as your duties towards your husband. They have stolen you from me and from your people and made a little republic here in m-my court, and I will no longer suffer it.'

Henrietta fell to her knees at his feet. 'Please, Your Majesty, do not do this, I beg you.' The tears were streaming down her face. 'If you have any feeling for me at all then I pray you will take pity on me.'

But pleas that would move even stones to pity were having no effect on Charles. He was unyielding. 'It is not my intention to offend the F-French nation or my good brother King Louis, but you think and s-speak and act at the direction of these interlopers and I will not tolerate it a day longer.'

'I know you don't like Mamie,' Henrietta sobbed. She was almost grovelling now, all pride forgotten. 'But if I cannot keep her, at least let me have my lord chamberlain's wife. Let the Comtesse de Tillières stay with me . . . My priests . . .'

'Your priests have tyrannised you. I hope you will appreciate your liberty when they are gone.'

Henrietta raised her tearstained face to his. 'When? When do they go?'

'The secretary of state is even now breaking the news to your countrymen. The yeomen of the guard have been called to eject the lesser servants from your lodgings. They are to be sent immediately to Somerset

House where they will wait until a ship has been prepared to take them back to France.'

Henrietta scrambled to her feet and nearly tripped over the hem of her skirts as she ran for the door. Charles chased after her and grabbed her arm but she twisted herself free of him. 'I must say goodbye to them,' she cried, eyes wild and frantic. 'At least let me be allowed to say goodbye.' It was as if he did not hear her. She heard her ladies as they gathered in the courtyard below and rushed back across the room to the window. They were all huddled together, howling and lamenting as if they were going to their execution, while the yeomen of the guard rounded them up like a pack of animals.

Henrietta could see no way to open the window to call out to them. Suddenly all the anger and unhappiness and loneliness she had known in England overwhelmed her. She felt like a prisoner, trapped not only in this room, in this palace, but in this country, in this marriage. Overcome with a savage rage such as she had never experienced before, she smashed at the glass with her bare fists. She wanted to scream, to hit out, to hurt someone, herself even, to make Charles see what he had done to her, to smash all that he stood for, control and decorum and rules.

The king looked appalled and embarassed by such an unrestrained display of emotion. He grabbed her arm again and tried to drag her away. 'Stop this now,' he demanded.

Henrietta clung to the lead frame with such determination and fierce strength that when he tugged at her harder, the shoulder seam of her gown gave way and ripped apart. The metal of the window frame cut into her hands and she felt the stinging heat of torn and bloodied skin. 'You are behaving like a madwoman,' Charles protested.

She was beyond caring. If she was mad then he had driven her to madness. In desperation she hit at the glass even harder. Two panes shattered, shards of glass crashing to the ground outside and splinters of it driving into her already lacerated hands. She barely felt the pain.

Charles tried to contain her now by grabbing a lock of her hair. There was a knock at the door and he let go of her to allow the Earl of Pembroke to come in. The earl looked aghast at the scene. The Queen of England with her dress torn and her hands all covered in blood, her cheek too, where she had touched it to push her dishevelled curls back from her face. The earl then looked to the king whose face, flushed already with anger and exertion, now turned brighter red from shame. 'I command you to send all the French away,' he ordered peremptorily. 'Use fair means if you can. Otherwise drive them away like so many wild beasts – and the devil go with them!'

Henrietta ran to her bedchamber and slammed the door in the King of England's face.

Worn out with crying, she lay curled up with Mitte, motionless on the bed. The little dog had tried to lick clean her sore hands and tearstained cheeks but had now gone to sleep.

Henrietta had vowed not to eat unless she could keep at least one of her friends. She refused to go down to the hall for dinner, and when platters of various dishes were brought to her chamber to tempt her, she sent them all away untouched. At least not eating seemed to have cured her toothache, for now at least. Her belly growled angrily, though, but it was more than just her stomach that was hollow and empty. She felt like a rabbit being prepared for the pot, with all her innards ripped out of her. She could scarce believe what was happening, that it had come to this. Charles had permitted her dressers, cook and two priests to return, one of whom, Father Philip, had taken over the role of confessor. He was not French but Scottish, which was why he had been allowed back. A moderate, learned man, he had fled Scotland to escape the persecutions there and had headed for the Oratorians theological college at Lyons before Father de Berulle had asked him to join his English mission. Henrietta liked him, but she refused to see him. She could not imagine trusting anyone but Father de Berulle with her confidences.

She stayed in her chamber when the rest of the court went to break their fast next morning, and her resolve only increased when she learned that her ladies had been summarily replaced by the Duke of Buckingham's female relations, his sister, mother-in-law, and two nieces, whom the duke had been so determined to foist on Henrietta right from the beginning and who had been her enemies from the moment she'd landed in England. His father-in-law, the Earl of Rutland, became her chamberlain, while the role of chief lady of the bedchamber went to the Earl of Carlisle's vivacious wife Lucy. She was connected to the duke not by blood or marriage, but by virtue of the fact that she was his mistress. The duke had his own way at last. Henrietta was now surrounded by his people, day and night.

They treated her more like a prisoner under guard than a queen they were meant to serve. The king went off hunting and Eleanor Villiers slept that night on a pallet in Henrietta's room the better to watch her, even took to following Henrietta to the close stool. She felt like a captive. No Frenchman was permitted to come near her, not that there were many left at court. She was forbidden even to speak or write a word in her own language until she had been properly anglicised.

Never had she felt so totally alone. To be left all by herself amidst people whose language she did not understand, with no proper means of communicating with them, knowing that they all loathed and mistrusted her anyway, was hell. They even tried to make her despise her absent friends.

'We are no worse companions to you than those French people,' Lucy Hay said to her, not unkindly. 'They do not deserve your loyalty. You should know that they have robbed you.'

'Robbed me?'

'Stolen from you, ma'am. Taken your things. They have made off with most of your trousseau, including all your silver and gold, and left you only two smocks and one gown, not even a change of linen.'

Henrietta shook her head. She did not believe it, was sure that she had misunderstood.

Lucy took a letter from her pocket book, handing it over to Henrietta to read. It was from Mamie, claiming she had had no choice but to steal because she was still owed money for wages and for goods she had bought for the queen because the king gave Henrietta no money of her own.

People called Lucy Hay the Wizard's Daughter. Her father, the Earl of Northumberland, had earned the title of Wizard Earl because of his passion for alchemic experiments and there was a dangerous edge to Lucy's beguiling fair-haired beauty and quick wit, which made her appear not unlike a sorceress herself. It was all too easy to picture her casting spells, practising dark arts. Conjuring that damning letter from thin air.

But no, Henrietta knew this was no invention. Mamie had always openly envied Henrietta's gowns and cloaks, had always taken liberties. She set the letter down. 'She's welcome to it all,' she said, ignoring the order not to speak French. 'I do not blame or begrudge her.'

Lucy looked at the forlorn little queen as if seeing her for the first time. She said to her in her own language, 'Then Your Majesty is a better person than I. You are a generous and loyal little soul indeed, I'll grant you that.' A harsher light came into her eyes as she turned to go. 'If only you were more generous to your husband and *his* friends.'

Meaning the duke. Henrietta knew that all she said and did went straight back to Buckingham and via him to the king.

Well let it. For three days now Henrietta had taken nothing more than a little water.

She had no control over her own life any more, but her own person, her body, was a different matter. If the one and only way she could make her feelings and wishes felt was to starve herself, then she was prepared to do it.

The Buckingham ladies refused to starve with her, though, or miss out on one minute of the entertainments, so in the evening, when everyone else was dining and dancing, Henrietta was for a short time left alone. Having no idea if she'd be allowed to dispatch them, she wrote letters to her family in France. To Louis, and to Cardinal Richelieu whom she begged to help her by sending a diplomatic representative. To her mother she wrote: *I have no hope but in God and in you.* Henrietta imagined Marie reading that in her magnificent rooms in the Luxembourg Palace, realised the distress she must cause, how disappointed her mother was going to be in her, and a tear slid down her cheeks and splashed on to the paper, blurring the ink, making her remember her sister Christine's letters which had looked just the same. At that moment Henrietta wished with all her heart that neither of them had been born a princess.

Hunger had been replaced by a strange sensation of lightness, of being disconnected, floating away, which was not unpleasant. Though her limbs were weak and trembling she was strangely wide awake and alert. But when she finished writing she went back to lying huddled on the bed on top of the blankets, since there was nothing else to do.

She fell to thinking about her lost friends. It was true what she had told Lucy, that she did not begrudge Mamie and the rest taking her things but that did not mean she was not deeply hurt by their actions. It seemed she had not a true friend left in all the world.

There was a soft tap on the oak door. She had expected the women to be gone for hours and they'd enter without seeking permission anyway, so she didn't bother to answer. She didn't even trouble to open her eyes when she heard the door open. Footsteps sounded on the boards, approaching her bed. She ignored them. Her friends had been sent away. Whoever it was, it was not someone she would wish to see.

She sensed eyes looking down at her. They might have been her own. She had a peculiar sensation of seeing herself as if from above, outside her own body. A sorry sight. A tiny person curled up on the great bed in a torn and crumpled gown, black curls wild and tangled, face pale and tear-stained, small bloodied hands now scabbed.

Presently the mattress dipped as someone cautiously sat down beside her, breaking every rule of etiquette. She opened her eyes and saw . . . Harry.

Henrietta sat up and flung her arms around his neck, fell to sobbing against his chest. At first he braced himself as if against attack, held his body very rigid, more unyielding even than the king's, almost as if he was in shock or else afraid of her, did not dare to touch her. But presently he softened, tentatively enfolded her in his arms, and as she pressed herself closer, seeking comfort, held her tight. 'Hush now,' he whispered with infinite tenderness, in his beautiful forbidden French. 'Don't cry.'

Henrietta cried harder, clung to him more fiercely. It felt so good to be held that she abandoned herself to all the misery and loneliness of the past months. 'I want to go home. I am so unhappy!'

'I know you are. I know.' He stroked her hair, let her weep for a while longer. 'I came because, from what I heard, I feared you would cry yourself to death. Please try to stop now. Can you?'

He made it sound somehow as if he wanted her to stop for his sake as well as hers, because it hurt him to hear her so upset. She made an effort to compose herself as she drew back from him just a little. She sniffled, wiping her cheeks with her fingers. She saw then that her tears had soaked the luxurious black silk of his doublet and she reached out her hand and made a futile attempt to wipe at that too. Just as when she had wrapped him in her cloak to hide his nakedness, she became a little self-conscious of what she was actually doing, stroking his chest. It was Harry who made her stop, gently taking hold of her wrist and putting her hand from him. 'Don't do that. Please.'

She looked up at him, her black eyes still dewy and her long lashes spiked with tears. 'I am afraid it will stain.'

'It doesn't matter.' He still had hold of her hand, looked down at it as it rested, small and white, against his palm. He ran his thumb softly over the scabs. 'Dear God, what have they done to you?'

'Not quite broken me yet.' She even managed a faint smile. She felt so much better, just having him here. 'I didn't think you liked me any more.'

He raised his eyes to hers. 'How can you think that?'

'You never talk to me . . . not like you used to in France. You used to say such kind things to me all the time.'

He laid her hand gently back on the folds of her skirts, as if setting down a small bird with a broken wing. 'It's not that I don't care about you,' he said. 'It is that I care too much.'

She stored that away to think about properly later, together with the longing she saw in his blue eyes, a sort or loneliness or homesickness that was not unlike her own but which she could not fathom. He was home, he was one of the most popular people at court, garrulous and sociable with dozens of friends.

'I will always be here,' he said. 'For as long as you need me.' He made it sound like a pledge.

'Would you do something for me?'

'Anything.'

'Shouldn't you wait to hear what it is first?'

'No need.'

The amazing thing was that she believed him, believed that he really would do anything she asked of him, anything it was in his power to do. It made her think of knights being sent on quests. She was half tempted to tease him by setting him some impossible task. Instead she retrieved the letters she'd written to her family from where she'd hidden them beneath her pillow, giving them to him. 'Would you see that these reach France?'

'No sooner said than done.'

'What has become of my friends? Do you know?'

Of course he did. He always made it his business to know everything that concerned her. 'My Lord Holland is involved in arranging transport for them. A convoy of thirty coaches and fifty carts arrived in the Strand to transport them to Rochester, but they refused to leave until they had orders from their own king, your brother.'

'Good for them.'

'Quite right. Good for them.'

'There's something else . . . something you're not telling me, isn't there?'

'The captain of the guard came to turf them all out.' Henrietta could see it pained him almost more to impart this news than it did her to hear it. 'They have agreed to be gone on the next tide.'

'What is to become of me?' she asked forlornly. 'My husband hates me. All my friends have been torn from me.'

'No, they haven't,' he said gently. 'Not all of your friends. The king has granted my request to become part of your new household.' He let go of her hand and almost sprang from the bed, as if he had only just realised he was sitting on it and that it was improper for him to be doing so. 'Your Majesty is looking at the new gentleman usher of your privy chamber.'

Henrietta's mother wrote back to say that her daughter's letter had caused her much distress. That she had not in fact been so upset since the assassination of her husband King Henri. But she cautioned Henrietta that her predicament should come as no great shock. In her experience, the English traditionally broke their promises – spoke well and acted ill. Marie ended by instructing Henrietta to try to behave more diplomatically, while also reassuring her daughter that help was at hand. She was sending an ambassador, Maréchal de Bassompierre, brother-in-law to the Comte de Tillières, to try to repair relations between Henrietta and Charles. Henrietta had known Bassompierre from childhood. He was Austrian by birth and had fought with her father; was a fair-minded man experienced in the world since he must be well over forty by now. She felt more positive than she had done in weeks, had high hopes that he would be able to set everything straight.

'But what am I to wear to greet him?' she asked Harry, whispering to him like a secret lover because they had gone on speaking to one another in forbidden French.

As gentleman usher he attended her every day now, was responsible for the ordering of her household, overseeing the work of all her servants. It was not his duty to advise her on her wardrobe. But though he was a man, he was a very stylish one, and she'd far rather seek his opinion than that of one of the Buckingham women, whom she still could not think of as her ladies. Though in this instance she acknowledged she was not so much seeking an opinion as fishing for a compliment, flirting with him again. Just a little.

Henrietta ran her hands lightly over her dark blue silk skirts. 'I have only this one drab dress, and not even the wherewithal to buy a ribbon.' She sighed. 'I fear the ambassador will think me very plain.'

'You could never be plain, ma'am,' Harry said. 'You would look like a queen even in sackcloth.'

'It may yet come to that.'

He chuckled. 'You are very amusing.'

'I do try. I wish I were brave too,' she said. 'Brave people don't cry all the time, do they? The duke has forbidden me to cry in front of everyone.' She touched the string of pearls at her throat. 'He claims it is bad manners.' She felt the familiar sting of tears even now and tried to smile them away. 'The trouble is that lately, since I left France, I can't seem to help it.'

'Under the circumstances, that is totally understandable.'

'If totally unacceptable.'

'Not to Bassompierre, I am sure. Or to any man who possesses a heart not made of stone.'

The ambassador was brought to Hampton Court to be presented. There Charles and Henrietta waited in state, seated upon thrones on a red-covered dais. The Maréchal was a tall, bony, brown-haired man with an elegant demeanour and the quick, observant eyes of a judge. He bowed to her, and despite the duke's orders and Henrietta's best efforts to control her emotions, tears welled in her eyes as soon as she uttered the formal greeting to her countryman, the first French words she had been allowed to speak in public for weeks.

She asked after the health of her mother and brother, and Bassompierre gave his assurances that both of them were well. Charles then promptly led him aside to a private chamber, ostensibly to show off the crown jewels: the Grand Sancy, which had been acquired by Charles's father and was said to be the most valuable diamond in Western Europe, and another huge diamond known as the Mirror of Portugal, which had belonged to Queen Elizabeth. Henrietta knew it was just a ploy, that he would be taking the chance to air his grievances and complain about her, to try to win the ambassador over before she herself could do so. She could well imagine what divisive things he would be saying, words put into his mouth by the duke no doubt, words designed to damn her. Rather than do anything so improper as break down in front of the assembled court, she quickly rose, excused herself and fled to her rooms.

Later the court went by torchlight to the Strand, to the Duke of Buckingham's grandest residence, York House. Bassompierre and Henrietta were seated at the same supper table. Bassompierre made some small talk about the house, which he said was the most richly appointed he had ever seen, and the feasting and show, the likes of which he claimed never to have seen before either. The duke bragged that the entertainment that night had cost six thousand pounds, which was extravagant even by his standards. The dishes included swan, carp and caviar, mackerel, oysters, pheasant, and duck stuffed with anchovies. There were bowls of quinces and figs and oranges, plates of syllabubs and gooseberry tansies. With the aid of ingenious, well-concealed ropes, the food descended from above on mechanical clouds and every course was serenaded by music 'specially composed for the occasion in the ambassador's honour. The room had been turned into a stage-set for a short masque, with scenery depicting the sea dividing France from England. Above it sat a painted wooden likeness of Marie de' Medici enthroned. Henrietta's brothers and sisters were all readily recognisable too, beckoning for everyone to unite to put an end to the conflicts of Christendom.

'Would that they could,' Bassompierre mused. 'But I have to say, my dear lady, that from what I have heard and observed so far, it is my opinion that you have picked quarrels with the king your husband. I fear I shall have to advise your good mother and brother that you are chiefly responsible for this unfortunate estrangement.'

Henrietta felt all hope slipping away. She had assumed that since Bassompierre was French, had loved her father and been sent here by her mother, he would automatically take her side. She was stung by his lack of loyalty and support as well as by the utter injustice of his judgement. Did she truly have not a single friend, besides Harry? What troubled her most of all was the thought that her mother would hear misleading stories about her behaviour and would also turn her back on her in anger, disown her as she had threatened to do. If Bassompierre concluded finally that Henrietta was at fault, what would happen to her? Would she be sent home to Paris in disgrace? Or be forced to remain in England, to live out the rest of her life in misery? It was all so unfair. Her mother had ordered her to obey her husband in all matters. She had tried, she really had. She had tried to obey her mother *and* her husband, and much good it had done her!

'Please, sir,' she began, hoping she sounded proud and reasonable rather than desperate. 'You have allowed His Majesty to state his case. Grant me the same courtesy before you make your decision about who is to blame.'

Bassompierre gave a curt nod. 'Very well.'

After supper the guests were led into another state room, decorated with magnificent paintings and a thousand candles, where they danced country dances until four in the morning. In an attempt to show how she was trying to mix with English people and be friendly, Henrietta danced all night, with linked arms and crossed hands and slipping steps, casting off and falling back, curtseying and weaving in lines. She partnered the Earls of Pembroke and Arundel and Northumberland, even the confounded Duke of Buckingham, who, she had to admit, was by far the most agile dancer she had ever met. Thankfully he was so busy concentrating on his performance that he barely spoke to her. But then, hardly anyone did and she felt more alone than if she'd been in an empty room. Then Harry passed right and ended up opposite her as they danced the circular hey. He took her hand and squeezed it. 'You dance so beautifully,' he said.

'Thank you.'

'You must not be nervous about your interview with Bassompierre. Just answer his questions truthfully and be yourself.'

His kindness and the fact he had known, without her having said a word, just how anxious she was feeling, brought tears to Henrietta's eyes. The duke might be the most accomplished dancer in that room, but Harry Jermyn was by far the most handsome and kind. She did not want him to pass down the line, not ever, but to keep him all to herself.

The private interview with Bassompierre took place later that same morning. Despite Harry's assurances, Henrietta had spent hours lying awake in the dark, fretting over what she was going to say and what might be said to her. Bassompierre did most of the talking, and even though she was seated upon her throne in her own audience chamber she felt more like a criminal brought before the assizes than a queen.

'I understand that your priests have laboured to create in your gentle mind a repugnance for all His Majesty desires of you in private?' was Bassompierre's opening statment.

'My priests are not to blame for that,' Henrietta whispered shyly.

'*Pardon?*' He spoke French with a guttural Austrian harshness.

'My priests are not to blame,' she repeated a little louder. 'Nor anyone but myself.'

He let that drop. 'Furthermore, I understand your bishops have converted your house into a rendezvous for Jesuits. That they have imposed upon you strict penances, made you eat out of wooden dishes and wait upon your own servants. What do you say to that?'

What could she say? She had not realised that the duke was capable of telling such blatant lies. The accusations were absurd. She sat back and refused to respond, not caring if her silence was taken as an admission.

The ambassador thoughtfully pressed his forefinger across his lips. His eyes were as harsh as his accent. 'I also hear that at their insistence you walked barefoot to the site of the gallows at Tyburn, where you prayed so openly that people were scandalised. They say you fell to your knees under the gallows with your rosary clutched in your fingers. And yet you must have known that the Catholic martyrs are regarded as enemies to Protestant Londoners. One of the most notorious, Henry Garnet, was a ruthless traitor who was hung for his part in the Gunpowder Plot. You must see that, to your husband, prayers for such a man, one who tried to assassinate the king's own father and the whole of Parliament, are an abomination?'

'I was not aware of that. It is true that I did visit Tyburn during Holy Week,' Henrietta admitted. 'I could not help but meditate on the pain and misery suffered at that horrid site. But I whispered my prayers in French, which most English people do not understand.'

'Which brings us neatly to your own neglect of the English language. That you cannot deny, unless you are willing to converse with me now in the language to prove your fluency?'

'I cannot do that, sir. I am not fluent.'

'Which lack is put down to your former companions, who endeavoured to instil you with contempt for this nation and a dislike of its habits.'

'I was ready to love this nation and its people with all of my heart.'

'Was?' he posed. 'Is that no longer the case?'

Henrietta was swamped suddenly by a sense of debilitating despair. His tone was accusatory, confrontational. She was certain he was still of the opinion that she was to blame, and that nothing she could say or do would change his mind in her favour. 'I thought you came here to help me, sir?'

Her voice was tremulous and faint as a child's, but that did not touch him.

'Your good mother sent me as an impartial arbitrator in this conflict,' he replied sanctimoniously. 'And in my role as such, my advice to you is this. If you wish to please her and your brother, do your best to please your husband. And be swift about it.'

Henrietta no longer cared about pleasing her husband. Why should she? When he did not care at all about her. But she wanted very much to please her mother, or more to the point did not want to displease her. Since childhood, for as long as she could remember, she had done her best to avoid that. One stern look from Marie had been enough to make her behave and do exactly as she was told, for a short time at least. Despite being a child no longer, a queen herself now and a wife, she still felt that same strong need for her mother's approval. Once she had made her decision about what she must do, she wasted not a moment in acting upon it. As soon as Bassompierre left her, she sent for Harry. She was quite excited by her little scheme, which would please the ambassador, her mother, the king, as well as herself, since it meant she would have the perfect excuse to command Harry's full attention for hours and hours!

He arrived promptly and Henrietta came straight to the point. 'You once kindly offered to teach me to speak English, sir.'

'Indeed I did, ma'am.'

'I should like you to do so.'

'What? Now?' He grinned. 'Foolish question. It is always now with Your Majesty, is it not?' He sat himself down in the chair Bassompierre had vacated, opposite Henrietta's throne. 'Where shall we begin? Your Majesty is already familiar with the basics, I'm certain. Please and thank you and suchlike?'

'Suchlike?'

'Means others of the same kind.' He waved his hand. 'Never mind about that. Not the must crucial word to learn. Hello and goodbye. Yes, no. *Oui?*'

Henrietta nodded. '*Oui*. I mean, yes. But of course!'

'How about far more important words? Palace.' He pointed at her, then circumscribed an arc with his arm. 'Crown.' He pointed to her head and drew an invisible circlet round it. 'Throne? Horse and carriage?'

'Yes, yes,' she giggled. 'I know all of this, obviously.'

'This,' he corrected gently. 'Not zis. French people always scatter the English language with Zs. Zis and zat. Eez. Personally I think it rather exotic, but it is not correct.'

'And we must be correct!' she said, reverting to French.

'Your Majesty knows far more than you reveal. Why do you never use the words you do know?'

Henrietta shrugged her shoulders. 'I'm too obstinate, I suppose. The more I'm told to do a thing, the more I want to do the opposite.'

He laughed too. 'Obstinate but honest.'

'Is that bad?'

'*Très bon*,' he said. 'Very good.'

'Very good,' she repeated.

'*Comment allez-vous?* How are you?'

'How are you?'

Harry inclined his head. 'Very well, thank you.' He stroked his short beard. '*Je ne comprends pas*. I don't understand. That's always useful.'

'I know the English word for Henri,' said Henrietta, her smile shyly flirtatious. She had never spoken his name out loud to him, though she'd whispered it in her head a thousand times over. She had a sudden urge to say it now, to his face. 'Arri.'

'Harry, you mean?' he said softly.

'That's what I said! Arri. I think I prefer it to Henri.'

'I think I prefer it myself,' he said. 'And Jermyn, the way Your Majesty pronounces it, like the beautiful place where you grew up near Paris.'

'Germain? Shall I call you that?'

'You may call me whatsoever you please, ma'am.'

'Goodbye then, Germain.' She smiled as she held out her hand for him to kiss when their first session was over.

\* \* \*

Henrietta had never thought she could look forward to English lessons with such eagerness but they became the highlight of her day. She had decided to learn English in order to please her mother and her husband, but it was her tall, handsome and beautifully spoken young tutor she really wanted to please now. She concentrated hard when she was with him and practised just as hard when not, repeating the words he had taught her quietly to herself and writing them down to help make them stick in her head.

Sometimes they sat together in her privy chamber, sometimes they rode in the park, sometimes she slipped her hand through the crook of his arm and they walked together in the garden and talked about gardens and flowers and trees and buildings. Within a week or so she had learned the words for most colours, all the numbers up to a hundred, as well as the terms for various animals, everyday objects, actions and descriptive words, plus some obscure architectural terms he thought she might like to know: column and pediment and lintel. And how to ask questions. Who, where, what, when . . . and suchlike! So that they could begin having short conversations in English, about commonplace things as well as subjects that interested them both. She found that she enjoyed chattering to Harry in his own tongue. She came to associate English words and phrases with him and thought it a beautiful language, because when she heard the words in her head it was his beautiful voice speaking them to her.

As a bonus, because she was now being so cooperative and diligent and the English ladies could see such rapid improvements in her vocabulary, they no longer watched her like gaolers.

Her household moved to Nonsuch Park and during the coach ride they all discussed the weather. Harry explained that this was a major topic of conversation for English people because their climate was so changeable.

'I can see that,' Henrietta quipped, looking out of the carriage window. 'Wet rain, cold rain, light rain, heavy rain. Very changeable indeed!'

'Ah, but the sun might come out tomorrow or at any hour, there is no telling.' Harry smiled at her and she felt it had come out already.

But all it did was rain, rain, rain, for the whole of June and July, making the gardens waterlogged and muddy and unfit for walking. Henrietta didn't mind that they were confined indoors for most of their stay, though. It was cosy and relaxed, sitting with Harry with candles lit and the rain pattering on the roof and lashing the leaded windows.

Sometimes he read to her or asked her to read to him, to help with pronunciation and new words. He read ballads and poetry and she loved just to listen to him. His voice had a strange power over her. It was like drinking wine, made her dizzy and languid with a glowing warmth that spread through her whole body.

They took to talking about food a great deal, since that was one of Harry's favourite subjects as well as close to her own heart. He complained that talking about it made him hungry though, so for their next lesson Henrietta ordered up a little feast from the palace kitchens. Things she knew he liked. Cheeses and wine. Fruit. Pork pies, pastries and tarts.

'This is very thoughtful of you, ma'am,' he said.

She wanted to tell him that no effort of thought had been required. It was not a case of being thoughtful because he filled her thoughts. He had once said that there was nothing he would not do for her, and though it was comforting to hear, it was, after all, the role of a loyal servant. It was not her role as his queen to give him things and do things for him. But she wanted to. The nuns and priests had always instilled in her the notion that there was just as much pleasure to be had from giving as from receiving. She used to think that pious nonsense, but discovered now that it was true.

These private feasts soon became a part of their routine, with varied menus that ostensibly encouraged Henrietta to try out new words.

They'd had a custart tart this time and he offered her a slice. 'Or a piece, you could also say.'

'I thought piece meant stillness and calm?'

'It does. Only that's spelled a little differently.' Harry grinned. 'Confusing, I know. Especially since you can have peace of mind and also give a person a piece of your mind . . . and they are entirely different things.'

'Now I am definitely confused!'

'Peace of mind with an "a". Untroubled thoughts. Piece of your mind with an "i". Sharing troubled thoughts.'

'I see.' She frowned. 'I think.'

'Peter Piper picked a peck of pickled peppers.'

'We don't have any pepper.' She gave the table a quick glance, wondering if she'd got the word wrong. 'Do we?'

'It's a tongue twister. They are very useful when learning pronunciation.'

'Oh.' Henrietta tried to repeat it, tripped over the words and giggled, helping herself to a hazelnut instead. The previous day they'd had soup and bread and cold meats, the day before that it had been candied fruit and oysters. Today it was a selection of nuts and cheeses as well as the tart.

Henrietta watched Harry effortlessly crack open an almond, drop the shell on to the table and toss the nut into his mouth. He was sitting slightly sideways on to her and had his left leg lightly crossed over his right, the muscles clearly defined through the black silk of his breeches. His left hand was resting lightly along the outer side of his long thigh, thumb hooked over the top, and for some reason she was transfixed by the sight of his slightly splayed fingers. They were long and slender,the bones somehow peculiarly defined, the nails short, clean and neatly trimmed. She could not help staring at them.

There was something about the way he was ever so slightly – and totally obliviously – stroking his own leg which made her ache to touch him. Why that small, inconsequential movement should so entrance her she could not fathom. She had thought there was something wrong with her, that she could not desire a man. But when she was with Harry, when she thought about Harry, she knew there was nothing wrong with her at all. Just to look at him, to have him smile at her and to hear his voice, caused the restless sweet swell of heat between her legs and in her heart which she now recognised as desire. There was nothing wrong with her at all, except that it was the wrong man she desired. A man she could never have. Could she?

She grabbed a nut and the cracker, lacking the strength, or dexterity, or something, to do anything effective with them. Harry cracked another almond, offered it to her wordlessly, still lodged in the half shell. As she took it and his fingers touched hers, she had the strongest temptation just to hold on to his beautiful hand. What had he done to her? It was as if that one glimpse of his naked body had etched itself on her brain and put her under a spell that had never quite been broken. She wished she knew how he felt about her. She had thought she did, but could not be sure.

'Sad,' he said.

'Pardon? What is sad?'

'*Triste*. The way you looked just now.'

'Oh, it's just that they have entirely forgotten me in France,' she said hastily. 'I have not heard from my mother in months.' She didn't want to sound sorry for herself, so made a joke of it. 'I don't think I shall speak French ever again, by way of protest.'

Alerted by her playful tone, one of the lapdogs appeared at the table and jumped up with her paws against Henrietta's leg, jigging about on her trailing petticoats and skirts as she begged for titbits.

'*Descendez*,' Henrietta instructed. 'She's going to have to learn English too, if I am to speak it all the time. What is the English for *descendez* anyway?'

'Down. But sit would perhaps be more useful. *Assieds-toi!*'

Henrietta held out a finger. 'Sit.'

The little dog continued thumping her tail so enthusiastically that her whole body wagged along with it.

'Hah! She doesn't understand. She's not as good a pupil as Your Majesty.' Harry tapped his thigh until the animal abandoned Henrietta and went over to him. He helped her to jump up into his lap and fed her a chunk of cheese.

'She's not a mouse.'

'She's not much bigger than one.'

'Shush! You'll hurt her feelings.'

'*Pardon*, pet. My most sincere apologies.' He tousled her white topknot. 'You're *très belle*. Very beautiful.'

'Beautiful,' Henrietta tried, not getting it quite right.

Harry turned to look at her and, gazing into her eyes, he repeated softly, 'Beautiful.'

It made her cheeks burn with a fire that ran down through her entire body and made her insides molten.

Without waiting to be dismissed, Harry stood up and set the dog down. 'That's enough for today, I think.'

Like a child, Henrietta's mood could transform itself in an instant from abject misery to heady joy. She had been so unhappy for so long, but now she couldn't stop smiling. The way he had looked at her! She hugged it close to her, and during the rest of the day relived it a hundred times. She began to fear that she might have imagined it. She did have the most vivid imagination after all. She lived in a fantasy world of ballads and ballets and troubadour poetry. But no, it really had happened, she was certain it had. It didn't matter at all to her any longer that Harry was just a courtier with no title. She was sick to death of kings and dukes. After months of having everyone criticise her with only scowls of dislike and disapproval, it was so wonderful to feel special, to feel desired by someone so handsome and amusing. Inclined to giddiness as she had always been told that she was, Henrietta felt more ready to skip and dance than she had done since she'd arrived in this God-forsaken, heathen country. At the same time she couldn't wait to go to bed, just so that she might lie in the darkness and think about him, about how he had gazed at her and said the word beautiful, so very beautifully.

She was wandering around the palace in a daydream and wasn't entirely sure how she came to be in the gallery or what had brought her there, why she was standing now before the king's impressive collection of Titian paintings. She stared in fascination at the image of a woman wearing a luxuriant fur wrap that daringly exposed one of her breasts. The painted stare was provocative, inviting, and the gleaming gold and pearly luminescence of her jewels was exotic against the pale, naked flesh and the softness of the fur. Beside it hung a painting of the goddess Diana bathing naked, beside Venus, Mars and Cupid. On the opposite wall was yet another mythological and sexually explicit image of gods transformed into satyrs, exposing their nakedness.

Henrietta had passed through this gallery dozens of times, had often paused to admire the pictures as she had been taught to do, for their composition, colour and form. But it was as if she had looked at them before but never really seen them, or had seen them with her eyes and her head, not her heart or her sex. They appeared entirely different now, arresting, disturbing even. She was looking at them in a new light, the light of her own desire, and she saw in them a beauty and eroticism that she'd never noticed before. Naked breasts and erect phalluses and ravishment. The images assailed her, fed the fantasies in her head, merged with her memory of Harry's naked body, of how it had felt to kiss him.

She became so aroused that she all but fled from the gallery.

She hardly slept, though she tried hard to and wished she could, because that would make the hours pass faster. She was so sure that the next time they met something wonderful was going to happen. When morning came at last Henrietta was ready for her English lesson long before it was due to begin.

Supposedly reading in her privy chamber after mass, she had watched the hour hand on the gilded mechanical spring-clock on the cabinet move from one quarter to another. Watched clocks always moved so much slower but that never stopped her from watching them. All time-keepers were unreliable, though, needed constant winding and resetting, so the chances were that the one Harry was consulting would be minutes ahead or behind hers. There was no telling when he would arrive.

But then there he was, well before the appointed hour by Henrietta's reckoning, as if he were as keen to see her as she was him. He had such presence that the whole atmosphere of the room seemed to alter when he entered it. The furniture and the paintings and the drapery all blurred around him, so that he was all she saw.

He bowed and wished her good day as usual, just like any other attendant, and she felt crushed as well as annoyed. In her mind everything had changed between them. She had wanted him to act differently towards her. She had fully expected a continuation of the thrilling conversation of yesterday. Better still that he would walk in and take her in his arms.

'So what are we going to talk about today?' he asked.

'We could talk about art,' she suggested on an impulse. 'The paintings in the gallery.'

'Since the purpose of this exercise is to enable you to converse with the king your husband, and since those paintings are his, that seems like a good idea.'

Henrietta immediately regretted suggesting it. She didn't want to talk about art any more. She certainly didn't want to talk about talking to the king! Damn it! All she wanted . . . and she wanted it so badly she felt as if she might cry or scream or explode if it did not happen . . . was for him to look at her as he had done the day before and say something lovely to her again. Well, she'd make him!

Instead of nuts, it was a bowl of fruit which sat waiting on the small table. Overcome with a mischievous impulse, she plucked a dark cherry from the bowl, her fingers hovering over the little pile as she paused for a second to select one with a long stem. She made certain that it had a knobble at the end. Some stalks did and some did not and a knobble was crucial. Holding Harry's eyes with the playful light in hers, she popped the cherry into her mouth, twirling the stalk lightly between her fingers as she ate.

The Duchesse de Chevreuse knew how to bewitch men, how to drive them half crazy with love and lust. And she had passed on a few of her tricks.

When Henrietta removed the stone and put the stalk itself into her mouth she wanted to laugh out loud at the look of consternation on Harry's face, but she managed to keep her gaze straight, playful, seductive. She swished and rolled the stalk around inside her mouth in order to moisten it and make it as flexible as possible. Then keeping her lips closed throughout, she positioned it so that it lay along the length of her tongue, bent it in half about a third of the way up the stem. Taking the folded stem, she used her tongue and teeth to cross the two ends over to form a loop. It required subtle contortions of her jaw muscles to achieve this and Harry watched her with fascination.

Flipping the loop in her mouth so the ends were pointing towards her throat, with the tip of her tongue she then pushed the loop upwards, and drove the bump on the longer end through into a knot. The Duchesse de Chevreuse had taught the trick to her and Mamie one rainy afternoon. Said that all men adored to see it done, or rather to see evidence of a girl with an agile tongue.

With a slow smile, Henrietta took the knotted stalk from between her lips and dropped it on the table before him. 'There's a real tongue-twister for you, sir,' she said.

He looked at the stalk in amazement, then at her. 'How the devil . . . ?'

'I have a strong tongue.'

She saw with delight that the blue light of his eyes grew more intense, somehow darker and also brighter. Her own eyes went to his mouth, to the lips she had once brushed with her own. Just to look at them caused her heart to pound and again came that strange leaping heat low down in her belly, between her legs, like a flame when sprinkled with wine. 'What is the English for *un bisou?*' she asked a little breathlessly.

He didn't reply immediately, as if she had asked the most difficult question and he had to think how to answer. 'A kiss,' he told her very gently.

She raised her eyes to his. 'Do you remember when I . . . ?'

'Christ, of course I do.'

The way he looked at her now made Henrietta feel fainter and more light-headed than she had ever done through lack of food. She stepped closer to him, so close she could see each individual golden whisker in his neat little beard. How she wanted to touch it, to stroke it as he did when he was thinking about something.

'Your Majesty, we must not . . .'

'Don't call me Your Majesty now.'

'Ma'am . . .'

'Not that either.'

What then?'

She didn't know. Henrietta? No, that wouldn't do. Why did he have to call her anything . . . say anything? Talking was not what she wanted him to do at all. 'You don't want to kiss me?'

His eyes searched her face. She did not so much hold her breath as stop breathing, because she could not breathe. He looked down into her eyes as if he were contemplating diving from a high bridge into a deep flowing river. It was not as if there were any real decision to be made now, it was more like being suspended, pausing before the inevitable. Like teetering on the brink, but having already leaned too far forward not to fall the whole way.

'I do want to,' he said softly. 'Very much.'

He took Henrietta's face between his hands and turned it up to his. His skin was warm and soft and dry. He bent his head and kissed her, lightly, softly. It made her legs go so weak that she fell against him. He pressed himself to her. He was trembling but somewhere at the back of her consciousness she was aware of the strength of him, an animal yet tender strength that excited her. She put her hands on his hips and gripped him, drew him closer. His mouth opened slightly. His tongue licked inquiringly against her lips. She sensed what he was inviting her to do and she opened them, letting him lead her, just as he did in the English lessons. The tips of their tongues touched. It was the most extraordinary sensation, the taste and the texture. He pushed deeper inside her mouth. Again she copied, did the same to him. He cupped the back of her head in his hand and she moved her own hand up around his neck, entwined her fingers in his hair. His tongue went around hers, around and around.

He took her hand and led her to a chair. She sat in his lap and they kissed and caressed with languorous kisses that grew simultaneously more passionate. Impatiently, she swept her skirts out of the way, reached down and cupped the place where his own hands had once been so tantalisingly cupped. She felt the bulge in his breeches, the long hardness of him pushing into her palm. He made a little moan and moved her hand away. She moved it back. He moved it again. So did she, pressed a bit harder.

'What is this part of you called?' she asked softly, pretending that her English lessons were continuing still.

He seemed to struggle even to find his voice. 'There are lots of different words. Some more polite than others.'

'Teach them to me. The polite ones and the not so polite.' She turned her face into his neck, nibbled his ear and whispered into it. 'Tell, Monsieur Germain. A girl needs to know these things.'

'The correct term is penis but the most well-used term is cock.'

She giggled. 'Like . . . cockpit?'

'Like that. A cock is also a male chicken, you understand?'

English can be a very nonsensical language, I think.'

'Can't it just?'

'What else, besides cock?'

'There's prick. Yard. And rod.'

She repeated the words slowly, softly, rolling them on her tongue.

'Your accent makes them sound so beautiful.'

'Tell me some more.'

'Member.'

'Like Member of Parliament?'

'Yes.'

'I want to see you,' she whispered. 'Can I?'

She went on caressing him for a moment, with her palm and then her fingers, and all at once he unfastened himself, guided her hand inside. She took the shaft of him in her hand. He was larger than the king, as much as her hand could grasp. She drew him gently out through his breeches, the most beautiful and magnificent part of him.

There was a fold of skin towards the tip of him which uncovered a head like a huge red cherry. She ran her finger over it. It was soft as silk, as pleasant to the touch as anything could be. She dipped the tip of her finger in the little hole and as he flexed in her hand he gave a moan as if she had hurt him, but she knew she had not.

He took hold of her hand again. 'Here, lower.'

'What are these called?' she asked as she cupped them.

'Stones.'

'That's a good word. Like diamonds and rubies.'

'They are precious stones.'

'So are these, I think'

She went on stroking him, his stones and his cock, up and down and around, changing the pressure from light to hard. She watched his face as she did it and it seemed as if he must die with joy at each caress. She felt such a sweet and overwhelming pressure between her own legs that she feared she might die too if she did not have him, and she understood then why that part of a man is considered the object of all female desire as well as the means of satisfying that desire.

But he showed her that there are other means. Other places and other ways he could be inside her. The next time he came to her rooms he did what she had wanted him to do before. He took in his arms, lifted her and carried her to the bed. From then on, in the quiet of the afternoon, in her bolted chamber, it was a different kind of lesson he taught her, an altogether different language, sensual and, though not always silent, wordless.

What she did with him was different in every way from trying to make an heir with the king. They never saw each other in just their smocks. Since their time together was snatched, they never dared take off all their clothes, just unfastened them, or hitched them up, or down, as need be, and in the disarray, imagination provided what their eyes could not.

He seemed to know just where she'd like to be touched, and how, and he taught her how and where to touch him and hold him. He taught her to make a ring with her thumb and forefinger and slide it up and down his erection, caressing his stones with her other hand. How to slide her fingers beneath them and rub. How to drum her fingers lightly down the shaft of him as if he were a flute. How to put him in her mouth as if he were a flute too. She learned how to do all these things and bring him almost to the crest of pleasure and then stop tugging or stroking or sucking. Wait. And do it again. She delighted in teasing him and tormenting him, until he was practically begging for her to give him release. He brought her to her own pleasure by rubbing the little peak just above her opening, sometimes with slow circular movements and sometimes more vigorously. Sometimes with his fingers and sometimes his cock. He put his fingers in her. Not like the king had done on their wedding night, but softly and thrillingly, reaching parts she had not known even existed, taking her to a place she had never before been.

He never put his cock inside her, though. She knew that he desperately wanted to and she wanted it just as desperately, but it was the one way they could make what they were doing seem less wrong, less dangerous. This way, he could not get a baby on her. In any case, he taught her that she did not need his seed in her in order to know the ecstasy she had despaired of ever experiencing. The first time he brought her to her own climax it was so strong and wonderful it made her cry. She could not believe it could happen once, let alone over and over.

One day, he turned on to his side and said, 'Shall I teach you something else? Do you want me to?'

'Yes.'

He inserted his finger between her legs but held it very still. 'There's a muscle here, inside you,' he said. 'Squeeze me with it.'

At first she could do it only weakly. The stillness of his finger was tormenting. She wanted to pull it deeper. She tried to tighten her womb and then she felt herself opening and closing around him, as if she were sucking him with her privates as she did with her mouth. And when later she took him in her mouth, she thought how the physicians and writers of conduct books were entirely in error about bodies and about love. What was written about penetration and the moment of release being the only way to achieve exquisite pleasure was entirely mistaken. It was very true what the Duke of Buckingham said about her, though, that she was French through and through. But if it was French tricks she learned and perfected, it was an Englishman who had taught them to her, albeit one who had lived in France and spoke the language like a Frenchman, and by his own admission loved all things about her country.

'The English may have some strange names for a man's privates,' he whispered, slipping his hand over her belly and between her legs. 'But they have a lovely name for a lady's.' He stroked her there. 'They call it a garden.'

The king's and queen's households both moved to Hampton Court, and on the first day of the new month Henrietta insisted her entire train of lords and ladies squeeze into a hundred and fifty coaches to go on a maying procession through the woods and fields around the palace. It was a perfect spring morning of pale gold sunshine, enamel blue skies and fluffy white clouds. There were new lambs in the fields, the birds were singing, the leaves were bright and fresh on the trees, the grass lush and green. In this instance nobody seemed to mind taking part in what was a Catholic custom.

Henrietta was the first to spy a beautiful thorny may tree laden with its enchanting white blossom. She knocked on the roof of the carriage to halt it then sprang out without waiting to be handed down, calling everyone to follow her. She ran across the long sunlit grass to break off a stem of blossom. She bent it into a circle, twisting the ends to make a may crown, reached up both arms and placed it on her own head, securing it amidst the mass of glossy black ringlets. Soon all the ladies were running around doing the same, holding up their skirts, laughing and picking flowers, wearing flowers in their hair, tucked behind their ears and in the tight bodices of their bright silken gowns. Some of the gentlemen sported a sprig along with the feathers in their hats. Henrietta looked for Harry. He was leaning against the carriage, one foot hitched up on a spoke of the wheel, not joining in.

She plucked another sprig of the blossom and ran over to him with it. He was not looking at her, but over her head, his eyes scanning the meadow almost as if he expected an ambush. She reached up and tucked the flowers behind his blue feather. 'There. For you.' He smiled at her, but only faintly. 'What's the matter?' she asked. 'Why so gloomy?'

He pushed away from the carriage and stood straight. 'No reason, ma'am.'

She glanced around to make sure nobody was near and whispered, 'Are you missing me? Do you want me?'

'Yes, I want you. I always do and I always will.'

'Later then. I will say I need to rest.'

'Maybe.'

'Maybe! Please don't feel obliged if you have something better to do?'

'I do not.'

Everyone was very talkative and merry as they travelled back. Henrietta led the way into the palace, her ladies still chattering almost as light-heartedly as her French companions had once done. But as she entered the door all behind her went suddenly quiet.

She turned round and saw that Lucy and Eleanor were staring at her in horror, staring not at her face but at the crown of white flowers on her head, as if it had suddenly turned into a crown of thorns or a writhing serpent. Eleanor and Lucy were no longer wearing their own crowns, Henrietta noted. None of the women were. The gentlemen, including Harry, had removed the sprigs from their hats.

Nobody spoke or moved until Harry stepped forward. He reached out and gently removed the blossom from Henrietta's head. 'In England it is considered unlucky to bring may blossom indoors, ma'am,' he quietly explained.

'The smell,' Lucy added.

There was a faint but distinct odour coming from the flowers.

'Rotting flesh,' Eleanor said, pulling a face to show her revulsion. 'May blossom smells like the plague. It is the smell of death, an omen of death.'

Harry walked with the circlet of blossom to the door and discreetly deposited it outside on the upper step, but even with the flowers gone Henrietta could still smell the noxious scent. She was dismayed by what she had done. Omens and portents had loomed large in her life. Her father had long resisted crowning her mother because soothsayers had warned him that if he did, he would surely die. He was assassinated the day after the coronation. And now Henrietta had brought a crown of death into the English court.

That disturbing thought stayed with her while her ladies dressed her for dinner.

'So what new words has our Mr Jermyn been teaching you lately, ma'am?' Eleanor asked as Henrietta stood still while Lucy hooked the tabs of her bodice to her skirts.

Henrietta wondered what would have been the response if she'd told her: cock, prick, yard, member. It was tempting. 'Oh, about Parliament,' she said, hiding her pink cheeks in a wine cup.

Lucy looked up from her needlework. 'If the king has his way that word will be obsolete before too long.'

'I don't know what obsolete means.'

'Even so, perhaps your English lessons should cease,' Eleanor said with unprecedented malice. 'Do you know what scandalmonger means yet, I wonder?'

Henrietta shook her head, alert to the girl's belligerent tone.

'How about gossip then?' Eleanor inquired.

'Yes.' Harry had taught her that word.

'Well, Your Majesty should know that this court is full of scandalmongers and gossips, and they are saying that lately our little Queen Mary is looking with too gentle an eye on the handsome Mr Jermyn. I am not saying that I believe them,' Eleanor slipped in quickly. 'Only that you should be careful. A queen's adultery is treason. Two of Henry VIII's wives lost their heads for their loose morals.'

She sounded more like her uncle than ever so that Henrietta knew these were his words his niece had spoken, not her own. Which made them even more chilling.

It should have come as no surprise to hear that such gossip was circulating. Nothing was ever missed at court. Every word, every glance and action, was scrutinised, picked over for its potential for scandal. Foolish to think that her closeness to Harry had gone unnoticed. It was not enough just to lie with him and love him in secret. She wanted to be with him all the time, could not stay away from him. Talking with him, walking with him, riding with him, brightened her day. The joy she felt in his company must be reflected in her face for all to see. And to speculate upon. They had been careless, reckless. Touching and laughing together, snatching quick cuddles and kisses when they found themselves alone for a moment. What Eleanor said was true. She did look with gentle eyes upon Harry and he upon her. Gentle and passionate. In France, under the guise of courtly love, that would be entirely acceptable, a source of titillation, no more. To be encouraged even. But this was not France. The king himself had said that his family must set the highest moral example. Henrietta had chosen to forget that, or to ignore it. Perhaps to her peril.

At dinner the long table was laden with the usual plentiful spread but for once Henrietta was not at all hungry. The smell of the may blossom, of decomposing meat, seemed to overpower the aromas of the fresh, roasted dishes like the whiff of doom and scandal, and made her feel so sick that she excused herself just as soon as the main courses were finished.

'You have another of your headaches?' the king asked, with more derision than concern.

Her head did hurt, as if the may crown had leached poison into it, or else Eleanor's finely veiled threats had battered and bruised it. 'I just need to lie down for a while and close my eyes.'

She refused Lucy's offer to help her undress but retired alone to rest on her bed fully clothed. Not ten minutes after she had curled up on top of the blankets there was a light double tap on the chamber door. She knew who it was, knew that distinctive knock. The only person who cared enough to notice her distress and would trouble to come to see if she was all right. She almost sent him away. But it was beyond her.

'Come in,' she called softly.

She sat up as Harry came to sit on the bed. He took her hands in his. 'You could not have known about the blossom,' he said. 'There are so many customs peculiar to this country. I am cross with myself for not alerting you.'

She shook her head. 'It's not your fault.'

'It will soon be forgotten.'

'I'll not soon forget. I have brought bad luck into this court.' She glanced down at their linked hands, rubbed her thumb over the back of his hand. 'I don't want to bring bad luck to you too.'

'How can you ever think that you would?'

'There are rumours about us.'

'I know there are.'

Her eyes met his. 'You know?' So that was why he had looked worried earlier.

'The Earl of Newport claims to have stumbled upon us embracing and walked out again without either of us having noticed his presence.'

She knew the Earl of Newport only by sight and reputation. Mountjoy Blount. A rear admiral. Part of the Earl of Carlisle's entourage. He had straight black hair with a ragged fringe, fleshy cheeks and flared nostrils like a horse. Some women found him devastatingly attractive but Henrietta thought him rapacious and treacherous, did not trust him. 'It is possible he saw us.'

If that was what they were all saying, she might just as well kiss Harry now. How she wanted to! What more harm could it do? She could see he was thinking exactly the same thing, but when he glanced towards the unlocked door she couldn't tell if he was contemplating locking it or leaving, and instinctively she held on more tightly to his hands as a sudden dreadful fear struck her like a blow to the heart. 'They will not send you away, will they? Like they sent my other friends away? I could not bear to lose you.'

'Though rumours never die entirely, they do die down,' he said calmly. 'So long as they have nothing to keep them alive.'

'We must be more careful.' It did not enter her head to suggest that they should stop.

But already it was too late. Following a self-important rap on it the door flew open and in walked young Tom Killigrew, whose job it now was to light the king's way to Henrietta's chamber.

He stopped short like a horse balking at an over-high fence when he saw Harry sitting on the queen's bed, holding her hands. But Tom was Harry's nephew and the boy he had taught to play cards. Now he came willingly and enterprisingly to their aid. He created an instant diversion by dropping the taper he carried and setting fire to the rush matting which took light with a bright leaping flame.

'Stay back, sire!' he shouted to the king.

Harry made for the casement window while Henrietta frantically patted at the bedclothes where he had been sitting.

There was a great commotion as Tom yelped and leaped about like a jester or a boy with ants in his breeches. Henrietta could not help but laugh to see him. Allowing Harry more time to climb out of the window, he snatched a blanket off the coffer and beat at the matting, stamping out the flames with his boots while shouting frantically for the king to stay in the corridor, where it was safe. For good measure, he grabbed the ewer from the washstand and poured water on the smoking rushes.

By the time the flames were out and the king had entered, Henrietta had composed herself and Harry had made a hasty escape.

Bassompierre's negotiations had neatly sidestepped the rumours of infidelity in the absence of conclusive evidence, mostly because, had he given them any credence at all, his own position as agent of reconciliation would have been completely untenable. His final address before the king lasted a full hour and when he came out his voice was croaky as a frog's on account of having swallowed so much London coal smoke, he said. But he'd not lost his ability to speak before a resolution had been reached.

It was agreed that a Catholic chapel was to be built as swiftly as possible, equipped with twelve priests and a grand almoner. Bassompierre had also organised for Henrietta to have at least some French servants, including a seamstress and laundress, a squire and ten French musicians.

Bassompierre brought the king and queen together in the presence chamber and, like a parent mediating between two fractious children who'd squabbled over a toy, made them apologise to each other in front of him, as if that would be all that was necessary to wipe away the events of the past months, all the cruel words and misunderstandings, and make them the best of friends.

Charles embraced Henrietta stiffly. 'I am sorry for any distress I have caused you.'

She bobbed a little curtsey. 'And I you, Your Majesty.'

The situation felt laughably fake and forced. It felt far too late to be sorry.

# 1627

The rumours about Harry and Henrietta proved harder to stamp out than the flames that Tom Killigrew had so considerately ignited. At New Year, Charles formally presented his queen with the gift of Somerset House. A noble Renaissance-style building that stood on the Strand, fronting on to the river, it had high-ceilinged rooms full of beautiful objects and paintings, and had always been one of her favourite palaces. 'It was my mother's London residence,' he said as he rode with her into the wide courtyard. 'It is only right that you have it now.'

'Thank you.'

Henrietta knew he was trying to be generous, to be kinder, but his former unkindnesses to her had worn her down and closed her heart to him. She wanted only Harry. But even in her own house they were not safe from spies. In an attempt to aid the king in catching his wife in a compromising situation and win himself favour as a result, Mountjoy Blount led Charles and the Duke of Buckingham to the queen's rooms at a time when Harry was known to be there with her. But the three men found the door to her privy chamber unbolted and Henrietta and Harry merely talking, standing by the window looking out at the garden and deciding how best to improve it. Henrietta turned to the men with such a blameless and indignant expression that it was Charles who felt caught out for having even doubted her virtue.

'I am a good actress,' she smiled when they'd gone.

'I've never asked you,' Harry said. 'Does His Majesty appreciate your efforts to learn his language?'

'I wouldn't know. I barely speak to him at all now. In any case, I don't think you've taught me the words I most want to say to him.'

'What words would they be?'

'Leave me alone,' she said in French.

Harry looked unhappy, guilty.

'What would you have me say to him?'

He looked into her eyes which were flashing blackly. '*Je t'aime,*' he said. 'I love you.'

She didn't know if he was answering her question or speaking from his own heart, but never had those three little words sounded so ambiguous, or so beautiful.

It was not that Henrietta did not feel any guilt. If Father de Berulle were there, she would have confessed everything to him. It would have been a relief to confess and be absolved. But she could not bring herself to tell Father Philip. She did not know him well enough, and besides, he came from Scotland, where Charles had spent his childhood. She did not know quite where the priest's allegiances lay. She felt guilty but not sufficiently guilty to stop. She had grown up surrounded by adulterers and adulteresses. Her own father, most notably. Marie de Rohan, Duchesse de Chevreuse, who had had a series of affairs. Queen Anne, who'd become the Duke of Buckingham's lover when he came to France. The strange thing was, she felt unfaithful to Harry when she was with Charles, rather than the other way around. And when she knelt alone before the private altar in her closet and looked up at candles and the statue of Mary, she could not put aside the idea that he had been sent to her, given to her. She to him too maybe. The way he had come into her life just when she had been about to embark on what she had thought would be the great adventure of it, only to find herself isolated and lonely and unloved. He had been there all along. Like a very tall and strong and amusing guardian angel.

Then Charles betrayed her, in a very different but no less significant way. England went to war with France. Henrietta was not surprised to learn that, once again, it was largely the fault of the Duke of Buckingham.

'Villiers loaned eight warships to your country,' Harry explained as they walked in the garden with the dogs. He seemed keen for her to understand what was happening so she was listening carefully. 'Our ships were appropriated by the French naval fleet sent to suppress the Huguenots of La Rochelle, which your brother King Louis and Cardinal Richelieu have made their first priority. But given that the Huguenots are French Protestants, the Puritans here were not best pleased with that. They wanted their ships back. Villiers is now sending a whole fleet in support of the Huguenots in the hope it will weaken France and at the same time win him the position of Protestant hero, gain the affection of those same English Protestants and Puritans he has hitherto managed to alienate with his extravagances.'

It seemed to Henrietta symbolic, the greatest disloyalty, one she would find it impossible ever to forgive. Her husband had always put the duke before her. But now he had let his favourite lead him into war against her own country, her own brother. She had no choice but to watch as the land of her birth and her adopted nation prepared to annihilate each other. She was forced to participate even, in her own small way, by attending a dinner given aboard the warship *Neptune*, anchored at Blackwall. They travelled there by water and it made her shudder to see *Neptune*'s mighty guns and cannon that were soon to be deployed against her own countrymen. The Duke of Buckingham joined them in the low, cramped but plushly appointed cabin. He was proudly sporting a military costume with an immense collar and an ostentatious plume of red and blue feathers in his hat. He was not only her enemy now, but the enemy of her family, of all her brother's people.

When he sailed with a fleet of a hundred ships carrying a six-thousand-strong army bound for the Bay of Biscay and La Rochelle, Henrietta had to endure the torture of dining with courtiers who were drinking uproari-ously and unrestrainedly to the defeat of her brother, with toasts and cheers and anti-French jokes that grew coarser and more caustic as the evening progressed. The usual practice of crushing and smashing the leftover desserts, sweetmeats and sugar confections even took on a combative air, with cakes being thrown as missiles in mock battles.

Then a letter arrived from Henrietta's mother with the terrible news that Louis had been dangerously ill with a fever and Gaston's young wife had died four days after giving birth to a daughter, Anne Marie. Ignoring her household's complaints about mourning a princess against whose country England was now at war, Henrietta instructed Harry to arrange for black gowns to be made for all her court and ordered three months of full mourning.

The first day Henrietta dressed in her mourning gown, Lucy disappeared to her own chamber to fetch something and came back armed with a pot of rouge. 'Black may suit the handsome Mr Jermyn but it makes Your Majesty look very pale. Very French and elegant that is true, but pale. If you don't mind me saying!'

Henrietta was finding recently that it was impossible to mind much that Lucy said. She reminded her of the Duchesse de Chevreuse with her brittle beauty, acerbic wit, her supreme confidence and frequent romantic dalliances.

Were it not for the war being waged against her homeland, Henrietta might almost have been happy. She lived at Somerset House according to her own wishes. She had Harry and her French musicians. Not only was she growing increasingly fond of Lucy, but also of the duke's mother and his wife, Kate, who both accompanied her to mass each morning. Lady Mary Villiers was a passionate Catholic and Kate Villiers had admitted that she only practised Anglicanism to support her husband's position. Kate always spoke of the duke with such love and devotion in her voice, her hand resting protectively on his unborn child in her womb, that Henrietta wondered how she even bore the sight of Lucy. She could not help but know that Lucy was her own husband's lover. Everyone knew. But though the two women were not friends, they were not unfriendly towards each other. Once again Henrietta thought how there was one rule for the duke and another for everyone else. He could openly take a mistress, despite the king's strict moral code, and everyone accepted it. Even his wife.

Now Lucy waved the little pot of pink powder under Henrietta's nose. 'This is what you need. I wear it all the time.'

'What is it?'

'Made from cochineal.'

Henrietta was in a quandary. Lucy always looked so glamorous and vivacious. It would be nice to look even a little more like her. But it was extraordinarily vain to be so concerned with your appearance as to make your cheeks falsely pink. What should she do? Vanity quickly won out. 'I'll try it,' she said.

She let Lucy sit her down and show her how to apply the rouge, sparingly, under her cheekbones, with brushes and tissues.

Lucy leaned back, brush in hand, to study her work like an artist before a canvas, studying a portrait in the process of being painted. 'His Majesty is going to have to keep Your Majesty locked up in a tower, for chastity's sake,' she said. 'See.' She showed Henrietta her image in the looking glass.

Rosy-cheeked and red-lipped, she looked instantly older, more sophisticated, more like a woman than a girl, as if she had at last been transformed from a little princess into a queen.

'Just you wait until the king sees you,' Lucy said. Then, with a sideways flick of her almond eyes, 'Not to mention Harry Jermyn.'

Henrietta ignored that. But the truth was that she couldn't wait to see the look on Harry's face when he saw the effect of the pretty paint on hers. She was so unable to wait that she went to find him. He was talking to one of the king's laundresses, a strikingly tall girl with flame red hair, green eyes and a Scottish accent. Henrietta felt a twist of jealousy.

'May I speak with you, sir?' she said curtly.

The girl bobbed a curtsey and left.

'Is everything all right, ma'am?'

'Yes.'

'You look to be glowing,' he said softly. Henrietta was ridiculously glad that he had noticed. Only he did not sound as if he liked it at all. 'People will start saying it is pregnancy that has put such roses in your cheeks.'

She shook her head, dipped her eyes. He was jealous too, she knew he was. She had no choice but to allow Charles into her bed and to go on visiting his. She had told Harry once that she did not enjoy it, hoping that would make it easier for him. That she felt she was being unfaithful by lying with Charles rather than the other way round. But by Harry's silence she had known that he would rather they never mention it. The troubadours had written about how romantic love could not exist without jealousy.

'I am not pregnant,' she said. 'It is just Lucy's rouge.'

Henrietta wished that she were pregnant. It was her prime duty to produce an heir, and once she had one growing in her belly she felt sure the king would leave her alone, for a while at least. When Charles touched her now, everything shrivelled inside her. She hated the feel of his mouth when he tried to kiss her. The urge to push him away was far greater than on their wedding night. It was impossible, she had decided, to know that a man did not love you and then let him make love to you. Harder still to make love to one man while loving another.

The queen's inability to conceive was becoming a topic of public debate and was such a serious concern that Theodore Mayerne was summoned. The renowned French physician had attended Charles since he was a sickly child, and also his father King James before him. Mayerne was a rotund old man of five and fifty with benevolent blue eyes sparkling beneath white bushy brows and a domed forehead topped by thinning silvery hair. Henrietta liked him instantly and not just because he was French. The best advice he could give her, it seemed, was to recommend a visit to the waters at Wellingborough.

But he could not say if it would work or not, when or if she would ever fall pregnant, and Henrietta needed more certainty than that. Someone who could see into the future. So on All Saints Day she summoned the famous prophetess, Lady Eleanor Davies. The widow of an eminent lawyer, Lady Eleanor claimed to be in communication with the spirit world, claimed also that she was the reincarnation of a biblical character, he of the Lion's Den, as proven by the fact that an anagram of her name was Reveal O' Daniel.

'Give or take a few letters!' Harry joked.

Henrietta spelled out the words in her head. 'Oh, no! It doesn't quite work, does it?'

'Neither does Never So Mad a Lady,' Harry returned instantly. 'But it's a damn' sight closer to the truth.'

Henrietta let out a ripple of laugher. She knew he was not mocking but trying to lighten her mood. For that she was grateful to him. To her mind, practically nothing in life was too serious to laugh at. She did take the soothsayer's visit very seriously, though. She set so much store by prophecy that it was with apprehension she led a group of curious courtiers to the chamber where Lady Eleanor was preparing for her audience.

The prophetess had curly grey hair and a severe, fiercely intelligent face. She had not removed her dark cloak and in the darkened room, in which the shutters had been closed and only a few candles shimmered, appeared much like an apparition herself. She began the séance by closing her eyes and calling to the spirits to speak directly to her, her arms held rigidly down by her sides, palms facing forward, fingers slightly splayed. Her hands and eyelids fluttered a little but apart from that she was oddly still, as was her spellbound audience. All except for Henrietta, who saw no use in prevaricating. 'When will I be with child?' she asked forthrightly.

'Soon,' came the reply in dazed Latin.

Henrietta felt obliged to inquire after the duke's success in the current war.

Again Lady Eleanor spoke slowly, her voice sounding different from the way it had done before she'd entered the trance – deeper, more ponderous. 'His person will return in safety and no little speed, but as for his honour, he will not bring home much.'

Henrietta didn't think he'd had any honour before, but that matter duly dealt with, she returned to the original and most pressing topic. 'Will I have a son or a daughter?'

'Your firstborn will be a son and for a time you will be happy.'

'Only for a time? How long?'

'Sixteen years.'

At that moment the king burst through the door into the stillness of the room making everyone jump out of their skins, as if it was a spirit itself that had broken in upon them. 'How now, my lady?' he said, addressing the prophetess icily as her eyes snapped open. 'Are you not the person who foretold her own husband's death? It would break a man's heart to hear that from his wife, so it is small wonder your prophecy came true.' He took Henrietta firmly by the arm. 'Enough of this nonesense.'

'But Lady Eleanor has not finished!' she protested.

'That is as may be, but you are finished with her.'

Henrietta's ladies remained behind, and when Lucy and the others came to prepare her for bed she asked if the soothsayer had made any more predictions after she had gone. Lucy's fingers paused for a second on the laces of Henrietta's corset, then started working again more vigorously than before.

Henrietta turned, making Lucy stop what she was doing. 'She did say something, didn't she?'

Lucy's hands fell to her sides. 'She foretold that Your Majesty's firstborn son would be birthed, christened and buried within a day,' Lucy reported quietly.

Lady Eleanor's prediction about the duke at least proved uncannily accurate. Shortly after Kate Villiers gave birth to a son, the duke landed safely at Portsmouth, but his mission had been a total failure. The siege of the fort on the Île de Ré off La Rochelle had ended with the death of two thousand Englishmen. Those who were not already wounded or starving, sick with dysentery or the bloody flux, had been drowned or hacked to pieces on the causeway across the salt marshes down which they had been forced to retreat. The blame for this fiasco was laid firmly on the duke's delay in calling for assistance. But while the country at large cursed him, the king paid tribute to him for his courage and all the court was called to attend the glittering christening of his infant son, the king clad in a long soldier's coat covered all over with fine gold lace.

He and the duke were both hell-bent on continuing the war, which was all they discussed during the lavish christening supper.

'The French have no wish for peace,' Charles said, showing neither tact nor concern for Henrietta, who was seated beside him.

'It leaves us but one course of action,' replied the duke. 'They have vowed to destroy La Rochelle and we to save it. At any cost.'

# 1628

The king needed to summon Parliament in order to dispatch the second expedition to La Rochelle, and by the time it met in March Harry had won the seat for Liverpool. He returned from Westminster with the report that a lawyer in the House of Commons had stood up and shouted out that the Duke of Buckingham was the cause of all the country's miseries. It was a sentiment that seemed to be echoed across the whole land.

Monsieur Gouttier, a famous French performer and one of Henrietta's new musicians, was teaching her to play the lute, a skill which she had never properly taken the time to master. As with many things in life, she had lacked the patience to practise and persevere. She had wanted to be able to pick up the instrument and play a perfect melody immediately, and when she couldn't had been frustrated and rapidly lost interest and motivation. But she was determined to try again, and harder this time.

Gouttier was sitting beside her on a stool in her withdrawing room at Somerset House, showing her where to place her fingers to play a French country song. It was awkward and the strings made the soft pads of her fingertips sore. She did not enjoy her music lessons quite so much as she'd enjoyed learning English, but she was delighted to find she could pluck a few tuneful and recognisable chords. She also found a rebellious pleasure in playing a French song in a land at war with her country.

Harry was over at the far side of the room, dicing with his old friend the Earl of Holland and a young poet named William Davenant, who had very eloquent eyes and the strangest ruined nose, so eroded by the pox it resembled a spaniel's snout. He and Harry seemed to have struck up a close friendship. But Harry broke off from concentrating on their game and turned to watch Henrietta, to listen to her play. She felt his eyes on her, burning her skin, but it made her try especially hard to get the notes right.

'That's very pretty, ma'am,' he complimented her.

'I am glad you like it, sir.'

She was playing the tune through yet again when Lucy walked into the room. Despite her painted face, Lucy was horribly pale and walked as if in a daze, like someone wandering in their sleep. She all but collapsed into the nearest chair, not even bothering to arrange her skirts. She held a piece of printed paper in her hand. Not a letter but some kind of pamphlet or poster.

Henrietta stopped playing, set aside her lute. 'Lucy, what's wrong?'

The room had fallen entirely silent. Everyone stopped what they were doing, sewing, gaming, reading, gossiping, wondering the same thing.

Lucy turned her head slowly at the sound of Henrietta's voice, her eyes glazed. It was as if she could barely hear. 'The scaffold on Tower Hill has been burned down by a gang of ruffians,' she said dully. 'They say that a new one is to be built for my lord the Duke of Buckingham. The city has turned against him and all associated with him.' Her ringed fingers tightened on the piece of paper which Henrietta saw now was a billposter and she spoke in a rush of sudden emotion. 'John Lamb has been most brutally murdered.'

'Who is John Lamb?' Henrietta had never even heard of him.

'The duke's astrologer,' Harry supplied. And then more gently, 'How was he murdered, Lucy?'

'He was set upon and hacked to death by a London mob. They beat his head on the cobbles and kicked out one of his eyes.' Lucy crushed the billposter in her hand. 'It is too awful. They say that had my lord the duke been there himself, they would have minced and mangled his flesh.'

'My uncle had a nosebleed,' Eleanor put in, as if that affliction were also a matter of life or death. 'His father's spirit has been seen walking three times, telling him that he has but a short time left upon this earth if he does not mend his ways.'

'Come now, Eleanor, that's just superstitious nonsense,' Harry soothed.

'This isn't.' Lucy thrust the crumpled handbill at Henrietta. 'It was pushed through the window of my husband's carriage earlier today. They are being posted all over London.'

At any other time Henrietta would have been glad of the chance to demonstrate her new command of English in front of her former tutor.

But as she smoothed out the paper she shuddered at the words she now understood perfectly and must read aloud: 'Who rules the kingdom? The king. Who rules the king? The duke. Who rules the duke? The devil.'

The duke refused to take the threats to his life seriously, or to take any extra precautions to ensure his safety. He left for Portsmouth to inspect the warships preparing to depart again for La Rochelle. His wife and mother went with him and Charles later rode to the coast to join them. Following Theodore Mayerne's instructions, Henrietta departed with her entire household for Wellingborough, the waters of which were supposed to be so beneficial for ladies hoping to fall pregnant.

Wellingborough was an ancient market town, peaceful and pleasant, situated amid rolling meadows and pastures on the bank of the River Nene. Tents were pitched so that everyone could camp in the fields around the Red Well. Lucy poured Henrietta cup after cup of the waters, which being so iron-rich were tinged red and tasted like blood. But Henrietta drank diligently, three measures, at morning, noon and night. She considered it a small price to pay for being given the chance to enjoy the delights of camping, something she'd never experienced before.

Her four-poster bed was erected in the largest, grandest silk tent, and it was very homely and snug with tapestries swagging the walls to insulate them and thick carpets laid over the grass. But even with so many comforts it felt very different from being in a proper room in a proper building. It was a novelty for her to live so relatively simply, to be so at one with nature. The horses were tethered and put to graze nearby, with pens for the chickens and pigs and other livestock, and in the morning Henrietta awoke to the crowing of the cockerel. In the palaces she had to walk down what felt like miles of corridors and passageways to be outdoors, but here it was just a few short paces to the entrance of her tent, and sometimes she went out gloriously barefoot in the morning and felt the dewy grass between her toes.

Pages and gentlemen and ladies alike sat about on chopped logs and used the sawn-off tree trunks for makeshift tables for gaming or resting their mugs of ale upon. Meals were cooked outside over great open fires; hogs were roasted on spits, not in kitchens but right under their very noses. Mass was conducted beneath the natural arc of heaven. Since the evenings were so balmy, everyone ate supper on rustic trestle tables with only the sky and densely leafed trees for a canopy. As they watched the sun set, they were serenaded by the court musicians on their oboes and lutes. Alternatively, the village peasants entertained them with country songs and dances. Accompanied by tabors, tambourines and pipes, the spectacle was remarkably tuneful. The countrymen and women had a real ear for music, a great talent and lightness of touch. The songs had quaint titles, some of which Henrietta needed Harry to translate. There was 'The Shaking of the Sheets', which was delightfully bawdy, and the 'Cushion Dance.' 'Tom Tyler' was another favourite, and one entitled 'Put on Your Smock a' Monday.'

The fast pace of the music, fancy footwork, raised hands and snapping fingers, made it impossible for Henrietta to stay in her chair. She stood up and pulled Lucy out of hers too, glancing invitingly at Harry. 'Let's join in.'

Soon the entire court was on its feet, villagers and courtiers mixing freely, couples dancing on the grass in groups, the very opposite of mannered court dancing. Wine and cider and ale flowed freely. As the evening wore on people became more and more merry and rowdy. Cheeks were flushed, corsets and waistcoats and doublets were loosened, and the girls kicked off their slippers and danced about barefoot. There was so much amorous giggling and lusty jigging about that nobody appeared even to notice that the queen had been dancing solely with Harry Jermyn. Henrietta noticed only the intoxicating scent of woodsmoke and sunshine which clung to his skin and clothes, along with sweat, and horses, fresh air and grass. She breathed deeply, as if to draw it down into her own body.

Then the music changed and the dancers stopped. Henrietta looked round. 'Why is everyone kissing?'

'This song is called "John, Come Kiss Me Now" Your Majesty,' Harry said gently. 'It has kissing choreographed into it, as do many English country dances. That's why we are known by some in France as the Kissing English.'

He bent his head and lightly kissed her lips. It was the sweetest and tenderest kiss, and as arousing as having his tongue in her mouth, his teeth grazing against hers. Sad too. For it proved that, for her, any sense of freedom and simplicity was just an illusion. He could not take her as other men took their women. They must always stop at cuddling and fondling and mutual pleasuring with their hands, and even that only in secret, when there was no risk of being found.

What she wanted most then, and she wanted it with all her heart and her body, was the freedom and simplicity of lying naked with him, feeling his skin against hers, seeing him as she had only once before, but this time being able to touch him and know that, just for a while at least, he was hers.

The kissing that was going on all around lasted for exactly four bars of music. But it would resume later. This night would be no different from the nights before. As the light dimmed and a net of stars was flung across the black sky, couples would sneak off into tents or the trees or hollows in the ground to continue their kissing and caressing in private, and soft giggles and muffled sighs and moans would be heard all around the camp. Listening to those sounds, lying alone in her bed, thinking of Harry alone in his, Henrietta felt that she might go mad with longing and frustration. It seemed too great a risk to have him come to her tent, a room with no doors or locks and the flimsiest of walls.

The music and dancing lost its charm and she did not want to be there. 'Walk with me,' she said.

'Where to?'

'Does it matter?' She tucked her arm determinedly under his and they slipped away to the edge of the meadow, away from the camp. A gate led on to a field where the haymakers had been hard at work with their forks, gathering the grass into conical haycocks. It gave off a lovely summery scent in the still evening air and the stubble that lay over the fields glowed a gentle rich gold. Shadows were lengthening and deepening and there was an air of tranquillity, of time having slowed. They were out of sight, entirely alone, and Henrietta leaned on the gate as she had seen the farmer's daughters do. Harry leaned on it too and the silence between them was as charged as the air before a storm.

'When I was growing up I always considered myself very fortunate to have been born a princess,' she said. 'While we travelled about Paris in our royal carriage I felt sorry for people who had to live in a house, not a palace or château. It was my sole ambition in life to marry a prince and be a queen one day.' She turned her head and pushed her curls out of the way, looking intently into his blue eyes. 'Now I am wishing that just for one day, one night, I could live as other people live. I wish I could forget all about my royal blood, forget that I am a queen.' There was a moment's silence. 'Don't you wish you could forget that too?'

'I know that I never can.' Her hand was resting on the gate and he moved his close to it, slipped one finger up her sleeve and beneath the lace, stroked the underside of her wrist.

Suddenly she did not care about the risk. 'You could help me to forget. We could help each other.'

She knew he must come to her, but at the same time she knew nothing and doubted everything. She waited, and waited and when she felt she could wait not one second longer a shadow loomed on the wall of the tent close to the opening. He pushed aside the silk flap and ducked inside.

She stood before him in her nightshift, in the soft blend of golden candlelight and silver moonlight, her black curls tumbled loose. He was barefoot and had removed his doublet, was wearing only black breeches and a frilled white shirt, undone at the neck, revealing tantalising curls of chest hair.

She let her shift slip off her shoulders to the floor. She was naked beneath it. His eyes travelled the length of her body and she shivered as if they had been his fingers.

He lifted his arms and she dragged his shirt off over his head. He stepped out of his boots, undid his breeches and took them down. This time, he did not cover himself. She saw him, naked and erect. As she laid her palms flat against his chest and kissed him softly there, the hairs brushed her lips and her cheeks, and the hard heat of him pressed into her belly as she breathed in again the scent of his skin.

He lifted her as he had before and carried her to the bed, with no urgency this time but as if they had all the time in the world. They lay on their sides, facing each other. She trailed her fingers up the insides of his thighs while he ran his gently over her buttocks, her back, stroked the soft springy hair between her legs. She let her fingers wander across his hard belly and felt his muscles quiver at her touch. He turned on to his back and she straddled him, holding his arms above his head as she ran her fingers up the insides of them, then her tongue, her hair brushing his skin.

He sucked her fingers, her breasts, made of them a valley and pushed himself inside it. He rubbed his cock between her thighs and against that little mound in her groin, back and forth, until the pleasure grew so intense that he put his hand over her mouth to stop her moans and spent with a spurt of warmth and wetness across her belly.

She went to sleep snuggled into his side, her head on his chest, their legs entwined, and they woke in the morning when the sunlight burning through the silk filled the tent with its glowing golden warmth. He had turned half on his side, half on his stomach, one leg crooked, and she admired the strong lines of his thighs and buttocks and back. She thought about tracing them with her finger but she wanted to touch his penis again. When she did, lightly with her finger, it stirred and sprang up hard once more as he woke and took her in his arms.

A messenger arrived with a letter addressed to the queen.

It was from Dudley, Lord Carleton, one of the king's councillors.

*I am to trouble Your Majesty with the most lamentable news. This day betwixt nine and ten in the morning the Duke of Buckingham, coming out of his parlour into the hall to go to his coach to see the king who was staying on the edge of town, was by one John Felton, a former lieutenant in his army, slain at one blow with a knife through his heart.*

*The duke tore out the weapon and made an effort to draw his sword but after staggering a few steps cried out, 'Traitor, thou has killed me.' Thus we have lost the greatest man, the most remarkable favourite, the world has seen for many a century.*

*Madam, you may easily guess what outcries were then made when we saw him thus dead in a moment and slain by an, as yet, unknown hand.*

*Hearing the disturbance the duke's wife rushed out on to the gallery over-looking the hall in her nightgown, in time to see the blood of her dearest lord gushing from him. She let forth such a scream that it brought Lady Mary Villiers running. Never in my life before have I heard such screeching and tears, and I hope never to hear the like again.*

The letter was dated Saturday, 23 August. Four days past.

'Poor Kate!' Henrietta cried. 'His poor mother.'

'What is it?' Lucy asked anxiously. 'What has happened?'

Henrietta looked down at the letter, then reluctantly held it out to the other woman. 'Lucy, I am so sorry.'

For a moment Lucy did not take it, as though she knew already what it contained and wanted for a few seconds longer to hold on to hope. Then she reached for it, read it, crushed it in her hand. 'I cannot believe it,' she whispered. 'I cannot believe it. It cannot be true. It cannot.'

Henrietta went to her friend and put an arm around her shuddering shoulders.

She could scarce take it in herself. The great duke slain, in the manner that her own father had been slain. Much as she had loathed George Villiers it was impossible to imagine the court without him, still less the king. 'How is His Majesty?' she asked the messenger. 'How has he taken this news?'

'He is most profoundly distressed but is doing all he can to behave in a manner both manly and princely, ma'am. He was at morning prayers with his household when word was brought to him. The chaplain paused the service and the message was whispered into his ear and spread amongst the congregation. His Majesty ordered the service to finish as normal. Not until it was done did he retire to his chamber, where it is my understanding that he flung himself upon his bed, turned his face to the wall and wept. Since then he has not emerged or touched a morsel of food.'

'I must go to him.' She relaxed her hold on Lucy. 'Immediately.'

She looked for Harry but he was one step ahead, had anticipated what needed to be done and set about doing it. He was already overseeing the dismantling of her tent.

Henrietta hurried south, riding on horseback for speed, and was surprised as well as confused to learn that at the very same time Charles was hurrying north, in order that they might meet somewhere in the middle so that he could be with her sooner.

Henrietta's journey took her via Northampton towards the steep chalk escarpments of the Chiltern Hills before they reached Dunstable where they rested for the night in the old priory. They travelled on in the morning to Buckinghamshire and Slough, which was busy with stagecoaches travelling on the Great West Road to Bristol. Towards evening they came to the small town of Farnham in Surrey. Charles was waiting there in a noble's mansion that stood in the shadow of the castle.

The dimly lit withdrawing room was so hushed that it felt almost insensitive to burst in with her attendants in tow as well as the usual boisterous menagerie of lapdogs and monkeys.

The king was dressed in a long black mourning cloak that reached to his ankles, and all his courtiers were similarly attired in sombre black and were very subdued. They resembled a court of shades, which served further to heighten the absence of the luxuriously dressed, indisputably beautiful and exuberant duke who was once always to be found at its centre, by the king's side.

When the queen entered the courtiers discreetly filed out, leaving Henrietta alone with her husband. Even were he not dressed in black, he would have resembled a shadow. He looked wan, utterly lost and woebegone, and despite his previous unkindnesses to her, Henrietta's heart went out to him. With his slightly protuberant and doleful brown eyes he reminded her strongly of Mitte at her most forlorn, when she'd had her tail trodden on or had been scolded. At such times Henrietta felt so sorry for her that she immediately had to pick her up and kiss and cuddle her, no matter what she'd done wrong. Charles stirred in her that same sense of pity and she instinctively wanted to console him in much the same fashion, to take him in her arms. But given all that had passed between them, she did not know if that would be welcome, until he came to her and embraced her, as if it were the most natural thing in the world, something they did every day. For a moment she did not quite know what to do and stood with her arms by her sides while he held on to her. When eventually she took him to her, she tried hard not to do it in the sudden, quick, lively way she had of doing everything, which she was aware could make her seem impatient. As indeed she generally was.

Perhaps it was partly because she had grown used to being with Harry who was of such a different build, but Charles felt thinner and smaller and weaker than ever, crushed and diminished by sorrow. As he tucked his head in beside hers and she gave in to the inclination to stroke his back, his narrow shoulders heaved and he made a spluttering sound. He was weeping unashamedly and Henrietta was moved by the rawness of his grief and touched that he would not try to conceal it from her.

'It was a tenpenny knife that villain Felton used to run him through,' Charles sobbed despairingly, wiping his eyes with the heel of his hand as he moved away a little in order to talk. 'That's all it was. Not a sword or dagger, just a mean knife. All for some petty grievance about being passed over for promotion.'

'He has been caught?'

'He didn't even try to run, just came forward and announced it proudly. "I am the man. I am he." Felton will be executed, but that won't . . .' His voice cracked and he was unable to continue.

Henrietta completed the sentence for him. 'That won't bring the duke back. I know.'

For two weeks the Duke of Buckingham's embalmed body lay in state at Wallingford House, in a black-draped, candlelit room, before he was taken to Westminster Abbey for burial.

The king and queen were not present at the funeral, which despite Charles's wishes was not at all grand. It was conducted by torchlight at dead of night, with no more than a hundred mourners. A fake funeral, with a coffin full of rocks. The duke's body was not in the coffin led by the beadles and carried by half a dozen pallbearers, because it was feared his remains would be recovered and mutilated by an angry mob. Since his death, people had been lighting bonfires in the streets and rejoicing. Ferlton was hailed as a David who had slain Goliath and rid them all of a monster. So Buckingham was buried early and furtively, in the morning. But in the dignity of King Henry's chapel.

'He is the first commoner to be granted such a privilege,' Charles said to Henrietta after the sham funeral was done.

He was standing barefoot in his smock, before a full-length, life-sized portrait of the duke. In its ornately gilded frame, it had once hung in the Whitehall withdrawing room but now Charles had had it moved to a wall in his own chamber, right beside his bed, where it was the first sight to greet him when the curtains were opened in the morning, and the last thing he saw before the candles were put out and the curtains drawn at night.

The first thing Henrietta saw, too, when she lay with him in his bed.

In the painting Buckingham was dressed in white silk thigh-high stockings which emphasised his extraordinarily long and slender dancer's legs. He stood with one hand resting provocatively on his hip and that supercilious look in his jet black eyes that Henrietta knew so well and which still made her feel nervous and defensive. No matter where she stood, those eyes seemed to follow her, always to be watching. Try as she might to convince herself that he was gone from her life, she still could not quite believe it to be true. Would Charles ever love her as much as he had loved Buckingham?

Her husband seemed so completely changed as to be a different person entirely. It was as if a part of him had literally been removed. As if he had been posessed by Buckingham's vital, malign spirit which had now deserted him, revealing the real man. But without Buckingham's energy and confidence and swagger to bolster him and shore him up, Charles had been left empty, weakened and vulnerable. Henrietta joined him in the coach to travel back from Farnham to London and had watched tears slide down his hollow cheeks into his beard throughout the journey.

She was still wary of intruding upon his grief but trusted now to her strongest instincts, which were always to offer kindness and comfort wherever and whenever they were needed. She took his hand and he immediately tightened his fingers around hers as if he needed something or someone to hold on to; as if grappling for an anchor to replace the one that had been taken away and protect him from the storm of emotions that his loss had stirred. She noted that his hand wasn't much larger than hers, a delicate, almost feminine hand, the fingers thin, skin soft and pale.

She did not want to hear Charles mourning Buckingham. It hurt her to hear, in his voice and in his every word, just how much he loved him and missed him. But she sensed that he needed to talk and talk about his lost friend, and knew that she must let him do that. Must listen to him for as long as necessary.

'The world was much mistaken in its opinion of him,' Charles said. 'He was the most faithful and obedient servant. A great man.'

'Then where could be a more fitting place for him to be laid to rest?' Henrietta looked up at the likeness of the person who had made her life such a misery and did her best to be charitable. 'He will spend eternity as he most liked to live, in the company of monarchs and princes.'

Charles turned away from the portrait to face Henrietta. 'You are very gracious to speak of him so well.'

'You mean, considering he called me a foolish girl and all my companions confounded French freebooters?'

Charles gazed again at the towering portrait. Henrietta had said it kindly and had been jesting, but he did not even smile. In the past weeks she had grown used to being with a man who smiled and laughed readily, at everything. She had to remind herself that her husband was the opposite of Harry in every way. He rarely laughed, even at the best of times. No wonder he had found her frivolous. He probably always would. He had been cruel to her in the past, scathing even. She suddenly doubted and mistrusted his newfound love for her. How long would it last? Only until he had done with the worst of his grieving and had less need of her comfort? Until he found himself a new favourite? She wanted to forgive him and start anew, but could she?

He turned to her and kissed her and she closed her eyes, tried not to feel the duke's eyes watching her, scorning her, threatening her as they always had. When Charles led her to the bed and she climbed in beside him, she felt those black insolent eyes fixed on them both. She leaned over Charles and gave the curtains a firm tug, dragging them tight shut. That was better!

Her husband moved closer to her, nestled against her. He reminded her so strongly of Mitte again, needing the nearness and warmth of another living being in order to sleep, that Henrietta felt compelled to put her arm around him and hold him. Since the duke's death there had been no perfunctory coupling, no performing of their joint duty to produce for England an heir. That need had been set aside for now, replaced by a greater and more immediate one. Charles seemed content just to lie in her embrace and, after all they had been through, she found a surprising peace and contentment in having him do so.

'Try to sleep,' she told him now.

'I want to,' he said, his voice muffled against her breast. 'I want to forget, for just a few hours. It is a s-strange thing. For life to be so unbearable that the only w-way to escape nightmares is in the oblivion of sleep. Though there is no true escape even then. I have a picture in my head and it will not go away. The knife plunged into his heart . . . his b-body covered in blood . . . So much blood. It fills my dreams. And then, when I wake up, I remember he is gone, gone f-forever . . .' He broke off and started crying softly. 'Each time it hits me as hard as the very first time I heard.'

Henrietta felt his tears, hot and wet, though the linen of her nightshift and she thought for a moment then of Harry, of how she had wept on his chest because Charles had been so cruel to her and made her so very unhappy, by banishing her friends. It was all so confusing. She had hardly seen him since Wellingborough. She had been busy and preoccupied by the king's need of her. So much had changed with Buckingham's death, her whole life and world. Harry's had changed too, emptied where hers had filled, she realised. Or maybe not. Maybe she had been flattering herself. Maybe she had meant nothing to him. She had expected him to be downcast on seeing her again, jealous, angry even, like any rejected or deserted lover. Forlorn at least, like a childhood playmate left behind when a friend grows up and moves on to other pursuits, other friends. But he did not seem to be any of those things. He greeted her with his perfect courtier's smile, warm and dignified. Seemed entirely accepting of the situation. Maybe it was just that he understood where her responsibilities must lie. She felt hurt, though. Even if he did understand, she wanted him to miss her. To want her still. To find her new closeness to the king difficult, painful. It was not that she wanted him to be jealous and unhappy. Well, actually, she did! A little.

As soon as she had arrived back in London from Wellingborough she had visited Kate Villiers. To lose her husband in such a violent manner, while she was carrying their third child . . . Henrietta could not imagine what she must be suffering.

Harry had commended her for it. 'You have no reason to mourn this man, ma'am,' he had said, when he accompanied her to Wallingford House. 'Yet your first concerns are for those who do. His Majesty and now Buckingham's widow. To seek to comfort those most in need, irrespective of your own feelings, must surely be the mark of a great queen, such as I always knew you would be.'

There had been no bitterness in his voice, only admiration. She should have been glad of it. She tried to be. A great queen was what she had always most wanted to be. Her sole purpose in life. And the only way for her to fulfil that purpose was to be a good wife to the king, something that she had also once dreamed of being but had so far been unable to accomplish. That now looked set to change, and with that change must inevitably come many others. The trouble was, she still wanted Harry. But she wanted to be here with Charles too. She needed to realign her head and her heart somehow. It was Charles she must think of now. Charles who needed her. Her place was with him.

He was still crying.

'Hush,' she whispered, and stroked his back in a way she intended to be comforting. But it aroused him, or something did. She felt him grow hard against her leg. When he penetrated her, rocking silently and slowly back and forth inside her, it was almost as if he were seeking consolation through that act too, needed that physical contact and release. Or just to remind himself that he was still alive. There was something infinitely right about it. She found it consoling too. It was as if she were a little ship that had been blown off course, or had been battling against a headwind, and now all was smooth sailing again. She had the winds with her rather than against her. She was heading for the right destination, the right destiny. She was with the man she was supposed to be with, was exactly where she was supposed to be. With the husband who had been chosen for her to love. She was a queen and she was with her king.

All was as it should be. Just so long as she kept the bed curtains closed against that overbearing portrait!

News reached court that the Huguenots at La Rochelle had surrendered in the same week that Charles took on the guardianship of the duke's young son and heir, the next George Villiers. It was what both he and the late duke had wanted and planned, in the event of the duke's death, for little George and the baby yet to be born to Kate Villiers, should it be a boy, to be raised in the royal nursery. Henrietta was only sorry that Mall would not be coming to Whitehall too, but was to live instead at Wilton House, near Salisbury, the family seat of the Herbert family into which she was to marry.

'George Villiers and his brother, if it is a boy that Kate is carrying, are to be raised as brothers to whatever princes and princesses it pleases the Good Lord to grant us,' Charles said to Henrietta.

From the way he looked at her when he said that, she wondered if he guessed what she had not yet dared to tell him, or even to hope. Perhaps one of her ladies, though sworn to secrecy, had whispered something about her courses being a few days late. Everyone was waiting so eagerly for it to happen that there was no way it would stay a secret for long.

When Henrietta had not bled for six weeks Theodore Mayerne questioned her, examined her and confirmed that she was with child. 'Wellingborough worked its magic then,' he concluded, sounding pleased.

She had such a vivid and sudden picture in her head then. The tent, the scent of hay and woodsmoke and sun-warmed skin. 'I suppose it must have done.' She wondered for a panicked moment if the peasant girls were right in their belief that it was possible to fall pregnant just from kissing and touching. It seemed almost miraculous that she was with child now, after three barren years of marriage. Then she remembered the tender way Charles had loved her after the duke's murder. That must be when the child had been conceived. It would be fitting. Life after death.

Etiquette dictated that royal children had their very own residence and St James's had been designated for this purpose, with Buckingham's son soon to move in. The Palace of Richmond was to serve as the children's summer retreat. Given her interests, Henrietta was curious to know more of the history and construction of the palaces in which her children would grow up.

St James's was a red-brick hunting lodge a short and pleasant stroll from Whitehall across the park. Yet another Tudor building, it had flat lead roofs edged with ornamental battlements. It was dominated by the crenellated towers of the gatehouse with its four octagonal towers, that guarded the approach up Pall Mall. The chambers were hung with bright tapestries from the factory at Mortlake, depicting Venus and Mars.

Richmond Palace was far grander. It had been built by Henry VII, and until Henry VIII had acquired Hampton Court after the downfall of Cardinal Wolsey, had been the great show palace of England. It was a moated gothic castle of white stone, with octagonal and round towers capped with pepper-pot domes with delicate strapwork and decorative weather vanes. The privy lodgings faced the river, with a bridge over the moat linking them to a central courtyard with a fountain at its centre.

Henrietta took to wandering round its beautiful rooms, imagining the happy family life she had longed for. These empty rooms, filled with children's voices and laughter. And servants. One day Charles came to Richmond with her and they walked in the park there, discussing the appointment of the Countess of Roxburghe as lady governess to the little prince or princess. She would head up a household of thirty rockers, nurses, wetnurses, physicians and apothecaries.

The countess was devoutly Catholic and Henrietta wondered if Charles's willingness to allow her to raise his son or daughter might signal a new leniency towards all people of her faith. Henrietta hardly dared hope that it might be so. Her mother had never let her forget, reminding her in every letter she sent, that God Himself had sent her to England as queen in order to do His work. Her estrangement from the king had made it impossible for her to achieve anything at all. But now? She bit her lip, deciding how best to broach the subject.

'So you don't think Catholicism so wicked after all?' she asked, her tone light, underlying the serious intent behind her question.

'It is not nearly so wicked as Calvinism and Presbyterianism.'

Henrietta was not sure what Calvinists and Presbyterians believed, but knew they were definitely more Protestant than Catholic. 'Really?'

'I have great respect for your Pope Urban,' Charles said. 'And for the thousand years of Roman Catholic doctrine which went astray only ninety years ago at the Council of Trent.'

'In that case, you could put it right. You could change the laws,' she suggested boldly. 'Your Majesty could suspend the penal laws and stop this country persecuting people of my faith.'

'For you, dear heart, I could certainly give it some serious thought.'

She wanted to ask him to repeat what he had just said. He had never called her 'dear heart' before, or used any term of endearment. She was sure she would never tire of hearing it. But at the same time she could hardly believe her ears. That he had called her that in the same breath as offering to consider leniency towards Catholics, for her sake! She was astonished afresh by his changed attitude towards her. But she made the most of it. 'And might Your Majesty also allow the Pope to send an envoy to England?' It was something else her mother had long been pushing for.

'I might allow that,' he said cautiously.

Charles kept finding every excuse to touch Henrietta's belly, even though it was still entirely flat.

He had the perfect opportunity to do so while teaching her a very curious sport called golf. It was much played in Scotland apparently, and Charles, who had spent his early years in Scotland and had a fondness for all things Scottish, had a passion for it. He wanted to share that passion with his wife, just as he now wanted to include her in everything he did. They were at Hampton Court and, the morning being warm and bright and still, he had asked Henrietta to come to the golf lawn with him. He was showing her how to wield and swipe the crooked club with its curved end of horn and lead, to drive a little leather ball into certain holes made in the ground. In order best to demonstrate how this was achieved, he was standing close behind her, his arms around her and his hands covering hers.

It seemed to require a good deal of skill to hit the ball high and far and straight enough and Charles had evidently spent many hours practising, since he required only a few strokes to get it very close to one of the holes. Henrietta, on the other hand, was not doing nearly so well, could not get a ball within yards of any hole, let alone the right one!

'Oh, I give up,' she protested. In truth it seemed a silly and pointless sort of game and she far preferred to go off and chatter with her ladies as usual. Before she left Charles to continue without her he insisted on kissing her again, even though she wasn't really going anywhere since her ladies had all come to watch the game and were standing not two feet away at the edge of the lawn.

It really was extraordinary, the way her husband behaved towards her now. The love he had showered upon her after the duke's death had blossomed with the news that she was carrying a baby. Where once they were hardly ever even in the same room as each other, now they were scarcely apart for five minutes. Where once they had exchanged only harsh words, if any words at all, now he was always talking and whispering with her, sharing with her the smallest details of his day. He talked about what he had seen when he was hunting and riding, what he had read, the paintings and artworks he was intending to purchase, what his councillors had said to him, his worries and concerns. Formal and stiff as he could still sometimes be, he was forever giving her little presents and kissing her in public.

'His Majesty kisses you at least a hundred times an hour,' Lucy said. 'He has fallen utterly in love with you, I think.'

Henrietta watched Charles take aim, swing his club. 'Do you honestly think he's in love with me now?' She hardly dared to believe it.

'Oh, it has become the greatest romance,' Lucy gushed. 'Everyone says so. There is such a degree of kindness between you, the whole court cannot stop talking about it. It is such a tender affection the king has for you now. Isn't that so, Harry?'

Harry had been heading towards the golfers. With a glance towards them, he halted as if unsure whether to continue on his way or change direction and come over to Henrietta and her friends. He did the latter, turned and strode across. He had a golf club slung over his shoulder and one of the small hard leather balls in his hand, but he was without his ready smile. 'Isn't what so, Lucy?'

'That our dear king and queen are deeply in love? It is to be the model for every court in Europe. Theirs is the greatest royal love story that ever there has been.'

Lucy was known for her cutting repartee and barbed quips. It was one of the things Henrietta had grown to love about her. But she would not have believed her friend had the capacity for such unkindness. She wanted to slap her. No wonder she and Buckingham had got along so well together. They were startlingly similar. Henrietta didn't know what to do, what to say. It was all so utterly bewildering still. Charles's kisses did not make her heart thump, did not cause that liquefying sensation in her insides that Harry's did. Harry didn't even need to kiss her, to touch her even, his voice and his presence, the mere sight of him, had been enough to make her melt. Love was not like a candle that could be snuffed out in an instant. It could not be relit with a tiny spark. Nor switched at will from one person to another overnight. And yet, for all that, she returned Charles's kisses with eagerness. It was apparent even to her that he had become dependent on her in a way he had previously depended on the duke, and though Henrietta was wary of such a sudden about turn, unnerved by it and mistrustful of its longevity, it was extremely flattering, headily so. She could not forgive him, just like that, for the great unkindness he had shown her in the past, but she was more than willing to try. She had half forgiven him already. Was half in love with him already. It was so lovely to feel appreciated by her husband at last. She had always dreamed of being happily married, and now, when she had all but given up hope, it seemed a real possibility.

Harry was contemplating the ball in his hand, easing one of the feathers, with which it was stuffed, out through the stitches with his smooth, oval thumbnail. Henrietta found herself staring at his familiar long fingers, remembering what he had done with them, where he had put them when they were alone, the feel of them on her skin. How she had loved sitting in his lap. Perching on Charles's stiff, bony knees was never going to compare, she feared, no matter how much she grew to love him. Charles could never lift her in his arms and carry her with such effortless grace.

Harry seemed unhappy, tense. Henrietta could not help but feel a momentary gladness, sure that she must be the cause. And then she felt horribly guilty for it. She did not really want him to be miserable. As if to prove he was not, that in fact he did not care one jot what Lucy had said, or that Henrietta was loved by the King of England now and was carrying his child, he gave the ball a lazy toss in the air and caught it.

When he spoke he looked directly at Henrietta, not Lucy. 'The evidence would suggest that His Majesty has now so wholly made over his affections to Your Majesty that we are out of danger from any other favourites. For which court and country are eminently grateful.'

His tone was casual, conversational. There was no irony in it, no sarcasm. No bitterness. But the words did not quite match the tone. They stung. Sarcastic, bitter words, even if his voice did not reflect that. She wanted to tell him to stop.

'Were Your Majesty not so very young,' he said, 'I dare say it would be an easy matter for you to make the king do whatsoever you pleased, so much has he become attached to you. I hear he hurries to your side as soon as he returns from hunting and can scarce bear to be parted from you for a moment. The councillors are all complaining they never get a chance to speak to him alone.'

'Are they?' Henrietta had changed her mind. She didn't want him to be jealous and bitter at all. She couldn't bear it. Nor for him to feel that she had rejected him, or had treated him in any way unfairly. It made her angry too, though. What choice did she have? What was she supposed to do? Could he not see this was how it had to be now? Yet when she had thought he understood, that had irked her too. Oh, it was an impossible situation.

'I hear that His Majesty has vowed to grow more gallant every day,' said Harry. 'Which is why, I expect, we are to be treated to a tournament to celebrate Your Majesty's birthday in November.'

'A tournament?' Eleanor's face lit up. 'I didn't know. I thought Your Majesty preferred masques.' She cursorily flicked her eyes in Henrietta's direction but didn't wait for her to respond. It was Harry Eleanor wanted to talk to and jealousy spiked Henrietta's own heart now. 'I thought that there were to be no more tournaments,' the girl said to him, smiling with her dead uncle's wickedly charming smile.

'Perhaps this will be the last one,' Harry said to her. 'We'd best all be sure to enjoy it.'

'So when is it to be, this tournament?' Eleanor asked.

'Ten days' time.' Harry gave his stick a careless swipe. 'Damn' sight more exciting than golf anyhow.'

The tension Henrietta had sensed in Harry at the golf course erupted a day or so later on the great enclosed tennis court which was another legacy of Henry VIII. Or something erupted. Perhaps it was just his dislike of Mountjoy Blount, the bothersome Earl of Newport.

A good-sized crowd of courtiers had come to sit on tiered benches along the sides of the court to watch the match, with hefty bets being laid as to who would win. First the Earl of Pembroke had worked up a sweat defeating the Earl of Holland. Then the Earl of Arundel, stocky but possessed of great stamina, had ably thrashed George Goring. Now Harry was competing against Blount, with long volleyed shots that sent the ball ricocheting off the high roof and smashing down on to the opposite side of the net which divided the court in half.

Henrietta could not take her eyes off him. How she loved to watch him. The way he moved. Knowing he was hers no longer, that she could no longer be intimate with him, seemed to make him more alluring and captivating than ever. His long legs and the ground he could cover with them, coupled with the power that came from being such a tall and strongly built man, made him appear unbeatable. That was not the only, or even the chief reason why she had placed considerable bets on Harry to win. She'd have done it out of loyalty to him even if he stood no chance. But it was Blount who looked to stand not a chance right now. Harry was playing with a single-minded and ferocious determination she'd never seen in him before. He had his long red-gold curls tied back to keep them out of the way, his white shirt was open, revealing his strong, smooth neck and tufts of thick curly gold chest hair. His skin was faintly and tantalisingly visible through the fineness of the damp linen and he had to keep raising his arm to wipe the perspiration off his brow with his sleeve.

He was hitting that ball as if he loathed it. Henrietta winced every time, felt each contact like a blow to the heart. She was sure he must be picturing the ball as Charles. Or herself. Taking out all his anger and frustration upon it. She half wanted to leave, almost rose to her feet, but something compelled her to stay and watch him. She had probably got it all wrong anyway, and he simply wanted to trounce the Earl of Newport.

It was Harry who had patiently explained the complicated rules of English tennis to her some while ago. The English lessons seemed to have given him an appetite for teaching her things, imparting his knowledge. But Henrietta still found this game hard to follow. She knew at least that points were scored by hitting the ball through windows situated behind each player. She wasn't sure why it mattered precisely where the ball landed but evidently it did because Harry and Blount started having a row about it, a different sort of volley which was rapidly growing more heated.

'No question, I'm afraid. It hit the side of the net,' Blount stated peremptorily.

'You must be blind, man,' Harry hit back.

'And you, sir, must be a cheat.'

'That, sir, I am not,' Harry returned.

Blount smirked, casually swiped the air with his racquet, rested the edge of it on the ground and leaned on it. 'Why d'you do it? Trying to impress the girls as usual, are you, Jermyn, is that what this is about? Well, no girl likes a cheat, do they?' With that he turned and would have strolled away had Harry not dropped his racquet and grabbed the other man's arm. As Blount was spun forcibly back, a thunderous expression on his face, Harry lashed out, hitting him square on the jaw with his balled fist. Blood trickled from Blount's cut lip and a deathly hush descended over the court. It was broken by George Goring who started jeering. 'Get him back, Blount. Go on! Or is he too big and strong for you?'

As Blount clenched his fist, about to retaliate, Henrietta jumped to her feet, only just resisting the not very regal urge to shout at them both to stop. She wanted to run down on to the court and put a stop to it herself.

Thankfully the Earl of Holland intervened by doing exactly that, placing himself between them with his arms outstretched to either side, one hand against each man's chest, holding them apart.

Blount wiped the blood from his face with a cloth and examined the resultant red stains. 'Just you wait until the king hears about this, Jermyn.'

They didn't have to wait long.

Henrietta had taken to eating a simple supper in her rooms with her ladies and gentlemen and Charles would join them on occasion, which tended to restrain their enjoyment. He did not seem to know how to relax and be merry, and now he was in a particularly sour mood. Harry was noticeably absent.

'I gave your young usher a severe reprimand,' he told Henrietta. 'It is a respectable and moral court I keep here. I'll not stand for brawling. He'll abide by that rule or leave immediately. No matter that he's such a favourite of yours.' The indulgent way he said that made Henrietta realise that Charles was not at all jealous of Harry's relationship with her. He had dismissed or forgotten the rumours about them, or else never paid them much attention in the first place. There was a tiny part of her, an unpleasant vindictive part, that wished he were jealous. It would have served him right. She had a favourite, just as Charles had favoured the Duke of Buckingham. The difference was that she had been unable to do anything to get rid of the duke whereas Charles had the power to remove anyone he did not want at his court. He could send Harry away if he so chose. So it was as well he was no longer suspicious or jealous. She hoped his disapproval would be shortlived, and that Harry would do nothing more to antagonise it.

Charles picked at a chicken bone in his finicky way that, try as she might not to, Henrietta still found a little irritating. She could no more imagine him hitting a man and making his lip bleed than she could imagine . . . well . . . she could imagine most things. But not that. Which was a good thing, obviously. Except that she was French, and did not entirely trust controlled or inhibited behaviour. Charles had wept unashamedly when Buckingham had died but otherwise he kept his feelings on a tight rein. Henrietta naturally preferred people who were prepared to show their emotions, to give vent to them rather than hide them. She liked a man with fire in his belly. How many times had she longed to do what Harry had done? To hit someone! Something! Anything! She'd not really considered Harry as being quick to anger, like herself, but she didn't love him or respect him any the less for his losing his temper today. On the contrary.

Charles changed the subject, talking to her about the negotiations of an agent, Daniel Nys, who had gone to the north Italian lakeside city of Mantua to attempt to obtain the vast art collection of the overthrown

Gonzaga dynasty there. As he spoke of these things, Henrietta saw in his eyes a different kind of passion, a deep longing to possess these great works of art. She should have found that equally attractive, but she didn't. Not quite.

The incident on the tennis court made Henrietta anticipate the planned tournament with dread. At some point during the day Harry would come head to head with Charles, and she was afraid of the consequences should her favourite fight with the same aggression he'd displayed at tennis.

The day of the tournament dawned autumnally warm and bright. Henrietta dressed in a gown of bright marigold satin finished with creamy lace. She wore a string of pearls at her throat and pearl pendant earrings, a golden ribbon in her black hair. There was a great sense of occasion about the day, and it was all to mark her nineteenth birthday. She could hardly believe it.

Her stomach fluttering with anticipation, she went to take the place of honour with her ladies beneath the rich hangings of state in the tiltyard gallery. To one side of the long jousting field, the gallery offered them a clear view of the whole tilting ground, with a balcony looking out over the colourful fringed pavilions that had been erected at either end of the tilts and the tiers of benched scaffold stands behind the palisades, all adorned with arms and badges. The interior of the gallery was no less colourful. The ceiling was painted and gilded, embellished with yet more badges and arms. There were rich-coloured cushions and tapestries draped over the balcony for resting upon. Further tapestry hangings served as walls to divide the long space into different rooms, one for the merchants' wives, one for the mayor and aldermen, another for all the earls and barons.

The trumpeters arrived on the field in their lavishly embroidered coats, and all eyes turned in anticipation towards the turreted Holbein Gate that spanned the entrance to the tilting ground. The names of the knights were announced and the heralds with their fluttering banners led out the challengers, all clad in velvet and brocade, with gleaming embossed armour and dancing plumes on their helmets. They all carried gilded, lavishly painted lances at their sides, held perfectly straight, pointing at the clear blue sky. The horses were similarly gorgeously attired in plumes and fringed silk and wore their own armour of glinting metal to protect their heads.

Charles was mounted on a white mare fifteen hands high and clad in the polished suit of dark armour he had taken to wearing for his portraits. The gold medallion of St George hung from a blue sash across his armour-plated breast. On the reverse was now a miniature portrait of Henrietta in a golden case. He had made her cry when he showed it to her, happy tears for a change.

He carried his helmet casually under one arm. His hair, moustache and beard were as fastidiously groomed as the braided mane of his horse, its bridle adorned with tassels in the Stuart colours of green and gold and white. Usually seen as small and delicate, he looked surprisingly warrior-like now.

Being so tall and powerfully built, his armour and knightly trappings made Harry look extraordinarily imposing. Dangerous even. All the knights had their coats of arms emblazoned on their shields, and Jerymyn's was as simple and elegant as his clothing, a black shield showing a crescent moon between two five-pointed stars. If there were any battle to be fought you'd definitely want him on your side, and would choose to be on his if you had any sense. But in the crisp autumn sunshine and in the midst of such pageantry, surrounded by the gleaming turrets and battlements of Whitehall, there was not a gentleman on the field who did not look heroic as they paraded around, to cheers and shouts of applause.

Henrietta was almost envious. She wished, not for the first time, that she had been born of the opposite sex and could have ridden out heroically into battle.

'His Majesty has such grace and dignity and an excellent sense of theatre,' Lucy observed admiringly, giving voice to Henrietta's own thoughts as Charles approached the gallery.

He brought his grey mare to a halt before the balcony, giving Henrietta a gallant bow from his ornate, high-backed saddle. It was the red velvet one she had ordered to be embroidered for him in gold. He used it all the time now.

'May I beg Your Majesty's ribbon as a favour?' he asked.

'Gladly, sir.' She smiled back at him, reaching up to unwind the golden bow. She leaned over the balcony, her ringlets tumbling loose, and handed it down to him. It fluttered slightly in the breeze as he took it and secured it to his breastplate. 'I hope it brings Your Majesty luck.'

'I am certain that from now on you can only ever bring me victory,' Charles said.

'I do hope so.'

With another bow, he took up the reins and turned his horse in the direction of the pavilions.

Now Harry was nearing the gallery. He too bowed to the queen. Henrietta was sure he did so with a glance at her unadorned hair, minus the ribbon that she had given to her husband. Eleanor saw that too and wasted no time in seizing her opportunity. 'I realise you are Her Majesty's favourite, sir,' she said, her voice sugary sweet. 'But since Her Majesty has given her favour to His Majesty today, perhaps you could look to one of her ladies instead.' In case he had failed to take that unsubtle hint, Eleanor reached up and lightly touched the blue ribbon on her own head.

Harry laughed indulgently at her, cocked a brow. 'Do you happen to have some willing lady in mind, Miss Villiers?'

Eleanor gave a little pout, evidently not able to think of a witty enough reply, or any reply at all.

Harry came to her rescue. 'Miss Villiers, I wonder if I might ask, would you be so gracious as to let me wear your ribbon?'

'Help yourself, sir.' She leaned provocatively over the balcony, offering him a view of her full, creamy breasts as well as her head, so that he might untie the ribbon from her hair for himself.

Jealousy twisted like a serpent in Henrietta's belly, writhing around her heart. She knew she had no right to be jealous, nor any reason. Harry had not asked for Eleanor's ribbon unprompted, was too chivalrous and kind to offend her by ignoring such an open invitation, but Henrietta could not help wondering if a part of him were not also enjoying this chance to pay her back in a way. She wondered if there was already something going on between them, suddenly sure there must be.

Eleanor secured her ribbon around his upper right arm as if staking a claim or attaching a leash, tying it with a double knot as if to make doubly certain it would not come loose.

The first combatants were being announced. Two names were called. George Goring and the Earl of Pembroke.

All Henrietta could think about was Harry and Eleanor. Eleanor and Harry. His mouth on her mouth, his hands on her body, that she had sat in his lap and lain with him in bed, felt his arms around her and the warmth of his naked skin against hers. That he must have said to her all manner of intimate things. That she had held in her hand that part of him which Henrietta had never felt inside her but still considered to be hers alone. She couldn't blame Harry. He was a man. Since he could not have her, she could not blame him if he invited Eleanor to his bed or visited hers.

She glanced at Eleanor's face, comparing herself to the other girl's willowy form. Might Harry find her beautiful? Of course he would. She was. More beautiful though? Might he come to love her more deeply, desire her more ardently? Might he marry her? Never so strongly had Henrietta wished she could just do what a man could do and challenge the girl to a duel. Or whip out a sword and fight her at the lists. Instead she tried to reason with herself, to talk herself into some sense. She was married. She had Charles. She loved him. She did. It shouldn't matter to her whom Harry loved, whom he married. But, oh, it did matter. At that moment it mattered to her more than anything else in the world.

The Earl of Pembroke had won the first round and now faced Harry, who had been casually awaiting his turn, drinking a cup or two of wine with the saddlers and bit-makers and grooms who were milling about near one of the pavilions.

Henrietta's stomach clenched with apprehension as his name was called and he donned his helmet, lowered the visor and took his place at the opposite end of the list to the lord chamberlain. Both men were sitting erect in their decorative high-backed saddles, lances held at an angle in readiness, legs out straight in the stirrups. Swept up as Henrietta was in the thrill and triumph and glory of these mock battles, she felt a shiver of dread. For all its show and the strict rules designed to protect combatants, jousting could be lethal, as her family had discovered to its cost. Her great-grandfather, King Henri II of France, was killed when a lance poked through his visor and went right through his eye and into his brain. If one's love of a person could somehow be measured by the degree of fear felt for their safety, then she must still care for Harry Jermyn very deeply, for the thought of him being wounded, or even suffering the mildest injury, was intolerable to her.

'Let him win,' she whispered under her breath. Then, far more importantly, 'Let him not be hurt.'

There was a roar from the spectators as the opposing chargers thundered towards each other. The knights kept their lances levelled for attack, shields clutched close to their bodies. Hoofs thundered and clods of earth flew. Henrietta's fingers tightened on the balcony and her heart pounded as hard and fast as a galloping destrier. She braced herself for the impact, managing to resist the urge to shut her eyes and clamp her hands over her ears until it was all over.

There came the thud of wooden lances striking metal, the sound of splintering wood, accompanied by much cheering. Harry's lance hit Pembroke's with such force that it snapped with a reverberating crack. Pembroke was thrown backwards in the saddle. He looked for a moment as if he might topple, then righted himself, turned his horse to ride round and prepare for another try. The same thing happened again, and again, until Harry was declared the victor.

'All thanks to you, I'm sure,' Lucy said to Eleanor, cattily.

When Charles rode to the lists in his distinctive dark armour he was greeted with by far the loudest cheer of the day and for that reason Henrietta did not worry for him as she had worried for Harry. The crowd was behind him. And since he was the king, he also fought with God on his side. Perhaps that was why he so effortlessly defeated the Duke of Buckingham's strapping young nephew, Basil Feilding. Or maybe he was right and Henrietta had brought him victory, just as Eleanor had brought victory to Harry.

The jousting went on all afternoon before a group of young boys took turns at tilting at the ring, a loop of wood suspended from a pole, which they had to spear with their lances.

Harry finally met Charles in the tourney, when lances were swapped for blunted swords. The low October sun had started to sink lower still in the sky when announcements were made that the tourney was to be fought just beneath the gallery window, followed by a mock battle at the barrier.

'Since Harry's much the larger of the two men, he's bound to win,' Eleanor predicted.

'If size were all that counted, the king would always lose,' Lucy pointed out. 'Whoever he fought.'

Charles might have been much smaller than Harry, but when the two men rode out to face each other, he was again greeted with by far the loudest cheer.

'He may find it hard to win the people's love, but he does at least command their respect,' Lucy said appreciatively.

He turned to the gallery to acknowledge Henrietta, brought the end of her ribbon to his lips and kissed it with a theatrical flourish that raised yet more applause.

Henrietta could hardly bear to watch. Her heart was in her mouth. She could feel it, pounding in her throat, as if it had travelled up and lodged there. It was agonising, to feel so torn between two men who were fighting each other. She did not know who she wanted to win. Both. Neither. She didn't even know which one of them to watch. No. That wasn't quite true. Her eyes sought Harry entirely of their own accord, but then she could not imagine a girl whose eyes would not seek him, so commanding and handsome did he look.

Charles was holding this tournament in Henrietta's honour. He was wearing her favour. He would desperately want to win, for her sake. She had brothers, had witnessed the fierce competition between them. Being the younger brother of the tall, athletic and golden Prince Henry had made Charles insecure about his own lack of stature and physical strength and prowess. And now he was facing another tall and golden man named Henry with whom he was also in competition, though of a different kind. Even were he not jealous, Charles would not want to be beaten by Harry of all people. The tourney ground, in front of hundreds of spectators, noble and common, was the one place where men needed to prove their worth and ability.

As Harry wielded his sword Charles met it ably, lunge for lunge. Each strike of Charles's weapon on Harry's armour met with an even more enthusiastic cheer, which seemed to be all the encouragement both men needed.

The sparring came so fast that Henrietta could not see how the judges could keep a proper count of strokes and blows. The two horses seemed almost locked together, so that as one stepped agilely forward, the other moved back. As one swung to the side, the other swerved round to follow. For a moment both stood off, snorting, heads tossing while their riders considered the next move. Swords were raised, descended, sliced. For a moment the tip of Harry's sword was pointed directly at Charles's throat and Henrietta had to remind herself that the weapon was blunted and her husband was in no real danger.

Charles drew back on the reins and manoeuvred his horse with dexterity, so that in a matter of moments it was his sword doing the pointing.

The tourney was taking place so close to the gallery that the clatter of sword upon sword and upon armour was deafeningly loud. Charles's sword clashed with Harry's again, the two weapons making the shape of a silver cross between them as each held the other off. It was brute strength that was called for now. There was surely no way that Charles could overpower his opponent. For a moment there was silence and then, with a loud grunt of effort, Charles gave a push and a simultaneous twist of his arm. His sword swung up in an arc, the sun glinting off it so that it was like a fork of lightning as it sent Harry's sword flying from his hand and clattering to the ground.

There was a great cheer. Harry gave a gracious bow to the crowd and earned himself his own display of appreciation, in the true spirit of the occasion.

Only Eleanor did not cheer or applaud but instead gave a petulant sniff. 'He didn't try hard enough,' she complained, pushing back from the balcony, her arms sullenly folded across her chest.

Harry did not spare her a glance. He turned and bowed to Henrietta. As his eyes met hers, he held the gaze. She felt a gentle pressure in her chest like a hand around her heart, softly squeezing it, because she knew then that, despite wearing Eleanor's favour, Harry had not been fighting for that lady, but for her.

For Henrietta's sake, he had let Charles win. He had allowed himself to be defeated by the man who had already defeated him in other ways, had taken her from him. What could be more heroic or noble than that? He had once promised Henrietta that he would do anything for her. If she had ever doubted him before, she must never do so from now on. To do his worst at a tournament, to lose willingly, was as strong a proof of his devotion to her as there could be, wasn't it? She herself must show utter loyalty to the king, put him first from now on, and with his actions today, Harry was telling her, showing her, that where her duty and love and loyalties must lie, his lay too. That no matter what the fight, he would always be on her side, on the side of the king, if that was the side she too was on.

When it came to the final foot fight at the barrier, he was battling shoulder-to-shoulder with Charles. It was almost impossible to keep tally of the scores as men on opposite sides of the waist-high divide made repeated pushes with pike and sword. The king had George Goring and the Earl of Holland with him too, while the Earls of Pembroke and Newport were opposing. By the time the battle was called to a close, the field was a churned mass of broken pikes and swords. The broken weapons were collected up to be counted and the judges eventually declared the king's army triumphant.

'It seems His Majesty was right and Your Majesty can bring him nothing but victory,' Lucy told her, smiling.

# 1629

Parliament was to meet again toward the end of January and since Charles had now taken to sharing everything with his wife, he went to great lengths to explain to her that he feared much trouble over the issue of finances, particularly something he termed customs duties on tonnage and poundage and ship money. It sounded deathly dull, but Henrietta tried to take an interest, to take it seriously. She was often accused of being frivolous and childish and she so wanted to prove everyone wrong about that. She was nineteen now, after all. But if Charles had been hoping she might comment, she found she could not, which made her feel inadequate and insecure. She was sure the Duke of Buckingham would have had plenty to say on the matter, would have freely offered advice for the king to follow. If Charles was looking to her now for the advice and support he'd once depended on from Buckingham, he was going to be badly disappointed. He'd realise soon enough that she was unequal to the task, was no replacement. Then what?

'Every monarch has a God-given right to such duties,' Charles told her on the journey up-river to Westminster. 'But I was only granted it for one year. One year,' he emphasised in pique. 'What was I supposed to do but carry on taking it regardless, since the treasury is empty?'

It was empty largely because of Buckingham's extravagance, as Henrietta understood it. But she didn't see why Charles should sound so timid about demanding what was his to demand. He had every right to exact revenues surely. But she did not feel confident enough to voice her opinions on politics.

She and her ladies watched from a private gallery at the side of the painted chamber. Charles in all his kingly regalia led the state procession. Beneath the colourful ceiling, surrounded by wall paintings illustrating stories from the Old Testament, he ascended his royal throne.

It quickly transpired that the Commons were no more interested in debating customs duties than Henrietta had been. Once again their primary concern was religion, the people's fear that the king would be swayed by his growing love for his Catholic queen to extend greater tolerance towards Papists. Bishop Laud preached the first sermon of the new Parliament but it was followed by strident complaints about Catholic influences upon the church.

'Are we to be flung headlong back into the arms of Rome now?' one of the Members bellowed, with a hostile glance towards Henrietta in the private gallery. 'England is already a nest of Papists.'

Others joined in with more of the same and Charles grew visibly morose and stony-faced. Henrietta bit her lip and clenched her fists so tight her nails dug into her flesh. She itched to remind these rude, ignorant people that their king was God's anointed ruler on earth and must be obeyed. Evidently they had seen fit to forget that inconvenient fact. How dare they insult him so? They deserved to be dragged out by the ears, the lot of them, Lords and Commons. How she wanted to stand up and tell them exactly what she thought of them, to their faces. But she couldn't, of course. She knew that would only make matters worse, far worse. It was her they all hated really, and they were just taking out their frustration on Charles for having married her and brought her to Engalnd.

Her bright dark eyes scanned their faces. It was always an advantage to know your enemy, and these men were hers and Charles's. They looked to fall into two distinct groups: those who dressed as courtiers, in bright satins and velvets, with ruffles and polished knee boots, lace collars and cuffs, and bold ostrich feathers in their hats; and another set who were far more soberly attired, in plain dark suits with starched, square white collars. It was this latter group which was causing all the trouble.

Charles retaliated by ordering the Speaker to announce a five-day adjournment, which made matters worse still. Violent chaos erupted. Several Members of the House leaped off their benches and on to the speaker, to hold him down forcibly. Henrietta sprang to her feet and Harry stood too, as if in readiness to rush to the king's aid, or to hers. It was terrifying, this scene of mob revolt. Charles rose and strode stiffly from the chamber with his sceptre held aloft and his cloak swirling behind him. Henrietta and her ladies hurriedly left the gallery too.

The order of adjournment was ignored. Laud came out to tell Charles that two Members of Parliament had locked the doors to prevent anyone else from departing and a man named Sir John Eliot rose to speak, or to shout, which he had to do in order to make himself heard above the pandemonium. He proposed the introduction of certain resolutions that were met with fierce shouts of approval and had been summarily passed. Anyone attempting to introduce Popery in opposition to the established church was to be condemned as an enemy to king and kingdom. And any merchant found paying tonnage and poundage without an Act of Parliament sanctioning such payments to the king was to be made an enemy of the state, to be punished by death. A Petition of Right would make it illegal for Charles to levy taxes without parliamentary agreement.

'Vipers!' he condemned them.

He donned his full regalia once more and went directly back to Westminster.

Henrietta felt very anxious for him while he was gone, wondering what was happening and fearing for his safety, given the events of earlier in the day. She was anxious for Harry too, still caught up in the affray. But Charles returned remarkably quickly and in a very buoyant mood.

'All is resolved, my lord?' she asked.

'Dissolved.' He gave one of his infrequent smiles for the simple pleasure of having conjured a rhyme. Henrietta's command of English was still not perfect by any means, but she understood that when you dissolved honey or sugar in wine or water, you made it disappear. Harry had shown her this in one of their teaching sessions. Was Parliament to disappear then?

Yes.

'I have dissolved Parliament,' Charles explained. 'For good this time. They mean to undermine me, and so from now on I shall reign without them. I shall never recall Parliament again in my lifetime.'

'Good for you, *mon cher*. Well done.' And serve them all right. His action made complete sense to Henrietta, since her family, the Bourbons, had attempted to phase out the French equivalent of Parliament, and the Spaniards had never even had one in the first place. They certainly seemed to be more trouble than they were worth.

But Laud, who had waited with Henrietta, now looked at the two of them as if they had both taken leave of their senses. 'If that is what you have done, sir, then as your trusted councillor, I must tell you that this is the most dismal day England has seen in five hundred years. God help us all,' he lamented.

'Indeed He will,' Charles replied, undeterred. 'His is the higher authority. He chose me to rule, and rule I can and shall. Alone. With no interference.'

The first thing Charles did, alone and with no interference, was to yield to Henrietta's fervent request. He suspended all penal laws against Catholics. She wrote with great pride and many happy tears to her mother and to the Pope, to inform them of her double success. New freedom for all English Catholics, and an heir to the English throne on the way.

In March the formal announcement was made that her first child was expected in the summer. Prayers were said for the safe childbearing of the Queen's Majesty, and the news was greeted with bonfires on street corners and church bells rang out all across London.

'The whole city is sharing Your Majesties' joy.' Lucy smiled as they listened to the jubilant clamour. 'A summer baby. How perfect.'

'Not that perfect,' Henrietta remarked. 'My timing could have been better. Poor Christine.' Henrietta's sister was also expecting and their mother was keen for both girls to have the services of Madame Peronne, the best midwife in France. Henrietta felt guilty that she was to take precedence because she was a queen, whereas Christine was merely Princess of Piedmont. 'I pray that it may work out so that Madame Peronne will be able to attend the birth of Christine's baby before travelling here in good time to deliver mine.'

Henrietta and her sister exchanged a constant stream of letters comparing their pregnancies and looking forward to the births of their babies. At the beginning of May the court moved to Greenwich but Henrietta travelled back up-river a few days later to Somerset House to hear the Te Deum sung in her temporary Catholic chapel. Her belly, though rounded now, was still quite small beneath her corset and voluminous skirts so that she kept half-forgetting that she was pregnant. But due to being weighed down in the front, she was not as steady on her feet as she usually was. With her customary impatience she stood up before the royal barge was securely moored. As it bumped against the landing steps there was a jolt, enough to make her lose her balance and topple backwards, landing awkwardly against the seat.

Harry was instantly at her side, taking a firm hold of her arm and helping her up. 'Are you all right, ma'am?'

Henrietta managed a nod, gripping on to his arm, her fingers sliding against the slashed silk of his sleeve. She was back on her feet, with not a scratch or a bruise, nothing broken and nothing sprained. No aches or pains . . . save for the one in her heart. Harry hadn't let go of her and she hadn't let go of him, didn't want to. The touch of his hand on her arm, supporting her, the way it burned through the delicate fabric of her gown . . . She saw that love had as many facets as a diamond. Charles brought out a protective, maternal instinct in her, made her want to be strong for him, encouraging and supportive. Whereas with Harry it was the other way around. He was the stronger. It was he who protected her. And it was lovely to feel thus protected. With him she felt safe, cherished.

'We must get you straight to bed, ma'am,' Lucy said, and for half a second Henrietta completely forgot that she was with child, that she'd just had an accident. She assumed Lucy must have read her thoughts. For at that moment, going to bed with Harry Jermyn was all that she wanted to do. She felt shaken and it had nothing to do with having taken a tumble. She felt as if she were tumbling still, headlong into chaos. She quickly realised what Lucy meant. 'Don't fuss,' she snapped, drawing away from Harry. 'I am perfectly well.'

She felt the first twinge of discomfort on the short walk to the chapel and decided it might be wisest to do as she was told and lie down for a while in her chamber after all. Lucy hastily drew curtains, lit candles. Within two hours the twinge had turned to a gripping, cramping agony in the pit of Henrietta's belly, unbearably tight, like the worst indigestion, only lower down. The pain reached like crushing tentacles around her back. She knew that her baby was coming, even though it was not due for another ten weeks or more.

Charles rushed to Somerset House to be with her as soon as he heard what had happened, and replaced Lucy at her bedside. She squeezed his hand on an upsurge of pain, waited for it to crest and subside. 'I'm so sorry. It's all my fault.' She had never been so angry with herself. 'If only I had not been so careless. If only I had not stood up too soon.'

'It's your fondness for walking up Greenwich Hill,' he chided. 'They're all saying that such violent exercise is unsafe for pregnant ladies.'

'What nonsense!'

The pain grew worse during the night, allowing Henrietta not a minute's sleep. By morning she was exhausted and sweating and had started to bleed, shockingly bright red blood that quickly stained her nightgown and the sheets. The Greenwich midwife was summoned and the bleeding grew so frighteningly heavy that Henrietta had to have cloths stuffed between her legs to soak it all up. She felt weak and light-headed, and all the while the paroxysms of pain were coming more strongly and frequently, unrelenting.

The windows were shuttered and the doors guarded. The queen's rings were removed from her fingers since that was believed to ease labour. Henrietta prayed the midwife would soon come but when she did arrive, armed only with sponges, poultices and ointments, she took one look at Henrietta, or rather at the ornate four poster bed hung with damask upon which the queen lay, and promptly fell down in a dead faint. Lucy caught her just in time before she hit the floor. If Henrietta had not been so afraid she might have found it amusing. 'Oh, for pity's sake!' she cried despairingly. 'Make her wake up, can't you?'

'It's the responsibility, ma'am,' Lucy said helplessly. She handed the insensible midwife to Harry and he hauled her out, not unkindly but with less than his usual care and attention, rather like a sack of faggots, her booted feet dragging a little on the floor. Henrietta could tell he was furious with her for proving so useless and wanted to be rid of her as fast as possible so that he might be free to help in some other way.

'We didn't reveal to the poor woman that it was Your Majesty who required her services,' Lucy explained. 'I imagine she assumed it was just one of your ladies, or a serving girl who had gone into labour. Attending a queen and delivering the heir to the throne . . . it was obviously far too daunting a prospect for her.'

'Then find someone else,' Charles ordered. 'And be quick about it! No,' he countermanded. 'Not just someone. Send for Peter Chamberlen in Blackfriars.' Charles turned to his wife, a trace of relief lightening his strained expression. 'Chamberlen's uncle, the first Peter, was my mother's surgeon. Their family is known to possess a great secret which they will not divulge and indeed go to great lengths to keep . . . a skill that has earned them a considerable reputation for safely delivering babies through even the most difficult of births.'

That sounded encouraging, but Henrietta was less sure when Peter Chamberlen turned up with two assistants, hefting between them a mysterious large wooden box, ornamented with carving and gilding. It was dragged in just as the previous midwife had been dragged out.

'What's in there?' She viewed it suspiciously while the physician felt her abdomen, pressing down hard around the swell of the baby.

'Instruments, Your Majesty,' he said, evasively and alarmingly. But he had a reassuring manner, a gentle face with clear calm hazel eyes, and strong, capable hands, which he removed from Henrietta's belly as her muscles contracted again. 'The baby is turned the wrong way in the womb, as is often the case with premature births.'

As the pain reached its pinnacle, Henrietta clenched her teeth, clutching the bedclothes in her fists rather than risk crushing her husband's fingers. She realised then that it was not only her baby who was in peril. She'd heard enough stories to know that infants who came feet or rump first were the most likely to die – and take their mothers with them to the grave.

Charles knew it too. She could tell by the way his face turned ashen. 'Save my wife before the child, Chamberlen, I urge you.' He looked every bit as wracked with pain as Henrietta. 'I can have other children. Far rather save the mould than the cast.'

Henrietta half wished that she could die though, quickly, just so the agony would end. The pain was so great she was sure it must be enough to kill her. She tried not to scream because she had already made her throat sore with it. Witnesses were required at royal births, to ensure that no substitutions were made, but now, confusingly, Peter Chamberlen was ordering everyone out while one of his assistants went over to the wooden box and began unlocking it.

'We can't leave Her Majesty alone, sir,' Lucy objected.

'We must,' Charles told her firmly, taking her by the elbow with a glance at the physician. 'It is the Chamberlens' way of guarding their secret. The one that could save my wife's life and that of our child. They will not risk revealing it, so we have no choice but to go.'

When everyone had gone, Peter Chamberlen approached Henrietta with a long narrow white cloth held between his hands. 'I am so sorry, Your Majesty, but do you mind? I cannot let you see what it is that we do.'

'You mean to blindfold me?' She was in too much pain and was too exhausted to feel more than a little surprised, let alone protest. In truth she did not care what was done to her, so long as it was all soon over. She nodded her assent. 'Do what you will.'

The cloth was very soft, and it was tied gently around the back of her head. When it was done she levered herself up on her elbows while her body started to force the baby of its own accord, an involuntary squeezing that was astonishingly powerful, even more so somehow because she could see nothing, only feel, every sensation concentrated in that one effort. She grunted and felt hands firmly but gently prising apart her knees.

'The little thing's shoulders are wedged fast, they just need a little help.'

There was a tinkling sound like the knocking together of metal, and Henrietta felt something cold and hard and metallic go up inside her. The mysterious instrument presumably. It did not bear thinking about. There was a wrenching and a torrent of heat. Two pushes, and there came a searing, stretching stinging between her legs. She cried out, but Peter Chamberlen's unruffled, disembodied voice told her to push again.

'The legs and posterior are already out,' he said. And then: 'A boy!'

There came a faint mewling wail, more like a kitten than a human child. Henrietta didn't wait for the blindfold to be removed but pushed it up and out of the way. She saw her firstborn son for the first time. Despite everything, he was breathing. Just as the queen's attendants filed back in, the baby was placed in his mother's arms, though he was so minute he would almost have fitted into her palm. He was the tiniest scrap of a thing, perfect in every way but unbearably tiny and weak, with birdlike ribs scarce covered with any flesh. His legs were thin as twigs. He had a faint downy fur covering his body, which made him look like one of the pet monkeys.

'What date is it?' Henrietta asked, not taking her eyes off him.

'The thirteenth of May, Your Majesty.'

His birthday. She gave the baby up to Dr Chamberlen to be swaddled and yielded to the urge to close her eyes, just for a moment. But she was so exhausted that she fell almost instantly into a deep sleep.

When she woke the following morning, Charles told her that the baby had died. His birthday, was also his death day, just as Lady Eleanor Davies had prophesied.

It was too much to take in. Suddenly there had been a baby, and just as suddenly that baby had gone. At least she had held him, just that once. 'He was christened?' Henrietta asked, the strangling knot in her throat making it hard for her to speak. 'He was admitted into the Catholic faith?'

'I insisted he be baptised by the royal chaplain,' Charles replied, rather than say no. 'He died an hour after the ceremony and last night we carried him to Westminster Abbey. William Laud led the service. They buried him beside his grandfather . . . my father.' Charles brought Henrietta's hand to his lips and kissed it. 'You must not listen to those superstitions that say the premature delivery of a first child bodes ill for the future of its family.'

Telling Henrietta not to give a care to superstition was like telling a farmer not to trouble about the weather. 'Would you leave me, please?' she said quietly. 'I should like to be alone for a while.'

Lucy did not go immediately. 'His Majesty begged for your life to be spared above that of his heir,' she said in wonderment. 'For a king to do that . . . he must love you very much.'

'I suppose he must.' Henrietta drew in a deep breath. These tragedies happened to women all the time. She would recover. She would have more children. She was alive. She had a husband who adored her, which was surely every pleasure a heart could reasonably desire. But all she could see was her baby's face, his perfect little monkey hands.

For a while she did not even see Harry at the doorway. He was bearing a letter. It was from her sister, bringing the news that Christine had given birth to a daughter, with Madame Peronne in attendance.

'Would you fetch me paper and a pen?' Henrietta asked him. 'I must send Christine my congratulations.'

Harry glanced at Lucy. 'You need not do that so soon, ma'am,' he said, very gently. 'Nobody would expect it.'

'Then even more reason to do it. I like to do the unexpected. I shall surprise everyone.' Henrietta forced a brave smile. 'Please do as I ask. Or are you going to go on standing there? Shall I have to get out of bed and do the job myself?'

There was a mixture of wonder and respect in his eyes. 'Your Majesty's spirits rise in adversity,' he observed. 'It is a great gift.'

'Only if I am to lead a life filled with adversity.' She smiled back at him. 'I do hope I am not.'

In July Charles left for Theobalds and Harry escorted Henrietta to the spa town of Tunbridge Wells in Kent. They travelled over the rolling North Downs to the northern edge of the High Weald, through woodland and past towering sandstone rock formations. A courtier to Charles's father, Dudley North, had discovered the chalybeate spring in Tunbridge Wells, and when he drank from it and found his health improved, he became convinced of its healing properties. His physician claimed the waters contained vitriol and could cure colic, melancholy and the vapours, as well as making the lean fat, the fat lean, killing worms in the belly and loosening clammy humours. In addition it was supposed to renew youth, make pale cheeks rosy and sad spirits cheerful.

The spring was pleasantly situated at the end of a tree-lined avenue. A small wooden pavilion had been erected around it. Henrietta was led to the front of the queue of ladies and gentlemen and handed a cup of the water. It tasted acidic but was cool and clear. She drank two cups.

They continued on their way, riding on horseback through the summer meadows of Surrey to Oatlands Palace with its red-brick profusion of turrets, gables and high chimneys. It stood on the south bank of the River Thames.

'Another Tudor building for you,' Harry said. 'King Henry had it built for one of his wives. I forget which one of 'em!'

King Henry VIII had left his mark everywhere. Every palace bore evidence of his reign and his power, the turrets and towers and gardens he'd had built in honour of his queens. And his other, darker legacy. Henrietta could sense the ghosts of those executed queens who had dared to love other men, or merely been suspected of loving other men. Who had lost their hearts and then their heads.

It didn't really matter which dead or executed queen Oatlands had once belonged to, it was to be Henrietta's now and she fell in love with it instantly. It was built around three courtyards, the outer two turfed and the inner paved in rough freestone. The entrance was adorned with a gilded dial decorated with planets and signs of the zodiac. The walls of every room were panelled, the floors boarded or matted. As well as bed chamber, privy chamber and closet, Henrietta's extensive apartment also included a gallery, coffer room and withdrawing room, plus what was called in England a crystal room.

From the vantage point of a hexagonal tower there were views over densely wooded parkland to the nearby village of Weybridge and the meadows of the Wey. In the distance lay the valley of the Thames and the rolling blue-shadowed downs.

'Is that Windsor Castle?' she asked Harry, pointing. 'Over there. Behind the woods?'

'I think it must be.'

Henrietta spun away from the window with a swish of her skirts and all but skipped towards the door, where she turned to find that he had not followed her. 'Come. I want to walk.'

'Walk, ma'am? What? To Windsor!'

She laughed. 'No, silly. In the gardens. It's such a pretty palace that the gardens must be equally enchanting. You know I have to explore the grounds wherever we go that's new to me. I still keep hoping I'll find somewhere in England to rival the gardens of France. Only so far I never have. Maybe this time.'

'Are you sure walking is wise?'

'Of course it is. I'm not pregnant now and am fully recovered.' She danced back to catch hold of his hand and drag him along. 'Hurry, Harry,' she said, giggling at the amusing similarity of the words. 'It'll be dark before we know it and I must see this famous silk house that our Mr Jones is so proud of having built here.'

There were various buildings scattered about the extensive grounds. With Lucy, Eleanor, William Davenant and a couple of other gentlemen including George Goring trailing behind at a short distance, they walked past a summerhouse with a blue slate roof set out with chairs and a table, a small banqueting house, and various other pretty garden buildings. There was a fountain in the form of a mermaid, an allée of rose trees, and a circular knot garden planted with herbaceous flowers, pinks and gilly-flowers. At the heart of a long flower garden stood a yew tree, its trunk ringed with a white-painted wooden seat. There was also a great orchard which must have contained upwards of five hundred fruit trees, as well as a pretty wooden and wirework birdcage for turtledoves. Henrietta imagined

King Henry's wayward wives using these places for clandestine trysts with their lovers, risking their lives here for moments of pleasure and passion . . . the moments all the more pleasurable and the passion all the greater for being snatched and forbidden.

It was a beautiful garden, but it could have been more so. The courtier who had been keeper of the gardens, orchards and silkworms had recently died and a replacement had not yet been made. There were already sorry signs of neglect: sprouting weeds and deadheads on the rose bushes. Henrietta itched to roll up her sleeves and set about removing them.

The silkhouse, though, was magnificent, a two-storey building comprising four small rooms below stairs and one large room above, which must have measured ten feet by forty. It was wainscoted in oak with oval and arched panels, the light shining in through an enlarged window incorporating the late queen's arms painted on the glass. There were carved mantels and shelves and pillared partitions for the worms themselves. The thought came to Henrietta unbidden: this would be the most wonderful, secret place to meet a lover. She struggled to suppress it.

'I have something to tell you,' she said to Harry. 'You are to be made surveyor of the petty customs'

'Thank you, ma'am.'

'It is the king you should thank, not me.'

'Your Majesty had no hand in it then?'

'I might have put forward your name.'

He looked at her as if to ask, was that really the best she could do? It *was* the best she could do, but Henrietta wondered if she'd have been better doing nothing. If, by putting his name forward, she had offended him. Though all she had done was offer him the time-honoured form of patronage, an office which involved little or no labour while conferring on him a title and extensive rewards. She hadn't meant merely to fob him off with this sinecure, pay him off even, as compensation for no longer being able to enjoy other of her favours. This was not his reward for having enjoyed them in the first place. Oh, could he not see? She had done it only because she wanted to help him, to see him fulfil his ambitions. Favour brought further benefits. That was how things worked at court. He knew that as well as she. It had worked for the Duke of Buckingham as well as for countless other courtiers. Why not for Harry, who was far more deserving and ambitious? She knew he was ambitous, even if now he looked as though it all meant nothing to him.

'It will make you extremely rich, you know. Don't you want to be rich?'

'Show me a man who swears he does not want that and I'll show you a liar.'

That was better, passed for some kind of acknowledgement that the advancement was welcome at least. There was more. 'Meanwhile your uncle, Sir Robert Killigrew, is to be my vice chamberlain,' Henrietta told him as they began to slowly walk back to the house. 'And I mean to make your father my master of the game. He'll be in charge of the deer and all other animals that are hunted on my estates.' She fell silent, realising that of course Harry would know the duties of a master of the game. Even were it not so plainly obvious from the title!

'Again, I thank you,' he said, eminently polite.

She stopped walking, making him do the same. 'You don't sound very pleased?' He didn't look it either. Not as pleased as she had wanted him to look at any rate. She so wanted all to be right between them. 'Please, do please, be pleased.'

'I am pleased, ma'am,' he said. 'Very. Of course. You are most generous.'

As they walked on she noticed that he kept enough of a distance between them that his legs did not once so much as brush against her skirts. She hated that. Hated the way he could be so controlled, as if he no longer desired her at all. She wanted him to be tortured with desire for her as she was for him. How could he put aside the passion they had experienced together?

Since Buckingham's death, Harry's behaviour towards her had been faultless. He had consistently behaved in a way that was totally appropriate, totally correct. It made Henrietta question everything that happened. Even his gallantry at the tournament. She had thought that in losing willingly to Charles, he was making some kind of declaration of devotion to her. Perhaps he was. That from now on he would offer only the devotion expected of any loyal servant and courtier to his queen. And his king. Treat them as if they were one and the same.

Henrietta half wished she'd not given him those sinecures. Maybe advancement was what he had been seeking all along and she herself meant nothing to him. That was the trouble with being royal, you could trust nobody. You never knew who was a true friend and who was on the make. You never knew what a person wanted, and every person wanted something. Everyone at court was there to serve their own ends. Why would Harry be any different? She had thought he was once. From the beginning, she had thought the lovely things he said to her were entirely genuine. But maybe he was just more skilled than other people at using his charm, at flattering her. He had flattered her, but he had never once said he loved her. He'd seen how much she liked him, loved him, and seen, too, his chance to become part of her household, to become rich and influential. Maybe he liked having been in a queen's bed. Maybe he bragged about it to his friends. Enjoyed the status and reputation of having been her lover.

Oh, but she knew none of that was true. None of it. She was being spoiled and petulant and possibly a handful of other sins which she could not name, just because she could not have it all her own way, have everything she wanted. The king's love and Harry's too.

Why couldn't she, though?

Her thoughts were so distracted that it came almost as a surprise to find that they were in the long garden again already, with the yew tree growing in the dead centre of it. Thrusting itself upwards with dense branches and leaves spreading from the top, the tree looked to Henrietta at once so suggestive of a man's erect and ejaculating penis that she smiled to herself and blushed at the same time.

Harry's eyes were on her face, watching her. 'What is so amusing?'

She shook her head teasingly, slid her eyes sideways to meet his. 'Sorry. Can't say.'

Or could she?

She couldn't touch him or kiss him any more, but flirting with him . . . being a little risqué . . . where was the harm in that? It was entirely in order. She was the queen after all. This was her court and he was her courtier. It was his duty to flirt and be flirted with, for her entertainment.

She reached out, plucked a petal off a pink rose, looked down at it as she ran her fingers lightly over the velvety smoothness. 'We are in a garden.' She smiled coyly, referring back to that conversation they'd once had about the words for private bodily parts. 'And that tree looks so much like a . . . well, you know . . . a man's . . .'

'Stop it! Please.'

'Why?' she flashed back at him.

'It is not . . . appropriate.'

She forced a laugh. He was being as stiff and starchy as Charles. 'How very English you sound,' she snapped.

'Is that meant to be an insult, ma'am?'

'*Oui. Certainement!*'

'I thought you loved England and Englishness now?'

Oh, he was too quick for her. She did not want to fight with him, just to flirt and play and feel that he still cared for her and wanted her. How nice it would be if they could just play with each other at least. She knew, from having two brothers, that games could be dangerous, that it only took a moment or one false move for a play fight to tip over into the real thing. But life was so much more exciting for having a little danger in it, wasn't it?

Lucy and the Earl of Holland and the rest of their little party were exploring one of the garden houses. Henrietta went over to the circular bench around the yew. Harry followed, sat down beside her. He dropped his head back against the trunk to stare up at the dark tracery of the leaves. He seemed so very far away from her it made her want to cry.

She made a study of the flowers, busy with lazy droning bees. Her mother had instilled in her a love of plants every bit as great as her love for art and architecture, and Henrietta couldn't help but see great potential here. Since this is my palace and my garden, I may do what I like with it, she decided. France had the most beautiful gardens in the world, in terms of harmony and artifice. 'How I'd love to create a French garden in this lovely corner of England,' she declared.

'You should do that, ma'am.' Harry leaned forward, resting his forearms on his knees, hands lightly clasped. It was impossible to tell what he was really thinking.

'We must hire a new keeper immediately,' she said. 'He must be someone who is knowledgeable and passionate and is willing to travel abroad for seeds and bulbs and cuttings. I'll have him fetch them from France and plant geometrical, ordered beds, just like in the Tuileries, segregated according to height and colour. Just think what we could grow!'

'Tulips?' he suggested.

'Anemones and Spanish gorse.'

'Ranunculi.'

'Indian cress. Irises. Maybe even the chequered daffodil that grows wild around Lyons. You know the one I mean?'

'Of course. Very pretty.'

'And an orchard is not an orchard without orange trees and lemons,' she announced, thinking how nice it was just to talk to him. 'Limes too. Would pomegranate trees grow in England? How about apricots, peaches and plums?'

'It's certainly warm enough today for them all to flourish. Even Bon Chrétien pears, I should imagine.'

And cherries, she thought but did not say.

He stood up, stretching his powerful shoulders and back, lazily and luxuriously, like a big cat flexing its muscles. Oh, but he was too beautiful.

'You should grow roses and lilies, side by side,' he suggested.

It sounded a bit like a riddle, but spoken so solemnly that she did not make light of it as was her usual inclination. 'Why?'

'They are calling you the Rose and Lily Queen. It be a pretty name and you should celebrate it.'

Celebrate the fact that she had bound the lily of France to the rose of England by her marriage? Henrietta supposed that she should, but found, in Harry's company, that she was not inclined to.

She slept at Oatlands with a miniature portrait of Charles by her bed. When he went off hunting, that was all that she had of him. As in the beginning, in France, as so often since, Harry was here and Charles was not. And Harry had such presence that with nothing and nobody to counteract it, the attraction Henrietta had always felt for him was too much for her to manage. She felt enslaved by her desire for him, a physical need, the ache. She lay awake, restless, frustrated, unable to sleep, fighting the temptation just to go this room, knock on his door. She had never truly realised before that it could take so much effort and strength to do absolutely nothing. To lie still. To make herself stay in her bed. And even if she did go to him, she was no longer at all certain that she would be welcome.

She saw no way to end her torment. It hurt too much. Wanting him and not being able to have him, not even knowing any more if he wanted her. All that she could do to end it was to send him away. Sometimes she thought it would be better if she did, that she must do it, tell him to pack his trunk and go, must never see him again. But the thought of never seeing him, never talking to him, was equally unbearable – more unbearable than seeing him and still wanting him. She was totally trapped.

It would have helped somehow to know for sure he felt just as tortured. But she did not think it was so. What had he meant by that comment about the Rose and Lily Queen? A subtle attempt to remind her that she had chosen Charles over him now? That she belonged exclusively to her husband. That he did not miss her. That he had come to accept the situation, was happy with it. That he had found someone else. No. She must not think of him with another woman or she would go mad.

Charles was missing her so much that he came to her at Oatlands several weeks earlier than planned and they spent each night together for a whole week. A month later, when Henrietta had a sudden craving for mussels, he sent a servant flying off to town especially to find some for her, sure what it must mean.

'On this new hope depends my happiness,' he said, holding both her hands in his.

She squeezed them. 'Mine too. I pray that God will grant me the favour of going full term this time. I shall take all possible care of myself, I promise.'

Her mother intended to take good care of her too, even from across the Channel. When Henrietta wrote to her to tell her that she believed she was with child once more, Marie sent her a present of a beautiful gilded French chaise so that her daughter would not risk excessive walking or the jolting of crude English coaches. Just to look at the beautiful equipage made Henrietta long to go out, and she took great pleasure in taking her daily air in it from then on. Her mother also sent her a pretty jewelled heart on a golden chain that Henrietta wore constantly, as if it might ward off all disaster.

# 1630

The anticipated arrival of an heir to the throne preoccupied the whole court as before, but after the loss of Henrietta's first baby the excitement was mixed with more than the usual anxiety. Everyone was tense and nothing was left to chance. In February, three months before Henrietta was due to give birth, a warrant for the sum of three hundred pounds was issued for the purchasing of childbed linen, and Henrietta's dancing master was sent to France to fetch Madame Peronne to ensure that she would arrive in plenty of time.

A messenger was also dispatched by Charles to order Lady Eleanor Davies to leave off her prophesying where this child was concerned. The order proved counterproductive however. Lady Eleanor used the very messenger sent by Charles to send back a message of her own, a prophecy that this time the queen was carrying a strong and healthy son no less. The message was delivered to Charles in his audience chamber and, as usual, he was furious to find that his direct orders had been ignored. As usual, Henrietta immediately saw the amusing side of the situation, and was entertained by Lady Eleanor's opportunism and ingenuity. More than that, she was heartened by the prophecy.

'Please don't be cross,' she said, touching Charles's arm, her black eyes dancing with merriment. 'Lady Eleanor should not have disobeyed Your Majesty. Of course she should not. It was very wrong of her. But she has been so accurate in the past, it has set my mind at rest that all will be well this time.'

The anger lifted from Charles's face. 'Well, if it pleases you, dear heart. That is all that matters to me.'

Henrietta's smile widened. Her influence over him still took her by surprise. And, increasingly, it delighted her. She had longed for Charles's affection and been deprived of it for so long that she did not take it for granted even now and every kind word or gesture felt precious as a droplet of rain falling in a desert. But she was beginning to let herself believe that the drought was over forever. To trust him. And if she could do that, fall in love with him, really fall in love, then perhaps she would be able to let Harry go. 'I am so longing to hold your baby in my arms,' she said. 'Just to meet him. Or her. Will you mind terribly if Lady Eleanor is wrong after all and it is a girl?'

'I shall not mind at all. Since she will be your daughter.'

But Lady Eleanor's prophecy seemed well on the way to being fulfilled. A messenger from Henrietta's mother arrived bearing the most lovely lacy baby clothes. They were far more elegant than any to be found in England and Henrietta could not stop looking at them. Several times a day she took them out of the carved coffer where they were stored, unwrapped the silver tissue folded around them to protect them and laid them out on the bed, sitting beside them with one hand resting on her taut rounded belly. She stroked the tiny smocks, whispering a prayer that this baby would live long enough to wear them and that she too would survive to see that happy day.

When it came time for her lying-in she withdrew to St James's. The birth chamber itself was appointed with a sumptuous bed newly hung with embroidered green satin curtains within which she would spend the coming days and weeks. They stretched ahead like a lifetime. She did not want this baby to come early like the last one, of course, but sometimes it felt as if it would never come at all. That she would always be pregnant, forever waddling about like her mother! Even lying in bed was uncomfortable, no matter what position she tried, how many pillows she used. She was used to being tiny and light and agile. Could not adapt to the fact that when she lay down now, she could barely get up again but was helpless as an overturned beetle. She just wanted the birth to be over. At least she knew more of what to expect this time around, though she wasn't sure if that made it more or less frightening.

As it turned out, everything was very different anyway. When labour finally began, at four o' clock in the morning in the last week of May, both Madame Peronne and Peter Chamberlen were already in attendance. Not that they had overly much to do, besides assuring Henrietta that all was proceeding well, that this baby was obligingly coming the right way, head first and of its own accord.

'What a big head it is,' Madame Peronne exclaimed, peering between Henrietta's legs. Madame Peronne came from a line of midwives and acted like the queen of her profession that she was. Her ramrod-straight back, refined features and air of serene confidence gave her an aristocratic bearing. She was entirely at ease in the presence of royalty, and was so accustomed to the sight of emerging babies that she spoke about the size of Henrietta's baby's head as casually as a countess commenting on the size of a breakfast boiled egg. But she'd also seen enough newborn heads in her life to know a large one when she saw one.

Henrietta could well believe it was bigger than average. Was sure she would be torn wide open by it.

'Almost there, Your Highness,' Madame Peronne encouraged her in French. 'The harder you push, the sooner it'll be over.'

That was all the incentive Henrietta needed. She bore down, feeling the hot rush and release she remembered from before. There was silence for a moment, followed by what must surely be the most welcome and wondrous sound in the world, a newborn's wail, far heartier than last time.

Madame Peronne ordered someone to hand her the knife to cut the slippery blue cord and Peter Chamberlen practically jumped to do her bidding. 'The new Prince of Wales,' she announced, lifting him high to display his miniature penis for all to see.

There were cheers and congratulations and bright smiles from the watching women all around the candlelit room. Tears of joy glittered in Charles's eyes, made Henrietta cry too. This baby was England's future, but also their own private future. The demise of the Duke of Buckingham had brought about a new beginning for them. But how much better to begin again with a birth instead of a death. To begin their new life together with a new life.

Exhausted as she was, Henrietta watched Madame Peronne wash the newborn prince. She felt complete and content and very proud. She had fulfilled her destiny and duty. She had provided England with an heir. So long as this baby survived into adulthood, she would be the mother of the King of England.

It looked as if he had every chance of surviving. There was certainly no question about his great good health. He was bonny as could be, and it was immediately remarked upon by all the ladies of the court who paid calls to the lying-in chamber how large and long he was.

'See how His little Highness never clenches his fists but always keeps his hands open.' Madame Peronne was playing with the baby's plump and dimpled fingers before they were bound tight to his sides by the swaddling bands. 'It means he will be big-hearted as well as big-bodied. My,' she exclaimed, 'he is going to be tall!'

The baby was to be named Charles, would one day sit upon the throne of England as King Charles II, but beside the king whom he would one day succeed, his namesake and father, and beside his doll-like mother, he looked like a giant baby cuckoo in the royal cradle. For the progeny of two such tiny parents, he looked like a changeling. As she carefully observed him, Henrietta was glad that his birth had been duly witnessed, that a dozen respected noble ladies could testify that no substitution had been made. She was too tired and too happy to worry about it now, but a thought did nudge the back of her mind. Her baby's birth might have been witnessed but his parentage could still be called into question. It was not so long ago that her name had been scandalously linked with that of the tallest man at court.

While Prince Charles slept peacefully in his cradle at Henrietta's bedside, his father King Charles rode in a great and colourful procession of state to St Paul's, to give thanks for the birth of his son and heir. Charles rushed to Henrietta's bedside as soon as he returned to Whitehall with a look on his face like that of a priest who'd heard the voice of God speaking directly to him.

'What is it?' she asked, almost afraid. 'What has happened?'

'There was the most miraculous occurrence,' he replied, his voice full of awed emotion.

'Be careful,' she said. 'Start talking about miracles and they'll call you a Papist too.'

He ignored her gentle mockery. 'As the procession was making its way to the cathedral a bright star appeared,' he told her in an earnest voice. 'Shining overhead in the noonday sky. People stood where they were in the streets, looking up at it, gasping in wonder. What further proof could one desire that God chooses the kings who will rule for him on earth? That he is rejoicing now at this birth, and will watch over our son's life and reign?'

'I wish that I could have seen it.' Thankful tears sprang into Henrietta's eyes so that in the darkened, candlelit room she suddenly saw stars everywhere.

What Charles omitted to tell her, though, what she had to find out later from Eleanor who'd had it from her cousin Basil Feilding, was that though God might have celebrated the arrival of Henrietta's son with a heavenly sign to match that of the arrival of his own, the usual earthly celebrations of bonfires, bells and fireworks had been severely curtailed in certain quarters. For all the celebrations that had greeted the announcement of the first pregnancy, the Puritan party did not welcome a new prince and heir born to a Catholic queen, and the arrival of the Prince of Wales had prompted a fresh wave of antipathy towards his mother. There were fears that if the king died it would leave the way clear for a Catholic queen to rule as regent. Puritan doors had remained firmly shut against any celebration. Wild rumours even claimed that there was to be another deadly Gunpowder Plot. A serving woman was arrested for saying she wished the queen could be ducked in the sea with a millstone around her neck. Pamphlets were circulating, naming Henrietta as an idolatress, a daughter of Heth.

'Would Your Majesty care to see one of them?' Eleanor asked.

'Of course Her Majesty would not,' Lucy intervened sharply.

'I do not need to,' Henrietta said. 'I already know how much people here hate me. Parliament at least.'

She had hoped that her providing the country with an heir would have won everyone round, not turned them more against her. But she was not thinking of herself now. People might hate her, but how could they not love her son? How could they not take him to their hearts as their future king? How could they not rejoice at the birth of a new prince and heir to the throne? How could they bear an innocent baby such ill will?

She leaned over and lifted the sleeping prince from his cradle, feeling guilty for disturbing him but needing to hold him close. For all that he was a big baby, he was so utterly helpless and vulnerable that her heart was filled with love and fear for him, a fierce protective love and fear such as she had never known before. She was naturally maternal, felt protective towards her husband, her pets, her friends, but this protectiveness she felt for her child was altogether different and terrifying in its power. Suddenly she no longer yearned to be free to leave this chamber, was glad that she must stay here for another forty days. She no longer saw it as a prison but as a sanctuary. She wanted to keep her little prince here with her for as long possible. The outside world had never seemed such a perilous place. She saw untold dangers for him everywhere and no way to safeguard him. Not even the appearance of that star soothed her now. In the face of such animosity, it seemed to her that it was not a bright, shining star that hung over the Stuart monarchy, but a dark and fateful one.

Charles changed his mind. Months after introducing new leniency towards Catholics, he decided that the little prince's baptism must allay all anti-Catholic fears. In total contravention of his marriage treaty, it was performed according to the Anglican rather than the Roman rite. Henrietta was annoyed and disappointed, but with a supreme effort of will she managed to keep her feelings to herself for once. There had been too many quarrels in the past. She did not want to revisit those days, though deep down she knew that at some point she was going to have to, in order to hold true to what was most important to her.

She was not expected to attend the ceremony anyway. Parents were never present at the font, had no role to play in christenings. She and Charles watched from the windows of her chamber in St James's as William Laud, Dean of the Chapel Royal, led the christening procession. The man lacked any social graces and looked rather absurd in his Episcopal regalia,but everyone else was very elegant. The Lord Mayor wore violet, the aldermen were in scarlet gowns, the lords and ladies in the state dress of the occasion, shimmering white satin trimmed with crimson and matching crimson silk stockings. The prince was carried to the font in the arms of another of the Duke of Buckingham's nieces, the Marchioness of Hamilton. Henrietta's mother and brother were to stand as godparents, but were represented by the Duke of Lennox and Duchess of Richmond. Outside the chapel crowds cheered, trumpets sounded, and cannons thundered from the Tower and ships on the river. The king and queen received the christening party in state, and there were bonfires and bells before the little prince was carried back to his nursery.

Afterwards, Henrietta went to the private altar in her closet. She took her rosary in her fingers and knelt before the icon of Mary. She prayed her own Catholic prayer: 'Glory be to the father, to the son and to the Holy Spirit, as it was, is now, and ever shall be, world without end. Amen.'

She was judged to be sufficiently recovered from the birth in time to go on the usual summer progress. According to royal tradition, she was to leave her baby behind at Richmond in the care of his newly appointed governess. Though, vexingly, Charles had changed his mind about that too. The role had gone not to the Catholic Countess of Roxburghe, as they had agreed, but to the Protestant Countess of Dorset. For now, Henrietta let that go too.

The very first thing she did upon arrival at Hampton Court was to sit down at her desk overlooking the garden and the river and write to her sister, enclosing a lock of her baby's hair and a little portrait of him. She also wrote a long letter to Mamie all about him. Henrietta had long ago forgiven the French girl Mamie for making off with her clothes. What were a few gowns and pearls between friends? Hardly worth the loss of a lifelong attachment, that was for sure. She told Mamie that Prince Charles's fingernails were like pearls, though he was not a very pretty baby because he was so large.

But rather that than he should be small and frail. It was a hot, dry summer and there was fever in every district of the city. Henrietta worried constantly for her baby's health. His governess wrote daily letters reporting that he was thriving, but a month after leaving him Henrietta was so concerned for him, and so longing to see the changes in him, that she returned to Richmond. Harry and Lucy went with her.

She found her son well, and growing larger and longer than ever. He'd be swaddled tight in linen bands from head to foot until he was eight months old, but already he looked as if he was about to burst out of them, like a seed from a pod. He looked old enough to be wearing smocks.

In her last letter to Mamie, Henrietta had asked her friend to send her a pair of perfumed chamois gloves and some bodices from Paris, as well as a set of boules and the rules of any other new games now being played in France. She looked forward to teaching her son the games she'd loved to play as a child at St Germain. Though that would be the extent of his French education. A wet-nurse had been hired from Wales in order to fulfil the ancient pledge that the first words uttered by a Prince of Wales should be in Welsh. But though his principality was Wales, his kingdom would encompass England and Scotland and Ireland too. Henrietta was in full agreement that English should be his first language.

The nurses and governesses had all made themselves scarce to allow the queen some time alone with her baby. She lifted him in her arms and settled with him in a carved chair beside the oak crib. As she cradled him in her arms with the English sun streaming in at the windows off the river to bathe mother and baby in warmth and light, she sang to him an English lullaby taught to her by Kate Villiers, who had sung it to her son George when he was small. It seemed particularly appropriate for Prince Charles.

*'Lavender's blue, dilly-dilly, lavender's green. When you are king, dilly-dilly, I shall be queen.'* It was a sweet song and Prince Charles seemed to like being sung to, looking up at his mother as if he understood every word she sang, even if it was nonsense! Henrietta loved to sing, and since stuffy English court etiquette prevented her from singing around the palaces where and when she wanted to, she was glad to have this perfect excuse. *'Lavender's blue, dilly-dilly, lavender's green. When you are king, dilly-dilly, I shall be queen.'* She stroked little Charles's silken cheek with the back of one finger and chatted to him. 'I am already a queen. When you become king, I shall have to share the title with another queen, your wife. I do hope I like her.'

Henrietta looked up to find Harry leaning against the doorpost, watching and listening to her singing and talking to her baby. Her heart still jumped at the sight of him, which made her feel annoyed with him, as if it were his fault that he continued to have that effect on her when she was trying to be a good and devoted wife. 'Am I needed?' she asked as if he required a reason now to be in her presence.

'No, ma'am.' He straightened up and stood to his full imposing height. He lowered his eyes to the child who had now started to blow bubbles at his mother. 'The little fellow is as dark skinned as a Medici duke.'

He was, with the blackest of eyelashes. There could be no doubting his lineage on that side. But that was not the problem. Henrietta felt the little prince wriggle inside his swaddling bands and marvelled at how strong he was, the opposite of her husband. But he was very serious too. He seldom smiled. He had that characteristic at least in common with his father. It was not enough, though, to stem the gossip. It had begun, just as Henrietta had feared it would. It was never conducted in her hearing and she tried dismiss all thoughts of it from her mind, but Lucy had relayed it to her, word for word. It was inevitable, given the baby's appearance and the earlier gossip. And it frightened her. In this land, maybe more than any other, it was dangerous even to insinuate that the legitimate lines of royal heredity might have been corrupted. The ghosts of King Henry VIII and his executed queens walked in Richmond too. The difference was that in this king's eyes his wife could no wrong. For now.

'Does His Majesty have any doubt that the child . . . ?'

'No,' Henrietta cut in. Was that why Harry had come? Not because he wanted to see her or be with her, but because he was worried about the gossip, about the king's opinion of him, about his own position, his future? 'His Majesty has absolutely no cause to be suspicious, does he?' She made it sound like a criticism. Which, in a way, it was. 'We must not give him any. You should leave.'

'You wish me to leave your service, ma'am?'

'No,' she said again, then shook her head. She did not know what she wanted. She was frightened, confused and sad, but she did not want Harry to leave court. Of course she did not. He had suggested it so casually, as if he would not much mind if she said yes, if she told him to go from her and never return. 'I meant only that you should not be in this room, alone with me.'

'As Your Majesty wishes.'

As he turned to leave, she wanted to call him back. To apologise. His manners had been impeccable, as always, but Henrietta knew she had behaved reprehensibly and despised herself for it. She wanted to tell him that his friendship was precious to her. That she could not imagine her life without him in it. He gave her something that Charles did not. Something she doubted he ever could. Passion, yes, but more than that. Henrietta could not define it, but her heart still yearned for it. And she was hurt by his apparent dismissal of her, his determined indifference. It left her always wanting more from him than he seemed prepared to give her.

# 1631

The Gonzaga paintings and statues had finally arrived from Mantua and Henrietta was just as keen as Charles to see the famous collection for which he had paid the enormous sum of twenty-five thousand. Not all the shipment had been unpacked. Some of the contents had been damaged by seawater and were awaiting repair, but even so the sheer magnitude of the treasures on display was astounding. As well as paintings by Titian, Raphael and Caravaggio, hundreds of statues and busts now peopled the audience chamber at Whitehall. All around stood Roman emperors and gods, silent, still and pale as ghosts. Standing amidst these hard won but almost priceless treasures, Henrietta had never seen her husband look so happy, and that made her happy too.

'Daniel Nys told me that my collection is transformed with this acquisition,' he said, face glowing. 'That it makes me one of the most important collectors in the world.'

Henrietta remembered how he had once told her he wanted to be a good king. It occurred to her now that it would have been better for him had he never had to wear a crown, never had to manage Parliament or his kingdom, but could have been left instead to collect art and to hunt, as had seemed his destiny when he was born the second son. If his brother Prince Henry had not died, then Charles might always have looked as content as he did now.

He took Henrietta's hand. 'You shall have the pick of the statues for your garden at Somerset House. As many as you want.'

'Thank you.' She realised something else then. He generally avoided words that began with the letter 's'. 'You just said "statues" and "Somerset" with no sign of a stutter,' she observed, smiling.

'So I did.'

'What a shame it is that Your Majesty cannot talk about art all the time.'

'What a shame that I can't talk to you all the time, dear heart. That is what it is. Not the art, but you. I hardly ever stammer when I talk to you.'

It was the greatest compliment he could have paid her and Henrietta felt warmed by it.

'It was just the same with Steenie,' he said, instantly spoiling the moment. 'I never stuttered when I was with him.'

Once some of the paintings and statues were in place, Charles took great delight in carrying his son around the galleries of Whitehall and St James's, encouraging the growing prince to repeat after him the names of the great artists, opening drawers of medals and coins while discouraging little grasping fingers from sending a piece of crystal crashing to the floor or knocking a bust from its plinth. Even though Henrietta was one of only two people at court, the other being Harry, who could be in no doubt that Prince Charles was the king's son, she still found it strangely disconcerting to see the two of them together, to see how oddly unalike they were.

It was no wonder that the speculation surrounding Prince Charles's paternity did not abate over the coming months but, according to Lucy who listened to gossip everywhere, grew steadily more vociferous.

'The trouble is that the more the child grows, the less he resembles the king,' she said.

'I realise that.' Those at court knew full well that King Charles had been a puny infant. Prince Charles, on the other hand, looked to be a year old even though he was only a few months. When he was a boy, the king's legs had been so feeble and crooked that he had not walked until he was nearly three. Whereas Prince Charles was toddling confidently down the long corridors and passageways of Whitehall on his long and equally strong legs well before his first birthday.

What Henrietta did not dare ask was if Lucy believed the gossip or not. If she knew the truth or not. Henrietta was sure somehow that she did know, and if she did not condone it, she did not condemn it either.

Even Father Philip had his suspicions.

It had been two months since Henrietta's last confession.

'Forgive me, father, for I have sinned,' she began. 'I have been impatient and hot-tempered and doubtless vain too.'

'Is that all?' There was no smile in Father Philip's voice, like there usually was. He, like Father de Berulle, had grown used to hearing the queen list these same sins. Now she wondered if he, like everyone else, suspected she was hiding a far greater one.

'That is all,' Henrietta confirmed.

'Ten Hail Marys.'

She was about to rise to her feet when the priest spoke again. 'I tell everyone you are full of purity and innocence,' he said levelly. 'That you are never tempted by sins of the flesh. But I am not sure they listen.'

'And I am not sure that you are entirely right in your judgement of me, but thank you for it. My son's blood is pure, father,' she said quietly.' Have no doubt of that.'

'I never did doubt it.'

But you did, she thought. And if you do, everyone must.

Before the new Prince of Wales reached the age of two, Henrietta discovered that she was pregnant for the third time. Since her lying-in at St James's had been trouble-free, she had a superstitious wish to deliver her next baby in the same palace, in the very same chamber. Only the bed hangings were changed, the embroidered green silk summer furnishings replaced with heavier and thicker tawny velvet, since this was to be a winter baby. It was due to be born at the end of November, so when Henrietta went into labour in the first week of that month she feared another breech birth, feared that even the haven of St James's would not protect her baby this time.

The labour was blessedly swift and marginally less painful than the previous two, as if her body knew what it was doing now. The little girl arrived on 4 November. She was named Mary.

Henrietta rested back against the pillows but she would not let herself sleep. 'I am afraid to shut my eyes in case she passes away while I am not watching, just as my first boy did,' she said.

'He was ten weeks early,' the midwife said. 'Little Mary here is only three.'

'But she is almost as tiny and weak as he.'

'You are tiny yourself, Your Majesty,' Lucy said. 'But look how strong you are.'

Princess Mary was strong too. Against all odds, she survived, even though she remained as small for her age as her eldest brother was large.

By the date that she should rightly have come into the world, Henrietta could have sworn that her eyes were already darkening, were flecked with a deep and soulful brown.

She was, in other words, her father's daughter, unquestionably Stuart.

But even that did not stop people whispering, louder than ever, that the princess's brother was clearly a bastard and that maybe she was too.

That their queen was Harry Jermyn's whore.

# 1632

For several days Charles had been complaining that his head ached and that he felt constantly tired. But nothing deterred him from keeping to his rigid routine. Henrietta worried about him. She tried to persuade him to rest but he continued to rise before dawn for prayers and spend long hours in meetings with his councillors and art advisors. He had not even given up his daily jousting and riding practice in the park. But when he woke one morning shivering, she insisted he stay in bed and let her send for the physician.

'It's just a chill,' he argued weakly. He pushed back the covers and swung his feet to the floor, but remained sitting on the edge of the feather mattress as if he could not summon the strength to stand.

Henrietta sat up with him, laid the back of one hand against his brow. 'You have a fever,' she exclaimed in alarm.

He gently removed her hand from his head but kept hold of it as he stood. 'A ride will do me good.'

'I absolutely forbid you to go riding.' She knew he liked it when she mothered him and ordered him about, like she did their son. But just like their son, he was inclined not to do as he was told.

'Very well,' he said. 'I shall play tennis instead.'

'Tennis!' Henrietta sat back aghast. 'Have you gone quite insane?'

'What better way to revive myself than with a hard game against my lord chancellor?'

It was no use trying to tell him not to exert himself too much or concern himself with winning. She knew him well enough by now to know that beneath the stiff regal exterior he was still the crippled little boy who'd been taunted by his older brother for his weak legs.

She stood up, kissed his clammy forehead. 'I shall make sure the kitchens have warm ale and a bowl of hot soup waiting for you when you are finished.'

He lost the game, but not by many points, and to please Henrietta he ate up all the soup, despite feeling sick. It was only later, when he was too tired to stay awake any longer and took off his shirt to prepare for bed, that he discovered a rash on his chest, the flat red blisters and lesions which were the tell-tale signs of smallpox. Fear gripped Henrietta's heart, making her feel as if she too were ill. Smallpox was deadly, almost as dreaded as the plague. Just as she had realised how much she loved Harry when he chanced his life in the joust, now she was knocked sideways by the terror of losing Charles, just when they had found each other at last.

The royal physicians, including Theodore Mayerne, were summoned to confirm the diagnosis. Henrietta stood aside as they made their examination, discussed amongst themselves the most beneficial treatment. There was much debate about whether to draw off blood or not. Mayerne attested that blood-letting in smallpox was more likely to kill than cure and that it was better to let the disease run its course, while relieving the symptoms with a potion of figs, currants, fennel, columbine seeds and saffron boiled in barley water. Someone suggested that the king could be saved from disfiguring pockmarks by opening the pustules with a golden needle. In the end it was agreed to administer the potion, stoke the fire, draw the curtains and leave the king to rest. Just as Henrietta had been saying all along. If only he had listened to her!

Mayerne cautioned her on his way out. 'Smallpox is highly contagious, ma'am. You must not remain here.'

'I am not leaving him.'

'It is Your Majesty's decision, of course.'

Charles's attendants were horrified when Henrietta went back to her chamber to undress only to return, determined to sleep with the king in his bed. She dismissed them all and climbed in beside him. 'Don't you start arguing as well,' she silenced Charles, before he'd had a chance to say a word.

'I wouldn't dream of it.' He smiled feebly. 'I want you to stay. You are the only *médecin*, I need.' She heard the fear in his voice. He shifted away from her a little. 'Only don't come too near me. I'd never forgive myself if you caught it.'

The lesions were worse the next day. He had developed some spots in his nose and his mouth which made it uncomfortable for him to eat and drink or even to breathe. His hands and feet were covered in them. But his face and body remained relatively clear and that made Mayerne hopeful it would prove to be a mild attack.

So it turned out. Within two days the spots had changed to blisters and Charles was able to sit up in a chair by the fire with a fur cloak around his shoulders. Henrietta never left his side. She chatted and read to him, played cards and parlour games with him to keep his mind off the pain caused by the pustules erupting. She scolded him relentlessly for scratching at the scabs and not letting them heal properly.

'Would you not rather take the air with your friends?' he asked as she gathered up the playing cards and shuffled them for another game. There was no mistaking the undercurrent of accusation in his question. It made Henrietta stop what she was doing and put the cards down. It was Harry who had taught her how to shuffle. Charles had said the word 'friends', but he had meant one friend in particular. Even if he had refused to believe the whispers and gossip at first, he might soon come to do so. Rumours were like water, dripping, dripping on to iron. One or two drops were harmless, but after a while the cumulative effects were corrosive, eating away until they caused a great hole. She did not want him to be jealous. Not only because a king's jealousy was always dangerous to invoke, but because she wanted him to trust her. More than that, she wanted so much to be worthy of his trust. To be as good and pious as Father Philip had said he believed her to be.

'I would rather be here with you,' she replied firmly, looking him in the eye. 'Now, what game shall we play next?'

'Backgammon.' Charles lifted his foot to scratch at one of the scabs on his ankle and she swatted his hand away as if he were a small child reaching for too many sweetmeats. He pretended to look cowed. 'Are you quite sure you'd rather not go outside?'

She giggled, 'Illness is evidently good for you. For your humour anyway.'

'It is being with you that is good for me, as I have said before. But I really don't mind if you've had enough of me and want to do something else for a few hours.'

She offered him a bowl of grapes. 'Would you not be terribly bored and lonely without me?'

He raised his hand to scratch his cheek but stopped himself in time. 'But not so itchy.'

Charles had recovered rapidly, with barely a scar, and shortly afterwards Henrietta and her ladies gathered in the candlelit great chamber for the first rehearsal of a new masque. It had been written by a clever young poet named Aurelian Townshend, a friend of William Davenant's. There were pages and pages of script, along with complicated notations on dance steps and formations. It was to rival the masques that had been held at the Louvre, a pioneering production, the first time that ladies had ever sung upon an English stage. The performance was to take place in the Banqueting House where Inigo Jones had already started work on the construction of a stage shaped like a gigantic picture frame.

He had explained with his usual exuberance how Henrietta's ladies were to play a cluster of stars that were to descend on a giant cloud, as if from the heavens, achieved by the use of an ingenious apparatus of pulleys and ropes suspended from a gallery above the proscenium.

'But what is the masque actually about?' Eleanor asked, looking at its author.

Aurelian Townshend deferred to William Davenant. 'Perhaps you would care to explain, sir, since it was you who suggested the subject matter.'

'It's an allegory based on a French fable,' William supplied. 'Circe and her court of lascivious beasts are conquered by Divine Beauty.' He glanced at Henrietta as if to make sure she was paying proper attention, which she was. 'The masque takes as its theme the ultimate ideal of the French notion of courtly love, which we'll call platonic love since it is based on Plato's teachings. A pure love between a man and a woman, which unites souls and minds rather than bodies.'

Eleanor wrinkled her nose in distaste. 'What can you mean, sir?'

'Love that is based on the deepest friendship, respect and admiration.' William did not look at Eleanor as he answered, but kept his eyes firmly on Henrietta. 'A chaste love, unsullied by carnal appetites and desire.'

'Love without lovemaking!' Eleanor exclaimed dismissively. 'I'm sure gentlemen would find that most . . . uncomfortable.'

The other ladies tittered.

Henrietta did not laugh. She wanted to ask William to repeat all that he had just said. But her musician, Bocan, began to play his violin and it was time to take up their places. Bocan always pulled the strangest faces as he moved his bow across the strings, which generally made Henrietta giggle, try as she might not to put the poor man off his playing. But now her mind was on other things, on all that William had said.

'Those are beautiful words Mr Townshend has written,' she commented to him later, when the rehearsal was ended.

'Platonic love is a beautiful concept, ma'am. Desire that is virtuously restrained and redirected to greater concerns. So that love can elevate the heart, inspire heroic deeds and true nobility of spirit.'

Poets had such pretty ways with words, but Henrietta was ready to believe these were more than just pretty, had some truth in them, some tie to the real world. 'Do you honestly believe that's possible?'

'I believe that love is the root of all virtue,' he said. 'So, yes, ma'am, I do.'

Masques were vehicles of court propaganda, always carrying some underlying message, and Henrietta had little doubt that on this occasion the message was directed at her and Harry. William had become Harry's closest friend; he had surely put forward this theme of platonic love for his benefit. What Aurelian Townshend had been directed to write by William was surely an attempt simultaneously to rewrite the past and to show the path forward. By revealing to king and court that the deepest love could be innocent, unsullied by lust and desire, he was excusing the extent of Henrietta's attachment to Harry, removing any grounds for suspicion while also showing a way for the two of them to be with each other, now and in the future.

Over the coming weeks the preparations for the masque involved stagehands, painters, tailors, haberdashers, goldsmiths, shoemakers, and hosiers. Rehearsals took place every day, moving from the great chamber to the Banqueting House for trials of the machinery, first with just Bocan's violin as accompaniment, then the whole orchestra; first with the actors and dancers in their regular clothes, and then in the 'specially made costumes. Preliminary versions had been made of cheap calico to get the cut right, all the skirts stopping just short of the ladies' ankles so that they could show off their fancy footwork.

The king's subjects had started complaining about the extravagance of his court, and of his wife's household especially. But the retainers paid no heed. The night of the performance finally arrived and the Banqueting House had been transformed. Tapestries woven with gold and silver thread were hung upon the gilded walls, setting off the spectacular set. There was an oriental sky, with a rising sun over a calm sea and a dazzling citadel opposite craggy rocks which would be split open by lightning. A revolving lighting display of lamps and flaming torches and hanging candelabra, decorated with tiny spangles of gilded metal foil, gave off a great amount of smoke and made the hall very hot. Costumes were also spangled, rich-looking and yet light enough for dancing, made of cloth-of-silver, fringed and decorated with tinsel that reflected and multiplied the light. White leather Venetian masks had been softly scented by the perfumer, and the combination of a headdress of plumed heron's feathers and high-heeled satin shoes made Henrietta feel almost tall.

Charles sat on his brocade throne beneath the red canopy of state. The assembly around him included the Muscovite and Persian Ambassadors, other notable guests and travellers, plus courtiers, nobles and ladies almost as grandly dressed as the performers.

The music started up and the Heavenly Spheres, or eight musicians in dazzling habits sitting on a gigantic cloud, were lowered first, before it was the turn of Henrietta's ladies in their starry troupe upon two more great clouds. They danced while the cloud descended, their flowing movements and the grand theatricality of it all bringing gasps of amazement from the spectators.

Henrietta was watching from the wings, awaiting her turn, and she couldn't believe what she was seeing. Clearly the notion of pure, spiritual love had made no impression at all on Eleanor Villiers, who was wiggling her hips and flashing her ankles far more often than was strictly necessary. She had been told time and again about how important it was to keep her gaze passive and level, with eyes cast neither too high nor too low. Now, disobediently, she had gone so far as to push up her mask the better to reveal her mouth. She was smiling an especially bright and twinkling smile, even for a star. All her smiles were directed at Harry who was sitting near the front, close to William Davenant. But like other members of the audience, he had fallen to talking and laughing with his neighbours rather than paying full attention. Until, that was, it was time for the queen's entrance.

Henrietta was to be lowered in a chariot, a heavenly being descending as if from on high. The chariot was a magnificent creation, worked in gold and gemstones. She was seated upon a velvet throne within it, wearing a gown of sky blue satin, heavily embossed and embroidered with silver stars and sunbeams, with a white ruff around her throat. More stars were woven around her crown.

'Let the queen's majesty and beauty draw us to a contemplation of the beauty of the soul,' Townshend's pretty verse instructed.

Now Harry's eyes were fixed on Henrietta as if he would do exactly that, as if he would look deep into her heart and soul and let a part of himself live forever there, would take back a part of hers to reside within him. It was a gaze which was not stripped of desire, but transcended it. As she alighted from the chariot, as the clouds rose once more and she was serenaded by a chorus of fifty magnificently costumed singers, his eyes never left her. She saw in them all the love, respect and admiration that William Davenant had spoken of and it made her feel as luminous as the blazing star sun she was portraying, as if she had been raised up far higher than Inigo Jones's pulleys could ever lift her.

Next morning, she wandered back to the Banqueting Hall, hoping to recapture some of the magic, but the lanterns and flambeaux had been extinguished, there was theatrical debris scattered about the floor, broken bits of wood and tinsel, droplets of dried candle wax. A forlorn, almost tawdry air hung about the place.

Inigo Jones was supervising the dismantling of his ambitious stage set. Harry and William Davenant were with him, not helping as such but talking to him. They greeted the queen with a courteous bow. Harry's smile was no different from William's and Inigo's. Friendly but remote. There was not a glimmer in his eyes of the grand and noble love she had seen in them as he'd watched her descend in her chariot. Or thought she had seen. Had it just been a trick of the light? A fleeting emotion, stirred by the poetry and the music and the drama of the occasion? Perhaps.

'You must feel sad to see all this taken down, sir,' she said to Inigo Jones. 'All that work, just for one night.'

He cast his eyes around at the empty Banqueting House, which he had also designed. 'I am glad that some of my constructions are more permanent, ma'am. At least this place will be still standing a hundred years from now, I trust.'

Harry had once suggested that in England Henrietta should become a builder and re-shaper of cities, like her mother and father. That she should bring some of the beauty and grandeur of Paris to London, just as her parents had brought the beauty of Italy and the classical world to France. She had thought it a glorious idea, something she would love to do. One day. Suddenly she felt that day had arrived.

'There should be more buildings like this in London,' she said, with a glance at Harry. 'Many more. Houses. No, whole streets of houses. For people to live in, I mean. Not just for feasting and entertaining.'

'That it is an excellent idea, ma'am.' Jones was being dismissive, not taking her seriously at all. Like an indulgent adult agreeing with the impossible whim of a child who dreamed of flying to the moon. A man indulging the whim of a woman who should not concern herself with such matters as building. 'You are humouring me, sir,' she said passionately. 'Please do not. My mother and all the Medicis have built the most beautiful buildings.

'I beg your pardon, ma'am. I meant no offence.'

'Your Majesty's dower lands at St James's,' Harry said. 'There, perhaps, would be a good place to start.'

She turned to him. 'St James's?'

'Would you like me to show you, ma'am?'

'Yes,' she said quietly. 'I would like that very much.'

'We may as well go right away then? No use in waiting, is there?'

Henrietta smiled. 'It is very underrated!'

'Hmm. Best avoided, if it can be helped!'

Horses were saddled and they rode side by side. Not far. Through St James's Park, past the pens enclosing the camels and the crocodiles and the elephant, the aviaries of noisy, exotic birds, and on through Spring Gardens. The sun was shining warmly on their faces, the leaves were still pale green on the trees, flowers budding. Soon the summer heat would turn everything dull and dusty, but for now there was a freshness and clarity. It was like a new dawn. Their horses clopped over the wide paved stretch of Pall Mall heading towards St James's Palace and Harry reined in at the corner of a track heading north from the palace.

St James's Park had been drained and landscaped by the king's late father, but the development had stopped short of this area. There were just a couple of ugly houses and a few scattered buildings. All else was damp pasture and scrubby grass where courtiers practised archery.

'Can you see it?' Harry asked eagerly. 'The mud and stubble replaced by fine mansions . . . around Parisian squares?'

'Yes. I can see it.'

'We could transform the whole of this west end of London,' he said, his voice deep and sonorous.

'And name a street in your honour?' she smiled. She could see it so clearly. As Harry turned to her and she looked back into his eyes, Henrietta could see his dream, his grand and beautiful dream. The dream which he had first dreamed with her, for her. Which had become her dream too. She saw something else. Aurelian Townshend's poetic definition of platonic love described an emotion that was channelled to a greater cause, redirected. When she had become a proper wife to Charles and could no longer be with Harry, she had still felt so much love for him that was blocked, had no expression and no release. But William's concept of platonic love unblocked it, gave it direction. A love that inspired and enobled. She saw now exactly what he meant. How it could be. How they might one day build these beautiful houses and squares, inspired by what she had shown him in Paris, by his love of Paris, his love of her. She would help him and together they would create a new London, fashioned upon the elegant squares of her homeland. This part of England would stand as a lasting tribute to the beauty of their friendship, would be there long after they had both gone.

But it was a hugely ambitious plan. Too ambitious? Impossible? No. With Harry she had always felt that nothing was impossible, that she could do anything, be anything. That was what he had always given her, a lightness of heart, a strength and a belief in herself. And now she had a belief in the transformative power of their love.

'We will conduct a proper survey,' she decided. 'That is what my father always did. A survey. That is what we need. So we can see how it would best be achieved.'

At Henrietta's request, construction was also resumed on a half-built house in Greenwich. Inspired by Harry's vision for the west side of London, it was to be completed now in the classical style, which pleased Inigo Jones.

'I am not sure I want him to build my house, since he was so disparaging before,' Henrietta protested to Harry. They were walking with Prince Charles in St James's Park, showing him the crocodiles and the elephant while also taking the chance to revisit St James's.

'Are you familiar with the concept of cutting off one's nose to spite one's face?' Harry asked, smiling.

'I am sure I do it all the time.'

They stopped beside the crococile which was basking in the sun.

'You'll find no man better qualified for the task of completing a classical house for you,' Harry insisted. 'Inigo's patron, the Earl of Pembroke, paid for him to visit Italy to study classical ruins as well as new buildings built in the classical style. He has read whole treatises on the subject.'

'I have employed a French artist to supply designs for chimneypieces and other decorative details,' Henrietta said. 'I'll show them to you, if you like. You can tell me what you think. Help me to decide which would look best.'

'I'd like that very much.'

The promise that together they would study illustrations of interiors and staircases, take the barge up-river to inspect the progress of the carpenters, stonemasons, gilders and glaziers, gave Henrietta a quiet contentment. It would be perfectly safe and acceptable to talk passionately of fluted Doric columns and classical porticos, even if they could no longer speak passionately of other more personal things.

# 1633

Greenwich was not the only building project underway. Finally, plans had been completed for the queen's new Catholic chapel to the south-west of the great court at Somerset House. Summer progress took the king's and queen's households west to Wilton House in Salisbury, home of the Earl of Pembroke, but everyone returned to London early in September for the ceremonial laying of the first cornerstones of the chapel.

The former tennis court had meanwhile been magnificently fitted out to represent a church. Tapestry, silk and arras hangings served for walls and roof, and the floor was strewn with rushes and sweet-scented flowers. At the far end stood a temporary altar, adorned with gilt candelabra and vases, glorious enough for Solomon's Temple.

The grand almoner led a mass as theatrical and colourful as the most lavish masque, with burning incense and gilded chalices and the most stirring, harmonious music. Hundreds of people had turned out to watch as Henrietta, accompanied by the French Ambassador and a number of other Catholic gentlemen and ladies, descended the dais to kneel upon plump red velvet cushions before the cornerstones the most prominent of which bore a silver plaque with a commemorative Latin inscription. Henrietta was handed a ceremonial velvet-trimmed trowel and used it to take a little mortar from a silver basin. This she threw on to the stone three times. As she passed down the lines of bowing craftsmen, dispensing gifts of silverware amongst them, there were rousing shouts of, 'Long live the Queen! Long Live Queen Mary!'

'I have won some hearts at last,' she commented to Lucy, who was walking a few paces behind carrying the basket of largesse.

'No doubt the Papists of this country will see the building of this chapel as a great triumph, ma'am,' Lucy replied, with a warning note of cynicism that Henrietta, in her happiness, totally failed to notice.

Soon afterwards, Charles left for Holyrood in Edinburgh to attend his Scottish coronation, which had long been postponed for political reasons. It would take him several weeks to ride north and he was then to tour the lowlands before returning to London. It would be the first time since their reconciliation Henrietta had been parted from him for months and the prospect of having to wake, go to bed and wake again without once having seen or spoken to him made her feel a little lost. She had grown so used to having him near that she couldn't imagine what it would be like not knowing exactly where he was, what he was doing and thinking, from one hour to the next, let alone one day to the next. She was also fearful for him. He had talked much of Scotland to her, a land he loved deeply, but it sounded like a harsh and inhospitable place of snow-capped mountains and misty glens and warring clans, totally at variance with the rarefied glamour of royal palaces, which was the only world Henrietta had ever known.

She fought back tears while she stood with her husband in the great court at Whitehall, their two slight, richly cloaked figures forming a still point in the midst of the throng of horses, dogs, and more than fifty carts preparing for departure. Charles's entire court was attending him: councillors and clergymen, musicians and buckhounds. The grooms had led his grey mare from the stables and were waiting to lift him into the red velvet saddle.

'Will you miss me very much?' he asked, wiping away a tear from her cheek with his finger.

'I shall be a complete mourning turtle without you.'

'And I without you. I wish I didn't have to go. I did request that the Scottish crown be brought to London to save me from so long a journey but the Scots have told me that if I delay too long they may be inclined to choose another king.'

Henrietta held his cold hand to her cheek before kissing it. 'England is wintry enough compared to France. I imagine it will be positively icy in Scotland. Make sure you keep warm.'

'I wish I could take you with me to warm me,' he said. 'But it is not wise for you to travel in your condition.' She was pregnant again. 'And I need someone to manage my affairs in England while I am gone.' She knew also, that the Scots despised Papists even more than did the English. 'You must keep busy while I am away,' Charles instructed. 'It will make the time go faster.'

'Nothing makes time go faster.' She smiled. 'Believe me. I have tried every trick.'

The best one was to seek the company of her children.

Prince Charles was nearly four and wearing miniature adult clothes, breeches and doublet and stockings. He was already being groomed for kingship, had dined with his parents in state and was receiving foreign ambassadors, giving audiences of his own with his little sister and accompanying his father to the annual garter ceremonies. His tutor, Brian Duppa, Bishop of Winchester, a man reputed to read men as easily as he could read books, was teaching the prince to write with the aid of ruled guidelines. After her husband had gone, Henrietta went to spend the morning in the nursery, sitting with her son, spelling out words for him and reading what he had written.

'Your handwriting is already far neater than mine,' she told him, and stroked his curly black hair. 'Clever boy. Well done. Now, would you like to come with me to mass tomorrow? Mary can come too.'

It was not too early to begin her children's religious instruction, and better to have them attend mass with her while their father was away. Until the chapel was ready it was still conducted in her closet. But even so, the two small children were enraptured by the sight of Father Philip in his flowing green chasuble and stole, and the way he bowed in reverence to the little altar with its matching rich green cloth. The candles in their tall silver-gilt sticks had been lit, their light shimmering on the gold crucifix; smoke mingled with the scent of burning incense, rising upwards to God with their prayers.

Through her children's enthralled eyes, Henrietta experienced the miracle of the mass as if for the first time. She felt afresh the beauty of the ancient rhythms that had soothed her soul since she was a little girl, the solemn reading of the gospels, the recitation of psalms and the creed through which God spoke. Then the most mystical moment, when a miracle happened and the bread and wine changed into the body and blood of Christ. Father Philip said the Lord's Prayer and broke the bread, allowing a crumb to fall into the chalice.

Mary pulled a face at the idea of drinking blood.

'It is the blood of Our Saviour,' Henrietta told her. 'Who sacrificed His life for our sins. And through Him, through this blood, we will never die but have eternal life.' She looked from one child to the other. 'Do you understand?'

They both nodded. 'We will go to heaven,' Prince Charles said.

Henrietta picked him up and kissed him. 'So long as you are good. And Catholic.'

Kate Villiers had requested an audience with the queen but Henrietta decided that it would be much more enjoyable if they all went to see her instead – all, that is, except for Kate's own niece. Eleanor was complaining of feeling sick, and said that the river journey would only make it worse. She did look pale but Henrietta suspected it was just an excuse, that she wanted to spend the afternoon with her lover. Or perhaps it was lovesickness she was suffering from. Eleanor no longer paid any attention to Harry whatsoever, but had transferred all her affections to Mountjoy Blount.

Blount's star was in the ascendant at court. He was now master of ordnance, selling gunpowder at exorbitant prices to the Spaniards. He had married too, the daughter of Baron Boteler, but Eleanor was following Lucy's example and not letting a man's wife stand in the way of her passion. She claimed that Blount loved her, and she loved him more than any man alive. Since she was the Duke of Buckingham's niece, the king turned a blind eye. And Henrietta did not much mind what Eleanor did, so long as she was not doing it with Harry.

It was George Goring's suggestion they should enliven the journey with a boat race, and before everyone embarked bets were laid as to who would win. Normally Harry threw himself into such entertainments with great zeal. Any activity which involved betting and chance particularly appealed to him, but he seemed to be taking part only under sufferance today. Henrietta wondered if he were jealous of Eleanor and Blount now.

She refused to let it spoil her enjoyment of the race. Her barge with pennants flying swiftly took the lead but George's craft was only a short distance behind and was fast gaining ground, drums beating to keep the rows of oars skimming the water in time and at a particularly swift pace.

George, standing with one booted foot up on the prow, bright silk cape swinging from his shoulders making him look a bit like a peacock, gave a gallant salute as his boat overtook the queen's, then turned to continue his shouts of encouragement, urging his oarsmen on to greater efforts.

'Come on!' Henrietta urged her own. 'We can't let them win.'

With renewed endeavour her barge managed to draw level again.

People were lining the riverbank to watch, cheering on the oarsmen. Skinny-legged boys ran whooping along the towpath, trying to keep up or to outrun the boats. Henrietta's own children were jumping around with excitement and she had to warn them not to go too close to the side of the boat lest they fall in.

Other river craft were also caught up in the spectacle which made for a magnificent display. The court barges were by far the most beautiful vessels on the wide river. With their banners and decorative woodwork, their velvet seats and gilding, they were a sight to behold, as was every single one of their fashionably dressed occupants. For a stretch the two boats vied for lead position but Henrietta's barge finally pulled ahead decisively and came in first.

They passed beneath the stone watergate built by the Duke of Buckingham not long before he died. George Goring helped Henrietta to disembark, still laughing with the thrill of the chase.

'Did you think we'd beat them?' Henrietta asked Kate Villiers, who had been waiting on the river steps, watching the contest along with everyone else.

'I hoped you would, ma'am.'

'Well, Mr Goring did not hope for it,' Henrietta said, as that gentleman leaped on to the jetty from the rocking barge. 'Did you, George? Or was it your plan to impoverish yourself for my benefit?' She held out her hand to him, not palm down to be kissed but palm up, waiting for him to place something in it.

He gave a sweeping bow. 'It is an honour to lose to so gracious a queen,' he said silkily, jingling a pile of crowns into her open palm. 'But I must not make too much of a habit of it or you will have so much of my wife's dowry that you might as well have wed her yourself! Seems we had a traitor in our midst, however. Jermyn here was riding in our boat but he had all his money on Your Majesty to win.'

'Her Majesty knows I would stake my life on her,' Harry said, as he stepped easily ashore.

Henrietta tilted her head and flicked her black eyes flirtatiously sideways at him. 'And you bet on everything, Mr Jermyn, do you not?' She could not resist taunting him a little by invoking their shared secret memory of the morning when she had found him naked after gambling away all his clothes. She wanted to see what effect it had upon him.

He looked away.

Kate asked Henrietta if they could speak for a moment in private and she gladly turned her back on him. She linked arms with Buckingham's widow and drew her away from the rest of the noisy party as it made its way up through the garden.

Kate seemed preoccupied.

'Is something the matter?' Henrietta asked her.

'My niece Eleanor is pregnant.'

Henrietta's own pregnancy was now nearing five months. It was causing a constant sharp digging pain in her ribs and making her feel sick and tired. She put her hand to her side now as she walked up the sloping lawn. 'Does Blount know? And, more to the point, does the King? No, he can't possibly, or I'd have heard about it by now.'

Charles would be outraged, determined as he was that all at his court should set the highest moral standard. He would make allowances for Eleanor, though. Fortunate for her that she carried the cherished name of Villiers, which had always excused all misdemeanours. 'There will need to be a hasty marriage,' Henrietta said. 'But it will not be the first, nor the last.'

'She is blaming Henry Jermyn.'

'She's what?' Henrietta stood stock still and stared at the Duke of Buckingham's widow. 'How dare she? It is the Earl of Newport she's been cooing over these past weeks.'

'She's hidden her condition for some months. It is too advanced to convince Blount that the child is his.'

Henrietta looked around for Harry but could not see him. That was why he had been reluctant to come here today, why he had said he'd stake his life on Henrietta, on her loyalty and belief in him. Why he had been in no mood to jest or flirt.

'I offered him the sum of eight thousand pounds as a dowry for Eleanor,' Kate continued.

Henrietta resumed walking. 'That is a generous sum.' Vast, in fact.

'He refused it outright.'

'Did he?' For all his ambition and great love of gambling, Harry was clearly not at all driven by the promise of fast riches then.

'I have to tell you, the whole family is incensed by such an insult,' Kate went on resentfully.

Henrietta was still absorbing the fact that Harry and Eleanor had been lovers. That he had refused to wed her, even when bribed with a huge dowry and entry into one of the most powerful families in the kingdom. Did that mean the baby was definitely not his? That he did not love Eleanor? Had never loved her? Or just that Henrietta did not know him nearly as well as she thought she did. Was he merely a rogue, who would carelessly get a girl with child and abandon her? Never mind all this talk of chaste love . . . platonic love. It was all very fine, a beautiful concept, but one that was deeply flawed. It was beautiful only until such time as one of the platonic lovers took a non-platonic one. So much for a love which elevated and ennobled the soul! Until that moment Henrietta had not known jealousy could be hotter than anger, tearing through her, making her heart race and her insides twist and knot so that she felt sick to her stomach and her heart. She could hear Harry's voice somewhere in the garden and it made her want to weep and shout at the same time, but she could not bring herself to look for him.

She only half heard what Kate said next. 'It is because of the slight to our name that Eleanor's brother Lord Grandison challenged Jermyn to a duel.'

Kate had her full attention now. 'Mary, Mother of God!'

'Jermyn refused.'

Henrietta relaxed again, a little. 'Thank the Lord for that.'

The queen's party did not stay long at York House, just long enough for everyone to drink a cup of ale and admire the display in the state room. The late Duke of Buckingham had been as avid a collector of fine art as Charles and the walls were hung with beautiful Renaissance paintings. Henrietta barely looked at them. There was no race back to Whitehall, the boats returning at a much more leisurely pace as the sun started to sink, the colour of the river changing from gold to pewter and a chilly breeze blowing off the water, making everyone draw their cloaks tighter about them. Henrietta wished that Eleanor had come, so that she could judge for herself how much the girl's belly was showing.

Charles had been writing to her frequently from Scotland. He reported how he had entered Edinburgh in triumph with music and cheering, and been crowned with great ceremony. What he did not tell her was that he was so keen to be home with her that he had ordered coaches to be ready all along his route, enabling him to travel post. He covered the distance from Berwick to London in only four days.

'I wanted to surprise you,' he said tetchily, when he arrived at Whitehall much earlier than expected. 'Instead I am greeted by everyone tattling about this affront to the Villiers family. The prospect of a duel combined with this tawdry scandal could lower the whole moral tone of this court, you do realise?'

'But Harry Jermyn refused the challenge!'

'Nonetheless, I have arrested all three of them, Miss Villiers, Grandison and Jermyn. They have all been sent to the Tower.'

Henrietta had heard enough talk of scaffolds and executions, of the beheadings of adulterous queens and their adulterous loves, for the very name of that place to fill her with horror. 'The Tower?' she whispered, dry mouthed.

'The Tower,' Charles confirmed.

It was not as bad as Henrietta had feared.

The Tower might have looked a forbidding place and the sound of its mighty guns have been enough to instil terror in even the stoutest heart, but she soon learned from Harry's father that life inside the fortress could be quite comfortable.

'He has a suite of rooms that are well furnished, and the food is good enough. He is allowed to drink and to play cards with friends and to walk in the gardens.'

Harry's father was not as tall or powerfully built as his son, but otherwise, especially in his blue eyes, warm laughing smile and beautiful cultured voice, he had a definite look and sound of him. It was easy to imagine that Harry would grow to resemble him closely in future years, would be as handsome with silver hair as he was with gold. 'He's a survivor, my Harry, and he's not faring too badly,' his father insisted. 'His biggest problem is that he hates being away from all the action at court, and from you, ma'am.' He looked straight at the queen, unabashed. 'I expect it's pointless my telling you not to worry yourself about him. Just as it's pointless my telling him not to worry about you.'

'He's worried about me?'

'Need you ask? He thinks your household entirely incapable of running without him, for a start.'

'It is.'

'More than that, he hates not having had the chance to explain himself properly to you. I have helped him to write a reasoned account of his relationship with that girl, but the trouble is, by refusing to marry her, he is dishonouring the sacred name of Villiers and thereby the memory of the great duke.' He sighed. 'If only he'd dallied with a maid of any name but Villiers.'

If only he'd not dallied with any maid at all! The Villiers name had not saved Eleanor from being flung into the Tower. If Charles were any other man, Henrietta might have suspected he had other reasons for imprisoning Harry, that he would leap at this chance to punish and banish his wife's favourite. It was surely a factor in his decision. But she knew her husband had acted less out of vindictiveness or jealousy and more from principle, disapproving as strongly as he did of fornication and duelling.

'You are aware that His Majesty has sent my son an ultimatum?'

'What ultimatum?'

'Wed the girl. Or be forced into exile.'

The two words battled inside Henrietta's head like the clash of sabres. Wed. Exile. Both options were intolerable to her. 'That is unwarranted,' she said, trying to remain calm. To think.

She marched straight to the Privy Council Chamber, the large, first-floor tapestry-hung room on the south side of the Great Court. A place she had never before entered and where her presence was not expected. She did not care. They were all seated round the polished oak table, the Earls of Arundel and Northumberland and Pembroke and a host of others, all in their cloaks emblazoned with the silver garter star. They sprang to their feet, chair legs scraping on the stone floor, as the queen swept in. All of them bowed. They'd barely had a chance to stand upright again before she launched her attack on the king. 'Your Majesty has threatened Henry Jermyn with exile?'

'I have.'

Charles at once came to her and took her arm, guided her out of the room and shut the door behind them.

'You know very well that he cannot marry a girl he has publicly disowned,' Henrietta said hotly. 'The scandal would ruin him . . . destroy all his chances of advancement.' Her own advancing pregnancy had made her short of breath, fury more so, but neither state prevented her from speaking at her usual rapid rate, and at some volume too. At the back of her mind she was thinking how proud Harry would be of her, that she possessed the words to argue his case so eloquently in English. 'You've forced him into an impossible position. His only honourable option is to proclaim his innocence by accepting banishment.'

'That is precisely what he said to me when he boarded a French merchant ship yesterday. If I didn't know it was impossible, I'd swear the pair of you had been colluding.'

For a second it was as if Henrietta's heart had stopped beating. She rested one hand against the wall to support herself, the other on her swollen belly. Charles grabbed a chair. 'Sit down,' he told her. 'For the baby.'

She sat, only because her legs gave way beneath her. 'He has already left England?'

'He is long gone from these shores by now,' Charles had softened his tone but done nothing to dispel the harshness of the words.

'How long must he be gone?'

'It is to be permanent exile. He's gone for good.'

Even though Henrietta was sitting down, she felt as if she might somehow collapse, slide off the chair and crumple in a heap. She gripped the sides of the chair, digging her fingertips into the hardened unyielding oak as if obliged to hold on to something solid. She stared at her husband for a moment and then she made herself stand again. Without a word, she turned and walked away. She heard him go back to his councillors then picked up her skirts and ran, fast, despite her condition, all the way to her chamber. Her belly was too large for her to throw herself face down on the bed as she wanted to. Instead she went to the window, flung it open, pressed both hands on the sill as she leaned out and gulped fresh air into her lungs.

She watched the river slide past, knowing it was the same river that was carrying Harry out to sea, and then she had a wild urge to throw herself into it. She had once toyed with the idea of sending him away from her, but now that he had really and truly gone she knew it was the very last thing she wanted. How could she bear it? They'd not even had the chance to say goodbye.

At least he could return to Paris. She tried to take heart from that. He loved Paris, had many friends in her brother's court. She could picture him there very easily. And it wouldn't be forever. No matter what Charles said, it would not. She would find a way to bring him back. They had houses to build, dreams to dream. She could not be without him.

Eleanor Villiers and Henrietta were due to go into labour within weeks of one another. Harry's father generously paid for a midwife to assist with the birth of Eleanor's baby while Henrietta retired once again to St James's Palace, with Madame Peronne, to await her own confinement. With nothng else to do all day but lie in bed in the darkened chamber and gossip and read and study her prayer book, her thoughts turned constantly to Harry in Paris. She wondered if he thought of her as often as she thought of him. It seemed unlikely. And then her mind began to torment her. She tortured herself with thoughts of all the French girls he might meet at court and elsewhere, beautiful, brazen French women who would be as charmed by him as most women were, who would want him for themselves and know exactly how to go about getting him and what to do with him when they had him.

Eleanor Villiers gave birth to a little girl and Henrietta was delivered of a third baby boy, on Monday, 14 October.

'A good lusty child, God be thanked,' Madame Peronne gave praise. 'Very fair and blooming.'

Like Henrietta's other babies, he was christened by William Laud who had recently been made Archbishop of Canterbury. The child was named James in honour of his grandfather, the late King of England and Scotland, and as next in line to the throne after his brother, he'd also be groomed for marine service. So along with becoming Duke of York, he was also designated Lord High Admiral.

'Such a grand set of titles for such a tiny boy,' Henrietta murmured, watching James, swaddled tight in his beribboned oak crib, sleeping the deep and peaceful sleep of newborn babies, oblivious to all the responsibilities that lay ahead of him. All the love and the heartache that adult life entailed.

# 1634

In May, Prince Charles's birthday was celebrated with a full day of bull- and bear-baiting. After he'd woken and dressed and eaten coddled eggs, the prince was taken to sit beside his mother and her companions in the raised spectators' seats which ringed the Whitehall bear pit. He had remained so remarkably tall for his age that it gave rise to an amusing incident when the Dutch Ambassador came to pay his respects before the baiting began, and bowed to Henrietta's dwarf, Geoffrey Hudson, mistaking him for the young prince. Everyone burst out laughing, Geoffrey and Prince Charles both finding it especially hilarious. The red-faced ambassador struggled to cover up his mistake by swivelling on his heel towards the prince, while still bent over in a bow, which only made everyone laugh all the more.

To Henrietta, however, the merriment sounded hollow. She missed hearing Harry's merry laughter above the rest. She knew for sure that he would have marked the date of the prince's birthday and would be sad to be missing it while so far away. For her own part, she would have far preferred to celebrate the anniversary with a theatrical performance or tournament, some activity with a little more elegance and chivalry to it. Unlike this barbaric sport which males of all ages seemed to relish. Some females too.

A high fence separated the spectators from the bear-baiting arena but the great brown bear with its leering pink eyes seemed alarmingly close, tethered as it was to a stick driven into the ground close to the perimeter. Henrietta put her arm protectively around her son's shoulders as the mastiffs were set loose. There was much fierce growling and snarling on both sides, and Princess Mary put her hands over her ears.

Prince Charles did not seem at all afraid of the vicious noise and the tugging, scratching and biting that made skin and blood and slaver splatter and fly. He did flinch though as the dog, having waited for its advantage, sank its fangs deep into the bear's throat. The bear gave a mighty roar of rage and pain, shaking its huge head to free itself, and the dog was tossed and tussled but did not let go until the bear lifted a great paw and clawed its scalp open, to gasps and cheer and applause from the spectators. A fresh dog was unleashed and the gruesome spectacle was repeated, until the bloodied bear was in turn replaced by a bull.

Henrietta was very glad when it was all over.

A few days later she went with Charles to Newmarket for the racing, a sport he relished and which Henrietta had grown to love too. Like golf it had been imported from Scotland. It was Charles's father King James who had seen how the flat plains of Suffolk and the spring turf of Newmarket Heath in particular were perfect for galloping horses, and he had built a grandstand there as well as a palace in the market town. Betting on which horses might win for their owners the silver bell or a hundred-pound prize gave an added thrill to watching the animals come thundering down the course.

If Henrietta had been able to write to Harry in Paris she would have told him how much she had hated the bear-baiting and loved the racing – the gambling as well. She'd have told him also that Mitte had died in her sleep one night and Prince Charles was begging her for a new spaniel pup which he wanted to call Mitte too. She wanted to tell him all these things. The small details of her day and the greatest secrets of her heart. She wrote such long letters to him in her head but set none down on paper, and even if she'd written them she would never have sent them. She could not write to him. There was too much left unsaid between them that could not be expressed in a letter. She needed to see his face. How she needed to see his face. As she watched the horses thundering down the track and saw the one she'd gambled on coming second, Henrietta smiled to herself sadly. Maybe it was because Harry was such a tall man that he left behind such a large void in her life. A void which nothing and nobody else seemed able to fill.

When Charles asked her in bed that night why she was unhappy, she could not hold back her tears. 'You have robbed me of my friend,' she said. 'Again. You sent all my French friends away and the only friend I had then was Harry. And now you have sent him away too. He is my friend, just as George Villiers was yours. And you have taken him from me, just as Felton took the duke from you. Why did you have to do that?'

'He is a scoundrel.'

'Maybe. I don't believe so. But in any case, so was the Duke of Buckingham. Did that make you love him less?'

'No.'

'No. Well, then.'


First stop on the summer progress was Windsor Castle, where Charles, the children and Henrietta were to have their portraits painted by the Dutch painter, Mr Van Dyck. The same age as Charles and no taller, with a debonair moustache and head of flowing auburn curls, the artist had recently come to England and was much in demand as a portrait painter.

For the sitting, Henrietta chose a gown of rich amber brocade with full lace ruffles and a little cape finished with a purple band, to match Charles's regal suit of purple velvet slashed with white satin. They were to pose seated on chairs of state, with their two crowns placed nearby on a small oval table. Prince Charles insisted on trying on both of these. Despite his size and strength they were far too big and heavy for him and Henrietta had to hold them on his dark curly head while balancing baby James in her other arm.

'I like wearing crowns,' her eldest son decided.

'Just as well, since you are a prince who is destined to be come a king.'

He picked up the king's crown again, which was considerably more ornate than the queen's. 'Will this be mine?'

'One day.'

'When I am dead,' the present king said, 'which I trust to God will not be for a good while yet, since there is much I still wish to achieve. Your grandfather unified the crowns of England, Scotland and Ireland but did not live to see unity of law, politics and religion. It is our duty to see that achieved. We must bring together those countries as one empire. Now, come and stand here.'

Prince Charles rested his hand on his father's knobbly knee but began fidgeting after about two minutes, clearly possessing all the patience of his mother.

'You must keep very still, darling, so that Mr Van Dyck can sketch you properly,' Henrietta instructed. Impatient though she was, she did not mind sitting still to have her portrait painted. Some would say that was because she was even more vain than she was impatient! They may have been right. But Mr Van Dyck was an entertaining companion whose topics of conversation had ranged just this morning from the mysteries of finding the philosopher's stone to the colourful lives of the great masters.

He was so short that when at work with his brush he disappeared completely behind his easel. It looked as if the canvas itself was talking, which gave Prince Charles endless amusement. Henrietta was pleased that although her eldest son had not been a smiley baby, he had grown into a happy, if still serious, little boy and was developing a great sense of humour. So much so that when, after a few sittings, Mr Van Dyck told them that they might see what he had done so far, it was Prince Charles's turn to complain that his mother looked too solemn.

Van Dyck stood back, still with brush and palette in hand, to let the royal family admire the painting. It was half finished, their faces complete but bodies still mere outlines to be filled in later. Already, though, it was possible to see how he had given the king a poise and elegance and majesty not captured in his previous portraits, while Henrietta appeared mysterious, remotely beautiful.

'This is excellent,' Charles pronounced.

'I am pleased it meets with Your Majesty's approval,' Van Dyck replied. He appeared to study the top of the real Henrietta's head, dabbed his brush in a spot of black oil paint and touched up one of the tiny curls which coiled on to her likeness's forehead and framed her delicate face.

Prince Charles too looked from his mother's beautiful real face to the one on the canvas. 'You look so sad, ma'am,' he remarked.

She smiled. 'It does not do to grin in one's portrait!'

'Perhaps it will cheer you to know that I have permitted Harry Jermyn to leave Paris and come to Jersey,' the older Charles said.

She glanced at him. 'Jersey?' Absurd, the rush of joy she experienced just from knowing he was a few miles nearer.

Having grown bored with the painting, Prince Charles was lured back to inspect the crowns once more.

'Jermyn's father is absentee governor of the island. I did suggest that

Jermyn himself should become lieutenant governor, but was told in no uncertain terms that the islanders do not want a young philanderer in charge of them. For which I can hardly blame them. So I have instead put him in charge of overseeing the destruction of the island's tobacco crop, which is undermining the new plantations in America.'

He would be kept busy with that task at least, but it didn't sound a very interesting one, nor Jersey a very interesting place for someone as sociable and ambitious as Harry. He liked to be at the centre of things and Jersey was in the middle of nowhere, except the sea. Henrietta expected he'd have been far happier to remain in Paris. He would be terribly bored, marooned on an island with a negligible population. Still, it was halfway home. And his move there gave her new hope that he'd be allowed to come the rest of the way. Soon.

She touched Charles's hand in thanks.

# 1635

On a snowy afternoon at the beginning of January, in the silk-panelled closet at Whitehall, Mall Villiers, who had now reached the great age of thirteen, was married to Charles, Lord Herbert, the Earl of Pembroke's son. The closet was still decorated with Christmas greenery and shimmering with candlelight. Mall's pretty auburn hair was dressed with evergreens, rosemary and white myrtle, and her champagne satin gown was decorated with scarlet taffeta and ribbons. Lord Herbert, boyish-faced, gangly and blond, was wearing matching champagne velvet and scarlet. Besides Eleanor, all the members of the extensive and illustrious Villiers family were assembled, and the gathering also included Mall's new relations, the Countess of Pembroke and the Earl of Pembroke of course, as well as the Earl and Countess of Caernarfon, all in their wedding finery.

Mall looked so very young, but then Henrietta had been only a few months older on her own wedding day, when she had become not merely a wife but a queen. She remembered so vividly the nervousness and expectation and dreams that had preceded that occasion. More vividly still did she remember the months of disappointment and misery which had followed, thanks largely to Mall's murdered father.

Henrietta still caught herself wondering if Charles loved her as much as he had loved the Duke of Buckingham. Or if she were merely a substitute, second best. Sometimes it was hard not to think that was all she was. That had the duke not been killed, nothing would have changed for her. Charles was so proud to stand in for him today, to give Mall away in his friend's absence, and it was in the duke's honour that a sumptuous wedding banquet was to be served on the king's command, to which the highest-ranking nobles in court were invited.

To further mark the occasion, William Davenant had composed a commemorative verse. But Mall and her new husband were not the only ones to whom William had dedicated a work, as he explained to Henrietta when they were waiting for the coaches and horses to be brought round to take them all to York House for the feasting. It had started to snow, and Mall, full of excitement, had insisted that everyone go outside into the courtyard in order to watch the soft white flakes drifting down from the laden sky, to dust ermine-trimmed cloaks and ringlets and feathered hats.

'I have also composed a poem for Your Majesty's favourite,' William said to Henrietta. 'It is entitled, "To Henry Jermyn". Perhaps Your Majesty would like to be the first to read it?'

Henrietta watched a snowflake land and melt on the end of William's ruined nose. She shook her head. 'Mr Jermyn should have first sight of it,' she said. 'If it's actually about him. Is it?'

'Very much so. Since it is intended to inspire statesmen with decency and dignity.' William recited a few lines criticising leaders who sought power only out of arrogance, and compared them with someone named Arigo.

'Arigo?'

'A pet name Jermyn acquired in his boyhood, ma'am, did you not know?'

She didn't. She had talked to Harry about so much, had shared so much with him, that she had thought she knew all there was to know about him. It gave her an odd sense of loss to learn that this childhood name of his should have escaped her, that he should have told William about it but not her. She had the sense that he might have kept it from her on purpose and there might be more that she did not know, more of himself that he had purposely withheld.

What William said next seemed to confirm that, in a way.

'On first sight it's easy to see him as just another jovial fellow who enjoys a drink and a game of cards and the company of pretty ladies.' There was an edge to the poet's voice that Henrietta had never heard before and didn't understand. 'A loud and arrogant fop who laughs at bawdy jokes and is quick to end every argument with a brawl or a duel. But that is not what I see.'

'Nor I, sir.' That said, she knew very well that if Harry had been there now, he'd have been laughing loudly in the snow with Mall's illustrious new relations, the Earls of Pembroke and Caernarfon. 'Well, only some of the time.' She smiled.

'He is a man of great depth of character.' William's tone had turned almost defensive, as if he thought she might disagree with him. 'He is a consummate courtier and a shrewd politician, and might not have the showy wit of the likes of Goring but has a way with people nevertheless. All who meet him love and trust him. He is fiercely loyal and, despite appearances to the contrary recently, entirely honourable.'

What was William trying to do exactly? Make her love and miss Harry more than she already did? Henrietta saw these admirable qualities he spoke of all too clearly, had always seen them. She was glad to know she was not the only one. 'You are a good friend to him, William. And therefore a good friend to me. But I, of all people, do not need convincing of his worth.'

'I believe he has the potential to achieve true greatness, to secure his place in history even.' William grinned. 'Now if I were a poet . . .'

'You *are* a poet, sir.'

'If I were a poet, I would say this of Harry Jermyn: that he has a soul composed of the eagle and the dove.'

Henrietta let the words settle in her head like the snow drifting down on the cobbles all around them. 'William, I think that is the most perfect description of him.' The dove, symbol of purity and of peace. The eagle, representing great power, dignity and grace. By joining these two symbols William had pinpointed the contrasts in Harry's character and nature that Henrietta had always seen and been fascinated by and drawn to, but had never really identified before. His gentleness and strength. His tranquillity and hot temper. His ready humour and considered judgement. The loud and the quiet, the dark and the light. 'You are not only a poet, William. You are a great poet,' she told him.

'And Harry Jermyn is my great patron.'

That was something else she hadn't known. Some months ago Harry's father had been appointed comptroller of the royal household, a post which entailed checking the accounts of the clerks responsible for buying provisions. He'd performed so well that shortly afterwards Henrietta had promoted him to become her vice chamberlain. She'd also secured for Harry's quieter elder brother the role of gentleman of the king's privy chamber, a highly privileged position that involved his keeping Charles company and helping him to dress. Before being banished, Harry himself had held a succession of sinecures and, together with the grants of land such as his holdings in the St James's area, these had provided him with the huge income of four thousand pounds a year. Such gifts had been Henrietta's only real way of thanking him and letting him know how much she appreciated him. But she wasn't aware until now of how he had shared his good fortune and put it to good use by patronising poets.

Not only had William Davenant entitled his poem 'To Henry Jermyn', but soon after he dedicated a whole play to him too, with those same words. 'To Henry Jermyn'.

This new drama was entitled *The Platonic Lovers* and Henrietta turned its pages at first with keenness and then with mounting consternation. Not only was it openly dedicated to Harry but, to Henrietta at any rate, the main protagonists seemed to be only thinly disguised versions of Harry and herself. Though William had once promoted and supported the ideal of platonic love, now he seemed to question that ideal and challenge it anew with every word he had written. Characters made reference to 'a sad servant', to 'an odd kind of lover'. Most damning of all was the line: 'He comes to my lady's chamber at all hours. Opportunity is a dangerous thing.'

'What do you mean by writing this, sir?' Henrietta asked, brandishing the script at him. She ordered him to step into her private closet and closed the door so that she could discuss it with him in private. 'Just what are you implying?'

'I imply nothing, ma'am. It is a work of the imagination . . . pure theatre.'

'I know you are Harry's true friend,' she said. 'And thought you approved of what we . . . of platonic love. It's largely because of you and your writing that it's become such a craze here at court and is becoming increasingly fashionable further afield, I understand. I believe that the gardener and diarist Mr Evelyn also has a platonic lover?'

'I believe he does. But just because a thing is fashionable does not necessarily mean it is admirable.'

For a moment she did not know what to say. 'You no longer believe it is possible for a man and a woman to be no more than the closest and dearest of friends?'

'Do you, ma'am? Honestly?'

She did not answer.

'When he returns to court, as soon he surely must, I expect all will continue as before. He will be in your company from morning until night. He will sit and talk with you in your privy chamber, and walk with you in the gardens and in the park. He adores you and you adore him. It is perfectly understandable. Your Majesty is a beautiful young woman and he is a young, red-blooded man. I don't know how a man can survive such a regime of non-physical love.'

Or a woman?

What Henrietta could not bring herself to ask, because in truth she did not want to know, was if William had drawn this conclusion merely from his own instincts and observations, or whether Harry had confided in him, corresponded perhaps from Paris or Jersey. She dropped the script on to her writing desk. 'So, you have changed your mind entirely?'

'No. But as a writer my role is to explore and to question, from all perspectives. And in doing so I have come to see what I should have understood long ago.'

'And what is that, sir?'

He seemed reluctant to answer.

'Speak your mind.'

'That there is no love as intense as a love that is unconsummated.'

In the following weeks, Henrietta thought much about what William had said. The plot of the Shrove Tuesday masque centred on evil magicians who strove to control human nature through the elements of earth, air, fire and water, corrupting the bodies of men and women with sensuality and lust . . . until the magicians were defeated, nature and the elements tamed, and a Temple of Chaste Love established on the island of Britain. The scenery was a seascape with a lagoon ingeniously filled with real water and fringed with vegetation, across which Henrietta glided in a chariot decorated with seaweed and coral, shells and pearls. Dressed in blue silk and tulle, she represented a water nymph. Accompanied by a baritone and soprano, she did battle with the elements, and with fire spirits cloaked in red satin.

But it felt to her as if she had been cast in entirely the wrong role.

*She* was the fire spirit. There was fire in her soul and in her heart, and since she had arrived in the English court, where that was neither accepted nor understood, she had been trying to quench the flames within her. She had been doing battle with her own nature. She had been trying to contain or put out the fire that burned inside her, the fire that Harry had lit and that still burned for him, and only for him. A fire that her feelings for Charles could never match.

Her request to visit the northern parts of England resulted in both her household and the king's journeying in June to the rugged and starkly beautiful county of Derbyshire as guests of William Cavendish, Earl of Newcastle, a man with such a passion for building that he had constructed a little castle for himself at Bolsover. It stood perched on the edge of a dramatic escarpment, tiny and toy-like, its ornate stone battlements creating an almost fantastical silhouette against the lowering sky. It was a scene such as Inigo Jones might have designed as the backdrop for another masque, with exaggerated arrow-slits and balustrades topped with gleaming golden orbs. To pass under the gateway into the courtyard was to be transported to another world, another time. To the imaginary, medieval world of courtly love and troubadour romances.

Only not quite. For the Earl's version of the age of chivalry which he had set out to recreate at Bolsover was very different from the one Henrietta had envisaged and read about. As she was taken on a tour of the sumptuously decorated castle, it was revealed to be not truly a fortified refuge at all but a pleasure palace. Candlelight flickered across heavily gilded walnut panelling, winged white horses galloped and flew across ceilings, and the air was heavy with the exotic scent of burning orange water. Rooms of black-and-white marble were hung with crimson silk and paintings of naked women and gods. The garden had for its centrepiece an elaborate fountain, a white marble statue of a voluptuous bathing Venus emerging from a basin surrounded by horned satyrs, griffins riding on the wings of swans, boys squirting water from their stone penises, and bizarre dragon-like creatures with enlarged genitals.

Charles pronounced it obscene. Henrietta thought it all utterly magnificent. But since there was nothing chaste or platonic about any of it, it made her wonder. She was the daughter of King Henri le Grand, a descendant of the Medici. Perhaps the Earl of Newcastle's version of love was more suited to her true nature than platonic love would ever be.

\* \* \*

For weeks Charles had talked of little else but the nine ceiling canvases for the Banqueting House which he had commissioned from Peter Paul Rubens. The interior of the building was being prepared in advance of their arrival, nearly a thousand pounds having been spent on new white paint and gilding. If the paintings were half as beautiful as the friezes Rubens had completed for her mother in the Luxembourg Palace, Henrietta was sure they would be the talk of London.

Charles did not let her see the ceiling canvases until they were properly mounted. Only then did he take her by the hand and lead her into the magnificent white-and-gold space. And only when she had taken the seat of state upon the royal dais did he instruct her to look up.

What Henrietta saw made her catch her breath.

The central square panel, directly above her head, depicted King James as a wispy-bearded, fiery-eyed King Solomon, seated on a baroque throne in a temple, surrounded by rich drapery and foliage. He was flanked by two naked women gazing up at him, between them a baby. The images that surrounded it were no less extraordinary and powerful. Mesmerised, Henrietta pushed herself up from the throne, wandering slowly around the hall, face tilted upwards, as if in a trace. Above her was King James being crowned with the victor's laurel, attended by winged figures. The God of War. Wild beasts. Swirling deities.

She did not know quite what to say or how to respond. She had not been prepared for this. She had expected the paintings to depict her husband and his reign just as the paintings Rubens had done for her mother celebrated her life. Instead, the Banqueting House had been turned into a mausoleum to Charles's dead father. The images were a glorification of his reign. It was as a revelation to Henrietta. She saw suddenly all that Charles was striving to achieve, all that he had to live up to, all that he expected of himself. She'd had some sense of it when he'd read to her from the book he kept by his bedside, his father's instructions on kingship, but only now, as he literally stood beneath these majestic, myth-making images of King James, did she understand the degree to which Charles lived not so much in his dead brother's shadow as in his father's.

Henrietta ended up back where she had started on the dais, with Charles beside her. 'These are the personifications of England and Scotland,' he said of the naked women above them. 'The infant represents the birth of Great Britain.'

'Or you,' Henrietta said, only now lowering her eyes to meet his. 'Your father's heir. Heir to a unified throne.' She reached for his hand. They were so alike, she and he. Apart from their both being born royal and small and loving art, she'd never understood before how very much they had in common. Had seen only the differences between them. His formality and seriousness and Englishness. Her passion and impatience and humour. But they were both striving to fulfil the ambitious dreams of powerful parents. King James's dream had been to unify England and Scotland. Marie de' Medici's to rejoin England and Rome. It was left to their children, to Charles and Henrietta, to make those dreams reality, to change the world and the course of history.

But given the Scots' vehement hatred of Papists, did their two dreams run completely contrary to one another? Might they be absolutely opposed?

'I have granted Jermyn permission to return to England,' Charles said, breaking her train of thought. 'He will arrive sometime next week, I believe.'

Henrietta had dismissed everyone else and Harry was standing before her in her privy chamber.

It was if he had never been away, and at the same time as if he had been away forever. Everything about him was achingly familiar and yet it was as thrilling as a chance encounter with a handsome stranger. He had lost a little weight, which suited him, made him appear even taller and more elegant. From the way he stood and held himself, she could see that his extended stay in Paris had given him extra confidence and polish. His boots were of the finest leather, his black silk suit and lace-trimmed shirt were of the most exquisite cloth and cut, yet his skin was lightly tanned like a country boy's from working outdoors in Jersey. It was a devastatingly attractive combination.

She remembered what William had said about the intensity of unconsummated desire. When she held out her hand for Harry to kiss, it trembled. When he took it and bowed to her, she caught the unfamiliar aroma of tobacco on his clothes and in his hair, glamorous and exotic.

He waited for her to sit then sat down himself, with one long black silk-clad leg slung casually over the other, looking at her and waiting for her to say something. She had so missed talking to him, had so longed to talk to him. There had been so much she wanted to say to him, so much she wanted to tell him. So many questions she wanted to ask. But now he was here none of it seemed to matter. She could not find the words, was more dumbstruck than the first time they'd met.

She watched him take out a clay pipe, fill it with crumbly brown tobacco, pressing it down with his long fingers. He lit it, wreathing himself in a mysterious, fine cloud of smoke.

'I thought your task was to eradicate Jersey tobacco by uprooting it, not smoking it.' She smiled.

'Spoils of war.' He smiled back. 'Everyone who works with it smokes it. Besides, there is nothing much else to do in Jersey.'

'You missed Paris?'

'I missed London more.' He put the pipe to his mouth, inhaled. She watched his lips press around the stem, suck on it gently. 'Your family send you their affection and best regards,' he said. 'They were all well, when I left.'

'I am glad. You look well yourself.'

'As do you, ma'am.'

His eyes seemed to tell her she looked not merely well, but beautiful.

'Thank you,' she said, with a fluttering sensation in her belly. 'I am well.' Now, she might have added. Now that you are here.

'I trust the children are all thriving. The Prince of Wales and Duke of York and the Princess Mary?'

It gave her a strange quiet joy just to hear him say her children's names. 'They are.'

'So tell me, what's been happening while I've been away?'

She gave a short laugh. 'You surely don't expect me to believe you don't already know full well? Your web of spies and contacts must have kept you informed of all the goings on. I expect you probably know more about what's been happening here than I do myself. Or the king for that matter.'

'I have been eager for news,' he admitted. 'All I have really heard lately is that this new kind of love called platonic holds much sway here now.'

She turned aside to the sunlit window, presenting him for a moment with her delicate profile, framed by a mass of tight black curls. She touched the strand of pearls at her throat. 'You know what courts are like. There must always be one craze or another and everyone follows everyone else.'

'Quite so.' There was a moment's silence. 'I did not love Eleanor Villiers,' he said quietly. 'Not platonically or otherwise. That is why I could not marry her. She knew that. She realised that though I gave her my body, I could never give her my heart.'

'Why not?'

'Because, ma'am, I have already given it to another lady and she has not yet given it back. I trust she never will.'

Henrietta was silent for a moment, taking that in. 'I thought you no longer cared for me,' she said. 'When Buckingham died and the king . . . reclaimed me, you became so . . . so proper! You would not even flirt with me. You did not seem to like it when I flirted with you.'

'Because it tortured me,' he said. 'It is a torture, wanting what you cannot have.'

'But I cannot . . .'

'I know you cannot. It doesn't matter. I had much time to reflect during my exile. Too much perhaps. But let me ask you something – what is the purpose of love? What is it for?'

She frowned and, not quite understanding the question, repeated it. 'What is it for?'

'To be given away,' he replied. 'And, as with anything, we should not give simply in order to receive. We should not love in order to be loved. We must love simply to love.'

'What are you saying?'

'This. I liked Eleanor well enough. There are plenty of other pretty girls I like well enough. But I will not settle merely for someone I can live with, when I have found someone I cannot live without. I am willing to remain a bachelor all my life, so that I may devote myself to your service.'

'No. I cannot let you make that sacrifice.'

He sank back in his chair, inhaled from his pipe and looked at her through the smoke. 'It is no sacrifice. It is not even a choice. I make it sound as if I have a choice when in reality there is no choice to be made. I fool myself that I can leave court and never see you again. I cannot. From the minute I met you, my love for you has directed my life, every decision and action I make. It gives it meaning and purpose and clarity. Without you, without the promise of seeing you and serving you and loving you, everything is pointless. I have no reason to rise from my bed in the morning. I have no reason to live.'

# 1636

S pring was marked by two deaths. Lucy's estranged husband, James Hay, Earl of Carlisle, who had fallen out of favour with his wife as well as with the court, passed away quietly and was grieved for just as quietly. Mall's young husband, Lord Herbert, died in Florence of smallpox while he was on the Grand Tour. He was just sixteen. In honour of the great esteem in which the king still held Mall's father, he cancelled all entertainments and put the whole court into deep mourning.

Death was in the air. Plague was rife in London, forcing the court to leave early. It did not stop at Greenwich Palace where the contagion had already taken hold but went first to Hampton Court, from where the queen journeyed on to Oatlands while Charles went to hunt in Salisbury.

They met again in Oxford. Two miles outside the city the royal train was received by Archbishop Laud, as chancellor of the university, leading a procession of doctors, masters and citizens. They proceeded to St Johns. The college had been rebuilt with colonnades and classical pillars in greenish marble from a local quarry, and over the new gatetowers presided bronze figures of the king and queen. Everyone alighted in order to admire them properly. At six foot high, they were significantly taller than life-size.

'I always wanted to be taller and . . . *voilà*. Now I am,' Henrietta said to Harry as they looked up at them. 'I am as tall as you.'

'Not quite,' he teased.

She had not spent much time with him since his return from Jersey. He seemed always to be busy, drinking or playing tennis, not with William Davenant and his regular friends in her circle but with the king's privy councillors mostly. After his extraordinary declaration he had retreated once more into propriety, so that she wondered if it had been just a lapse, a moment of weakness stirred up by the emotion of their reunion; if he had not really meant what he had said or else had changed his mind. At any rate, it was as if he were avoiding her now, keeping his distance, holding her at arms' length. She hated it, felt that she was always striving to get his attention.

And maybe William's poem about what a great statesmen he was destined to become had gone straight to his handsome, curly head. 'You seem to have grown very popular and influential,' she chided him as they made their way to Christ Church for a banquet.

'Ah, there you are wrong, ma'am' he said. 'It is Your Majesty who wields all the influence.'

'The king is not in the habit of talking politics with me. Everyone consistently overestimates my ability to sway him.' She was not really interested in affairs of state in any case, unless one of her friends was involved.

'Still,' Harry said, 'if Your Majesty can be convinced that action needs to be taken, then you can persuade His Majesty to take it. Courtiers and councillors wishing for a small favour or a major change in policy know that the real person they need to win over is you. Some even say that you are the man in your marriage.'

Henrietta laughed at the very idea but was secretly rather pleased she gave that impression. 'Do they really?'

'They really do. But since etiquette prevents all and sundry from clamouring for your attention, the shrewdest have learned that the best way to engage Your Majesty is to share a flagon of wine or a game of tennis with me. Once I have been persuaded, I can persuade you, and you in turn can persuade the king.'

'Hah! So now I know!'

'So now you know!'

As the court sat down to a banquet of venison, fish, poultry and ham, melons and grapes, Henrietta watched Harry in conversation with the Earls of Pembroke and Northumberland and realised then that William's poem had not gone to his head at all. William had made an observation, not a prediction. Harry was already a great statesman.

The papal envoy, Monsignor George Con, landed at Rye in July. He was Scottish, good-looking and affable, and had come laden with gifts from the Pope which he distributed at a ceremony in the Banqueting House, beneath the newly installed ceiling paintings. He presented Henrietta first with the most beautiful rosary beads of agate and buffalo horn, and with a miniature portrait of St Catherine.

She thanked him, saying, 'I shall have the portrait fastened to the curtains of my bed where I can look upon it when I'm saying my prayers before I go to sleep.'

He also gave her a beautiful diamond-studded crucifix, with the stones arranged in the form of bees. 'The badge of the Barberini family. The Holy Father's kin.'

She fastened the cross around her throat and showed it to Charles who examined it very carefully, letting it rest in the palm of his hand. 'Such a fine and generous gift,' he exclaimed. 'I shall have to change the opinion I have hitherto held of the priests of Rome.'

It was not so much the ambiguity of the comment as the way he delivered it that sent stifled exclamations all around the hall.

'His Majesty hardly ever jests and was definitely not jesting about my gift,' Henrietta said to Harry the next day, during one of their regular walks in the park at Richmond. 'He was entirely sincere. Did you notice?'

'Everyone noticed, ma'am. And read a far deeper significance into his avowal about changing his opinion of priests.'

It being a warm and sunny summer day, they were accompanied by the Prince of Wales, Princess Mary in a little white pinafore, and and Prince James in a crisp white lace bonnet. The children were in turn accompanied by a large gaggle of nurses and governesses, plus the Countess of Dorset and the Countess of Roxburghe, who had charge of Mary and James. In the middle of the park there stood an enormous oak tree and Prince Charles and Mary loved to clamber and scramble among its huge twisted boughs. They had a rickety wooden ladder leading up to an arbour seat at the top where they played, joyous and carefree, their laughter drifting down from the leafy treetop.

'So, tell me,' Henrietta asked Harry, referring back to the conversation they'd had in Oxford, 'what is everyone currently so keen to persuade you, me, and the king to do?'

Harry broke off from craning his neck to watch Prince Charles rather perilously yet regally perched upon a high branch. Charles had taken to wearing a tambourine on his head, like a mock crown. 'To recall Parliament.'

'Well, that's not going to work, is it? I'll never be convinced of the need for Parliament, and even if I were, I'd never manage to convince my husband.'

She had expected Harry to agree with her. He did not.

Henrietta's eyes widened. 'Oh, don't say . . . surely they've not persuaded you, have they?'

In that disarmingly astute way of his, Harry answered a difficult question with a more pertinent one. 'Where is His Majesty now?'

'You know full well. He has gone to Deptford to inspect the ships he is having repaired and refitted.' It was part of an ambitious programme of naval expansion to ensure there were enough well-armed vessels to safeguard the coasts of Britain and Ireland.

Harry stepped forward in time to grasp Prince Charles under his arms and swing him down from the tree. 'Allow me, Your Highness.' And then to Henrietta in the same light tone: 'And how is this refitting being funded?'

'That you also know full well. Ship money.' Harry had taken great pains to explain the confusing tax to her the previous autumn, when writs demanding payment of it had been issued to all maritime counties. Charles had once tried to make her understand its significance. For some reason, Harry had believed it vital that she did. 'Such levies have not been collected since the days of Queen Elizabeth,' he said now, moving back to the tree again to help Mary down this time, swinging her wide as if he were dancing a country dance with her, so that her skirts flew out, making her giggle. How well Henrietta remembered country dances with Harry among the peasants on the grass at Wellingborough. And what had followed.

'People are complaining that only Parliament has the right to impose them,' Harry continued.

Concentrate, Henrietta chided herself. Taxes. They were talking again about damned taxes.

'They are refusing to pay, and by refusing are exerting pressure for the recall of Parliament.'

'They'll all pay in the end, of course they will, if their king and country need it.' Henrietta threw up her hands in exasperation, losing all patience with the lot of them. 'Oh, for sweet Mary's sake! Just tell everyone to stop complaining and do as they are told.' She linked her arm through his. 'The children need to go back to the nursery for their dinner. Come with me to Greenwich.'

The queen's new house there was nearing completion and she had recently appointed Harry to the lucrative position of keeper of Greenwich Park. Besides which, it was an excuse to have him all to herself for the whole afternoon.

'Your Majesty does realise there are grumblings about this house too?' he said as they walked up from the river steps at Greenwich towards the gleaming white house with its perfectly straight walls, clean corners and elegant proportions. 'The Puritans are calling it a foreign house, built by Papists.'

'I don't care.'

'Then you should care, ma'am. Public fear of foreigners and Papists grows stronger by the day.'

Henrietta knew it was true and that it was her fault. Though 'fault' was not at all how she saw it. She might not exercise any influence over Charles when it came to politics, but it was a different matter when it came to religion. It was widely known that it was as a result of her persuasion that Charles was more lenient towards Catholics than ever he had been in the past, that the strict anti-Catholic policies had been discarded.

Henrietta was proud of what she had achieved so far. But she still hoped for more. Charles's new tolerance and the fact that he was such a high Anglican meant that her Catholic circle of friends had begun to talk in earnest about the real possibility of his conversion, of England's eventual reconciliation with Rome. Henrietta had renewed hopes for that too. But no doubt if her court was talking of this return to Rome then others were doing likewise, others who did not want it to happen at any cost. Harry and she had had only one debate about religion and since then had stead-fastly avoided the topic. Though she feared for the salvation of his soul, she had long since given up any attempt to try to convert him, or not at least until he was an old man and facing imminent death. Then she might try again. She knew, by the very fact he had raised this issue now, that it must be worrying him considerably.

But she forgot all about that on first sight of her beautiful new house.

'Oh, but how could anyone not love it?' she cried as they climbed the steps leading to a grand classical portico. It was so elegant, all pale, smooth grace and curves. The first Italianate villa to be built in Britain since Roman times, Inigo Jones had said, and it shone in the spring sunshine like a

Parisian pearl among the hotchpotch of red brick and topsy-turvy timber-framed houses surrounding it. It was either referred to as the Queen's House or the House of Delights, and both names were fitting, for it was hers and it was very delightful, even though the paint and plaster were not yet quite dry, and there were windows that still needed glazing.

The portico led into a great hall, decorated in white and gold, a perfect cube shape, with gleaming grey and white marble on the floor and richly hued paintings on the ceiling. The spiral staircase had turned out magnificently. It was made of stone and wound up and up in long graceful lines and elegant curling flights, its delicate ornate wrought-iron balusters decorated with fleur-de-lys and the tulips after which it was named 'the tulip staircase'. It led upwards to the bridge room which joined the two wings of the building.

Henrietta picked up her skirts and darted for the bottom stairs.

Halfway up she stopped to hang over the railings and look down at Harry, her glossy raven curls cascading around her pale face and shoulders, her small breasts bursting out of her low-cut russet gown. She knew very well just how alluring and provocative she looked. But then Harry too was being provocative just standing there, so tall and imposing and handsome in his black silk suit. 'You still love foreign houses, don't you?' she asked, needing to bring him closer through this shared project of theirs.

'I do,' he said.

She lifted her skirts and ran back down the stairs to him. She wanted so much to take hold of his hand. There was a time when she'd have thought nothing of it, but since he had returned from Jersey and said what he had, everthing seemed even more confused between them than before, volatile and precarious and unsettled. There was the sense of treading on dangerous ground, that the situation was unsustainable, something had to give, that they could not go on this way indefinitely.

'We *are* going to build more houses like this?' she asked, all that she could safely say. 'Many more, aren't we?'

'Yes,' he said, looking down into her black eyes that burned as warm and bright as hot coals. 'As soon as there's enough money for such an expensive project.'

They took the dogs and went to walk up Greenwich Hill, past grazing sheep and a shepherd sitting in the lee of a tree reading the Bible to his little boy, past milkmaids returning home with their pails of milk. At the top they turned to admire the prospect. It was one of the most prized views in England, across fields and hedges to the twisting River Thames, dotted with tall-masted ships, and the city beyond. Closer to hand stood Greenwich Palace, with the Queen's House now dominating the vista.

'One day, the whole west end of London will be as beautiful. Square, elegant classical buildings like the Queen's House spreading out all across it,' Harry said.

The queen's chapel was nearing completion and there was to be a grand opening, timed to celebrate the Feast of the Immaculate Conception. Twelve Capuchin friars had come over from France to take up residence and Henrietta had ordered that the service be held with all possible pomp and magnificence. The friars had approached a Flemish sculptor to design a special stage-set for them. In contrast to the plain exterior of the chapel, the hundred-foot space inside now glittered with gold and silver reliquaries, crucifixes, statues and chalices.

When the congregation had taken their places the curtains were drawn back to reveal the grand altarpiece. Archangels were depicted on clouds with at their centre a dove carrying the Holy Sacrament in its beak. Surrounding this were over a hundred figures of cherubim and seraphim. Two gigantic stone pillars supported an arch, with space on either side for the choir which began to sing an anthem, making it seem somehow as if the angels themselves were singing.

Henrietta's cheeks were wet with tears and many of her Catholic ladies were weeping openly. Charles, at the queen's side, looked to be enthralled and Henrietta noted that, staunch Anglican though he was, Harry's blue eyes were also glistening in an unaccustomed way.

'This is the Lord's doing,' the grand almoner preached. 'And it is marvellous in our eyes.'

It was marvellous to Henrietta that this was happening at all in England. That it was happening because of her. She had made it happen. She had done it primarily for her mother, as well as for the Pope and for God, but for the first time she saw why it was so important to them. This sacred ceremony must be allowed to take place freely in England. She grasped for the first time just how wrong it was to forbid it. It was evil to deny English

Catholics the right to practise their faith, evil to deny English Protestants the chance to experience such holiness, to learn what they had been missing before it was too late. To deny them the chance of comfort, of beauty, of eternity. They wanted it, needed it. You only had to look at the throng of English sightseers, so great that the congregation packed tightly into the pews had difficulty forcing its way outside when the service ended.

It was marvellous too, miraculous even, the way the chapel continued to be besieged. The crush lasted so long it was impossible to close its doors for three days.

When on the third night Charles ordered it to be completely cleared, Henrietta assumed he'd had enough of it all. But that was not the reason at all, far from it. He wanted the chapel emptied so that he could spend some time there alone. He told her later that he'd stood for a long while just gazing at the altar.

'I have never seen anything more beautiful,' he admitted when he came to find her in her rooms in Somerset House.

Henrietta was being helped into her cloak by Mall. 'Then come with me and Father Philip to visit the Capuchins,' she suggested, fully expecting him to decline. 'Tell them what you have just told me. They would be so honoured by your visit.'

'Very well, dear heart,' Charles decided without hesitation. 'If you wish it, I shall do it.'

They shared a frugal supper with the friars, served in rough wooden bowls in the sparsely furnished refectory.

'It is hardly what you are used to,' Henrietta said, wondering if Charles was hating it.

'I am enjoying it every bit as much as a royal banquet,' he said. And so he seemed to be.

Father Philip and Henrietta shared a hopeful smile across the table, then Father Philip spoke to the king. 'I have been meaning to speak to Your Majesty about a matter that has been brought to my attention.'

'What is that, sir?'

'Four lay Catholics, old and extremely poor, who have been imprisoned for years at York Castle for unpaid recusancy fines.'

'I expect you want me to order their immediate release?'

Father Philip glanced at Henrietta.

'Could you?' she asked Charles, laying her hand pleadingly on his arm.

'I shall release not just them but all who are detained for matters of faith. See Sir Francis Windebank in the morning and he will write out the orders.'

'I know what you are going to say,' Henrietta pre-empted Harry when next they were walking with dogs, ladies and children in the garden of Somerset House. Populated now with more than a dozen of the Mantuan statues, it had become a garden of gods and emperors. Frost and sunshine had given the statues glittering bejewelled cloaks and the water in the fountains was laced with ice. Henrietta's hand was tucked into the warm crook of Harry's arm. 'His Majesty dined with the Capuchin fathers purely to please me, but I expect it has given rise to plenty of talk?'

'The fear is that His Majesty will do anything to please Your Majesty,' Harry said. 'And I mean anything. People realise it is His Majesty's devotion to you that is making him more susceptible to the Catholic cause, and it terrifies them. They see that his affection for you is such now that he sees through your eyes, is determined by your judgement, and desires that all men should know how he is swayed by you. That is not good, for either of you.'

Henrietta glanced at Harry's face, the set line of his jaw. He was always open with her but not usually so blunt. Was he being so disparaging because he especially found the king's devotion to her hard to bear? 'Go on,' she said.

'They are watching very closely. They are noting those cosy suppers you and His Majesty have been sharing with Father Philip and Monsignor Con and are assuming the discussions turn to matters of theology, as I imagine they do?'

'From time to time. Sometimes the monsignor and the king talk about art or else play cards.'

'They are saying that it poses a threat to the quiet of the realm.'

'What? Talking about art and playing cards? I'll have you know that once, when the stakes were Catholic trinkets, crucifixes and relic cases and the like, His Majesty refused to play on the grounds that he did not wish to win such prizes!' She removed her hand from Harry's arm as they paused by a statue. 'It is right what I am doing,' she stated.

Now that she had her chapel at last, and with the full support and encouragement of Father Philip and George Con, Henrietta felt unstoppable. The Capuchins taught Catholic doctrine in English twice a week. Mass was said from six in the morning until noon. Every Saturday litanies were sung with great solemnity, and on two Sundays every month Henrietta and her priests led a solemn procession to confess their sins and take communion. The throng was so great that people had to wait three hours for their turn. The queues snaked all the way down the aisle, out through the door and around the chapel. It was not just Catholics who came, and there was not a day went by now that one of the queen's attendants did not convert.

'Even Toby Matthews is a Catholic now,' she told Harry, as if to prove a point. 'He used to run away when he saw me on my way to mass.'

'And Lucy? She seems very attached to Con. Is she a Papist now too?'

Henrietta laughed. 'She is drawn to the monsignor as she is drawn to all charming men. Monsignor Con himself told me that he believes she has never given thought to any other religion than that of beautifying herself.'

Harry laughed too, but emptily. 'Some say that even the Archbishop of Canterbury is a closet Papist.'

'Laud?' Henrietta repeated in disbelief. 'He's about as Papist as . . . well . . . you.'

'He has brought back ceremony and altar rails and reverence for the Eucharist,' Harry said, sounding almost as humourless as Charles now. 'That is more than enough these days to see him accused of preparing the Church of England for Roman domination. As far as the Puritans are concerned, the Anglican church is now being run by an emissary from hell. They are calling Laud "The Pope of England". And if that does not pose a threat to the quiet of this realm, then I don't know what would.'

His words sent a sudden explosive anger sweeping though Henrietta, like a spark along a fuse. She did not know where she stood with him now and so every word carried the weight of a thousand. His criticism stung her like nobody else's. 'I think perhaps it is not such a good thing that you are spending so much time with the king's councillors,' she retorted. 'You are beginning to sound just like them. Next you'll be telling me I'm silly and frivolous!'

He looked at her, as if the comment were beneath response.

She stared back at him fiercely. 'How dare you be so impertinent! You forget your position, sir.'

'No,' he said levelly. 'That I never do.' There was a peculiar intensity in his eyes. Like desire. Like anger. Like pride.

Around them the statues stood in silence, staring with cold blank eyes as if in mockery. Harry reached out a hand and rested it on the carved shoulder of an emperor, and the casualness of the gesture, the contrast of his long elegant fingers, living flesh and blood against the stone, was somehow suddenly too much.

She could have left it there, but something drove her on, some need to goad him, fight with him. 'Is it that you don't like how much influence I have with the king? How devoted he is to me and I to him?' She was shouting at him now, not because of what he had said but because she wanted him . . . wanted him to kiss her, to crush her in his arms and against his lips. Because she needed him. 'Is that what this is really all about? Is that why you are so set against what I am trying to do? You forget, first and foremost, I am a queen. A Catholic queen.'

'You insult me,' he said. Now there was no mistaking Harry's anger. The light in his eyes was like frost. So cold it burned. 'Those things I never forget. I am well aware that you do not take kindly to being told what to do. But I believed that you valued my advice along with my friendship. It seems that I was wrong.' His tone was measured, controlled, in a way that her own anger seldom was. Instead of raising his voice, he had lowered it. It only served to make what he said more forceful, lent every word a sharper edge, an added impact. 'I believe that you are stirring up untold trouble and danger for yourself, and I cannot stand mutely by and see you make such terrible mistakes.' He took a deep breath. 'I should never have come back.'

Henrietta watched him turn from her, stride away through the frozen garden, and it was as if she too had been turned to ice or to stone. What had she done? Her heart jolted back into life and she was running after him, with no concern for the slippery pathways. She nearly fell, grabbed the arm of a statue to right herself. The frost made her fingers stick to the the stone as if the statue were holding her back. By the time she had reached the stables, Harry had already mounted his horse.

'Where are you going?' she called.

He looked down at her from the saddle and she had never felt smaller or more insignificant or foolish in all her life. 'For a ride,' he said.

She could have ordered him not to go but she did not want to order him to do anything. Ever again. She wanted to do nothing to emphasise her status as queen, to remind him of his position as her servant. She had always admired him for his honesty, for not fawning on her as other courtiers did. Now that admiration was multiplied a hundredfold. For his pride and integrity, and the purity and goodness of his heart. The eagle and the dove.

He must have noticed that she gave him no order when she could have done, but he acted as if it was of no significance, as if he had the right to do exactly as he chose. He raised his hat as he dug the heels of his boots into the horse's flanks, tugged on its reins. 'Good day to you, ma'am.'

Henrietta watched his horse canter away and it seemed to her as if the world had come to an end, that the sky was falling in on her head.

Her feet led her back to her new chapel, though she walked blindly, as if she were walking in her sleep. It was empty now, but the candles still glowed on the golden chalices and crosses, on the cherubim and seraphim. Yet she felt no peace there. She knelt at the altar, looked up at the angels and cherubs and the face of Mary. Tears streaming down her face, her hands clasped, she did not speak the words out loud but cried them from the bottom of her heart.

*Dear God, let me see his face again.*

*Dear God, let me hear his voice.*

She knew what it was to be without him when he was in exile, but to have lost his friendship, his respect . . . She leaned forward, her breasts against her thighs, her brow on the hard stone, arms spread at her sides, palms flat against the floor. Faith had always been her comfort and strength, but so had Harry. 'Bring him back,' she prayed.

When at last she left the chapel, she told herself she would go nowhere near the stables, would not check to see if his horse was there.

She did. It was not.

She avoided his apartment. He had left without taking any of his belongings. But he could have them forwarded to him. She went to bed and taunted herself with memories of all that they had shared, the good and the bad.

In the morning she did not send for him but made herself wait. And there he was as usual, as always.

It was not as if nothing had happened. He had come back to her on his own terms and of his own free will. He did not apologise for anything and she did not expect or want him to, and as a result she knew that something had changed for ever between them. That he was in effect her equal now, an equality borne out of need and love and respect. She loved him and needed him more than ever she had. He was more precious to her than life itself and she would never risk losing him again.

# 1637

On 17 March, after only two hours' labour, Henrietta was safely delivered of another daughter. A pretty cherub with a round face and fair hair, she was a minature version of Queen Anne of France, but she was christened Anne after her paternal grandmother, Anne of Denmark.

Her brother the Prince of Wales, now aged six, and sister Mary were the proud godparents. The service was taken from the Archbishop's new Book of Common Prayer, a large folio which set out fixed forms of liturgy and worship. At Charles's urging, Henrietta had examined Laud's book the night before while her husband explained how large numbers of them were to be sent to the Scots with the strictest orders for its universal adoption. Henrietta wasn't much interested, one form of heresy being the same as any other as far as she was concerned.

It was the only thing Laud and Charles spoke about at the christening supper.

'My new daughter is named in remembrance of my mother,' Charles said to the Archbishop over the christening wafers. 'But it is my father in whose memory I do this. Through your Book of Common Prayer, we shall continue his work and see Scotland and England united in a common faith.'

Mall had been listening to the conversation. Now she leaned in closer to Henrietta to whisper, 'There are rumours circulating in Edinburgh, ma'am.'

'There are always rumours, Mall,' Henrietta sighed. 'About one thing or another.'

'To the Scottish Kirk, the new prayer book signifies Popery.'

'People see Popery in a pepper pot these days.' Henrietta smiled at her. 'Anyway, how would you even know what the Scots think, might I ask?'

Mall's little face turned red as she glanced down the hall at James Stewart, the king's young cousin. 'James and I have been talking.'

This Henrietta knew very well. She couldn't have failed to notice that Mall was spending more and more time in the company of the king's melancholy relation, a slender young man with soft fair hair and a temperament more anxious even than Charles's.

'James is a Scot,' Mall reminded Henrietta. 'He knows the Scots. And he worries that His Majesty's announcement that he and not they are in charge of their own Kirk will not be borne. This new liturgy is seen as the first step to the restoration of the Roman church in Scotland.'

'I wish that were so,' Henrietta sighed.

Mall and James Stewart were married in the summer, one scorchingly hot afternoon in August. The ceremony took place in the chapel at Lambeth Palace and the wedding party travelled down-river by barge. This time, instead of evergreens, Mall had daisies, violets, pansies and roses in her hair and in her posy, and the little Stuart princesses wore matching flowers. They made an enchanting sight, following in the bridal procession that led past the rose terrace and the fig trees and Lollards' Tower, down the aisle that was illuminated by tall lancet windows filled with bright stained glass. As at Mall's first wedding, the king gave her away and Archbishop Laud performed the ceremony. There was once again a wedding banquet in the splendour of York House. Harvest-time fare had been turned into a lavish spread to which were added capons, partridges, woodcock and swan.

As had become routine, while Charles went off hunting, Henrietta went with Harry and the rest of her household to Oatlands, from where she paid frequent visits to the royal children at Richmond Palace.

Charles had recently ordered the creation of a new park at Richmond, enclosed by a stone wall and stocked with red and fallow deer, secretive, delicate creatures which the children loved to watch from their vantage point high up in the branches of the great oak tree. The younger ones were just as intrigued by the stone figures of two trumpeters adorning the middle gate of the palace as they were by the apples ripening in the Great Orchard. The boys especially liked being taken to the piece of open land beside the moat stretching down to the riverside, where a crane stood to unload the goods and provisions brought by water to the palace.

Prince Charles practised his archery and played with his model fort and in the artillery house with its child-sized cannons. James, short-haired and round-faced like his baby sister Anne, was usually to be seen with a tennis racquet in hand.

Henrietta spent many long afternoons sitting on the grass near the archery butts with Lucy and Mall. As often as not she had baby Anne in her arms while close by Mary made impossibly long daisy chains.

She watched Harry showing her eldest son how to hold his crossbow, after he had spent nearly the whole morning showing James how to hold his racquet, and told herself that she must be the happiest princess alive. She had her children. She had a husband who adored her. She had Harry. She had her friends and her chapel and she was fulfilling the great destiny that everyone believed to be hers. She had all that her heart could desire.

# Part II

# 1638–41

When, during the darkest of days, Henrietta looked back to that long sunny summer in Richmond, that last peaceful summer with Harry and her children, the deer grazing in the long grass beneath the oak trees, the little princes with their bows and arrows and tennis racquets and the princesses in their frilly petticoats with crowns of daisies atop their shiny heads, it did not seem like a dream of hers, as treasured memories so often do, so much as a borrowed dream, someone else's dream entirely. The delicate little queen, with her ebony ringlets and silks and pearls, whose only concerns in life were music and dancing, whether the king loved her more than he did a dead duke and whether or not Harry Jermyn still wanted to kiss her . . . she had become unrecognisable.

What happened as that summer drew to a close and over the following months changed Henrietta's life as radically as it changed the country she had grown to love and to call home.

She could not even remember exactly how it all began, still did not understand how it came to pass.

That sequence of dire events that led to revolution and war was as unlike a nightmare as the idyllic summer was like a dream. For after a nightmare, the sleeper wakes to find that all is well, just as it was before. Henrietta woke to find herself forced to leave behind her husband and children, branded a traitor to the country where she had been queen, unable to return without risking imprisonment or execution. Harry was forced into exile too, accused of high treason. All that she loved was lost. All her hopes destroyed and turned to dust.

Calamity followed calamity so swiftly that it was like being at sea, at the mercy of a violent storm. Battered and tossed by a relentless onlslaught of pounding, roaring waves that kept coming and coming, one after the other, so that there was no time to regain strength or perspective. Just a swirl and collision of wild, cold, dark terror, threatening to engulf her, drag her down and drown her.

It had something to do with ship money. A wealthy Buckinghamshire landowner, John Hampden, had refused outright to pay it, which had resulted in the king's right to collect it being debated in the law courts. And the Book of Common Prayer . . . that fatal prayer book, as it became to her. But primarily, tragically, it was the king's love for her that plunged the country into civil war. Not his marrying a Catholic queen, but his loving her so much that he would be persuaded by her and seek to protect her.

The fatal prayer book . . . When it was used for the first time in St Giles's Cathedral in Edinburgh people rose to their feet and hurled their wooden stools at the Archbishop, tore the vestments from his body, screaming that the mass had come amongst them. The Scots drafted a pledge, a National Covenant to oppose Popery at any cost. It was signed by thousands, many writing their names in their own blood. They warned that if the king wanted the prayer book read in Scotland, he must send an army of forty thousand men to defend the minister who was to do it. Charles condemned the Scots as traitors for defying him. He commanded they drop all opposition or be charged with treason. That they must give up the Covenant or be suppressed by arms. Even if it proved ill work and bloody.

A council of war was called. The king marched to York with an army twenty thousand strong. But morale collapsed and he backed down, agreed to negotiate with the Scots. Treaties were made and broken and made again, with the result that the king's enemies knew he could be intimidated. He had shown himself to be indecisive and weak.

Charles summoned the truculent Yorkshireman Sir Thomas Wentworth to return from Ireland, where he had been appointed Lord Deputy some years ago, to advise him. Wentworth, newly made Earl of Strafford, shared Charles's deep-seated conviction that it was essential for a king to maintain absolute power and to command complete obedience. Parliament was called for the first time in eleven years, but a short, shaggy-haired man named John Pym took command of the Commons and spoke for two whole hours, listing complaints about the way the country had been run in Parliament's absence. About what he termed the unchecked spread of Popery. As a result, Parliament failed to grant the king the subsidies he needed and it was dissolved after just three weeks.

Soon placards were posted all over the city, claiming that the Catholics had stirred up the Scottish crisis for their own ends. Rumours spread like lice, of Popish, Irish, Spanish and French plots against England.

There could not have been a worse time for Marie de' Medici to come on a visit to the country. Henrietta's mother had been sent into exile from France after a disagreement with Cardinal Richelieu and, having outstayed her welcome in Brussels, had then sought refuge with the Prince of Orange in The Hague, from where she wrote to Henrietta to say that she feared she would soon have to move on yet again. Charles warned that she was a troublemaker who had such a reputation for bringing bad luck wherever she went that it would be the beginning of new evils if she came to England. But to please Henrietta, he opened the ports to her mother and sent a flotilla to escort her. Marie arrived with a train of six carriages, seventy horses and nearly two hundred attendants, all of whom had to be housed in the greatest luxury at England's expense.

To make matters worse, she went around telling everyone that she was more hopeful than ever of the king's conversion to the one true church. Her very presence in the country was inflammatory. While the Scots were saying the whole crisis over the prayer book was a Papist conspiracy, she could have said nothing more dangerous.

One night Henrietta was woken in the small hours by the sound of scratching against the window of her antechamber. It sounded like a tree branch knocking and scraping against the glass in the wind. Only the night was very still and there was no wind, and no tree grew near that particular window. She wasn't afraid. It wasn't a threatening sound, more irritating, like a door banging in a draft or mice scurrying about in the wainscoting. She knew she would never get back to sleep while it went on. Not wanting to leave the warmth of the bed, she considered waking Charles or calling for one of his attendants to go and investigate and make it stop. But then it stopped abruptly. She lay awake for a while listening, but all remained almost eerily quiet.

In the morning she saw what had made the scraping sound. Letters had been scratched across the greenish ancient glass. A message for them.

*God save the king.*

*God destroy the queen and all her offspring.*

It came to seem like a curse.

Shortly before Christmas 1639, little Princess Anne died of a suffocating catarrh.

That same year, Henrietta gave birth to a daugher who lived but a few hours, dying in her cradle just after she had been baptised with the name of Catherine.

For days the queen seemed close to death herself, drifting in and out of consciousness.

Meanwhile the situation around her grew desperate.

She was aware of a constant clamour which invaded her fitful sleep and gave her no rest. A mob was roaming the streets of London and had gathered outside the gates of Whitehall and Somerset House. Chanting and yelling. Shouting abuse and vicious insults. Singing riotous songs. Threatening to kill all Papists.

On Queen Elizabeth's Accession Day, 17 November, a day held sacred by English Protestants, ministers all across the kingdom delivered sermons from their pulpits urging the people to put down the Catholic religion in England. As the congregation left the queen's chapel they were pelted with mud and stones. The Capuchin fathers packed up their belongings and fled.

Arhchbishop Laud had already been forced to flee from Lambeth Palace by river when a gang of apprentices and journeymen and dockhands marched there with drums and guns to slay him. The riot was driven purely by a fierce hatred of Catholicism. Laud had been attacked just for having a crucifix on the communion table in his chapel and for bowing to the altar. After bringing down Laud's houses the rioters vowed to destroy Marie de' Medici's residence at St James's and Henrietta's chapels, all the haunts of Popery.

There were guards everywhere now. Charles had redoubled the night watches, ordered cavalry troops to patrol the streets and had summoned six thousand militiamen to guard stairways and doors with muskets and pikes. Two hundred were sent to protect the royal children at Richmond Palace night and day.

In April 1641 the Scottish Covenanters issued a manifesto justifying plans for their invasion of England on the grounds that the preservation of their religion and liberty was of vital concern to both kingdoms. Whitehall was turned into a garrison, readying itself for an attack either by the invading Scots army or by rebel English mobs. The palace grounds rang with the sound of banging and hammering as gun platforms were erected at the corner of the Banqueting House and along the privy gallery. Soldiers dragged armaments into place there, around the great court, at the palace gates and along all the approaches.

The cries of the mobs still rampaging in the streets brought with it the constant terror that at any moment they might storm the palace, overpower the guards, cut everyone's throats or else murder them in their beds.

When Henrietta needed to leave London to give birth to her eighth child, it was Harry who conducted her to the safety of Oatlands, through gangs of drunks and past placards that were fastened to gates and doorposts all across the city, threatening all Papists with death. They were ransacking churches, and outside church doors lay the broken and charred communion rails that had survived the Reformation that had been torn up and burned because they still reminded people of Catholicism. Some were smouldering, some still on fire. The streets were littered with broken candles, ragged and dirty shreds of ripped and trampled altar cloths, shattered stained-glass windows.

Henrietta was delivered of a son and named him Henry, in honour not of her own father or the king's dead brother, but of the man who had cared for and protected her.

But it seemed even Harry could not protect her now.

Parliament had been recalled and had demanded those it called 'the king's evil councillors' be brought to justice. First Strafford was impeached and thrown into the Tower awaiting trial. Then Laud was also arrested and imprisoned. Parliament was picking off the king's most faithful councillors, one by one.

Seated in a latticed box that was itself like a prison, Henrietta and Charles were present at Westminster Hall during every day of Strafford's trial. Henrietta had called him their *Très Bon Ami*. He was not merely fighting for his life but for something far greater: to defend the methods of government in which he believed so strongly. To preserve the sovereign power of the king. If he were acquitted it would be a mortal blow to the king's opponents. If he were found guilty . . .

Henrietta was certain she would be next.

When it looked as if Parliament might actually fail to prove Strafford guilty, it passed the Bill of Attainder, an ancient and wicked mechanism that allowed for the putting to death of a man without any need to prove the case against him.

It was the strangest of times. While the Lords and Commons retired to debate Strafford's fate, Princess Mary was quietly married to the Prince of Orange, a strategic alliance designed to secure the support of the powerful Dutch States General. The date for the wedding had been set some weeks before and could not be postponed because fourteen-year-old Prince William and his retinue had already made their plans to travel to England.

The Prince, with his pink cheeks and long curling brown hair, a gold sword worn at his side, was a handsome boy, amiable, rich and Protestant. In normal times he would have been welcomed with open arms by the people of England. But his train of fifty coaches arrived with a guard of four hundred heavily armed Dutch soldiers. In normal times, too, the marriage of the king's eldest daughter would have been cause for great public celebration, with masques and banquets, bonfires and firework displays, across the whole land. But there were to be no masques, no banquets, no bonfires or fireworks, to mark this wedding.

At least Mary looked like a royal bride, despite everything. Henrietta had been determined that her daughter would have the most beautiful, elegant wedding gown. It was made of silver tissue and Henrietta's chief embroiderer had decorated it with silver roses. Mary had matching silver ribbons for her ringlets and a pendant of pearls around her neck. The bridegroom wore a costume of satin and velvet the colour of ripe raspberries.

Because of the differences in religion, Henrietta and Princess Elizabeth watched from a curtained recess in the gallery while Mary was escorted to the altar by her two dashing elder brothers. In the absence of Archbishop Laud, the Bishop of Ely officiated, and, as Charles had directed, he used the order of service set out in the very prayer book that had caused so much disorder and disruption.

Later that evening the newlyweds had to go through the ritual of the public bedding. Henrietta recalled with dread the humiliation and pain of her own wedding night and was glad that Mary would be spared that, would have a very different experience. Since Mary and William were both so young still, all that was required was for their bare legs to touch. Then the marriage could be pronounced officially consummated. Even so, Mary looked quite petrified at the idea of actually lying in the same bed as William. But as soon as Henrietta's ladies started unlacing and unhooking her dress, her mood was transformed and she started giggling and squirming and complaining that they were tickling her. She was still giggling when she climbed into the state bed with its blue velvet curtains and silver fringe. A crowd of lords and ladies and the four ambassadors of the Dutch States had gathered around it, and William, in his nightgown, was led towards it by Charles and Henrietta's two sons. After gingerly kissing Mary as if she might bite him on the nose, William tentatively lay down beside her to cheers of encouragement from around the room.

Both children looked so shy and nervous now that even moving close enough together to allow their legs to touch seemed beyond them. It was Henrietta's dwarf, Geoffrey Hudson, no bigger than a child himself, who saved the day. Diving under the covers and setting the children off laughing again, as well as creating peals of hilarity amongst the spectators, his muffled voice informed them all that Mary's nightgown was far too modest and reached to her ankles. His head popped out from under the blankets and he produced a pair of shears. With a flourish he slit the garment, creating more hilarity that again turned to cheers as William boldly touched his bare skin to Mary's.

For a few moments at least Henrietta felt like a child too, with a child's ability to live only in the present moment, where there was no place for either despair or hope. She was able to put from her mind the dire events of the past years and not worry what tomorrow might hold.

When Charles obligingly took William to spend the rest of the night on a little pallet in his bedchamber, Henrietta found Harry at her side. 'Is there somewhere private that we can go?' he asked very quietly. 'Where there's no chance of us being seen or overheard?'

For a second her errant heart leaped at what he might be suggesting. Almost before she knew what she was saying or could stop herself, she said that they could meet in the chamber of one of her ladies who was away in the country.

Which was how it came about that at dead of night, alone, her way lit only by a flambeau which she carried herself, she went by way of the narrow backstairs to an empty bedchamber for a secret rendezvous. Even as Henrietta said the word to herself in her head, she thought it must be one of the most enticing of French words, for which she could think of no adequate English substitute.

Having used the torch to light one of the candles on the small dressing table, she sat down on the bed to wait. It was a half tester, less ornate than a royal bed but prettier for that in a way, draped in a canopy of green silk. She wished she'd suggested somewhere else to meet, anywhere without this one tantalising piece of furniture.

There was a knock on the door and she sprang to her feet almost guiltily, calling out softly for him to enter. Harry was carrying a torch too but he had not come alone. William Davenant was with him.

'Why all this intrigue?' she asked. 'Do you have a cunning plan to save my Lord Strafford from the executioner's block?'

He said nothing.

'Sweet Mary in heaven! You do, don't you?'

Harry was smiling. 'One that I think will appeal to Your Majesty. Since it holds the promise of immediate action and fast results.'

'Are you are implying that I am impatient?' She immediately proved his point. 'Oh, just tell me! Tell me what it is you propose we do.'

Harry glanced at William so it was evident they had cooked this idea up between the pair of them, whatever it was. 'The remains of the king's army are still on standby in York, are they not?' Harry said. 'Several hundred foot and nearly as many cavalry?'

'Indeed.'

'And a gentleman belonging to Your Majesty's household still holds command of this army?'

George Goring. Colonel Goring. 'Yes.' Oh, but she knew where this was leading now. 'You propose to bring the army down from York to intimidate Parliament and free Strafford from the Tower?'

'Only if Your Majesty is in agreement.'

'Need you ask? It's a brilliant scheme. Of course I am in agreement.'

'Aye.' Harry smiled with some satisfaction. 'Thought you might be. It's a risky plan. You do realise?'

'Risky. Not rash.'

He smiled. 'A gamble.'

'You believe it is the right thing to do?'

'Gambling? Most definitely.' Then, more seriously: 'I believe extraordinary circumstances call for extraordinary measures. The king may disagree however.'

Henrietta shook her head. 'He's easily persuaded.'

'That's half the problem,' William mumbled under his breath.

Henrietta ignored that. 'William, fetch His Majesty right away.'

William gave a nod, took the flambeau, and with a glance over his shoulder at Henrietta and Harry, standing beside the bed in the little candle-lit chamber, he left them alone, closing the door softly behind him.

Henrietta moved to stand by the darkened window. 'I was wondering earlier,' she began softly, harking back to the English language lessons he had once given to her, which had come to symbolise so much else in both their minds, 'What is the proper English word for rendezvous?'

'Tryst,' he said. 'Assignation.'

She turned to face him. 'Rendezvous is much better.'

Directing her mind on to safe ground felt like pulling on the reins of a wild horse determined to gallop free and in the opposite direction. 'Lord Strafford would be grateful to know that you have gone to so much trouble to think of a way to rescue him,' she said.

'I did not do it to help Lord Strafford. I did it for you.'

They stood inches apart, looking at each other for what felt like an hour and was probably only a few seconds, until there came a sound at the door.

William and Charles.

Charles looked from Henrietta to Harry and to the bed with some wariness. But Harry, consummate courtier that he was, immediately sprang into action and explained the proposed plan as if that was all that was on his mind. Charles pronounced this Army Plot, as he named it, an excellent idea. So that left only one matter to decide. Someone must be sent to negotiate with Colonel Goring. 'If it is to be done,' Charles said with uncustomary decisiveness. 'It is he who must do it.' He nodded his head at Harry.

'No!'

All eyes turned to Henrietta and she knew that with that one outburst she had revealed her heart as surely as if her body had been cut open like a deer after the hunt. She did not care. It was too dangerous. If Parliament should get wind of this plot . . . 'He must not do it,' she said, thinking fast but making herself sound more calm and rational. 'And . . . when you learn why you will be of my mind.'

'Speak then, madam,' ordered the king. 'That I may know why what I have commanded you forbid.'

'Mr Jermyn is our most trusted friend,' she said, trying to sound practical. 'Think how fearfully inconvenienced we would be if his part in this were discovered and he too driven from us.'

Charles set her argument on its head. 'It is because he is our must trusted friend that he must go. There is nobody else we can entrust with such a vital and sensitive task.' Now he looked at Harry, not with suspicion or any hostility but in the way he had once looked to the Duke of Buckingham and Thomas Wentworth, as if he were placing all his faith and hope upon those broad and capable shoulders. 'Jermyn is well respected and possesses great tact. There is none to whom Goring will listen better than to him. What say you, Jermyn?'

'I am honoured that Your Majesty would place such trust in me,' Harry said. 'I will go proudly and gladly.'

So it was all decided. He was to leave in the morning.

All that Henrietta could do by way of bidding him farewell before he mounted his horse was to give him her hand to kiss. He took it, brought it to his lips and then held it for a moment longer than decorum dictated. His thumb pressed gently into her palm, and it felt more intimate and thrilling than if he had run his fingers down the length of her naked body.

He let her go and as she watched him ride on with William Davenant her heart was a curious mixture of heavy and light. Like a feather with rock tied to it.

The Army Plot lifted the mood of the whole court. The very air at Somerset House and Whitehall buzzed and crackled with barely contained excitement and relief. Those in the king's and queen's inner circles were sworn to the utmost secrecy, but the plot was the topic of endless and fervent conversations whispered in corners and closets throughout the palaces. Harry and William were hailed as heroes and all thoughts and prayers were riding with them on their journey north to meet George Goring and the remnants of the King's Army.

But all did not go according to plan.

Ten days after the men had left for York, Edward Hyde came hotfoot from the Commons. Hyde was a puffy-faced, thick-set man, a pompous and pretentious lawyer who had sided with Pym and once voiced criticism against the king. He was also the man the Villiers family had called upon to try to persuade Charles to force Harry to marry Eleanor. But now he too seemed to have switched sides. 'The plot to free my Lord Strafford is discovered,' he baldly informed the king and queen. 'I do not know how, or by whom, but Your Majesties have been betrayed. John Pym revealed the existence of the plan to the House of Commons not an hour ago.'

'How much do they know?' Charles asked.

Icy panic had seized Henrietta at Hyde's opening words but she made an effort to pay proper attention to the rest of what he had to say.

'Pym knows that Your Majesties are involved. He said he was in no doubt that persons of the greatest quality at court had their hands in it. He has called it as desperate a conspiracy against Parliament as there has been in any age.'

Hyde's eyes flicked from Henrietta to Charles and then back to Henrietta again. She was certain there was something he was not saying, did not want to say, and it made her mouth turn dry as ash. Had Harry been caught? Instead of freeing Strafford, had he joined him – was he even now being held captive in the Tower? Or lying wounded? Dead?

'Continue, sir,' she said.

Extraordinarily Edward Hyde's cheeks flushed bright red, like a young boy asking a girl to dance with him. He shuffled his feet, lowered his eyes as if he did not know quite where to look. 'John Pym accused the man suspected of leading this conspiracy of too great an intimacy with Your Majesty.'

The rumours were not new but never had they been more lethal. At a time when she was under such scrutiny and attack, Henrietta needed to remain above suspicion.

Parliament's agents began searching Harry's rooms without any respect for the place or for his belongings, rummaging through his papers in search of incriminating evidence. Harry was so discreet, Henrietta was sure they would find nothing. When word reached London that William Davenant had been apprehended and imprisoned, she did not know whether to believe it or not, whether to be relieved or dismayed that there was no mention whatsoever of Harry.

Where was he?

The question was answered a few nights later when Tom Killigrew came running to her rooms as Lucy was undressing her. He said he must speak to Her Majesty in private. When she had thrown a gown over her bodice and petticoats and made her way through to the presence chamber, she found Tom hopping from foot to foot with impatience, as if he needed the pot. He whispered to her urgently that Henry Jermyn was waiting for her in the empty Banqueting House. As she made her way there by torch-light she tried to shut her ears to the angry roar of the mob that was still besieging the palace gates.

The heavy doors of the Banqueting House only partially shut out the din.

Harry was sitting on a bench that was pushed against the far wall. He had his elbows on his knees and his head propped in his hands. He stood when Henrietta entered but it looked as if his legs were not strong enough to hold him and he might collapse at any moment.

'Please sit,' Henrietta quickly instructed, but knowing that he would not break with etiquette, weary as he was, until she was seated, quickly went to take a place on the bench herself that he might do likewise.

He did so with relief. Close to, even in the dim and flickering light, she saw that his fine black suit and white calfskin boots were covered in a film of dust and dirt from the road, his face lined with it, pale with exhaustion beneath.

Yet still he thought only of her. 'I am so sorry that I failed you.'

'Oh, I wish you had not gone!' cried Henrietta, clutching his hands. 'I did not want you to go.'

'I would do so again, and readily. Even knowing the outcome. William too.'

'Were you with him when they took him? '

'There were five soldiers against the two of us. I wanted to stay and help him, but when we heard them behind us he insisted I try to outride them if I could, saying it would not help anyone if both of us were captured. I confess that my first concern was reaching London and you.'

'They will come for you, won't they?'

At the sound of the king's boots ringing out in the cavernous hall Harry staggered to his feet once more. For once Charles looked to be the stronger of the two men.

'You must leave these shores immediately, Jermyn,' he said. 'Before daybreak. Or risk death for high treason just like my Lord Strafford.'

'Only not like Strafford.' There was the usual note of humour in Harry's voice, albeit blacker than usual. 'For I am not an earl, merely a commoner. Which means I should not have the privilege of being beheaded.'

'What do you mean?' Henrietta asked in alarm.

Harry gave a small shake of his head.

'Tell me.'

'Commoners in England are hung, drawn and quartered,' the king replied. 'I'm sorry, Harry,' he said. 'There is nothing I can do to protect you so long as you remain in England. The best I can do is to provide you with a warrant that will enable you to flee to France.'

Henrietta's eyes flew to her husband, imploring him. 'There must be another way?'

'There is no other way,' the king said. 'He has no option but to seek exile.'

There was another threatening outburst of noise from the mob outside. 'I won't go,' Harry decided. 'I'll take my chances.'

'No,' Henrietta said decisively. 'His Majesty is right. You must leave.'

'Is that an order, ma'am?'

She shook her head. 'No. I am asking you. Begging you.'

He had vowed to live his life in service of her, but she could not let him give his life for her. He had risked doing exactly that when he'd devised the Army Plot in the first place, and had offered to ride as instigator to York.

Henrietta forced a smile. 'You are not much good to me dead, are you? I need you alive, and free.'

As she watched Charles finish scratching out a warrant granting him safe passage she thought of something. 'Tom, go at once to my closet and bring whatever money you can find, and bread and cheese and a flagon of ale from the kitchens.'

When the boy opened the doors to go and do as the queen had ordered he was met with a noise like the baying of the hounds of hell. Harry looked at Henrietta with mute despair and rage in his eyes. Rage that he must leave her now, in so dangerous a place and in such desperate circumstances.

Tom returned with the provisions and pouches of money and these Harry stuffed into his pockets. Henrietta went with him as he hurried to the privy steps. It was all so rushed and too swiftly done. She could barely think or take in what was happening. 'Wait,' she called as he put his foot on the top step. She hastily unfastened the pearls from around her neck, handing them to him. He put them in his pocket as he had done the money, but rather than remove his hand he kept it there, wrapping his fingers around the necklace which was still warm from her skin.

There were tears rolling down his cheeks. She had never before seen him cry. There was something so heartbreaking about seeing a strong man weeping that she clutched at his hand. 'What if I never see you again?'

'You will,' he said, making it sound like a promise. 'You will.'

She watched him descend the steps to the wherry that would take him across to Lambeth where he would take passage on a barge down-river. As the boat pulled away on the swirling black tide and Harry sat looking back at her on the shore, she raised her hand to him and did not know if it was harder to be the one who was leaving or the one left behind.

'What happens to people who are hung, drawn and quartered?' she asked Prince Charles later, sure that as a small boy he would know all the gruesome details and would relish the chance to share them.

'First they are strung up on the gibbet until they are half-dead of strangulation,' he said. 'Then they are cut down to watch the executioner's knife plunge into their belly and wrench out their intestines. Then the axe comes down and chops off their legs and arms, one by one, until pain and loss of blood finally kill them. It is the most painful way to die. Why do you want to know?'

She shook her head. 'No reason.'

The House of Lords passed the Bill of Attainder against the Earl of Strafford by twenty-six votes to nineteen.

Outside, the mob appeared to have quadrupled in size. They were flinging themselves at the carriages of the peers now, attacking their houses, threatening vengeance, yelling that if they did not have Strafford's life, they would have the king's. From the alleys around Whitehall they could clearly be heard shouting for vengeance, with violent threats to storm the palace and massacre all inside. Courtiers began gathering up their jewels and hiding them in their clothes, ready to flee. At St James's, Henrietta's mother was calling for the priest to hear her last rites, so convinced was she that they were all going to be murdered at any minute. Charles ordered a hundred musketeers from the Middlesex militia to defend her but they refused to go. At Whitehall guards were stationed on all the staircases.

By 4 May a vast crowd over two hundred thousand strong was waiting on Tower Hill to see the Earl of Strafford beheaded. It was a day of dazzling sunshine and the birds were singing, but to Henrietta the sky looked dark and the sound of the birdsong was the saddest she had ever heard. While the rest of London celebrated in the sun, she sat quietly at Whitehall with Charles.

Strafford's head was severed from his body at a single blow. When the executioner lifted it, dripping with blood, the crowd went wild with rejoicing. The chilling cry of 'His head is off! His head is off!' rippled through the streets all the way to Whitehall.

Henrietta had hoped, as had everyone at court, that Parliament would be appeased by the death of Strafford. It was not. A Commons committee now convened to investigate the Army Plot. It had been granted full authority to examine witnesses without exception. Which meant that the king and queen were to be subjected to its inquisition.

The investigations now singled out Henrietta as the real instigator. Two black-coated men came to the chapel to arrest Father Philip as he was lighting candles in preparation for morning mass. They led him away in his vestments, one on either side of him, like gaolers. He went peacefully, but when he refused to betray the queen by answering any of their probing questions, was flung into the Tower. Parliament also demanded Marie de' Medici should leave the kingdom, claiming that she had instilled evil counsels in her daughter.

As Henrietta said a tearful goodbye to her mother, she had never felt so alone. She feared she might go mad at this sudden reversal in her fortune. The king deprived of his power, Catholics persecuted, loyal servants lost and hunted for their lives. She was like a prisoner, with no one in the world to whom she could turn for comfort and help.

At least Harry was safe. She had word that he had reached Portsmouth and slipped away by boat, just as soldiers galloped into town with orders for his arrest. And, thankfully, William Davenant had been released. John

Pym decided it was unwise to execute poets and risk turning them into martyrs. So William had gone to join Harry in France.

Mall and Lucy and all Henrietta's ladies of the bedchamber and courtiers were cross-examined one by one regarding the queen's actions over the past weeks. When the questioning was over and Henrietta was permitted back into her rooms, she saw that her desk had been ransacked, papers rifled and the enamelled casket in which she kept her private correspondence opened and emptied.

The Commons committee took three weeks to produce its preliminary report, but when it was completed in June it was revealed that it was George Goring who had leaked the details of the plot to Parliament.

Henrietta refused to believe it. 'No,' she said. 'Not George. He would not betray me. Or Mr Jermyn. He is our friend. There must be some mistake.'

'He has freely admitted it with his own tongue, Your Majesty,' Edward Hyde confirmed.

'But why? Why would he do that?'

'He claims he disapproved of the plan. It's either that or he resents not having been appointed lieutenant general of the northern army. Whatever the reason, as soon as Harry Jermyn put the proposition to him, he sent a messenger straight to Mountjoy Blount to inform him of everything.'

Mountjoy Blount. Lord Newport. The man who had loathed Harry since they'd both been involved in the scandal surrounding Eleanor Villiers's pregnancy.

'I suppose the report made much of the fact it was Harry Jermyn, my favourite, who had been sent to negotiate with Lord Goring?'

'I am sorry, ma'am.' She assumed he meant he was sorry to confirm that was the case. But it was for something far more serious. 'I have to tell you that Henry Jermyn has been tried in absentia and sentenced to death, should he ever again set foot on English soil.'

Henrietta might just as well have been sentenced to death herself. Even though she knew Harry was safe in France, just to hear those words in connection with him filled her soul and her heart with dark despair. She barely heard what Hyde said next and the implications failed to register.

'Parliament is now consulting ancient documents to determine what was done with previous queens in similar circumstances . . .'

She stared at him blankly, her thoughts miles away, with Harry in France.

'You know what this means, sire?' Hyde asked Charles.

Henrietta realised then. 'They are preparing the way for me to take Strafford's place,' she said, without emotion. 'It is I now who will become the enemy of the people and the most hated figure in this kingdom.' She gave a short laugh. 'They are not exactly starting from scratch though, are they? It is not as though the people once loved me with all their hearts.'

Parliament had threatened to impeach her. She was accused of attempting to change the religion of England. It had been decided that a queen was no different from any other subject, and could be punished in just the same way.

'They mean to execute me too?'

'The vengefulness of Parliament against Your Majesty is so great that it is my duty to warn you that your life is now in grave danger,' Edward Hyde told her with the utmost gravity. 'If they can, these Puritans will rip you to pieces.'

Her thoughts were still with Harry and how he would never see England again. How she might never see *him* again. 'Sir, they have ripped me to pieces already,' she replied.

'They will not,' Charles said, reaching for her hand. She had never felt his grip so firm, or heard him sound so sure. Or maybe once. When he was defending the Duke of Buckingham. She had noted before how staunchly he came to the aid of those he loved when the world had turned against them. 'It is high treason to threaten a queen,' he said. 'Those who have done so will be arrested.'

# 1642

On 3 January when the Members of Parliament returned to the House of Commons, Charles sent his Lord Keeper and Attorney General to the House to charge six leading opposition members, John Pym and his associates, with high treason.

The Commons ignored the king's order, refusing to surrender the men. 'Then we must strike a bolder blow,' Charles said. 'If the House of Commons will not obey me willingly, I will force them to do so.'

By morning Whitehall was thronged with gentlemen and army officers.

Henrietta and Charles took their midday meal as usual and then she retired to her cabinet where Charles embraced her. 'Tell none where I have gone,' he instructed her. 'Trust no one. My success depends upon the element of surprise. But if you find one hour elapses without hearing ill news from me, you will see me when I return, master of my kingdom.'

She felt suddenly so light of heart that she threw her arms around his neck and kissed him on the lips. 'Go and pull the rogues out by their ears,' she encouraged him.

Charles climbed into his coach and left Whitehall at the head of five hundred men, guardsmen, servants, loyal gentlemen and army offices, all armed in warlike manner with halberds, swords and pistols.

It was the longest hour Henrietta had ever known, and she had known many long hours. She knelt at her private altar to pray. She tried to read the psalms. She took deep breaths and attempted to stay calm.

When the hour was almost done and there was no news, Lucy happened to come into the chamber to see if she required anything and Henrietta could not contain her excitement and relief. 'Let us celebrate, Lucy. For the King, I hope, is now master of his state and John Pym and his men are under arrest.'

Lucy looked at her, showing a strange lack of emotion at this startling announcement bar the flicker of a triumphant smile, which served to remind Henrietta how she had once thought The Wizard's daughter a sorceress herself.

'I must leave Your Majesty to your rejoicing,' was all Lucy said and, having excused herself, walked rapidly out of the room with a swish of her skirts, leaving Henrietta wondering what had just happened, if something were wrong.

When Charles eventually returned it was to tell Henrietta that he had failed. He had entered the chamber of the Commons at the head of his guards, with their hands on the hilts of their swords and pistols ready cocked. No English king had ever been inside the House except for King Henry VIII and he only once. Charles walked straight down the middle of the chamber, bowing to members on either side who all bowed back. He went to stand beside the Speaker's chair and demanded that the accused MPs be handed over.

'I could not see them,' he said. 'I asked whether Pym were present or not and there was general silence. The birds, forewarned, had already flown the nest. I could not do what I went to do.'

'But how could they have been forewarned? When only you and I had prior knowledge of . . .' Henrietta realised in an instant what must have happened. She dismissed it as out of the question. 'But by the time I told Lucy you'd already have been at the Commons . . .'

'A coach and five hundred marching men move only slowly. We were detained in the streets by petitioners.'

They had been betrayed yet again by a person Henrietta had thought to be one of her dearest friends. Lucy had sent word to Pym. 'Is there no one we can trust? No one at all,' Henrietta said in despair.

Even as she spoke the words she remembered how Charles had ordered her to trust no one. She had betrayed his trust even as Lucy had betrayed hers. It was thanks to her own careless prattling that the coup had failed. It had been mounted in her defence and in order for Charles to regain his honour. Instead, because of her foolishness, he had walked into a trap. Of all the idiotic things she had done in her life, of which there were a great many, this was by far the most idiotic. She threw herself into his arms. 'Oh, it is all my fault! I am totally to blame. I was not worthy of your confidence. Of your love.'

He stroked her black curls, kissed her forehead. '*Mon coeur*, do not judge yourself so harshly.'

She stepped back from him. 'Can you ever forgive such an indiscretion?'

'It is already forgiven,' he said. 'It cannot be helped.'

But he looked so despairing it broke Henrietta's heart.

She had enough political acumen to realise that by attempting to stage a coup and failing, he'd lost every shred of credibility. Not one word of reproach did he give her, but she knew that, in trying to save her, he had ruined himself. She had ruined him.

The king's actions were deemed unjust and illegal, a traitorous design against Parliament. Printed libels proclaiming more Papist plotting laid all the blame firmly on Henrietta now, claiming that Charles was a good Protestant in his heart. It was the queen and the Catholic lords who had always misdirected the king. She had advised him to arrest the MPs. She had employed all her wit to inflame the king's violent purposes. Charles was enslaved by his affection for her, though she had no more passion for him than served her own designs.

The city was preparing for war. Cannons had been wheeled in, weapons were being stockpiled, all the trained militiamen were standing to arms in expectation of a counter-attack by bloodthirsty hordes of Royalists. Shops were shut up as if an enemy were at their gates. The cry went up for citizens to arm themselves and within an hour over a hundred thousand men turned out, armed with muskets, halberds, swords and clubs. A hundred sailors were stationed on the Thames, defending Parliament from attack by water.

The terrifying news reached Whitehall that the tables had been turned and Parliament was preparing to accuse the queen of high treason. Charges against her had already been prepared and the Commons had determined that it was legal for the local sheriffs to come for her with guards.

Henrietta and Charles, left with no other option but to flee, bundled themselves into the royal coach and headed for Richmond. They were accompanied by only thirty of their bodyguard plus a handful of courtiers who had remained loyal. Their baggage was carried in carts by peasants.

Henrietta wanted to take all the children but Charles assured her that the younger ones would be safer left where they were, so they took only the two eldest boys and Mary. En route to safety their coach passed westwards through Hyde Park, past thousands of Roundheads, as all now called the supporters of Parliament. They made a terrifying sight, cramming the narrow streets and alleys, waving placards inscribed with the single word: Liberty. The rivers were swollen after the recent rains, making the journey even more difficult. The princes saw it all as a great adventure while Mary clung to her mother's arm in fear. For her sake, Henrietta tried to keep her own apprehension hidden.

'Are you not afraid, Father?' Prince Charles asked.

'It is shame more than fear that I feel,' the king replied. 'This barbarous insolence of the people is too much to bear.'

The family reached Hampton Court late in the evening but nothing was ready, the servants were in a fluster because no food fit for royalty had been provided and not even enough beds were made up.

'No matter,' Henrietta said. 'We shall eat cold meat and bread tonight like everyone else and the five of us shall sleep in the same bed.'

It did not make for the most comfortable night but it was cosy and consoling to huddle altogether, aside from the inevitable squabbling and jostling for position between the boys, the fighting over pillows and a fair share of the blankets.

'All of you hush now,' Henrietta instructed. 'Close your eyes.' She glanced at her husband across the heads of the three children. 'That includes you,' she said softly. 'Sleep.'

One by one the children drifted off, with limbs tangled together like a litter of puppies, and there was peace for a while, until James grew hot and sweaty and in his sleep tried to kick off the blankets. Henrietta moved to the edge of the bed to give him some air, and closed her eyes.

In the morning the Commons sent orders that they should return to London at once.

'We cannot remain here with no military defences,' Charles decided. 'We shall go to Windsor.'

While the children were getting ready Henrietta put on her own cloak and out of habit, glanced at her reflection in the gilded mirror on the wall of the chamber. For once she was not admiring her own appearance: reassuring herself how beautiful she looked, how well a new gown fitted, that her hair was prettily curled and dressed, how bright her jewels looked against her black hair and milky white skin. For once she did not gaze into her own face and see large black eyes sparkling back at her, did not tilt her head beguilingly and adjust her ringlets around her face. Instead she looked into her eyes and tried to summon an inner strength and courage. She lifted her hand and lightly touched the jewels around her neck, not to assess their lustre but their worth.

If they were sold, how much would they fetch? How many muskets would they buy?

She discussed her plans with Charles as they travelled to Windsor, passing through dangerously high fords that threatened to wash away horses, coaches and carts. Having no one left in whom they could trust, there was no one else for them to consult. But one thing was clear.

'I must leave England,' Henrietta decided. 'As soon as possible. You must be free to do whatever you need to do, and must not be hindered by fears for my safety as you would be if I were to remain in the country.'

Charles did not argue.

'I shall go to Holland,' she decided. 'Mary's husband is keen for her to join him, so I will escort her.'

'Would you not rather go to your family in France?'

'Of course I would.' Harry was in France. She immediately pushed the idea from her mind. 'But the Commons will surely object, assume I do so only to gather Catholic support. They can hardly raise similar objections to my taking my daughter to her new Protestant family. And once at liberty there, I shall be able to continue serving Your Majesty's cause.

'I have already ordered the Earl of Newcastle to take command of Hull. We must secure it,' Charles said decisively. 'All the military stores collected for the Scottish campaign are there and it is vital that we have an east coast port to which any money and military supplies you raise may safely be sent. And letters.'

Parliament made no objection to the queen's request to leave England. On the contrary, the idea was seized upon with alacrity. They made it as easy as possible for Henrietta to go, and to go quickly. Their only stipulation was that Prince Charles must not leave the country with her.

'Do you suppose they imagine you will be more amenable to their demands with me out of the way?' She gave the king a smile she hoped was braver and more confident and optimistic than she felt. The only thing she did not have to feign was determination, she had enough of that to motivate an army. 'Little do they know that I plan to do them far more damage in Holland than ever I could do here.'

Only a very small party was accompanying her, no more than a dozen attendants including Mall and Father Philip, her dwarf Geoffrey Hudson, and two of the remaining Capuchin friars. Mary's governess was coming with her too. They were to leave in just three weeks and there was so much to be done, so much planning and preparation and so many different affairs to think about, that Henrietta felt her head might explode. There was no time to sleep, barely enough time even to breathe.

'Everything is being done in such a rush! I never heard the like of it before for the voyage of persons of dignity,' Mall complained as she hurried between trunks and cupboards, folding and packing bed linen, table linen, gowns and cloaks, shoes and stockings – the queen's and her own too. 'I don't see how we are ever going to be ready in time, unless Your Majesty is to do entirely without coaches and horses!'

The Countess of Roxburghe was similarly flustered, packing up Princess Mary's needlework and petticoats and making sure her charge had enough pretty gowns and jewels ready to wear to meet her young husband. It was not just the preparations that were making Mall and the countess agitated. The whole court was in a state of nervous anxiety, everyone fearful of the outcome of this journey upon which so much depended.

How Henrietta longed for Harry's soothing presence, his energy and skill for organisation. He would have made sure that everything was planned and completed on time and with minimal fuss. He'd even have managed to make them laugh about it all too, she was sure. She had written to him in France to tell him she too was to become an exile, but had explained only that she was escorting Mary to be with her husband. She could share with him none of her real plans for fear of her letters being intercepted. Given the scandal surrounding them both and that his name was already so blackened in England, she did not dare risk suggesting he should join her. Though if he was enjoying life back in France as much as he seemed to be, he might not even want to. At first he had written to her regularly, but over the weeks the letters had grown less frequent and shorter. He told her that he had renewed his connections with the Frenchmen he had met on the diplomatic mission to arrange her marriage but his letters were so carefully worded, in case they fell into enemy hands, that it was impossible to glean much from them anyway, except that he seemed busy, happy.

As before when he was in exile, it was an agony for Henrietta to think of the people he must be meeting and mixing with now, the women who shared his company when she could not. Who shared . . . she did not allow herself to think of what else they might be sharing because to think of it crushed her. She wanted to write to him in anger and say: You forget me so easily and I never forget you. You put me out of your mind so readily. And every time you do, it is as if you put a knife in my heart.

But she could not even bear to ask him to come to her, because she could not bear to have him give some reason, some excuse, why he could not.

In truth, she was not even sure that it would be wise or right for him to come. Many times in the past they'd been left alone together while Charles was hunting, but she knew it would be entirely different if he were in a different country, if there were a whole ocean between them and their separation indefinite.

Not only was there a shortage of time to prepare for the journey but also a great shortage of money. Parliament had frozen all the king's income and Henrietta had to sell off gold plate just to pay for the most necessary provisions. It was not enough to pay her retainers' wages, so when the party left for Windsor to return to Hampton Court, where Princes Charles and James were to remain, they were forced to travel without guards.

At Hampton Court she and Mary said a tearful farewell to the boys, who both demanded to know why they could not come too.

'I wish you could come,' Mary wept, putting her arms around her oldest brother and kissing him.

Henrietta smiled. Her daughter spent most of the time being teased by all the boys and telling tales about what nuisances they were. 'Parliament does not permit them to come,' she said. Then, turning to her sons, 'Besides, your father needs you.' She kissed them once more on the top of the head and tried to smile. 'Be brave, both of you.'

'You be brave too, Mam,' Prince Charles said.

'I am trying to be.'

Before she had left Hampton Court Henrietta had piled into her baggage the choicest of the crown jewels. In went gold coronets, circlets and collars, a set with rubies and pearls which had belonged to Henry VIII, as well as the two famous diamonds, the Grand Sancy and the Mirror of Portugal. At Greenwich she emptied her own jewellery casket of strings of pearls, pendants, earrings and rings. She did not even retain the most treasured items, the cross given to her by her mother and a set of pearl buttons belonging to Charles. As she softly closed the door on her chamber, walked across the gallery and down the twisting tulip staircase which she had taken such care and pleasure in designing and seeing installed, she was overcome with sadness, wondering if she would ever see her house again.

It seemed that she was always saying goodbye – to places and to people – and with each goodbye she said, she left a little part of herself behind, so that it felt as if she were gradually being chipped away, like stone beneath a chisel, shaping her into something different, eating away at her until there was nothing of her left.

Their coach retraced the journey from Canterbury to London that she had made on first arriving in England sixteen years ago. Only this time there were no flowers in the hedgerows, no smiling, cheering faces lining the route. It was the depth of winter. The trees were stark and bare. The rutted road was frozen, the wind just as icy. There were flurries of snow and sleet, showers of hail and rain. Instead of leaning out of the litter to wave, Henrietta huddled into her cloak, tucked the fur blankets tighter around Mary and shivered.

The party reached Canterbury at the beginning of February. They stayed there for a few days since vessels suitable for transporting them were still being hastily made ready. Then they proceeded to Dover where five ships were waiting, a small flotilla led by a flagship named *The Lion*.

The castle there had looked so gloomy to Henrietta when she had first sighted it, but now, even in the bleak winter light, it looked friendly. It was she who felt gloomy, looking upon it with a heavy heart, for it was there that she had spent her very first night in England. She had been so unimpressed then, so haughty and homesick, but now England felt like home and she must say goodbye to it too. It was also in Dover Castle that she had first met Charles and he had kissed away her tears.

This time he had tears that needed kissing away. He went with her to the water's edge and they both cried and clung together, buffeted by the bitter winter wind that whipped off the restless grey sea.

Mall and the Countess of Roxburghe were weeping too, while Princess Mary looked somewhat alarmed to find herself surrounded by emotional adults when it was generally their place to dry *her* tears.

In Charles's pocket and sewn into the lining of Henrietta's cloak was the key to the cipher in which they were to correspond. It had been tried and tested by Mary Tudor's ambassador over a century ago. They were also to make use of codewords. *Les Malheureuses* meant the Catholics. Mall was to become Isabelle. Charles was a number for some reason: 189.

'Take good care, I beg of you,' he implored Henrietta, holding on to her hands still. 'Write nothing to me which is not in cipher. And whatever you do, do not let it be stolen.'

'I will guard it with my life.'

'I cannot bear to say goodbye to you. I cannot bear to see you go.' His voice broke. 'It is only your love which sustains me.'

Henrietta embraced him again. 'It will go on sustaining you from Holland,' she assured him. She was overcome afresh with passionate anger at being forced to abandon him, her children and her adopted country, without hope of returning to them except in peril. But worse than her sorrow and anger was her fear of what Charles would do if she were not there by his side to sustain him, to keep him strong. Her growing love for him had not blinded her to his faults. The events of the Scottish wars had proved him to be hesitant and indecisive, too reluctant to stand up for his God-given rights, and she feared he would not be able to manage the current crisis alone.

She drew back a little from him. 'You have already shown your goodness sufficiently and it has been very ill repaid,' she told him firmly. 'To settle affairs it is necessary to unsettle them first. I am risking all we have left in the world to get money for you. You must play your part, too, or my efforts will be in vain.'

'I promise you, I will not make any peace that is disadvantageous to our family.'

'Stand firm against our enemies,' she stressed, squeezing his hand. 'Remember, you must make for Hull straight away. Hull must absolutely be held. Continue strong in your resolution and do not falter. And lose no time! You have lost enough already.' She realised she must sound strident and critical, but did not care. These things needed to be said.

Charles nodded assent, seeming almost glad to have her take charge and tell him what to do. He let go of her then and took Mary's face between his hands. He kissed her forehead and Henrietta saw in his eyes the fear that he might never see his daughter again.

The royal barge was waiting to take them out to the ship but as Henrietta turned towards it Charles grabbed her hand, holding on to her fingers with arm extended. She came back to him for one last kiss and then made him let go. Blinded by tears and with a fierce pain in her throat, she picked up the new Mitte, climbed into the barge and the oarsmen took up their oars. The wind being favourable, the little fleet put out to sea with no delay. As the sails filled and billowed, Henrietta stood on deck with Mary. They looked back to the white cliffs of England and her heart twisted and leaped to see Charles on horseback, in his plain brown wool hunting suit, galloping along the winding shoreline, racing with the vessel and frantically waving his hat in farewell.

She laughed with delight to see it and she and Mary leaned out over the rail as far as they dared to wave back just as frantically, as if warning him back from danger rather than saying goodbye. They carried on waving until there was no chance that Charles could see them, and they could barely see him. Henrietta kept on waving until he had faded from view entirely.

But the image of that small lone rider galloping along the clifftop to keep her in sight and stay as close to her as he could, for as long as possible, was an image she would carry with her to Holland. It would urge her on to greater efforts on his behalf. It was that which would sustain her until she saw him again. She did not let herself for a moment consider that she might never do so.

Mary went down to the cabin with Mall and Geoffrey and Father Philip, but Henrietta stayed up on deck alone. As the coast of England grew hazier she travelled back in her mind to St James's. She was standing there with Harry, at the very place where the first great square might have been built.

The survey of his land had been completed before the Scottish wars erupted. But the beautiful classical houses they had once envisioned building together seemed no more substantial now than spun sugar, castles in the air that had crumbled like the empire of Rome upon which they were fashioned, never to rise again. That empty, muddy field had been a foretaste of the country's future: a ruined, war-torn, devastated landscape. Houses that had been razed to the ground rather than raised up.

Henrietta had so wanted to build those houses and streets and squares, just as she had wanted to ease the lives of English Catholics and be a beloved queen.

She had failed.

# Part III

# 1642

The sea voyage, only the second Henrietta had ever taken in her life, was remarkably smooth, completely different from her first experience. She was determined that everything would be different for her daughter. She remembered her own ignorance as a new bride, what a disadvantage it had been to arrive in England with no knowledge of its language, customs, history or people. She wanted Mary to have some understanding of the country in which she was to make a new home with her husband, so she asked their captain to point out some landmarks.

He was a jowly man with a long beard and a thick English country dialect Henrietta found almost impossible to comprehend, but after about fifteen hours they sighted a town which he said was called Flushing. Its large harbour contained a vast forest of masts, sailing ships plying in and out continually. These were the mighty vessels of the Dutch East India Company, he said, which traded in exotic spices from the orient. *The Lion* then passed the island of Voorne, its shore lined with sand dunes, to reach a place called Brill, where the Prince of Orange's vessel came to accompany the English fleet as it sailed across the wide mouth of the River Maas to land at Hounslerdike.

Coaches and horses were unloaded and the convoy set off towards The Hague. They were met a short distance from there by a grand procession led by Mary's young husband, Prince William, and Charles's sister, Elizabeth. She had been a celebrated beauty in her time, with chestnut hair and strong, almost masculine features. She had married Frederick V, Elector Palatine, and they had been crowned King and Queen of Bohemia. But within a year they had lost everything, their home territory invaded by the Spanish, forcing them to flee to Holland where Frederick had died some years ago.

Elizabeth remained regal and dignified in a tattered, faded velvet gown. The jewels that had once embellished it were missing, the stitching coming loose and the hem frayed. Her coach too had seen far better days, its velvet seats threadbare, woodwork and paint scratched and chipped. She and Henrietta sat side by side. In the boots, the seats above the wheels, were two of her daughters and her son, Prince Rupert. All the youngsters, including the newlyweds, Mary and William, sat very quietly, regarding one other with cautious interest.

Elizabeth by contrast was very vocal. She made it instantly clear that she held Henrietta responsible for her brother's reversal of fortune and that she wholly disapproved of Catholicism. 'You are against any agreement with Parliament but by war,' she criticised. 'If you had witnessed the fury, misery and desolation that has torn my country apart, you would not be so keen to plunge Britain into battle when it alone has so far flourished in peace and plenty. But war it will be now for England, since my brother does nothing without your approbation.'

'I assure you, madam,' Henrietta replied, 'I advise him as I think best, for him and for his family and for England.'

Elizabeth sniffed. 'You will find that many people in this country share my views. Many of our citizens are Calvinist, so they have as much time for Catholics as do I. The burghers hold great power here, this being a trading nation, and they are not impressed by this alliance with England which they believe will be bad for trade.'

Henrietta struggled to hold her tongue. For Charles's sake as well as for her own, she did her best to make friends with his sister as the procession rolled across the wide rainy lowlands of Holland beneath stormy March skies. She chatted about the children she had left behind in England, Elizabeth's nieces and nephews, and she talked to Prince Rupert about his passion for horses. Though only fifteen years old, the boy had an air of swaggering confidence, which together with his black eyes and rather cruel mouth reminded her a little of the Duke of Buckingham. Elizabeth's only comment was a bitter one: that it was a pity her son had had to learn to ride on old nags instead of fine stallions.

Henrietta sympathised with Elizabeth's hardships and was also made uneasy by them. Might she find herself similarly dressed in a faded gown and travelling in a battered carriage before too long? Could war in England bring the privation that the Thirty Years' War had brought to Bohemia and Elizabeth's family?

The towns and cities they were passing through were a stark contrast to Elizabeth's tattered clothes and battered coach. This was a golden age for Holland, its trade, art, scientific achievement and military might acclaimed across the world. The Dutch economy was thriving and its cities expanding. There was building work going on everywhere, rich merchants erecting country houses, and town houses with ornamental façades along the canals that were being dug in and around the cities, for defence and for travel.

Henrietta was to stay in one such gleaming new building, aptly named the New Palace on Staedt Straat in The Hague, which had been made ready for her use. The Hague was an elegant city on the North Sea, with wide streets bordered by more rich houses, an impressive sixteenth-century city hall, churches and many fine palaces, outside which fireworks were discharged and cannon sounded a triple salute for Henrietta's arrival. Otherwise the reception was less than enthusiastic. An assembly of principal citizens accompanied the queen's procession to the New Palace and was presented to her once she had been enthroned in state in an audience chamber. She was, however, astounded and insulted by their great discourtesy. Some sat down in her presence before she had given them leave to do so, while others did not even trouble to bow.

'They are so rude, ma'am,' Mall muttered later.

'Never mind them,' Henrietta said. 'We are not here to make friends, but money.'

Wasting no time, she set to work the very next morning. She ordered trestle tables to be erected around the walls in the audience chamber and, like a market trader presenting her wares, set out the glittering crown jewels and all the beautiful gifts that Charles had given to her over the years. They made a brilliant display and soon word spread around the city. Merchants and pawnbrokers began to arrive at the New Palace.

'They have strange faces, ma'am,' Mary whispered, leaning in towards her mother while eyeing them in curious fascination. 'Such hooked noses.'

The men's swarthy complexions, black fur cloaks and beaver hats gave them an air of the orient, from which came the exotic spices upon which the Dutch East India Company had grown so rich. But Henrietta was not at all interested in appearances or how they had grown rich. Only that they were. 'Don't stare,' she told her daughter quietly. 'We want them to buy from us. We must not make them feel uncomfortable.'

But the merchants looked unlikely to spend anything. They seemed singularly unimpressed with what was on offer. Henrietta seethed with impatience as they made their ponderous examinations, fingering the diamonds and holding them up to the candlelight as if they were at a common market stall and the jewels merely pieces of fruit rather than priceless treasures. Although priceless no longer. For Henrietta was a merchant too now and ready to trade her dearest possession. Sweet Lord, but they were taking their time!

'Don't you think that a very beautiful piece, sir?' she encouraged one of the men who had picked up a gold collar.

'Indeed it is,' he agreed, not very enthusiastically. Then he set down the piece and sucked in his breath through his teeth in the most aggravating way. 'But too large and costly for me, I am afraid.'

'And for me,' echoed his companion who was admiring another collar, or not admiring as the case might be. 'Not five people in Europe could afford to consider such a purchase or risk offering a loan against it and locking up such a large amount of money for any protracted period of time.'

Henrietta tried not to mind that neither of them had the courtesy to address her properly, and tried harder to hide the impatience and despair she was feeling inside as she turned her attention to a third merchant, who did at least bow to her. 'How about you, sir? Are you not tempted?'

'It is not my business to be tempted but to purchase with prudence. And I fear that you'll find we are all in agreement. These baubles are too costly for The Hague. Besides which . . .' he broke off and glanced at the other merchants as if for confirmation '. . . it is only fair that I tell you there are doubts about Your Majesty's authority to pledge such treasures.'

'What doubts?'

'It was written from London that you carried off the jewels secretly and against the king's wishes. We cannot risk lending money to you against them if you have no right to them in the first place.'

Henrietta took a deep breath. Now was not the time to unleash her temper. 'My husband gave me permission, I assure you.' She flashed her most becoming smile which made her cheeks dimple and black eyes sparkle far brighter than the jewels on display. 'In any case, many of the jewels you see before you are my own personal property.'

The first merchant was won over. 'To break up the larger pieces would be bad business and an act of barbarism, ma'am. Part of their beauty and value lies in the way they are so perfectly matched. These smaller pieces you speak of, however . . .' He picked up some pearls and a pair of ruby earrings, then put then down again. 'I find myself spoiled for choice.'

Why choose? Henrietta asked silently. Buy them all!

After much deliberation, his hand hovered over a little chain and the cross which had belonged to her mother.

'Those were once worn by Marie de' Medici of France,' Henrietta told him.

'Very pretty. I should like to buy them for my wife.'

That Henrietta had not expected and it threw her. 'Will you not take them in pledge, to be redeemed later? So that your wife may have the pleasure of wearing them for a few years and then return them?'

He shook his head. 'I will only buy outright.'

Henrietta did not want to part with the items forever, but she could not afford to be sentimental. She named her price.

He shook his head. 'Too much.'

He looked to be about to move on so she quickly gave a lower amount. 'Still too much.'

She bit back a sigh. 'Perhaps it would be better if you told me how much you are prepared to give, sir.'

The sum he suggested was insultingly small, half of what the items were worth. She took it.

'You could have held out for more, ma'am,' Father Philip said, taking the bill she handed to him and putting it safely in his pocket. 'He obviously wanted them.'

She disagreed. 'The trouble is, they know how badly we want money. They have their foot on our throat.'

Another merchant who had been admiring Charles's little pearl buttons now asked if he might string them on a chain to see what they looked like so arrayed. Once that had been done, he said he would buy them. They were Henrietta's most cherished possessions and looked very handsome all linked together. It tore at her heart to think she must let them go. She had been so sure the merchants would be far more enticed by the grander jewels.

'Can we not keep those for a while longer, ma'am?' Mary asked, seeing her mother's sorrowful expression. 'They're my father's, aren't they? I remember him wearing them.'

'It is him we must think of,' Henrietta said, resolute. 'I give them up with no small regret, but keeping them will not help him and we must do only what will.'

Again she had to agree to a price that was a fraction of their true value. She fixed her mind on the prospect of writing a letter that evening, in cipher, to tell Charles proudly of her small success as a pedlar of jewels. 'They will buy guns and cannonballs,' she said to Mary after the merchant had departed with his bargain. 'That is all we must consider.'

But after several weeks there was still precious little gain to count. Henrietta had even taken the more valuable crown jewels to Amsterdam to try to sell them there but had been unsuccessful. Now she stood at the window of her chamber in the New Palace, looking out over the mist-shrouded street, trying to think what to do. She felt weary, having been talking all day. She had written to Charles but feared her letter would make no sense, that she had jumbled the cipher and he would have trouble reading it. She had told him that if she did not turn mad it would be a great miracle, but provided it be in his service she would not mind. She could barely gather her thoughts together. She had such a bad toothache again she scarce knew what she was doing. And it was not only her tooth that ached. She put her hand to the small of her back and made herself straighten. 'The damp air of this low country is giving me such aches in my bones, I am starting to feel like an old lady,' she said to Mall, who had come in with a gown to dress her.

Herietta's back and shoulders ached and her head was pounding and she had such a pain behind her eyes she wanted only to close them. But she could not sleep, had hardly slept in days. How could she? How could she rest for even a minute when she had achieved so very little? So far she had amassed no money worth forwarding. In any case, it was proving very hard to send messages to Charles, or to receive them, since Parliament's ships were beating up and down the coast waiting to capture any messages and supplies sent by her to England. Henrietta was also nervous about using the cipher. It was so time-consuming and she was always afraid of getting it wrong. Afraid also of her letters falling into enemy hands. Scattered with numbers as they were, they could never be mistaken for innocuous documents.

Letters from Charles reached her as infrequently as hers were reaching him, leaving her desperate for news. But when it came at last in April it gave her no respite. Though Charles and James were still with their father, Elizabeth and Henry were now in the hands of Parliament.

Henrietta pushed away her plate of Dutch cheese, almost choking on it. 'They are with their nurses and governesses, ma'am,' Father Philip consoled her, with a steadying hand on her arm. 'They are not imprisoned, only under watch, and they will be perfectly happy and safe. If Parliament wishes to retain the people's sympathy it will never harm small children.'

Henrietta tried to believe this was true but could only think of the vile message scratched on to the window at Whitehall, threatening death to her and all her children.

Charles's own news was equally distressing. His letter was full of excuses as to why he had still made no attempt to secure Hull. It made her furious with impatience. 'Parliament controls the navy. If they send a fleet to Hull to remove our arsenal we will be powerless to retrieve it.' Oh, the folly of it was so obvious and so great that she could not understand it. She stood up abruptly, walked a few paces from the table and turned back, her hand pressed to her head. 'I am beginning to wish I had never left England. The whole point was to leave His Majesty free to act. But if he's just going to sit around at York and do nothing, I might as well have stayed there with him. He writes that everyone dissuades him from taking Hull by force. But why? He would not be attacking but defending himself against the rascals who refuse it to him. I cannot understand this reluctance to fire the first shot.'

Mall and Father Philip looked on in bemusement to hear her talk so heatedly of battle strategy. But it did not take experience of war to know what needed to be done, just courage and common sense. Her husband clearly lacked both, as well as proper advice.

Henrietta lacked the latter too. The people who had come with her to Holland between them ensured her spiritual and bodily needs were well taken care of, and they kept her company and entertained her, which was all that a queen generally required of her attendants. But now she needed advisors, just as the king did, and those were sadly lacking.

She was visited fleetingly by one of the king's former councillors, George, Lord Digby, an accomplished and handsome politician who'd spoken out against the attainder condemning Strafford and had also backed Charles's disastrous plan to enter the House of Commons. But Henrietta was not inclined to trust him and the last she heard he had returned to England disguised as a Frenchman, of all things!

Mall and Father Philip's best advice was that she should write to Charles again and let him know her concerns, reminding him that occupying Hull must be his priority.

Her headache had grown worse rather than better and writing only intensified the pain behind her eyes. But she sat doggedly at her desk as the light failed, painstakingly working out in cipher what she wanted to say. She had written out the proper words first to get them right and before she burned this copy she gave it to Father Philip to read. 'I have apologised to His Majesty in advance in case I have said too much. Do you think I have? Do you think it is too harsh to say that my whole hope rests in his firmness and constancy, and that when I hear anything to the contrary it makes me mad?'

'I am sure His Majesty will understand,' said Father Philip, whose job it was to show understanding and compassion to everyone.

'I am right too in saying that Parliament is simply toying with him, like a cat with a mouse?'

'It seems as if they are doing exactly that,' he replied without conviction.

Henrietta begged the king's pardon if she had said anything that was too forthright, explaining that it was only her affection for him that made her so. The letter was sent and Charles sent one back. He had finally led a troop of horse to Hull but the governor had ordered the city gates to be shut in his face. The messenger who brought the letter had picked up alarming rumours that the king was now turning back for London. Worse still, that the queen's enemies had made a declaration that her life was not to be spared.

For a time Henrietta sat and stared at the decoded letter in disbelief, her head in her hands. She pressed her fingers against her aching eyes for a moment. When she stood up, her legs nearly buckled beneath her.

'Are you all right, ma'am?' asked Mall, alarmed.

'I'll lie down for a while.'

Henrietta tried to think how best to respond to this letter, but a dark despair sapped her spirit and paralysed her, so that her mind seemed not to work at all. She was incapable of making the simplest decision or completing the simplest task. She had not even removed her shoes before she climbed on to the bed. She felt as if she would never have the strength to rise from it again.

She was trying so hard but all her efforts were utterly pointless if Charles did not play his part. She could not help but take his actions personally. She felt bitterly disappointed in him. How could he be so weak? How could he let her down like this? How could he contemplate making an agreement with a Parliament that wanted her dead? That would mean she could never again live with him in England. Did she mean so little to him? Did his crown mean so little to him? She knew that it did not. Oh, but how could he be such a fool?

Henrietta felt suddenly unequal to the tasks ahead of her. She had been brought up to dance and to sing and be pretty. Not to haggle with pawnbrokers and cut deals with merchants to fund an army. She felt like the most wretched person alive. The burden she was carrying felt too great. She was no longer capable of bearing the weight of it. How she wished she could set it down at least for a time, that there was someone who could relieve her of it. But there was no one. She must bear it alone. She loved Charles deeply and truly and would go on doing so, no matter what he did. Nothing would change that. But she could not depend on him for anything. Through the fog of despair and fear there was one point of clarity, one realisation. She saw that she loved him more in the way that she loved her children than as a husband. There was nothing she would not do for them. No effort or sacrifice that was too great. She would willingly die for them and she would die for Charles. She would kill anyone who hurt them or him. The fierce, protective love of a mother for a child was the way she felt towards her husband too. But it was an unequal sort of love, for like a child he could not be relied upon.

Henrietta curled up and sobbed, drawing her knees to her like a child herself, knowing that there was no one in the world for her to turn to.

The next morning she summoned all her strength and wrote to Charles. Once again it took a painfully long time to translate the message into code. She read it through so many times that the words grew meaningless. She knew she sounded bitterly angry and frustrated with him, but so she was. She saw no reason to disguise that, could not disguise it.

*You see what you've got by not following our first resolutions? That governor is a traitor and, for treating you so abominably, deserves to be flung over the walls. I will believe nothing of these rumours of your return to London and trust you to be constant in your resolutions now. But I am troubled almost to death by fear to the contrary. If you really have gone to reach an accommodation with Parliament, I shall have to retire to a convent, since I could never trust my life to those persons who want nothing but death for me. You have already learned the cost of lack of perseverance. If you abandon our friends it will be worse than abandoning your crown. You are lost for ever.*

*Always remember that we have justice on our side. She is a good army and one that will at last conquer all the world. She is with you and therefore you should not fear. If I knew Latin, I ought to finish with a word of it, but as I do not, I will finish with a French one. I am yours after death, if it be possible.*

*Adieu. Go on boldly, sweetheart. God will assist you.*

She wrote also to Mamie.

*Pray to God for me for I am wretched. I am separated from my lord, from my children and from my country, without hope of returning there except in imminent peril. I feel as if I have been abandoned by all the world.*

But she had not been abandoned. Another letter arrived. It was from Harry.

Just to see his neat handwriting, his name, his signature at the bottom of the page, was both a comfort and a pleasure. If he knew how much it meant to her, he would surely write to her every day. Or never. But what he had written gave Henrietta even greater comfort and pleasure.

He was trying to join her in The Hague. He had already reached the Dutch frontier in the southern part of the Duchy of Brabant, which was under the control of the Spanish Hapsburgs. The border guards had refused to let him pass. They had told him the Dutch States General, whose sympathies now lay firmly with the English Parliament, had refused permission for any of those they called 'the queen's traitors' to cross. But he had made a personal appeal to the Prince of Orange and was hopeful that he would soon be allowed to come to her.

Henrietta read the letter through again and then, very gently, she brought it to her heart and held it there with both hands, pressing it against her. Then she lifted it to her lips and kissed it with a flourish.

'Fetch my coat, Mall,' she said eagerly, jumping to her feet. 'And have the carriage made ready.'

'Certainly, ma'am. Might I ask where we are going in such a rush?'

'To see the Prince of Orange and beg him to bring his influence to bear on the States General.'

Days later, she was sitting at her desk by candlelight, struggling to decipher another communication from Charles, when Mary came running in to tell her that the Prince of Orange had persuaded the States General to order the border guards to turn a blind eye to Harry and William crossing into Dutch territory. Even now they were travelling north to her.

'Have Father Philip send my coach right away to meet them,' Henrietta told Mary. 'So that they may travel in comfort, and faster.' It was like waking up to a day of sunshine after a month of cold and rain. Suddenly everything looked totally different, brighter, warmer. She grabbed both her daughter's hands, her face alight with hope. 'Courage, Mary! I have never felt so much.'

When she turned her attention back to the letter it seemed suddenly not such an effort to read. Miraculously, the pain in her eyes had gone. Her head felt clearer and the letter practically decoded itself, even though Charles would insist on using the cipher incorrectly. When she worked out that what it said was that the precious Royalist arms and ammunition stored at Hull had now been removed to London, by order of Parliament, she was not remotely surprised. Had she been able to make any sense of it prior to Mary's welcome interruption, she'd have been so disheartened she would have laid her head on the desk and wept, or else fired off the angriest reply to Charles.

Now, she responded with restraint.

*It will not be easy to find the money to make up for this loss. I must say that if you had not delayed this going to Hull as long as you did, I think that you would not have lost your magazine. I am ever returning to the old point, lose no time for that will ruin you. Believe me,* mon cher, *that I am moved to speak by no consideration in the world but yours.*

She had not seen Harry for so long, months of extreme anxiety and stress which she feared must inevitably have taken their toll on her appearance.

'Your Majesty is as beautiful as ever you were as a girl,' Father Philip assured her, catching the queen studying herself in a mirror.

'As vain as ever, you mean.' Henrietta smiled at his reflection, scowled at her own. She leaned forward a little and with her finger tried to wipe away the shadows beneath her eyes. She needed some of Lucy's rouge. And food. She had grown so thin. At least her hair was still thick and glossy and Mall was very skilled with the curling tongs. Only . . . she yanked out a white hair that she was horrified to see glinting against her black curls and blue ribbon. She turned round, holding it up between thumb and forefinger like a slug found lurking in the lettuce. 'All this worry is turning me grey.'

'Nonsense!' Father Philip said. 'You are as lovely as a girl of sixteen.'

She felt as happy as a girl of sixteen a few nights later, or perhaps a girl of fourteen – the age she had been when she'd met Harry for the first time and he had made her heart skip in that wonderful way.

Unable to sleep, largely because of the excitement of seeing him again, she was standing leaning against the shutters in her closet, idly looking out into the quiet moonlit street, having taken a break from writing yet more begging letters to peers and cardinals. She had stopped writing because the strain of doing it by candlelight was making her eyes hurt badly. But the sight they saw now was enough to gladden even the saddest, sorest eyes. A coach. Her coach. Rocking up the deserted silver-lit street. She picked up her skirts and, not even bothering to grab her cloak, ran outside just in time to see it draw up in front of the stables.

The door was opened and out stepped William. Then Harry. She resisted the urge to run to him and fling her arms around his neck.

Both men bowed to her.

Henrietta's first thought was that Harry did not look much like an exile! Not in the way that Elizabeth did. Suave as ever, dressed in black cloak, silk breeches and knee-high white boots with his sword at his hip, his hair tumbled but tidy and his blue eyes so warm and alive, he looked no different from the image of him she always carried in her memory and in her heart.

'I knew you'd come,' she said as he took her hands in both of his and looked down into her face. 'I knew it.'

'I am only sorry it has taken me so long, ma'am.'

He was looking so intently into her eyes that she lowered them, feeling suddenly shy. William had discreetly turned his head aside. 'Don't tell me I look well,' Henrietta said quietly. 'I know that I don't.'

'You look well to me,' he said softly.

They stood staring at one another until William shuffled his feet and cleared his thoat, as if to remind them he was there.

'Are you hungry? You must be? You always are.' Henrietta linked her arm through Harry's, and smiled at William. 'Come in and have some Dutch cheese. It has holes in it that make it look as if the mice have been at it, but is very good. Though not so good as French, of course. But the ale here is excellent.'

She fetched tankards and poured for them herself, though both men tried to relieve her of the jug. 'We are short of servants now,' she told them. 'I don't stand on ceremony. We don't have much to eat either. I send all I can to England and am left without a *sou*, but it matters not. I would rather be in want than that the king should.' She sat with them both at the table and, while they ate and drank, told them all that had happened in England and what she had been trying to achieve in Holland.

'We are here to help you now,' Harry said gently. 'We will talk properly tomorrow and devise the best plan.'

She felt a calmness settle over her then, like a snowfall in the night that softened all sounds and made everything beautiful.

She showed them to the chambers she had made ready for them and said goodnight before going to her own bed. Just knowing that Harry was here, down the corridor, she slept deeper and longer than she had in weeks.

She rose late to find him already up, dressed and shaved, and looking about for something to do.

'All I do is write letters,' Henrietta told him. 'Letters, letters, letters! Come and see.' She took his arm and led him through to the closet where she had been working the previous night. It was as she had left it, strewn with quills and candles, wax and paper.

'I would have tidied it away,' she said. 'Only I was disturbed by a certain person's arrival.'

'Why was Your Majesty writing in the middle of the night?'

'What else is there to do?' She could not resist flashing a flirtatious smile at Harry. He did not respond to it but she did not care. She was so pleased to see him that for now she did not mind what he did or did not do. 'I have given up trying to sell the jewels because nobody wants them or even believes I have the right to sell them in the first place. I shall likely have to give up writing too.'

'Why?'

'I have such terrible headaches.'

'I am sorry to hear that, ma'am. You have seen a physician?'

'They can do nothing. I don't know if it's caused by the damp air here or by the strain of all the writing. Or maybe it is just that I have been crying so much.'

He looked at her for a moment in such a kindly way that it made her want to cry again. Then he took up one of the letters which she had not yet sealed. Henrietta snatched it back off him with a grin. It was one of the ones she had written very late at night. Too late. It was a mess and she could not bear for him to see it. So many blots and crossings out. 'You are not to read it,' she said. 'If you even *can* read my little hand.'

Her hand was anything but little. He'd received enough letters from her to know that she was being ironic. She was still embarrassed by her own clumsiness with a pen though she took great pains, especially when writing formal letters to important people. Even so, her writing was large, slanting and spidery, the looping tails of her letters hopelessly long and unsteady. She used capital letters rather randomly, and even though she knew, in principle, where full stops and commas should go, tended to use colons to serve all purposes and to scatter them randomly also.

'Writing is a pain and a grief to me,' she admitted, setting the letter aside. 'Pathetic, since for the larger part of my days all I do now is write letters. I have also been driven well-nigh mad by the difficulty of making out His Majesty's meaning because he's as bad at using the cipher as I am at using punctuation.'

Harry glanced at the pile of correspondence. 'I would offer to write all your letters for you from now on, if it would not offend you?'

'It would not offend me,' she said. 'How could it?'

'Don't cry now,' he said gently, seeing the tears sparkling in her eyes. 'If crying gives you a headache, you must be done with it. There is no need. Now tell me, why don't the Dutch want to buy your jewels?'

Henrietta wiped her eyes and sighed. 'These people are so Parliamentarian that it is only with the greatest trouble we get anything from them. Besides which, it is no use hurrying them. The more they are hurried, the less they do.' It was such a relief to be able to share this with someone, with him, that she grinned. 'I declare that being patient is killing me!'

He laughed. 'I can well believe that. In which case, we must do something to remedy the situation immediately, before it is too late.'

The first thing he did was take complete charge of all her correspondence. She asked Charles for permission for Harry to cipher and decipher their personal letters, on the grounds that he was far quicker and more skilled at it than she and that he already knew their affairs anyway. So from then on Harry ciphered Henrietta's letters to Charles and deciphered Charles's letters to her. It was a little odd and confusing sometimes, to hear her husband's words read to her in Harry's voice or to read them transcribed in Harry's writing, but it meant there was nothing now that she did not and could discuss with him, no personal or state secrets that they did not share.

With Harry at her side, Henrietta felt fearless, tireless and ruthless. She even began to enjoy herself, seeing their joint work as a challenge and an adventure. Cunningly, they sent letters in English without cipher which were designed to fall into enemy hands, misleading them about plans and provisions. In one she acknowledged receiving messages from John Pym, with the aim of discrediting him.

'Who thought of that one?' Harry asked. 'Was that your idea or mine?'

Henrietta folded the paper, let fall a red blob of scarlet wax and pressed into it the signet ring which hung around her wrist, making a tiny impression of a rose and a lily, mark of the Rose and Lily Queen. 'Do you know, I can't remember. Both of us?'

They worked so closely together and were of such like minds that it had become almost impossible to know where his ideas stopped and hers began.

Equally cunningly, Harry lured back the merchants and pawnbrokers by offering to show them the king's signature empowering Henrietta to pledge crown property. She did not possess such a document but Harry assured them it could be obtained if they wanted to see it, and he was so charming and confident that everyone was convinced by him. The result was that they agreed to take every item of the queen's personal jewellery in pawn for fairly large sums. Against her pendant pearls she borrowed over two hundred guilders, and she put her rubies in pawn for forty thousand. Harry also helped finalise loans. The money started rolling in. A wealthy Rotterdam family lent forty thousand guilders, their bank another twenty-five thousand, while the Bank of Amsterdam came up with a loan of nearly a hundred thousand.

'How do you do it?' Henrietta asked Harry after they'd sat down together at the table with more ale, counting up the coins, notes, bills and pledges.

'Do what, ma'am?'

'Make everything all right? You are my magic charm!'

He smiled. 'There is more than enough now to buy ammunition and hire ships and men,' he said, with a nod at the pile of money in front of them.

'How do we go about doing that? I don't even know where to begin.'

'Ships? Sailors?' Harry stroked his beard, pretending to ponder. 'The harbour maybe?'

She gave his arm a playful slap. 'Such impudence!'

First they went together to visit Frederick Henry, Prince of Orange. He was a short, round man with a plump face and dark hair that sat like a mat upon his head. He had proved himself a capable general, statesman and politician, and it was under his guidance that the republic had grown so powerful, through great military and naval triumphs and maritime and commercial expansion. The prince was also responsible for fostering advances in art and literature. His palace was more like a burgher's mansion than a royal residence, constructed in symmetrical blocks with plain large windows and unadorned by any ostentatious flourishes. It had a hall as large as the Palace of Westminster, hung with trophies captured from the Spaniards which he was keen to show off, while readily listing for Henrietta and Harry the names of those who had supplied his own army.

So to the harbour. An East Indiaman had just put into port and the quay was swarming with sailors and merchants and sea captains. Barrels and trunks were being carried down the gangplank and loaded on to horse-drawn carts. On another ship that lay at anchor, carpenters were at work on the deck mending planking and masts. The air smelled of tar and fish and spices, and was alive with shouting and banging, horses neighing and snorting, and the rumble of cartwheels. There were sailmakers and rope-makers and men at work in the rigging. Harry kept tight hold of Henrietta's arm and steered her past a great barrel of smoking pitch and a cage full of chattering monkeys that had been left in the middle of the walkway.

They made their way to an inn at the side of the harbour, a dark, low, lamplit place with an earthern floor and beer-stained tables and barrels for stools. It smelled of stale beer and smoke and sweat, and was packed with the most dangerous, unsavoury-looking characters Henrietta had ever seen.

'You don't have to go in if you'd rather not, ma'am,' Harry said, seeing the expression on her face.

'Are you?'

'I am.'

Henrietta squared her shoulders and raised her chin with a brisk nod. 'Then so am I.'

With one hand in the small of her back, Harry guided her towards the bar, past leering faces with blackened teeth or no teeth at all, men with scars on their brows and tattoos on their knuckles. With shaggy beards that looked as if they'd never been groomed, and tattered, dirty cloaks and breeches that looked as if they'd never been washed. Men who looked ready to cut their throats as soon as look at them. The women were scarcely less intimidating, with brightly painted faces and brightly dyed hair and the bodices of their dresses so low-cut they might just as well not have been wearing any.

But with his sword at his hip and his pistol in his belt, Harry strode through them all with ease. No one gave him any trouble but rather stepped aside to let him pass.

He gave a name to the barman who nodded across the room to a muscular man sitting at a nearby table. He had heard his name mentioned and looked up from his jar of ale. He had veins in his neck as thick as ropes and was in possession of most of his teeth but none of his hair. 'Who wants me?' he said, in a strong Dutch accent.

Harry introduced himself. 'I am Henry Jermyn. And this lady is Her Majesty the Queen of England.'

The man belched. 'And I'm the Emperor of Rome.'

'Just the man we need, then.' Harry smiled. 'We're looking to buy muskets and cannonballs and gunpowder. We also need men and ships. I was told by the Prince of Orange that you could help.'

'You're starting a war?'

'Starting, averting, ending. Hard to say. Is there somewhere we can talk?'

The man stood up. Taking his ale with him, he led them to a dingy backroom with one grimy window. There they sat on rickety stools and talked for an hour.

In the days that followed Henrietta accompanied Harry when he went back to the harbour and the inn and into other back rooms in the city to haggle with shipowners and armaments manufacturers. She drank tankards of warm beer and bargained along with him, handed pouches of coins into dirty, callused hands and in return took possession of crateloads of guns and lead shot.

It was not at all the way she had imagined her life as Queen of England would be, but she found it exciting and exhilarating and was certainly no longer brought low by the wide, grey lowland skies.

They were kept so busy that Charles complained of not receiving letters often enough.

'"I would rather you chide me than be silent,"' Harry deciphered, reading out loud to Henrietta after they'd sat down together one afternoon in her closet to deal with her correspondence.

'That makes me sound such a . . . what is the word?'

'Nag? Harridan? You are neither of those things, ma'am.'

'I do chide my husband, though. But with good cause.'

'Evidently he does not mind it at all, and why would he? I would not mind being chided by you either.'

'You do not need chiding.'

'May I have that in writing?'

'In cipher, if you like?'

He smiled at her and it made her heart turn over and her body flood disconcertingly with heat. When she stood up, she felt a little dizzy. 'Let us go and count our weapons.'

'Again?'

'It is very satsifying, don't you find?'

Through their joint efforts, the stockpile of armaments had slowly built up. The salon at the New Palace had been cleared of all its ornamental furniture and treasures and turned into a giant storeroom, locked and bolted and guarded night and day.

By July they had painstakingly assembled:

one thousand muskets;

one thousand pikes and swords;

three thousand pistols;

one thousand saddles;

five hundred carbines;

two hundred flintlocks;

ten loads of powder;

twenty cannons.

Wagons arrived to remove part of their supplies. They were to be loaded on to a supply ship that was sailing for the North of England, and transported overland to York. Harry had engaged a Dutch convoy to escort it. Possible landing places had been discussed: Scarborough, Holy Island and Whitby.

They stood together on the harbourside watching the ship set sail. As the gulls wheeled overhead and the wind whistled in the rigging, Henrietta saw how wonderfully low the ship lay in the water, its hold filled with the vital supplies that she and Harry had bartered and haggled and striven so hard to obtain. Nothing in her life to date had given her such a sense of achievement.

As they watched the sails unfurl and fill with wind, she kept her face fixed ahead but reached discreetly for Harry's hand. He took it, and she slipped her fingers between his and held it firm. She wanted to thank him, to say that she could not have done it without him, but words seemed superfluous.

Due to forces beyond anyone's control, the shipment went catastrophically wrong. The supplies bound for York got no further than Hellevoetsluis, when the wind changed and the ships had to lower their sails and drop anchor to wait for it to shift direction. No sooner were they underway again than they had to turn back in order to avoid capture by Parliamentary ships. Frustratingly, the captain then refused to embark on a second journey without better information regarding the location of the enemy fleet. Harry found a replacement ship and William offered to sail with it. When news reached The Hague that this vessel had been seized at Whitby and forced to surrender its cargo, and that William had been taken prisoner by Parliament, Henrietta covered her face with her hands and burst into tears.

She felt Harry's hands gently taking hold of hers. He lowered them, forcing her to look at him. 'Don't cry,' he said, almost as a command.

But she was inconsolable. 'All our weapons,' she wept. 'We worked so hard to buy them and now Parliament has them. And William is captured. Damn the wind and weather! Why did they have to be against us like everything else? Oh, it is a disaster.'

He put his arms around her and she felt his strength enfolding her. His hand on her head, stroking her hair. 'All is not lost,' he said, softly.

'Oh, but it is,'

'No,' he said. 'It is not.'

He sounded so sure about that she stopped crying and drew back a little to look at him, blinking away her tears.

He took her hand and Henrietta let him lead her to the salon, where the rest of the guns and cannonballs were still stockpiled. 'Just in case you need reminding that we still have half the arms left.'

'I know, but what if they are lost too? How can we risk . . .'

'I have found a merchant who has assured me he can deliver them wherever we please. He is accustomed to avoiding pirates and says he can run the Parliamentary blockade and slip into any fishing port on the north-east coast.'

Henrietta half laughed, then frowned. 'But . . . we've only just heard about the loss of the first ship. How did you know to . . . ?' She answered her own question instantly. 'You have not only just heard, have you?'

'I was given news of the seizure of our vessel yesterday,' Harry admitted, a little warily. 'I could not bear to tell you about it until I had found a solution.'

'You should not have kept it from me.'

'I know I should not, ma'am. Forgive me. You told me you never needed to chide me and now, see, you do. You are!'

'I am not childing,' said Henrietta. 'Of course I forgive you. You are a wonder and a marvel, Harry Jermyn.'

'You are a wonder and a marvel yourself, ma'am.' There was a warm light burning in his eyes that she had not seen for such a long time but recognised well. She wanted to kiss him, to be kissed by him, in this room filled with cannons and gunpowder and muskets. Unconsciously, she leaned a little towards him. He drew back, away from her, and it was as if he had slapped her, or grabbed one of the muskets and shot her with it.

Thwarted desire and loneliness tore though her like a storm. Why did they never speak of what had passed between them? Those glorious weeks that had begun with a lesson in English and ended in Wellingborough with the Duke of Buckingham's assassination. Why was it they never even acknowledged it? As if they were ashamed, as if it had never happened, as if they wanted to pretend it had never been.

Her lips parted to speak but Harry spoke first. 'Prince Rupert is keen to join His Majesty in England. He seems a brave and resourceful young man and I propose that we should send him with this next shipment of arms.'

'If you think so,' she replied, distracted, wanting to stop his mouth with kisses. Then she remembered. 'William! What about William?'

'William can take good care of himself. He knew the risks and was entirely prepared to take them, as are we all. And he will be released, I am certain. This is not the first time he's been imprisoned by Parliament, after all. They let him go before and I'm certain they will again. On the grounds that they do not wish to make martyrs out of poets.'

'Yes, of course. I'd forgotten.'

Inside she was screaming: Have you?

\* \* \*

When news arrived at the beginning of September that Prince Rupert had landed safely at Newcastle, Mall grabbed Henrietta's hands and started dancing around the room as if the arrival of one supply ship in England meant the war was as good as won. Henrietta knew it would take more than that, much more, but for now she allowed herself to be content. 'I just hope His Majesty appreciates all our efforts on his behalf.'

He did not.

Information reached Henrietta from England, via Prince Rupert, that the king was in fact displeased with her efforts. He believed she was being lazy, not trying hard enough.

After all the criticism she had suffered from him while the Duke of Buckingham was alive, about not trying hard enough to learn to speak English, to be a better wife, a better queen, to please her husband in bed, this was especially hard to take. It was not so much like having an old wound ripped open again, as ripped open and a knife stuck into it, deepening and widening it. She'd thought Charles had changed, that everything had changed between them. But his letter made it seem that nothing had, after all. She could not see him or speak to him to smooth things over so instead she nursed her hurt and it seethed inside her.

'It is so unfair!' It was Charles she wanted to shout at but instead it was Harry who bore the brunt, just because once again he was there when Charles was not. 'How can he say that I am lazy, that we are not trying hard enough? How can he even for one moment think it? We've both been working night and day to serve him.'

They had been eating a frugal supper and Henrietta tossed down her spoon. Her eyes flashed with anger as brightly as ever they did with merriment or mischievousness, and her pale cheeks were flushed with indignation. 'I send him every guilder I can. We live on soup and one meat dish a day. All the hours we've spent battling with those miserly pawnbrokers and arms-dealers count for nothing, do they? All those letters? We have followed all his instructions. I cannot be held responsible for Parliamentary blockades. I do not have command of the winds!' As she stood up she banged one fist on the table, making the silver rattle and the candles gutter and everyone flinch. 'Damn it, it is not my fault that Hull is in enemy hands, leaving us with no safe landing port!'

She ran out of breath, realising that Harry had still not said a word. She had not given him time to, but she realised also that she'd placed him in an impossible position, as so often she did. He would not want to criticise his king. She sat down again. 'Oh, I know that it should be enough reward that God blesses our pains. I should not need praise. But I do, and he knows that.'

'We all like to be praised, ma'am,' Harry replied, putting down his own spoon. 'And you deserve to be.'

'I thought he loved me,' whispered Henrietta. 'I thought I loved him. He can be so unkind.'

'I am sure he is not entirely to blame.'

'How can he not be to blame for his own thoughts and feelings?'

'I am sure mischief is being made by those determined to reach a settlement with the enemy. Since they know you will never consent to that, it serves their purpose to malign and belittle you in the king's eyes. Do you see? They will try to persuade His Majesty that you are unable or unwilling to aid him, and use that to force him into negotiating with Parliament.'

'*This* is supposed to cheer me?' But she saw the wisdom and sense in what he said and did feel cheered by the hope that her husband was being manipulated and these cruel sentiments did not come from his own heart. It meant she could still trust in the goodness of that. But what did it say about the strength of his backbone? Nothing she did not already know. If the mischief-makers succeeded and a settlement were reached, it meant she could never return to England.

But as she looked across the table at Harry in the glow of the candlelight, she realised that England was the last place she wanted to go. She was despised by the English people and her husband did not appreciate her. Moreover, England was a place where Harry could never be.

'I am sorry for shouting at you.'

'No need to apologise.'

'If I am despised and hated, I fear I shall become despicable and hateful,' she said, with a wry smile. 'If I were loved, I should be . . . lovely.'

'You are loved, Your Majesty,' he said simply. 'And very lovely.'

'Let's do something different in the morning,' she suggested impulsively. 'Since we have worked so hard and have had no thanks, let us reward ourselves.'

'How?'

'Let's saddle the horses and go exploring. We can look at the architecture. The houses and gardens here are beautiful.'

In the hot summer sun they rode out towards the city hall, past rows of elegant houses several storeys high, which took their sober and restrained style from classical antiquity. The gardens were neat and precise, like those in France, with flowering shrubs and ornamental plants set in geometric patterns between gravelled paths, marble statues and fountains.

But Henrietta was not looking at the beautiful gardens or the beautiful houses. She was staring at Harry's beautiful hands resting on the reins, the thread of the leather through his long fingers, the line of them, the shape of his nails, the fine gold hairs, the shape of his strong bones beneath the lightly tanned skin. She wanted to take those hands and turn them palm upwards and bury her face in them.

'It is not Paris,' Harry said, looking up at a rigorously steepled church. 'But these buildings are impressive.'

They rode on out of town and onto the polders, where there was nobody to hear them but the herons in the rush-filled dykes.

'Why did you come here?' Henrietta asked.

He turned to her looking puzzled. 'Because of your letter. Because I knew when you said you were going to Holland that you would not just be escorting Mary. I came to help you and I trust that I have.'

Henrietta reined in her horse, knowing that it was all that she could rein in, that this frustration and desire and anger which had been building in her for weeks, months, years, had to have its release, that she could hold it back no longer. 'You came to serve me.' She made it sound like nothing, worse than nothing. 'As you promised always to serve me?'

'Yes.' He had brought his horse to a halt too. 'I did.'

'I don't want you to serve me,' she said, fighting tears. 'I don't want you to do anything for me out of duty, or obligation, because I am the queen and you are a courtier.'

Harry looked down, away from her, and she saw his shoulders slump a little, as if he had been expecting this conversation for some time and dreading it.

'You are just upset, ma'am, because His Majesty . . .'

'It is not just that.' Now she had begun she could not stop until she had said all that she wanted to say. She was not even sure what that was or why she must say it, but the words were pressing unformed against her lips, against her heart, making it feel as if it would burst, or collapse, or both, if she did not let the truth out.

Henrietta slid from the saddle and he did likewise. They stood facing one another, hands on the bridles of the horses.

'Don't you see?' she asked. 'You torment me with your help and your kindnesses. Everything that you do to serve me, out of kindness, or duty, or gratitude, out of the goodness of your heart . . . it tortures me. I do not want you to do these things because I am your queen . . . because I have rewarded your service with sinecures and you are grateful to me. I want you to do it for love of me.'

'You have a husband who loves you,' he said, very quietly.

'And you are being very noble and honourable and proper, I know.' Her hand tightened on the bridle and her eyes were flashing like black stars. 'Well, damn your nobility and your honour! Damn you for respecting my marriage and the king! I want you to be . . .' she broke off. 'What is the opposite of noble?'

'Ignoble. Ma'am.'

'Then I want you to be ignoble and dishonourable and improper. All of those things. Your honour insults me. Frankly.'

'Insults you?'

She lifted her chin. 'If you wanted me as I want you, you would be unable to control yourself . . . to resist me. It is an insult that you can. I want . . . your desire and love for me to sweep aside all notions of honour. For nothing else to matter.

'Sometimes . . . sometimes I wonder if perhaps you use your honour as a convenient excuse. That you do not want me at all. Oh, but that does not make any sense! I believed in William's concept of platonic love. I did. I thought it a beautiful ideal. Sometimes I think it is truly beautiful, special, what we have. And sometimes I think it is horrible. Intolerable. This love is not the beautiful love of poets, it is a humiliating enslavement. Wanting more from a person than they are willing to give. That is a dark and desperate place to be.'

She was trembling with emotion, talking even faster than usual, barely pausing for breath. She had so much to say that had gone unspoken for too long.

'Courtly love. Platonic love. Love without its proper physical expression and release . . . It does not work. Not when there is desire. It is a road only to madness. I want you with all that I have and all that I am. My heart and my soul and my body cry out for you and you are deaf and blind to me, or choose not to hear or see. I want you so much that sometimes I cannot breathe. Sometimes I almost hate you. I want to hit you and scratch you and bite you. How can you be so controlled, so cold? I thought it would be enough to have you as a friend. To have you in my life. To see you every day, to talk to you. But it is not enough. Because when I see you and talk to you, I want so much to touch you. To taste you. To feel you. I cannot sleep for wanting you. I can think of nothing but you. You have filled my head and my heart and my body and yet . . . you have left me empty. You awakened something in me, and then you denied it to me and now I am not allowed to love you and so I have all this love for you that is trapped in my heart and . . . between my legs . . . and has no release and nowhere to go. And it is devouring me and destroying me!'

He moved towards her but she backed away. 'Don't! Don't touch me. Don't try to comfort me. There is only one way you can. One way. Damn your honour,' she repeated. 'Just fuck me.'

Harry was looking down into her eyes and she tried to read his face. She knew him so well but could not read him at all. This keeping of his thoughts from her made her break down in a passion of weeping. She wished instantly she had never spoken. For having him serve her and be her friend was better than not having him at all. Now she feared that she had upset some fine balance between them and made it impossible for them to go on even as they were. She wanted to unsay all that she had said, to feel his arms around her again, just because she was crying, to hear him laugh and see his smile and for everything to be all right between them.

He gave her a kerchief from his pocket, knowing that even though she often cried she never did keep one on her person. It smelled of him. Henrietta looked at him through the mist of her tears. 'Now you are angry with me.'

He shook his head. 'Why would I be? When all you have done is give me a piece of your mind. As we are all entitled to do.'

'You give me no peace of mind,' she said quietly. His remembering and mentioning that silly conversation they'd had so long ago, when he was teaching her to speak English, seemed like a kind of a code. Like a private cipher of their own.

342

'I do not wish to be ignoble,' he said. 'I cannot treat you with dishonour and disrespect. I honour and respect you too much to do that. What is more, I don't believe you would respect me if I did cast aside all honour. And I want your respect more than anything. I do not believe that you could be dishonourable towards His Majesty either. Not now.'

Henrietta knew that he was right, completely right, but almost hated him for being so. 'England is tearing itself apart for honour,' she said. 'And we must do the same.'

It was only as they rode back in silence that she realised she had said so much and he had said nothing. Not really. She still did not know if it was all an excuse, if he did not really want her any more. They supped in silence on soup, with Father Philip, Geoffrey and Mall who must have known something was wrong but were too tactful to comment.

Henrietta felt sick, poisoned, fragile and raw. I could die of this pain, she thought. I was sure I would die of the pain of childbirth but this is far worse. It goes on and on, with no respite. And there are no ointments to soothe it. I cannot scream out with it. I have to smile and get through the day.

As soon as she could, she escaped to her chamber and, like a young girl in the first agonising flush of love, seized the pillow and wrapped her arms around it and held it tight against her. She was so lonely. It was so long since she had been held or had someone to hold.

She pictured Harry in his own bed, an image that merged with a memory from Wellingborough of him lying naked on his belly on the tangled white linen sheets in a tent suffused with soft early sunlight. She could still see him so clearly. How he lay slightly turned to one side, with one leg hooked up, while she wanted to trace the strong lines of his buttocks and his back with her finger. In an agony of loneliness and desire, she pushed the pillow down between her thighs and squeezed it.

And then there was a soft knock at the door, a distinctive double knock. His voice, whispering, 'Are you awake?'

For a moment Henrietta was sure she had imagined that too, but then she knew she had not. She tossed aside the pillow and sat up. 'Yes. I am awake.' She climbed out of bed and almost ran to the door, reaching for the latch.

'Don't open it,' he said. 'I don't want to come in.'

Her arm fell to her side. 'Then . . . what do you want to do?'

'I can't sleep.'

She rested her forehead against the door. 'Neither can I.'

'I am curious. Tell me, do you think in French now or in English?'

Why did he want to know that now? She had never considered it. So she thought for a moment. Found that she was doing it . . . 'In English!'

'And when you dream?'

'French. Mostly.'

'I too,' he said. 'Since it is you I dream about.'

She closed her eyes and pressed her body against the door, her hands beside her face, the flat of her palms against the wood. There was a sound at the other side and she moved back a little, thinking he would open it now. But then there was a rustle against it, lower down, and she realised Harry had just slid his shoulder or his back down the length of it, to sit on the floor outside.

She sat too, sideways on, curled against the door.

'I had a dream about you last night,' he said. 'I dreamed that I was hard and inside you.'

She bit her lip. 'I dream about you too, and I wake in the morning wanting you so much. I go on wanting you all day and so I walk around with this . . . bursting flower between my legs.'

He gave a soft moan that made her imagine him hard, and the image of him with a painful erection which she could neither touch nor relieve made the liquid heat between her legs so unbearable that she turned so that her shoulder blades were against the door, her head arched back against it. She pressed her hand against her belly and her legs together, as she had done against the pillow.

'What are you doing?' he said softly. 'Talk to me.'

'I would rather listen to you,' she said. 'The king has never satisfied me. He has never made me spend you know. Not once. You can do it just with the sound of your voice.'

Harry brought the news of Marie de' Medici's death in Cologne to Henrietta as she was writing to her sister. She saw from his face that something was terribly wrong and her first thought was for Charles and her children in

England. She had not expected to hear that it was her mother who had died. Even though Marie was old and had been ill for some time, it came as the greatest shock. She had always seemed to Henrietta to be indestructible.

She looked down at the half-written letter to her sister, preoccupied as it was with the war in England and Henrietta's own efforts in Holland. Did Christine know already? Should she send word? Henrietta tore up the letter. Either way, it would be a very different one she must write now.

She stared at the torn pieces of paper. What struck her hardest was that her mother had died thinking Henrietta had failed to to do what had mattered to Marie more than anything else: to bring England nearer to Rome. Even if by some miracle she achieved it in the future, Marie would never know now. Given her own predicament, Henrietta also hated to remember how her mother had died, impoverished and in exile. 'She should have gone home to die,' she said, tears stinging in her eyes. 'In her beautiful new palace in Paris. Not in Germany. I have never been to Germany.'

'The River Rhine will lead us straight there,' Harry said gently. 'I will make the necessary arrangements.'

But when he requested permission of the Dutch burghers for the queen's party to travel to Cologne they forbade it. So all Henrietta could do to mark her mother's passing was to put her tiny court into mourning and write to Charles to tell him to do likewise.

She received no reply. The leaves were drifting down from the trees and when she woke there was frost on the window pane. For six long, tense weeks there had been no reliable news from England bar agonisingly vague scraps of conflicting information from random sources: sailors whose ships had sailed close to English shores, merchants who'd traded with the leaders of the Parliamentary party. Holland was seething with rumours. One thing seemed beyond doubt: England was now in a state of full civil war.

They said that the king had raised the royal standard at Nottingham but that during the night a gale blew down the flag. They said this foretold certain disaster for the Royalists. They said King Charles had been defeated. Then that he had been captured.

Then that he was dead. And that the Prince of Wales had died with him.

This news was brought to the New Palace by a young English sailor whom Harry had met at the harbour and was paying for intelligence. He said that there had been a great battle and that King Charles and the Prince of Wales had both been killed in the fighting. There were those who claimed to have seen and touched their dead bodies.

Harry handed the man some coins, made Henrietta sit down. He drew up a stool before her and held her gently by the arms. He made her look at him, focus on him. 'You must not listen to this.' There was a fierce light in his blue eyes and she fixed on it like a candle in a cavern. It was her only tether to life and to hope. But it was as if a widow's veil had fallen over her already, a heavy black mantle which blocked out all light and sound so that the world turned at once dark and silent.

'I refuse to believe this,' Harry said quietly. 'I refuse to believe any of it, until I see with my own eyes a letter from someone we can trust informing us that it is so. If the people of this country are to be trusted, not a day passes without us losing one battle or another. Rumour mongering has become their chief pastime, and the very nature of rumours is that they become further exaggerated the more they are spread.'

But what if it were true? What if Prince Charles was dead? And his father? Her husband's last words to her had been to express disappointment that she had not done more to help him. She had been so angry with him. In her mind she pictured him galloping along the cliffs, waving goodbye. *It is your love that sustains me.*

'I should have worked harder,' she said weakly, the tears rolling down her cheeks. 'Bargained harder. Begged harder.'

'Nobody could have worked harder than you.'

She was shaking her head. 'I should never, never have left him.'

'Then write a letter to him,' Harry said. 'Ask him if you should come home.'

The idea of writing to Charles as if there were no question but that he was still alive to read the letter was so heartening that at once Henrietta felt better.

'What if a letter comes back from him saying that I should?'

'Then go. And I'll go with you.'

She was sure she could not have heard him right. 'To England?'

'We have done all we can here. Perhaps it is time.'

'You are a convicted traitor!'

'And your enemies have made a declaration that your life will not be spared. In addition, you know very well the rebels may try to take you, in order to barter with the king for your life. It will be no more dangerous for me than it is for you. But where you go, I go too.'

'Even if it is into danger?'

'Especially if it is into danger. Not out of duty or obligation,' he added softly. 'But because by your side is the only place I want to be. The only place I can be.'

As had become their habit, Henrietta drew up a chair next to his at the desk in her closet and they worked side by side. She knew what she wanted to say and dictated it without hesitation. 'For my own part you may imagine my inclination leads me back to England now. But I beg you not to think of that which will please me most but will serve you best.' She paused, giving time to let Harry catch up, but he ciphered with great speed and was keeping pace. 'Only let me have a quick answer.'

Instead of a letter, it was James Stewart, Mall's husband, who arrived at the New Palace out of the blue one morning, while Mall and Henrietta were walking the dogs in the autumnal garden that was strewn with golden leaves. James had always had an affinity with dogs and it was Mitte who spotted him first and bounded up to him through the drifts of fallen leaves, barking a welcome. Henrietta stared at him in dread, sure he had brought the worst news, that he had come in person to tell her Charles was dead. But though of a naturally melancholy disposition, he did not look very melancholy now. And the first thing he did after he had fondled Mitte's ears and returned Mall's emotional hugs and kisses was to assure Henrietta that the king and all their children were alive and well.

'Thank God.'

'They cannot wait to see you, ma'am.'

'So I am to return to England?'

'His Majesty wishes to have you with him at the earliest opportunity,' James said, with a smile for Mall who was still clinging to his arm and gazing up at his face as if she could not believe he were really there.

James also brought the first reliable news of the war which finally put paid to all the false information and speculation. Once inside the palace, having sat by the fire with Mall beside him, he told of how the first major engagement had been fought at a place called Edgehill in the Midlands. The Royalists had won an opportunity to advance on London, but by the time the army reached its outskirts the capital was on the alert. 'His Majesty was forced to turn back and is now setting up winter quarters at Oxford.'

Yet again it seemed Charles had not acted swiftly enough, but Henrietta was so relieved he was alive and safe that she felt no annoyance and instead made a joke. 'We will sail by All Saints' Day. But before we start preparing for our journey, I'll go and pray for the man of sin that has married the Popish brat of France, as the London Puritan preacher has surely said.'

# 1643

The queen's party was to sail for England from Scheveningen, a short distance up the coast. It had a small quay at the foot of gently sloping hills upon which stood a windmill and a church. The *Princess Royal*, a first-rate man-of-war, was to be accompanied by a fleet of eleven transport vessels carrying a final consignment of ammunition and stores. Thanks to Jermyn's tireless negotiations with the Dutch, they were providing an escort of eight warships under the command of Admiral Von Tromp, a tall middle-aged man with spiky hair which stuck up in all directions like a hedgehog's quills.

The Prince of Orange, Mary and Elizabeth came to see them off, along with half the population of Holland or so it seemed. The tiny quay was thronged with coaches, carts, horses, dogs, and countrywomen carrying baskets on their heads. It was a blustery January day with spitting rain, so a fringed tent had been put up to provide the royal party with an elegant shelter until the time came to board. Inside, seated on cushioned chairs, everyone was very quiet, all lost in their own unquiet thoughts about returning to a country now at war with itself and with them all. Even before they landed they would face grave danger. They had been forewarned that Parliamentary ships had been ordered to keep a look out for the queen's arrival and to open fire without ceremony.

The gangplank had been lowered now and it was time to embark. Time for Henrietta to say another goodbye, this time to her daughter. Mary clung to her mother's hand, reminding Henrietta how she had once clung to her own mother's, and her tears were for them both, Mary and Marie.

'Be happy,' she told Mary tearfully, kissing her and pressing her own wet cheeks against her daughter's. 'Your husband is adorable. And Holland is a fine country.'

'Give my love to my father and my brothers and sisters,' Mary sobbed. 'Tell them all that I love them and miss them.'

'I will.'

Somehow Henrietta extricated herself and boarded the boat. The anchor was slipped and the convoy fired a salute which was answered from the shore.

Mall visibly flinched at the boom of each cannon.

'There's no need to look so terrified,' Geoffrey told her chirpily. 'We're not being fired at by Parliamentary guns. Yet!'

'Are you not afraid, ma'am?' Mall asked Henrietta.

'I fear none but God,' she replied.

However it was not Parliament which made the journey fraught with danger but the forces of nature. As soon as the convoy left the shelter of the Dutch coast a fierce north easterly gale blew up. Henrietta settled herself in her little bed in the oak-lined cabin, and Mall, Geoffrey, Father Philip and Harry did likewise while the ship bucked and pitched, battered by unrelenting waves, wind and torrential rain. It was far worse even than the storm that Henrietta had faced on her way to England the first time. The noise of it was terrifying: a deafening roar and hiss, crashing and creaking, which was made worse by the sounds of people moaning with seasickness and crying out in fear for God's mercy. On and on for hours it went. And in the midst of it, as the ship pitched wildly, the captain's servants insisted on attempting to serve Henrietta in full state.

'I am too sick to eat,' Mall moaned as the table was laid with linen and in came platters of steaming beef and potatoes along with sauce boats and flagons of wine.

'I too,' Father Philip moaned, taking one look at the food and putting his hand to his mouth.

The ship suddenly tipped so violently it was nearly on its side. Salt cellars rolled off the table, the servants tumbled over each other splattering the wine and gravy and sauces, and the joint of roasted beef flew across the cabin and landed in a hammock. Surrounded by yelling and cursing and messy chaos, Henrietta started giggling.

'How can Your Majesty laugh when we are all going to die?' Mall wailed.

'We are not going to die,' Henrietta assured her. She glanced at Harry, remembering what he had told her. 'No Queen of England has ever yet been drowned. Is that not right, sir?'

'It is, ma'am.'

'I simply cannot die,' she added cheerfully. 'I refuse to. Think how it would delight our enemies!'

Harry laughed at that and Mall looked at them as if they were both mad, or hysterical. Or both. But she looked a little braver, and when the ship listed violently again she did not scream.

But as darkness fell, the storm worsened. Never mind her courageous words of earlier, Henrietta half expected to sink beneath the waves at every second, but kept her fears to herself. She vowed that if she were spared she would send a silver model ship to the shrine of Our Lady of Liesse in Picardy. Candles could not be kept lit and for a while, in the darkness, the ladies were tied with ropes to their narrow beds. But seeking comfort in numbers, so many people crowded into the queen's small cabin that she insisted she be released. They were joined by some of the officers who swore this was the greatest storm they had seen for many a year.

In the morning there was still no change to the weather and when Admiral Von Tromp tried to locate the other ships in their little fleet, it was discovered that one was missing. It had gone down in the night with the loss of eighteen men.

'Oh, how awful!' Mall cried.

Along with great sorrow for those who had drowned, the disaster only made the prospect of them all sinking more real and increased everyone's terror. Night came on once more and still the storm did not abate. Nor the day or night after that. On and on for nine dreadful interminable days and nights. Everyone was violently sick and the stench in the cabins grew overwhelmingly bad. Nobody could eat or even wanted to, and the violent pitching and tossing made sleep impossible. Despite the depth of his faith, Father Philip looked petrified. He crossed himself repeatedly and his lips moved permanently as he muttered a string of prayers. He caught Henrietta watching him and stopped, not wanting her to see his fear.

'Please do keep praying for us all, Father,' she said. 'There is nothing better that you could be doing.'

Throughout it all, Harry remained with her. When the ship lurched with the greatest violence, he held on to her to stop her being thrown about.

When she was sick, he held a bucket for her and kept her hair out of the way. When it was his turn, she did same for him, and in between times she clung to his hand in the darkness. But she never once wept in despair for her life, or screamed out in terror as others did, she merely told them to be brave. And the very fact that she seemed so serene and unconcerned gave everyone courage.

By the time the sea at last grew a little calmer, Henrietta, like the rest of the crew and passengers, was battered and bruised and bewildered with exhaustion. But she was so glad just to have survived, to be alive, that she persuaded Harry, Mall, Father Philip and Geoffrey to leave the unwholesome air of the cabin and go up on deck with her. The waves were still breaking against the sides of the ship, showering them all with icy seawater, but she held on to the rail near the rudder and breathed deep, looking out over the still turbulent sea and heavy skies. Even now the size and swell of the waves was alarming. But in the far distance she sighted land.

'Where is that?' she asked an officer, pointing.

'England, ma'am.'

'England,' she repeated wistfully. 'How long until we reach it?'

'I am afraid there is no hope of affecting a landing in these conditions.'

For two more weeks the ships went nowhere but up and down. Two more weeks of sickness and fetid cabins, or being lashed with icy seawater above deck. Two more weeks with England in sight but as unreachable as the stars. Two more weeks. Only finally to be beaten back, all the way to Scheveningen. They were carried to shore in a fishing smack, whereupon Father Philip fell to his knees at the water's edge giving thanks for their deliverance. Mall complained that their gowns were so stiff with saltwater and vomit they were fit only for peeling off and burning.

Though thankful for their deliverance too, Henrietta did not care about the state of her gown, only that they were not in England but right back where they had begun.

'We were so close,' she said to Harry, looking out across the sea. 'And we have not only lost time but a ship and valuable supplies too.'

'But Your Majesty has gained something invaluable, that which you can never lose.'

She turned to him as the wind whipped her hair. 'What is that?'

'A reputation for invincible courage.'

They were advised that it would be wisest to wait until the spring before attempting a second crossing, but Henrietta had no intention of waiting and Harry knew she would never be persuaded. Superstitious though she was, she was not even intimidated by Admiral Von Tromp's talk of a wild conjunction of the planets which had apparently occurred while she was at sea. She dreaded sailing again but would not let that fear stand in her way. 'God saved me from one great danger,' she said confidently. 'He will not abandon me now.'

They still had to wait ten days for the ships to be repaired and refitted but, while lodging in a local merchant's house, Henrietta and Harry put the time to good use, buying additional ammunition and collecting monies advanced by the King of Denmark.

They set sail once again and this time the sea remained calm and all went well. For once the weather was on their side. They had received word that Parliamentary ships were patrolling the waters off Newcastle-upon-Tyne, but at the last minute the wind changed direction which meant they could head south-west to the little fishing village of Bridlington where they arrived after dark.

It was a bitterly cold night. It had been snowing and now there was a thick freezing fog. But the whole party wrapped up in their cloaks and waited on deck, stamping their feet and blowing on their fingers while they strained their eyes for sight of the torches of the promised hundred-strong detachment of Lord Newcastle's cavalry that had been sent from York to meet them. When the valiant escort of Cavaliers appeared through the fog on the snowy hilltops above the bay, Henrietta thought she had never seen a more welcome or glorious sight.

Harry handed her out of the little landing craft on to the snowy sand where the leader of the Cavaliers bowed low. 'Welcome home to England, Your Majesty,' he said.

'Thank you, sir. I am glad to be back.' It felt like coming home, even though her home now was a place where she had been declared an enemy of the state and people, and where Harry was a convicted traitor.

'Where are we to lodge for the night?' he asked.

'The fishing families are to put you up in their cottages on the quayside.'

Harry glanced at Henrietta as if he feared she might object to such a humble arrangement, but she gave a little shrug of her shoulders. 'We are a pair of vagabonds,' she said merrily, as they were taken up narrow paths slippery with frost. 'Where better?'

The cottage she was to stay in was tiny and thatched, with just one room downstairs. It held a scrubbed table, and a pot was bubbling over the fire. Mall was to stay with her while Harry and Father Philip were in the neighbouring cottage.

Henrietta was quite happy. The cottage was clean and warm, and the fisherman, his wife and two young daughters who lived there could not have been more welcoming. The little girls curtseyed to Henrietta very prettily and then ran off giggling, came back and did it all over again.

'Enough now,' their mother scolded. Then to Henrietta: 'They have been practising all week, ma'am.'

'I can tell,' Henrietta said to the girls. 'Those are the most perfect curtseys I have ever seen. What are your names?'

'I am Jane, ma'am,' the eldest girl said. 'And my sister is called Anne.'

'I had a little girl called Anne,' Henrietta said to the youngest child. 'She was very good at saying her prayers. Are you?'

'Yes, ma'am.'

The little girls ran over to Mitte, who had found a place by the fire and rolled over with her legs in the air.

'She wants you to tickle her tummy,' Henrietta said. 'She thinks that is what children are for!'

The fisherman's wife offered Henrietta some warmed spiced ale. 'We are so honoured to have you here, Your Majesty.'

'I am honoured to be here.'

'We have always been for the king,' the fisherman said. 'As are many people around these parts.'

'I am glad to hear that.'

Henrietta was touched by their loyalty and hospitality. She was served a delicious supper of fresh-cooked fish, and as she ate the fisherman spoke of his dismay that Parliament should wage war against their own king and also of the terror that everyone now lived under, of sieges and riots and looting by both armies. How desperate the people were for peace and stability.

'I am desperate for that too,' Henrietta said. 'And doing all I can to restore it.'

She was shown to her room. The simple wooden bed was clean and comfortable, a quarter the size of the beds at Whitehall and Oatlands but twice as wide as the little bunk on the *Princess Royal*. The sheets smelled mildly of fish, as did the whole cottage, but Henrietta went to sleep as soon as her head touched the pillow, with Mitte lying peacefully across her feet.

She was woken by the sound of the door being flung open so hard it crashed against the wall. Harry burst into the room. She sat up, startled enough by his dramatic entrance, but then nearly jumped out of her skin as the sound of cannon shot ripped through the night.

'There are four Parliamentary ships in the bay and they have opened fire,' he shouted urgently.

By now the little low-ceilinged bedroom was crowded with people all urging her to hurry, but before Henrietta had a chance even to get out of bed there began a fierce bombardment. Cannonballs were whistling around the cottage and there was a deafening crash, the sound of crumbling stone and mortar and splintering timber.

Harry grabbed hold of her hand, dragging her from the bed. 'The cottage next door has taken a hit. We must leave this instant. Come as you are. There is no time to dress.' He grabbed a cloak and threw it around her shoulders and she ran out into the street barefoot. Mall was dressed likewise, trembling with fear and cold. It was five o' clock in the morning, pitch dark and freezing.

The last shot had totally destroyed the neighbouring cottage where Harry had been sleeping, the balls having fallen from top to bottom, ripping through the roof and pulling down walls in their wake.

'We must send an alarm to the harbour to secure our boats and ammunition,' Henrietta said breathlessly to Harry as they ran.

'Already done.'

But she dragged her hand from his and turned back.

'Where are you going? I told you I'd already . . .'

'Mitte,' she cried, as the cannonballs continued to whistle and crash. 'We can't leave her.'

Harry ran back with Henrietta and they found the little dog still shivering on the bed. As soon as she saw her mistress she leaped down and bolted to Henrietta's side. Harry pulled her by the hand out of the cottage again. It was so foggy they could hardly see, but there seemed to be Royalist soldiers running everywhere, vague shapes in the murky darkness.

'Why do not Admiral Von Tromp's ships defend us?' Henrietta shouted.

'Perhaps they cannot see the enemy in the fog. But the tide will go out soon and the ships will be forced to retreat.'

One of the soldiers was running towards them. Henrietta had just enough time to see his youthful face beneath his feathered hat and that he was elegantly dressed with lace at collar and cuffs. He was not twenty paces away when a cannonball ripped through his body. Blood sprayed, black in the darkness. His legs crumpled, knees hitting the road before he fell down face first in the dirt.

Henrietta faltered but Harry tightened his hold on her hand and pulled her on.

'Should we not help him?'

'He's dead.'

Henrietta was looking over her shoulder, thinking it was the first time she'd ever seen anyone killed, when Harry suddenly pushed her down into a ditch and threw himself on top of her. Cannonballs came whistling over them. One grazed the edge of the ditch, showering them with earth and stones. Harry pressed himself closer, shielding Henrietta's head with his arms as the bombardment continued to screech around them. On and on.

After about an hour all fell quiet. The enemy action appeared to have ceased. The sounds of cannon-fire were all out to sea now, the battle being fought between the rival fleets.

Harry relaxed his hold only slightly. Neither of them moved. Henrietta barely noticed the coldness and hardness of the frosty earth beneath her, just the closeness and hardness of his body lying along the length of hers, the weight and the warmth and strength of it. She thought that to lie with him on a bed of rocks in the cold, with cannon-shot raining down, was better than any feather mattress in a state bed in a palace. If she died now, it would be a good way to die.

'Is it over?' she asked.

'I think it must be.' He moved his arm so that she could turn her head and look at him, his face as close as if they were about to kiss. So close that even in the misty darkness she saw he had a little graze on his temple. She touched it with her finger. 'You are hurt.'

'It is nothing. Are you unharmed?'

'Yes, thank you.'

He shifted off her and they both stood up. Henrietta shook the rubble from her cloak, ran her hands over her tousled curls. Vain even in the face of death! she chided herself. But it was only because Harry was staring at her. He was dusty and dishevelled too, unshaven, his hair windswept and tousled, but it suited him. Deprived now of the warmth of his body, she shivered. He took off his coat and draped it around her shoulders and she was reminded of that other occasion, when their roles had been reversed and she had given him her cloak to wear.

'Come,' she said.

'Where to?'

'I shall find Mall and return to my lodgings. I will not have Parliament say it has driven me from this village. Besides which, I am ravenous.' Harry looked at her with a kind of wonderment that made her laugh. 'What? Did you expect me to quiver and quake at a few guns? I have been in danger by sea twice and now by land. But God has spared me as I always believed he would in aid of so just a cause.' She touched his hand. 'And while ever I have you to protect me, I need fear nothing.'

Henrietta stood with him for a moment longer in the misty darkness and then she stepped out of the ditch on to the road, Mitte scrambling after her. 'Once we have eaten, we will send to His Majesty and ask him to tell us how we might join him.'

While they waited for instructions from Charles and the arrival of the wagons to transport baggage and armaments, the queen's party rode three miles inland to Boynton Hall, an Elizabethan manor house near the village of Burlington. It was the seat of Sir William Strickland, now a Parliamentary agent, but he was absent on business and the ladies of the family, being related to Thomas Wentworth, had offered to let the queen establish herself there.

William Cavendish, the Earl of Newcastle, was their first visitor. A man of moderate size and middle age, with narrow features and a ruddy countenance, he had a reputation as a fine and fanatical horseman and rode in on a handsome high-stepping Spanish gelding. The last time Henrietta had met him had been at the little castle of Bolsover, in more peaceful times. Now, instead of masquing and feasting, discussing pleasure and admiring art as they had done then, they discussed the business of war. Warmed ale had been set out in the queen's rooms. The earl took out his clay pipe, gave a spare one to Harry, filled both from a pouch of tobacco, lit and inhaled deeply before he set about making sure they understood the challenges they were facing.

'A belt of country held by Parliament and including Leicester, Coventry and Northampton lies between us here in Yorkshire and the king in Oxford,' he said. 'Parliament also holds a large proportion of the south-east, including London. Your Majesty must be on guard,' Cavendish stressed.

'It is our intention to recruit men here and take an army south to the king.'

'Then make no mistake that the Parliamentary forces will do all they can to hinder your plans and oppose your march. Your enemies are vigilant, and the danger that Your Majesty may be snatched by them is very real. Our intelligence reports that the Earl of Newport and John Pym are planning to kidnap you, ma'am.'

'That does not surprise me,' Henrietta said. 'Pym is my husband's enemy and Lord Newport has long been Mr Jermyn's, which therefore makes him mine.'

Cavendish raised his eyebrows in bemusement at the queen's casual dismissal of personal danger. 'Apparently they have told members of the Lords who are pressing Pym for peace that if they would only have a little patience, they will win so good a pawn that they might make their own conditions.'

'Then I must make sure I have a regiment of lifeguards with me when we march,' Henrietta decided. 'How many of your own men can you let me have?'

Henrietta glanced at Harry as he suppressed a laugh. For weeks she'd watched him bargain and haggle and had seen how it paid to be bold when making demands. He looked as pleased with her for having mastered these skills as when he had taught her to master the English language.

'I can afford Your Majesty six companies of horse and three of foot, I should think,' Cavendish replied. He chuckled. 'You'll have heard no doubt that I have a reputation for lying in bed until nearly midday then taking an hour to dress, but my whitecoats are said to be the most formidable foot soldiers fighting for the king's name.'

'Then they are just the men we need.'

'I pray to God that Charles will think this the best course,' Henrietta said to Harry after Cavendish had ridden off. 'He had better do.'

She was also able to write and tell her husband that not only did they have the promise of Cavendish's men, but local gentry had started flooding to Boynton too with offers of arms and horses and able-bodied farm labourers and tenants, who wanted to ride south with the queen and fight for the Royalist cause. Men kept turning up at the door in homespun breeches, carrying pistols and pitchforks and scythes and any other weapons they could muster, ready and eager to fight for their king.

'We will have a whole army in no time,' Henrietta said to Harry. She was as moved by this support as she had been by the friendliness and generosity of the fisherman and his family.

While at Boynton she also secured a cache of plate. Having spied the Stricklands' array on the oak buffet in the hall at Boynton, she had told her hosts that she must take it to be melted down for vital arms but that she would consider it a loan. The ladies of the house were reluctant to agree until she handed over, as a pledge of her intention to refund its value, a bracelet engraved with her monogram, the letters H M R, Henrietta Maria Regina, in a delicate filigree of gold. She had brought several over from Holland for presentation to loyalists in return for loans or services and the Stricklands seemed delighted with the exchange.

Charles was delighted with her work too, for once.

When Harry sat down to decipher the latest letter to arrive from the king, Henrietta dreaded hearing more complaints. 'Is it going to make me cross?' she asked warily, as she took the decoded copy of the letter from him.

Harry shook his head. 'I don't believe so, ma'am,' he said tenderly. 'Quite the opposite, I should say.'

*'Til now,* mon cher coeur, *I never knew the benefit of ignorance. I am glad that I did not know the danger you were in from the storm at sea before I had assurance of your escape. I shall not be free of worry until I have the*

*happiness of your company, though. I am moved that for my sake you would face such perils and I confess it is impossible to repay you by anything I can do, much less by words. My heart is full of affection and admiration for you.*

Henrietta's heart was full of affection for her husband too. She was in the greatest impatience in the world to join him, wanted to see him so much, and yet she did not want to see him at all. It was so long since she had and so much had happened, so much had changed. She felt she was now an entirely different person from the one to whom he'd waved farewell at Dover. She loved him deeply, but could not truthfully say that she admired him, as he said he admired her. Harry, on the other hand . . .

She had loved and desired him, but now that love and desire had grown into so much more. His loyalty, his courage, his resourcefulness and energy. His kindness. *A soul composed of the eagle and the dove.* There was no one she respected or admired or needed more in her life.

'I am glad you will be riding south with me,' she said. For some reason, having said so much in the past it was all she could find to say.

'I am glad too.'

By the last week in May the wagons and equipment had arrived and Henrietta and Harry were preparing to ride out to a field south of Boynton Hall to meet William Cavendish's regiment and the other men who had volunteered as recruits and had mustered there.

Harry had procured a litter for the queen to travel in, but she told him to send it back. 'I shall be needing no more than a saddle,' she said. 'I mean to ride on horseback like you.'

'All the way to Oxford?'

'Yes, all the way to Oxford.' Looking around as the wagons were being loaded, she saw that the pieces of a great four poster bed were being stacked into one of them. 'I'll not be needing that either. Nor a grand royal tent. I shall sleep upon a simple camp bed in a simple tent, the same as you and my men.'

'Very well then.' Harry smiled. 'I had better tell the fellows who are packing up the bed to unpack it again.' He made to go and then turned back, unfastening the belt that was slung around his hips from which hung a holster and pistol. He handed it to her. 'If you are going to ride like a cavalry soldier, you need to be armed like one too. You need to be able to defend yourself,' he added seriously.

She took the pistol, weighed its cold, heavy solidity in her hand, turned it around and rested her finger on the trigger.

'D'you know how to fire it?'

'My brother had one just like this and let me have a turn.' Henrietta slipped it into the holster, wrapped the belt twice around her tiny corseted waist, buckled it over her skirts and straightened her shoulders.

Once her horse had been saddled, she and Harry said their goodbyes to Mall and Father Philip and Geoffrey, who were to travel independently to Oxford, and rode out of the village side by side at the head of the soldiers and the train of wagons.

'It's like a scene from a great masque or theatrical,' Henrietta said. 'I am a warrior queen. Boudicca . . . or else Helen of Troy . . . or Joan of Arc maybe.'

'You are as brave and and as beautiful as all three,' Harry said.

As they passed through the cobbled market square they came upon a procession of country people walking behind a man in a horse-drawn cart, his hands and ankles tied tight with rope.

'Find out what is going on,' Henrietta told Harry.

She watched him walk his horse over to the bulbous-nosed man who was driving the cart, then ride back. 'The prisoner is the captain of the Parliamentary ship that directed the cannonade at Your Majesty's lodgings at Bridlington,' Harry said. 'He was captured, has been tried by a military tribunal and been condemned to be hanged.'

'Tell them I have forgiven him,' Henrietta said thoughtfully. 'He did not kill me so he shall not be put to death on my account. Command his captors to set him free and send him over to speak to me.'

Harry rode back to the cart. As the prisoner's arms and legs were untied, alternating expressions of fear and disbelief crossed his face. Finally realising it was not some mistake and that he really was a free man, he burst into tears. Still wiping his eyes, he scrambled from the cart and hobbled on stiff, sore legs to where Henrietta sat upon her horse. He took her hand in his and kissed the back of it, wetting it with tears, then bowed so low that his face was almost pressed into the dirt of the road. 'A thousand blessings on Your Majesty,' he wept. 'A thousand blessings. You are a good, good lady. If there is anything I can ever do for you . . .'

'All I ask is that you do not persecute a person who would not harm you when she could.'

'I am in Your Majesty's debt forever and will never fight against you. I do not really know what we are fighting for anyway. But I would fight for Your Majesty,' he said fervently. ' I would willingly die for you. I will come over to your side and will persuade the crews of the other ships that attacked you to do the same.'

Henrietta smiled at him.

'Be on your way then.'

They watched him hurry off, as if he feared his captors might have a change of heart and come after him once the little queen was no longer there to protect him.

'That was a very gracious thing you did,' Harry said as they rode on.

'I believe it is what my father would have done,' she said plainly. 'Just as he rode with his men and lived as one of them, as I also intend to do.'

She was sure that Henri le Grand would have been mightily impressed with the army his youngest daughter had amassed in the field outside Burlington: three thousand foot, thirty companies of horse and a battalion of dragoons. She saw now why the tenants William Cavendish had put into arms were called whitecoats, since they were clearly distinguishable by their surcoats of coarse undyed wool. Aside from them the army was a complete hotchpotch, but what they lacked in uniformity and elegance they more than made up for in number and enthusiasm, giving such a rousing cheer when they saw the queen ride up that it brought tears to Henrietta's eyes. She had left England thinking everyone there despised her.

It struck her suddenly that it was not just the throne and Charles she was fighting for, but his people too. These people. Her people. These men. Their wives, children, mothers, fathers. She was fighting for king and for country. She was the Queen of England and she was fighting for her homeland.

The ranks stood in line as Henrietta and Harry surveyed them and then the flag of the new army was hoisted and unfurled above their heads: a red field with a glittering gold fleur-de-lys representing France, surmounted by the golden crown of England.

'The Queen's Army,' Harry announced with pride.

'Commanded by Colonel Jermyn, newly promoted,' Henrietta said. Then, seeing the expression on his face, smiled. 'Don't look so surprised! Who else would I trust to command my forces but you?'

So began the long march to York, horses and oxen straining in their harnesses to pull great cannons and mortars and over a hundred wagons laden with money, arms, ammunition and supplies. Under heavy skies, the dark clouds whipped by a fierce cold wind that blew straight off the North Sea, they made steady progress. For a few miles they travelled along a coastline of high chalky clifftops and sandy beaches, isolated fishing villages and colonies of sea birds. Then they struck westwards over the Yorkshire Wolds, a landscape scattered with ancient standing stones and tumulus mounds, then on over the rolling North York Moors and into the Vale of York. There were intermittent showers of icy rain, but they did nothing to dampen the army's spirits.

Harry made up a marching song, singing it quietly at first, as if he were merely serenading Henrietta. 'Plague take Pym and all his peers,' he tried, testing the tune and rhythm and rhyme. 'Huzza for King Charles and the Cavaliers.'

Henrietta picked it up so that it became a duet which soon passed behind them down the ranks until there was a choir of three thousand gruff voices, all chanting in unison, if not quite in time or tune.

> *Plague take Pym and all his peers.*
> *Huzzah for King Charles and the Cavaliers.*

Then one of the men began another song.

> *Let's hope for peace,*
> *For the wars will not cease*
> *'Til the king enjoys his own again.*
> *Yes, this I can tell,*
> *That all will be well,*
> *When the king enjoys his own again.*

His lone voice and the rousing words made goosebumps stand out on Henrietta's skin. And then the other men joined in and began singing the same refrain. She twisted round in the saddle and spoke to one of Cavendish's men who was directly behind her. 'What is that song? You all seem to know it well.'

'It is much sung by all the Cavaliers across England, ma'am.'

'It is lovely.'

Henrietta started to sing along. She loved to sing but always before she had been accompanied by lutes and flutes, had performed in the finest surroundings, before an audience of genteel ladies and gentlemen. Never had she belted out a song at the top of her voice from the saddle of a horse on a wild moorland, with a chorus of labourers and tenant farmers. And never had she enjoyed herself so much. It was cold and wet and they were on constant lookout for Parliamentary troops come to kill or capture her, but strangely she could not remember a time when she had been so happy. This felt like the greatest adventure, very far removed from the frivolous, feminine pursuits which had previously filled her days. She felt she was finally doing what she had been born to do.

They set up camp for the night on high open moorland strewn with rocks and boulders that the men used as tables and chairs, while the cooks set up their pots over the fires and wine was unloaded from the carts and handed round in stoneware jars. After a day of riding and fresh air, Henrietta was famished and thirsty. She found a comfortable flat rock for herself, spread her cloak and sat herself down.

'Your Majesty cannot sit there!' Harry exclaimed.

'Why not? I am and I can. And before you have men bring me a table and start laying it with linen and plate, know that I mean to dispense with all ceremony from now on. A wooden bowl of stew and a hunk of bread will serve me very well.'

Harry brought these to her himself, the stew steaming hot. 'As requested, ma'am,' he said, sitting himself down on another rock opposite her to eat his own supper.

Henrietta put the wooden spoon to her mouth. 'Delicious,' she pronounced. The extravagant dishes she'd eaten at banquets had never tasted half so good.

'I think you are enjoying all this,' Harry chuckled.

'I am Boudicca. Or is it Alexander the Great?'

Her tent would hardly have been fitting for the Great Alexander though, she thought later, turning over again as she tried to get comfortable on the hard, narrow camp bed. It was as basic as the supper had been, but even so she was reminded of the last time she had slept out in open country, at Wellingborough. She wondered what she would do if Harry came to her now as he had then. Oh, it was pointless wondering, pointless wishing, because there was no chance that he would. It seemed the time when he might have done so had passed forever and she must school her heart to stop longing for him.

Wellingborough was another age, another life. There was no place now for the tender emotions of love, only the brutal reality of war.

The Queen's Army gathered strength as it advanced. As they passed through each village, Henrietta distributed alms and more men and young boys came to join the march south, armed with pikes and pitchforks, the wealthier with flintlock muskets slung over their shoulders, all in good fighting spirits. Even the men who had been marching for days in wind and rain still had smiles on their faces.

'I thought they'd resent me, mock me even,' Henrietta said. 'A woman leading an army.'

Harry shook his head. 'They are all inspired by your bravery. You eat with them and treat them as brothers, and in return they give you their love and their loyalty.'

'There are doubtless some who would say I am fonder of this life than is right for a virtuous woman.' Henrietta laughed. 'Perhaps they are right.'

After all the warnings of assaults and kidnappings they'd barely had sight or sound of any Roundheads. But the Queen's Army actively sought them out. A detachment of horse and foot with dragoons was sent to Lancashire, the plan being that they would clear Parliamentary rebels from that county within two weeks and rejoin the queen at Newark. Meanwhile the rest of the army reached York where Henrietta and Harry were given shelter in the house of Sir Arthur Ingram, in a twisting, narrow street close to the magnificent Minster. They were joined there for dinner by the Earl of Montrose, a slight, energetic man with mist-grey eyes and chestnut hair who, having been an enemy in the wars with Scotland, had now come over to the Royalist side. Before the first course of the meal had been served, he had pledged two thousand of his Cavaliers.

Escorted by them, the Queen's Army rode triumphantly into Scarborough. The little Yorkshire coastal town was an important strategic supply port, but the castle, standing bold and majestic on a high, steep, rocky promontory on the eastern edge of the town, was a Parliamentary stronghold occupied by Sir Hugh Cholmley. However, on seeing the pretty little queen valiantly riding towards him, with a pistol in her belt and a mighty army behind her, Sir Hugh immediately surrendered and declared himself a Cavalier too.

As Henrietta stood on the clifftop with the twelve-foot-thick castle walls behind her, commanding the harbour and the sweep of the bay and the dramatic and rugged Yorkshire coastline far below, she felt invincible. She felt also a fierce, passionate love for England. Not just for its people but for the land itself. It was such a beautiful country. Her country.

It hit her doubly hard then, when Harry came to her and told her what Sir Hugh had just told him.

Parliament had stripped her of the title of queen. It had now declared her a traitor to England, guilty of high treason for obtaining supplies and money and arms for the king. A crime punishable by death.

With several of her soldiers standing close by, she knew that she must reveal not even a flicker of fear. That if her men saw she was afraid it would destroy morale in an instant and all would be lost. She knew also that she must not let her own morale falter. She must not be afraid, for fear led to hesitation and nothing was achieved by that. 'The Roundheads know they need to be rid of me if they are to stand any chance of victory,' she said defiantly. 'But we are winning. That is all that matters.' Then anger asserted itself. 'Damn it, how dare they strip me of my title? Do they even have the right, the power? A queen is a queen.'

'You were never crowned,' Harry was forced to remind her.

She looked back over the cliffs, the wind setting her hair and skirts and cloak flying.

'If they have decided you are not queen, we shall have to give you a new title,' Harry said.

She turned back to him. 'Did you have one in mind?'

'Your Majesty is Field Marshal, Grand Admiral and Commander-in-Chief of this army, so as its colonel I name you Generalissimo. Or Generalissima, should it be?'

'Hmmm.' Henrietta's smile was thoughtful at first and then it broadened. She gave a nod, touching one hand to her pistol. 'That I like. Generalissima. Thank you, Harry.'

'You are very welcome, ma'am.'

The army left Scarborough at the beginning of June with four and a half thousand horse and foot, enough to intimidate the rebels at Tadcaster who quit the town without a fight. Royalist garrisons were left at Stamford Bridge and Malton, while the Parliamentary garrison of Burton upon Trent fell after a short assault by the queen's cavalry. At Nottingham, one of the queen's troops of foot overcame six Roundhead regiments.

Prince Rupert was doing equally well in the Midlands. He had already taken the little Puritan town of Birmingham, laid siege to Litchfield, and staged a dashing cavalry foray which ended in a bloody battle in the cornfields at Chalgrove, not far from Oxford. John Hampden, instigator of the ship money trial, had been mortally wounded, the enemy had scattered, and the Earl of Essex had been forced to abandon his advance on Oxford. Henrietta was hoping hourly to hear of the capitulation of Hull and Lincoln.

By mid-June her own army reached Newark on the River Trent where the flag was raised. Though Henrietta was keen to press on, she saw the wisdom of resting for a while, replenishing supplies and recruiting more soldiers. Together she and Harry gave directions for ordering the camp, setting men to work digging ramparts and trenches.

Her tent had barely been erected when she was visited there by three noble ladies of the town who had requested an audience. She invited them into her tent and they stepped gingerly across the grass in their silk slippers, lifting up their skirts as if walking through the mire of a pig sty, their eyes scanning the queen's appearance and living quarters with scandalised disdain. One corner of the tent was stacked high with swords and muskets, while Henrietta wore a pistol but no jewels and her windswept ringlets were pinned carelessly on top of her head. The hem of her cloak and her boots were muddied and dusty. Since she had been washing in streams and pools, she had a streak of mud on her cheek, too.

'For your safety's sake,' the oldest woman said, 'we petition Your Majesty not to march from Newark until Nottingham is properly taken.'

'And all the towns around it,' a younger woman added.

'Ladies,' Henrietta replied, summoning her small reserves of patience, 'I thank you for your concern. But you have no experience of affairs of this nature. I am commanded by the king to make haste to him, so I am unable to grant your petition.'

'But Your Majesty's life is in . . .'

'You may learn by my example to obey your husbands at all times,' Henrietta cut in imperiously.

She heard a low chuckle and, glancing up, saw Harry standing in the entrance to the tent, listening to the exchange. How was it that he could still give her butterflies in her stomach, even after all this time, when she was with him daily?

'What did you find so amusing earlier?' she challenged, after the ladies had gone and she was sitting with him in the warm evening sun, eating chicken off the bone held in her fingers.

'"You may learn by my example to obey your husbands",' he quoted. 'With respect, you are hardly the most submissive of wives yourself, are you?'

Henrietta tossed her chicken bone to one of the dogs and licked her fingers. 'Parliament has decided that I am guilty of treason, just like you. We are not merely vagabonds now but outlaws both.'

'So we are.'

She gave a little shudder. If captured and sentenced to death, they would die very differently. She had never forgotten how nobles were beheaded and commoners hung, drawn and quartered. How she wished she could protect him from that.

They had been through so much together, had faced perils on land and sea. He was dearer to her than ever now. She felt closer to him than ever she had been. And yet the distance between them remained. The war had brought them together, at the same time it held them apart. It had forced her to be apart from Charles for so long that his memory had grown dim for her. Much as she wanted to see him, the truth of it was that she had become accustomed to living without him. She could not imagine being without Harry. She needed him now, in a way that she did not need Charles. It was a case of knowing she was not alone. No matter what trouble one faced, so long as there was one person, just one, to depend on absolutely, then it was possible to go on, to have hope, to be strong. For her, that one person was Harry. Her strength derived from his strength. Without him, she could do nothing, was nothing. Sometimes she felt that if she did not have him in her life, she'd barely manage to draw breath. He made her so happy and yet . . . so sad.

\* \* \*

The Queen's Army marched from Newark at the beginning of July, leaving behind two thousand foot and twenty companies of horse for the defence of Nottingham and Lincolnshire. It marched through Ashby-de-la-Zouch, through Croxall, through Walsall and Kings Norton, and arrived at the riverside town of Stratford-upon-Avon to be met with cheers and chants of victory. Prince Rupert, now a general in the king's cavalry, and his followers were waiting to greet the queen by a wooden bridge across the Avon. They made an impressive and colourful sight. Rupert, like all his men, was gorgeously clothed in velvet and lace, his flowing locks of dark hair now reaching to his shoulders.

He swung down from his saddle, sword jangling, and swept off his feathered hat as he bowed to Henrietta. 'I have come to offer you protection, ma'am.'

She looked at this over-confident, dashing boy, even more full of swagger than when he had left Holland, and had to stifle a laugh. 'Thank you, Rupert. But I have ridden all the way from Yorkshire and have all the protection I need.'

Henrietta saw that she had wounded his not inconsiderable pride but thought that a good and necessary thing. Charles had been understandably delighted by his nephew's military triumphs but Rupert was young and it had clearly all gone to his head. 'I have to inform Your Majesty that a Parliamentary colonel by the name of Oliver Cromwell is gaining much power and is urging that every effort should be made to intercept you,' he said sulkily.

'Everyone is trying to intercept me, apparently,' she replied. 'So far they have failed. In fact, they have not even tried very hard because we have had not one sight of them.'

'The danger will increase considerably the closer we come to London.'

'Then I will be doubly on my guard.'

They were entertained for supper in the finest house of the town as the guest of Mistress Susanna Hall, daughter of William Shakespeare, a daunting old lady with fine bones, abundant silver hair and clear incisive eyes, which seemed to see far beyond what was in front of them. For someone who loved theatre and drama as much as Henrietta, it was a thrill to meet a relation of England's most famous dramatist, to drink claret with her and hear how, as a child, her illustrious father had sat her on his lap and read aloud from his newly written scripts, allowing her to try out the roles of Lady Macbeth, Ophelia, Juliet and Desdemona. It made a welcome change from all the talk of war and armies and armaments.

'I can still recite whole scenes,' said Mistress Hall. 'All the parts.' She brought her wine glass to her lips, sipped from it thoughtfully and set it down, looking directly at Henrietta. '"Of one that loved not wisely, but too well",' she quoted in a dramatic voice. '*Othello*. Act Five.'

'They're Elizabethan and Tudor,' Harry said to Henrietta afterwards as she walked with him through deserted streets of crooked, timber-framed houses towards the river and the palace where she was to spend the night. He was trying to distract her and she knew it.

'She meant the king, didn't she?' Henrietta said. 'Mistress Hall? She thinks my husband has loved not wisely but too well. I try to forget that I am a major cause of this war. His Majesty was forced into it for love of me.' She stopped walking. 'I think maybe Mistress Hall is right, and he does love unwisely.'

'Love is never wise,' Harry said simply. 'Nor should it be.'

They had come to the river. Two swans glided, luminous in the moonlight against the black water, their long white necks arched towards each other, forming the outline of a heart.

'I so enjoyed talking to Mistress Hall about her father and the theatre. It reminded me of before the war, when all I had to worry about was music and dancing and art.'

'Now you are living a life that is far more dramatic than any play you could act in or see performed. A life to which you are extremely well suited.'

She laughed. 'You think so?'

'Henrietta Maria Regina. A heroine to rival any William Shakespeare ever created.'

'I wish I were like Shakespeare,' she whispered. 'So that I had beautiful words to say to you, like the ones you keep saying to me.'

'You need no words,' he said. 'Only take mine into your heart and hold them there.'

Prince Rupert had told Henrietta that the king was riding north from Oxford towards her, bringing with him the Duke of York and the Prince of Wales.

They were to meet at the hamlet of Kineton, below Edgehill, a name she recognised as being the site of the battle that had marked the start of the war. As Henrietta rode on with Harry down the straight Roman road of the Fosse Way through a fertile vale, she saw, advancing in the opposite direction, the bright gold of the royal standard, Charles at the head of a procession of great pageantry. Riding to either side of him were two young men in armour. Henrietta realised with a wrench of her heart that these were her two boys. Who were boys no longer.

The armies halted. Henrietta and Charles walked their horses together and faced one another from their saddles, almost warily, more like conferring enemy generals than husband and wife, except that both of them had tears in their eyes. Charles seemed no better able to recognise Henrietta than she was to recognise their sons, waiting just behind their father. Dressed in a muddied cloak, her hair windswept, she was no longer the dizzy little princess in ribbons and pearls whom he had taken as his child bride. Nor was Prince Charles the small boy who was regularly to be found wearing a tambourine on his head, pretending it was a crown. He looked like a man now, and even James had grown tall. The four of them dismounted and there was much kissing and hugging.

'I am so glad you are here,' Charles said. 'And safe.'

Henrietta kissed his mouth, held his hands. 'And I you.'

The princes started talking at once. 'We nearly weren't safe,' Prince James announced with pride. 'We have been riding with the cavalry and men have been killed. Right in front of me!'

'*I* might have been killed,' his brother trounced that, talking as excitedly and as fast as his mother usually did 'There was a big battle at Edgehill. Just over there.' He pointed. 'I was given over to the care of Mr Harvey while my father was engaged in the fighting and we went to sit under a bank. Mr Harvey gave me a book to study but the bullets were whistling down around us and then a cannonball tore up the ground right near our feet. I might have been hit.'

'Well, thank God you were not.' Henrietta stroked his curls. 'I was nearly hit by a cannonball too.' She glanced behind her at Harry. 'Colonel Jermyn here saved me.'

'You are a colonel now, sir?' Prince Charles asked, raising his voice so that Harry could hear.

Harry gave him a pleased smile. 'I am, Your Majesty.'

'Is that true, Jermyn?' the king asked him directly. 'Did you save my wife's life?'

'I did no more than any man would do under the circumstances, Your Majesty.'

'What happened?' Charles asked her.

Henrietta could not think quite how to put it: Harry threw me down into a ditch and lay on top of me there. It had been an innocent, selfless act, but however she described it, it would seem somehow improper. Because her feelings for Harry had always been improper. And his for her?

'We came under fire in Bridlington,' Harry replied on her behalf. 'I made sure Her Majesty was safely out of her lodgings before they took a hit.'

'I am forever in your debt then, Harry,' Charles said stiffly.

'Will you not give him a title?' Henrietta pleaded with quiet urgency. 'One that will protect him should he be captured?' She had been thinking about asking for this as she rode and now allowed a moment for her request to register with the king. 'I have never forgotten what you told me . . . how commoners are hung, drawn and quartered. Save him from that, after all he has done. Make him an earl, so that he would suffer a less painful death should he be caught.'

Charles regarded her with a mixture of hurt, disappointment and anger. 'Your first thought on seeing me is of him?'

Henrietta bristled. 'My first concern for the past year, all the time I have been in Holland and travelling south, has been how best I might serve you,' she reminded him. 'It has been Harry's concern too. Now I need you to do this one thing for me . . . for him. Lord knows, he deserves to be an earl.'

'I shall make him a baron,' Charles declared. 'If that will please you.'

It was enough. Enough to protect him. 'Now? Will you do it now?'

'Very well.'

Seeing the king walking over to him, Harry dismounted, hooking his fingers loosely round the bridle of his horse as he waited. Henrietta had not noticed before how Charles had to look up at him just as she did. On being addressed by his king, Harry straightened, which served to make Charles look even smaller by comparison.

'In recognition of your services and the gratitude I owe you,' the king said, 'I am conferring upon you the title of Baron Jermyn of St Edmundsbury.'

Henrietta had wanted Harry to have the title as protection, to safeguard him from the most brutal death, but she could see that it meant far more to him than that. He was glowing with pride at receiving such a mark of respect.

'Baron Jermyn,' she said with a smile, wanting to be the first to call him by his new title. 'It sounds well, don't you think?'

'I promise Your Majesty that no peerage ever gave more heartfelt satisfaction to the recipient.'

'I promise you, no peerage was ever more deserved. I shall also make you my new lord chamberlain. Well, you may as well have complete control of my household as well as my army!'

The King's and the Queen's Armies travelled on together to Wroxton, a pretty Oxfordshire village of honey-coloured stone cottages, where they were to spend the night at the former house of Sir Thomas Pope, founder of Trinity College, Oxford.

Supper was served there with the customary royal ceremony. Courtiers stood in a semi-circle behind the king and queen. On side tables were ewers for hand washing, and by the sideboard a cupbearer waited with glasses and decanters. In came the procession of gentlemen bearing dishes of meat and fish. After the freedom she had enjoyed on the march south, the long-drawn-out procedure seemed faintly ridiculous to Henrietta, made her feel uncomfortable. And strangely isolated and lonely. She wished she could tell Harry and everyone who was standing so stiffly behind her just to pull up a chair, help themselves, share the wine and food and conversation as they had done these past weeks. She had not realised just how much she'd relished that freedom and companionship.

She was handed bread and was about to break it with her fingers, remembering just in time that she must use a knife. 'I almost forgot.' She smiled at Charles.

'Forgot what?'

She gave the knife a little wave in the air. 'Haven't used one of these in weeks.'

He was aghast. 'Haven't you?'

'You have?' She looked at him for a moment, casting her eyes around the table. 'Next you'll be telling me this is exactly how you ate at camp, with linen and cupbearers and carvers?'

'This court is renowned for its etiquette and ceremony,' he stated. 'To disregard that is to disregard the trappings of monarchy, and thereby forfeit all respect in the eyes of the men.'

'I disagree entirely. I used stones and logs and grassy hillocks for tables and chairs, and I ate with my fingers with my men and was loved for it.'

They consumed the rest of the meal in silence, Henrietta making a point of taking the salt from the cellar with a knife as was expected, tasting delicate bites of every dish, and dabbing her mouth with a napkin each time she was to sip the wine.

After supper Charles retired to his chamber and Henrietta to hers, but as Mall went through the routine of unlacing her and brushing out her hair, Henrietta was waiting for the summons to go to her husband. She was happy to go but not eager, and wondered at the meaning of that.

Charles was already in bed. Before she joined him there she went to throw open the latticed casement, leaned out with both hands on the sill and breathed in the warm summer night air, sweetly scented with honeysuckle and roses. 'I am so used to bedding down beneath canvas now that I shall not sleep without fresh air,' she explained, turning round and leaning back against the ledge.

'You have changed so much,' he said.

She climbed under the covers but did not lie down. Instead she drew up her knees beneath the sheet, propped her elbow on them, and with her chin in her hand, looked over at him. 'For the better?'

'I am not sure.' He reached for her, put his arms around her and kissed her. She kissed him back, thinking that if he were to judge by how it was between them in bed, then nothing had changed at all. The ceremonial meal had felt uncomfortable in contrast to the liberty she had enjoyed of late, whereas it felt very comfortable to lie with Charles again, as it always had since their reconciliation. Comfortable, comforting. But no more than that. And she wanted more, much more.

The queen's entrance into Oxford, now the king's headquarers, was celebrated by peals of bells and crowds of Royalists lining the streets, throwing their hats in the air. She was escorted through more cheering crowds to Merton College where her household was to occupy a fine set of apartments in the Warden's lodgings. Mall, Geoffrey and Father Philip were already waiting for her there and had done their best to make sure all was in order.

Her rooms were reached by an ornately carved oak staircase leading directly from the hall of the college, and they included a lofty reception chamber with mullioned windows looking south over the Great Quadrangle and a small west window with views over the Fellows' Garden.

Charles's residence was at Christ Church, and he took great pleasure in explaining how a door in the east wall of Corpus Gardens led to Grove Chapel, from which he could make his way across the bridge over Patey's Quadrangle and into Merton Hall, thereby allowing him to visit her rooms without having once to venture into the streets.

Henrietta's mother had not been dead six months when a letter arrived from Queen Anne to notify her of the death of her brother, King Louis. He had died of tuberculosis at the age of thirty-three. Anne related a touching story of how their six-year-old son, also called Louis, whom Henrietta had never met, had been taken to the king's deathbed and announced that he was Louis XIV. To which the king replied, 'Not just yet.'

As Mall dressed her in her mourning gown, Henrietta wondered when she would run out of tears to cry.

At least the weather was sunny and warm and everything was going well. Rupert took Bristol, a significant victory, which meant that though Parliament still held the south-east, the Royalists now had control of the south-west. There were even moments of merriment reminiscent of life before the war. There were supper parties and pastoral plays, and Henrietta plucked tunes on her lute while Mall and Geoffrey danced. She threw sticks and balls for the spaniels in the quadrangle, and walked and talked with Harry and Charles and her sons in the sunny college gardens and shadowy cloisters. She and her ladies took to going to mass in Trinity chapel *en déshabillé*, or half-dressed like angels, as Charles described them. Meanwhile he played tennis with Prince James or his courtiers and went hunting.

He also seemed to spend a great deal of time with a tall, green-eyed redhead.

The king's and queen's courts were out walking in Trinity Grove, which had become just like Hyde Park, so many nobles promenaded there. The redheaded lady was over with Charles by the lake, hanging on to his arm and his every word.

'Who is she?' Henrietta asked Harry, sure that he would have made it his business to know. The woman seemed vaguely familiar. Henrietta remembered seeing her about the Scotland Yard end of Whitehall. She was very distinctive on account of her hair which was a deep flaming red, the sure sign of a Scot, or else a witch. She was unusually tall too, well-fashioned, and her round face was strangely beautiful, despite being slightly scarred by the pox.

'That's Jane Whorwood,' Harry replied. 'Wife of Brome Whorwood of Holton Park, just outside Oxford. Her mother is Portuguese and was a laundress to the late queen. Stepfather is James Maxwell, Gentleman Usher of the Black Rod to the Lords and Usher to the Order of the Garter.'

Henrietta could picture clearly the man with the lowland Scots accent who was responsible for arranging all the chivalry of kingship. The man who was also the king's herald in Parliament, who had been the Earl of Strafford's jailer and chief usher at his trial.

'What does the king have to say to her I wonder.'

'She's an intelligencer and a gold-runner,' Harry said with some relish. 'She has smuggled literally tons of gold to us from the merchants of the East India and Levant Companies in London, as well as from a few loyal aldermen and knights.'

Henrietta's interest was aroused along with her admiration. 'How did she do that?' Henrietta was wondering how she might do it herself and couldn't arrive at a workable solution. It would be possible to conceal a few gold coins in a bodice or the hem of a skirt or in a book binding, but in such quantity they would be enormously heavy as well as bulky.

'Through the laundresses who bring us soap,' Harry informed her. 'The gold is hidden in the barrels of Castile that come from London to clean all our ruffs and cuffs and linen. As Jane's mother was a laundress, she is well acquainted with the routines of the royal laundresses and can easily pass for one.'

'Are they not searched? Do the sentries at the town gates just let her pass?'

'What roadblock picket wants to put his hand into one hundred and twenty-five pounds of greasy Castile soap? The barrels are too deep to reach to the bottom anyway. It is the perfect place to hide gold. And the sentries still have some respect for the crown. Traditional protocols and courtesies are observed for those about royal business, and a well-bred lady with confidence and a pass is less likely to be searched than a man.'

'Ingenious. You say she's a spy too?'

'As well as bringing soap and gold from London she brings private messages for the king, from his councillors as well as from the Parliamentary garrison, through a network of channels.'

'Can we trust her?' Henrietta asked dubiously. And then with a frown as she watched the two of them together: 'The king seems to trust her entirely, doesn't he?'

'Mistress Whorwood is exceedingly loyal and trustworthy, of good judgement and understanding, and she is ruthless in my service,' Charles said when Henrietta spoke to him about the matter at the first opportunity later that day. 'You may freely trust her in anything that concerns it. I have had a perfect trial of her friendship to me. I cannot be more confident of anyone.'

But he was avoiding her eyes and had spoken with a passion Henrietta had hardly ever heard from him before. Or only once. After the Duke of Buckingham's death, when he'd stood before the overlarge portrait, praising the virtues of the person he had loved beyond all others, beyond even herself. Henrietta had found Charles's praise so hard to win, and yet he was lavishing it freely on this green-eyed Scottish woman.

She doubted her husband even knew how hard she had continued to work for him. Since Henrietta had arrived in Oxford she had not given herself over entirely to pleasure, nor had she forsaken her role of army general. Every day pleasant pastimes were interspersed with giving audiences to the likes of the Earl of Montrose and, with Harry's help, corresponding with William Cavendish and Hugh Cholmley in Scarborough, valuable allies in the north. But Charles never seemed to notice or appreciate her efforts the way he evidently noticed and appreciated Jane Whorwood's. Henrietta's eyes fixed on the ring he wore on his left hand, two great diamonds set either side of an emerald. The colour of Jane's eyes. 'We must be grateful to anyone brave enough to smuggle, spy and embezzle for our cause,' Henrietta said carefully.

Charles had begun by saying that Jane was exceedingly loyal. Henrietta thought of the person she would describe as the most loyal, thought also that in English the word loyalty was not dissimilar to devotion, which was not dissimilar to love. The reason for Harry's devotion was that he loved her. And the reason for Jane Whorwood's devotion to the king . . . ?

'Where is her husband?' Henreitta could not help but ask. 'What does he make of her intriguing?'

'Brome Whorwood went into exile in Holland after the Battle of Edgehill.'

'She did not wish to go with him?'

'No. She did not.'

'I see.' But Henrietta was not sure what it was that she saw, only that it was something she did not care to see. Not now. Not yet.

For all the surface gaiety of court life in Oxford, it was impossible to forget that the country was at war. Hallowed places of learning were now commandeered for death and destruction. College plate had been melted down and turned into missiles. Scholars had become soldiers. Cavalry horses clattered through the ancient cobbled streets, their fodder stored in the law schools. New Hall Inn had become the royal mint, and the astronomy and music schools were occupied by tailors cutting out thousands of uniforms. The city walls had been strengthened by a great earthwork and Magdalene College Grove had become an artillery park, its bell tower piled high with stones to be cast down on invading rebels. By night hordes of roistering soldiers roamed the streets, drunk on ale and liquor, on bravado and the promise of victory. Prince Rupert and his men were particularly rowdy. They were luxuriously lodged in Laud's College but regularly rode off under the cover of darkness in order to surprise enemy outposts at first light, returning from Aylesbury or Reading at midday to march prisoners through the streets to the castle that was serving as a gaol.

'Rupert is earning himself a reputation for barbarity and devilry,' Harry commented to Henrietta one day as they walked to Port Meadow, where he was drilling his men.

'Most ladies I have spoken to think him and his men very dashing,' Mall defended, her cheeks turning a tell-tale pink.

'Mall, you don't by any chance have a soft spot for him, do you?' Harry teased.

'For all of them.' She gazed across the grass towards the glamorously dressed horsemen. 'What girl would not? Riding off into the night and returning victorious in the morning? They are our heroes.'

'The suggestion of barbarity only adds to the mystique, I suppose?'
Harry smiled wryly.

'Rupert has always put me in mind of the Duke of Buckingham,'
Henrietta observed later. 'With his dark looks and dash, not to mention
his arrogance.'

'The king believes we cannot win this war without him,' Harry said
thoughtfully. 'Which gives him as much power as Villiers ever had.'

'So long as we do win,' Henrietta said. 'I suppose that is all that matters.
Oh, why does the king still not move to take London? You know he is
considering sending Rupert in completely the opposite direction, to direct
the field army in a siege at Gloucester?'

'Gloucester is one of the few Parliamentary strongholds remaining in
the west. It occupies a strategic position, between Royalist Wales and
Cornwall, which makes it a key target.'

True. She knew that since the middle of August a vast army had been
positioned outside the city, determined to bring it to its knees. 'Gloucester
or London. I wish he would at least decide. I swear his inability ever to
make a decision will finish us all.'

In the end Rupert was dispatched to Gloucester, but soon after his
departure Charles came to visit Henrietta's rooms, arriving unannounced
by his usual private route, to tell her that the Roundheads, led by the Earl
of Essex, were now advancing towards Newbury. 'Rupert is going to see
him off,' Charles said. 'While I take my men to relieve him at Gloucester.'

There was a glorious sunset, firing the little west window with orange
and crimson and gold, bathing the room in its red glow. To Henrietta it
looked like a creeping stain of blood. She was horrified. Charles was not
asking for her opinion, but she gave him the benefit of it nonetheless. 'If
you leave here, you leave Oxford exposed to attack. You leave us completely
undefended!'

'The Roundheads are not yet strong enough to strike at our heart. They
will need to secure Gloucester and further towns in the west first.'

'Rupert has assured you of this?'

Charles's eyes hardened as Henrietta's flashed at him. 'You may call
yourself Generalissima, but a few weeks spent with Montrose's and
Cavendish's men does not make you expert in battle strategy.'

'Whereas Rupert, of course, is an expert? He is an arrogant, strong-willed boy! He is capable of doing anything he is ordered, but should not be trusted to take a single step of his own accord. And yet you will be guided solely by him!'

'If Parliament loses at Newbury it will clear the way for us to advance on London. Which is what you have been telling me to do all along, is it not? I shall be leaving at first light,' Charles said, and turning on his heel, he left the room just as Harry came in.

'Rupert has persuaded His Majesty to go to Gloucester while he makes for Newbury,' Henrietta told Harry. She was surprised to see that he did not look at all taken aback. 'You knew?'

'The plan is for George Digby and me to ride ahead and hold Essex off until Rupert catches up.'

'And the Queen's Army will go with you, I suppose? Meanwhile the queen herself must stay here and wait.' She turned to the window and folded her arms. 'Oh, be gone, all of you.'

When Henrietta said goodbye to Charles in the great quadrangle, Jane Whorwood was there to say her own farewell, standing in the shadows of the cloisters. Even from a distance, Henrietta saw love and fear blazing in the woman green eyes. She saw Charles's eyes turn towards her as he took up the reins. Saw the silent message that passed between the two of them. Saw also the way Jane looked at her before turning to walk away. And she knew. Even if she had not known before.

It was the strangest thing. Henrietta felt no twist or stab of jealousy. Indignation, but no condemnation. Just a sense of futility and waste. She had denied herself, all these years, and Charles had not. She had been honourable and faithful, and he had not. Yet she was not angry. They were at war. Normal rules and morality did not apply. Charles might die in battle today. For months he had been risking his life every day on the battlefield. They had been apart so long, he and she. She had not been there to comfort and console him. To rub muscles made sore by long days in the saddle; to hold him in her arms when he was afraid and could not sleep. Underlying it all was a strange sort of relief. Jane was strong, courageous, resourceful. Charles had someone else's love to sustain him now. Henrietta could not blame him for taking his pleasure and his comfort where he might. She wished only that she and Harry had felt free to do likewise.

And now it might be too late. Having said goodbye to her husband, she had to say goodbye to Harry and had such an overwhelming terror lest she might be doing so for the last time that she could not bear to see him go. Since she had a superstition that it brought bad luck to speak of death, she said nothing to him of her fears. But instead of giving him her hand to kiss, Henrietta put her arms around him and buried her face in his neck. She kissed him there, stroking his face before they parted. 'How I wish I were coming with you,' she murmured.

It was unbearable for her, watching him mount his horse and ride out with George Digby at his side instead of her. Leading out the men she had recruited, the men she had eaten with and ridden with and lived with, day in and day out. She had been so used to riding at their head, at Harry's side. Her place was to ride at his side. She felt that so strongly that in her mind that was where she was, riding with him all the way. Knowing from experience the distance her army would cover in a day, almost to the mile, she took out maps and calculated where they would pitch their camp each night. When she heard that Essex had reached Swindon she found that on the map too, realising that the two armies must almost be upon each other.

She waited in an agony of anxiety but heard nothing more until another messenger came galloping with news that there had been a bloody battle at a place called Aldbourne Chase. The troops of the Queen's Army, led by Harry and Digby, had clashed with a detachment of Roundheads. Harry had been badly wounded in his arm. Digby was bringing him home.

'How badly wounded?' Henrietta demanded. 'What does badly mean?'

'Just badly, ma'am,' the messenger repeated with a bewildered shrug. 'I have no more information. I can tell Your Majesty no more than I have been told myself.'

Henrietta sent for Mayerne and the royal surgeons and apothecaries, ordering them to wait in her privy chamber so that they would be at the ready. Then she ordered Mall to bed.

'Would you not rather I wait up with you, ma'am, in case you need help?' Mall sounded a little piqued to be denied a chance to share in the drama.

'Thank you but no.' Henrietta could not really say why, but she wanted to be by heself. After all Harry had done for her, she wanted to do this for him alone. She went to his room, taking a supply of clean linen and blankets from the linen cupboard; set water to heat in a basin over the fire. She lit candles and made ready a fresh supply. Then there was no more she could do, except sit by the hearth and wait. She seemed always to be waiting lately. Waiting for news, waiting for those she loved to return. But now her thoughts careered out of control, no matter how she tried to calm them. To imagine Harry wounded, suffering and in pain was intolerable to her. What if he must lose his arm? Those strong arms that so often had held her, that so often she had longed to feel holding her. His hands that she loved so much. What if he died? How would she go on without him? Those days when he was in exile had seemed so long and lonely to her. How would she face the rest of her life without him there, as he had always been? Even imprisoned in the Tower or exiled abroad, she had known he would be thinking about her, worrying about her, loving her, and that had given her strength and comfort. He could not die. She would not let him.

She heard laboured footsteps on the stairs accompanied by a dragging sound. She ran to the door and flung it open just as Digby was about to kick it with his foot. That was all he had free since both arms were supporting Harry, who was leaning heavily against his shoulder, half-conscious. Digby was a good foot shorter than Harry and could not carry him or support his full weight. He had Harry's good arm, his left, slung around his neck while the other, the wounded right arm, hung limp and bloodied at Harry's side. His doublet and shirt were ragged and torn, the top of his arm wrapped tightly in a bloody cloth. There was dried blood on his brow and in his hair, trickling down his fingers, so much blood that it had seeped out and stained Digby's tunic, making it look as if he too was severely wounded.

Henrietta went to Harry's other side, wrapping her arm around his waist to help support him, taking care to avoid going anywhere near his wound. Between the two of them they manoeuvred him to the bed. He moaned as they carefully laid him down and lifted his legs up on to the mattress. Henrietta turned her back, leaving Digby to remove his boots and breeches and cut off his shirt.

Mayerne arrived with the surgeon and apothecary and Henrietta stood away from the bed to allow him to unwind the bandages and examine the wound. The surgeon folded down the sheet, exposing Harry's body to the waist. The wound was wide as the rim of a cup, the ragged skin around it angry, red, raised in a ridge. The blood was mingled with a cloudy fluid that had formed a kind of a crust.

Henrietta did not allow herself to avert her eyes.

'Suppuration is entirely to be expected,' Mayerne explained, seeing her anguish. 'Infection is present in all wounds. He is a fortunate fellow. The artery is severed but there appears to be no extensive damage to the bone. With luck he'll not need amputation' The surgeon then set to work washing the wound with the water and cloths Henrietta had prepared, removing shreds of shirt and flecks of mud and grit. He opened his bag and took out a small bottle of lotion, needles and silk thread. Working methodically and dispassionately, he tied the artery with the thread and sewed the edges of the skin together before covering the wound with a dressing of linen soaked in the lotion.

'He won't die, will he?' Henrietta asked

'I can't say, ma'am. All I can say is that it is far better to take a hit to a limb than to head, chest or abdomen.'

The surgeon picked up his equipment bag. 'I'll be back in the morning to change the dressing. Let him rest until then.'

When Mayerne and the other medical men had gone, Henrietta noticed George Digby eyeing the bottle of brandy as if he would down it in one gulp. She poured him a hefty measure. 'Here. Drink it.'

'Thank you, ma'am.' He took a swig.

'Tell me what happened, George?'

Digby dragged over a stool. 'We were a few miles outside Swindon,' he said, pausing to drain the brandy. 'Surrounded. Trapped by the guns and pikes of Essex's infantry in the front and the cavalry at the rear. I tell you, they are a mightily terrifying spectacle, the Roundheads, in their dark clothes and with the grilles of their steel helmets covering their faces. We were vastly outnumbered. We should have retreated. But rather than do that, Jermyn drew his rapier and charged forward.' Digby paused for effect. 'In hindsight and even at the time it was a glorious moment, ma'am, to see Your Majesty's colours flying and to hear Harry Jermyn's battle cry.'

'His battle cry?'

'God for Queen Mary.'

Tears welled in Henrietta's eyes and her heart constricted as she looked across at the man lying unconscious and wounded. He must have been terrified. 'Go on,' she encouraged.

'Your name on his lips seemed to give Colonel Jermyn a kind of superhuman courage and power,' Digby continued. 'He was easy to spot, practically alone amongst all those Roundheads, galloping at them full pelt with his long fair hair flying, as if he had nothing to lose and everything to gain. I watched him lean down from the saddle and slash at those that got in his way. He seemed totally oblivious to the cannonballs whistling past his ears. But then I lost sight of him. There was a Parliamentary officer right in front of me and he fired his pistol at point blank range. Jermyn appeared as if out of nowhere, his horse rearing as he dragged on the reins to spin it round, wielding his bloodied rapier. He charged my assailant and ran him through the chest. The foot soldiers of Your Majesty's regiment were all fleeing for fear of being trampled, and a marquis from the north who was riding with us was struck and fell to the ground, stone dead, right before us. That's when Harry too was hit. Even though it was his arm that was wounded he somehow kept a hold of the reins, did not lose his saddle, and cut through the last ranks of the enemy to get away. He collapsed a few hours later, from loss of blood and shock, and I had to lash him to his mount to bring him the last few miles.' Digby glanced at the figure in the bed as he downed the last dregs of the brandy. 'I have never seen courage to match it.'

Henrietta did not sleep. For once it was not that she could not, but that she chose not to. Instead she sat by Harry's bed and watched him doze fitfully. His body trembled with the after-effects of shock. Sometimes he moaned softly as if in pain or else the grip of a nightmare. She imagined him reliving the battle. At one point he opened his eyes and groggily asked for a drink, but did not seem to know or care that it was she who put her arms around his shoulders to lift his head, who held the cup of warmed ale to his mouth.

By morning he was running a fever, his skin burning and sweat pouring off him, soaking the sheets. Mayerne removed the bandage, applied a fresh one, told Henrietta to keep the blankets piled high and the fire stoked. As the day wore on Harry became delirious, twisting his head from side to side, muttering rambling unintelligible words, crying out as if at some dreadful vision.

As beads of sweat trickled down his temples and into his hair, Henrietta took the cloth, dipped and wrung it in a basin of cool water. She gently wiped his face and his shoulders where sweat had made his hair cling to his skin and had pooled in the little hollows of his collarbone. She wiped him gently, lovingly, as if she were caressing him, which in a way she was. When she was not sponging him she sat and held his hand and talked soothingly to him, not knowing if he could even hear or feel her.

'I order you not to die. Do you hear me? I absolutely forbid it. You pledged never to leave me. That means I have to die first.'

When Mall came to ask if she should take over while Henrietta snatched some rest, she was sent away.

Harry's fever broke the second night. By daybreak he had quietened and his skin was much cooler. It was only then that Henrietta realised how very tired she was. She had not closed her eyes or even rested in over forty hours and exhaustion washed over her in a wave. How tempting it was, just to close the bed curtains and lie down by his side for a few moments. She leaned forward on her arms, her arms folded on the bed, rested her head on them and slept.

She woke to feel a gentle weight upon her head, warm but no longer burning. Harry's hand! She moved and he let it fall away. When she lifted her face he had opened his eyes. 'Where am I?' he asked.

'Oxford,' she said gently. 'In your bed.'

He tried to move his arm and grimaced in pain.

'Keep it still.'

'I am just checking it is still there. I was sure I would lose it. My arm, I mean.'

'You remember what happened?'

'Yes.'

He licked his lips and she reached for the cup of small ale, putting it to his mouth. 'Digby says you were very brave.'

He was quiet for a moment. 'I always hoped I would be, if and when it was necessary. There is always the fear that when one is tested, really tested, one will be found lacking.'

'You can never fear that now.'

'I believe that we are shaped by those we love,' he said. 'My strength and courage reflect the depth of my love for you.'

Henrietta took hold of his hand and held the back of it to her cheek. 'I have been very afraid for you.'

'All I was thinking on the battlefield, when I was surrounded by

Roundheads, was that if I died, if I let them kill me there, I would never see you again. I knew how wretched you'd be if I did not come back, and I did not want that. Most of all I was terrified by the thought of those Roundheads riding to Oxford and of you being surrounded by them as I had been. And of my not being there to protect you.'

'Digby says you rode into battle with my name on your lips.'

'And your face in my heart.'

Henrietta sent for some broth. When one of the pages brought it in, she set the tray on a side table, put her arms round Harry's shoulders and propped him higher with pillows. Then she took the bowl and dipped in the spoon, offering it to him.

'I cannot let you feed me.'

'Then you will starve! For I cannot let anyone else. Now . . . open your mouth.'

Within days he was stronger. His wound was healing slowly but satisfactorily and Mayerne declared him to be out of danger. But now that Henrietta no longer had to watch over him but had chance to sleep, she could not. She was once again plagued by chronic insomnia. It was not just her eyelids that were heavy. Her head and limbs too felt as if they were weighted with lead. Sometimes she became so exhausted during the day that even putting one foot before the other required the greatest effort and concentration. But when she lay down in bed, her mind started spinning and sleep eluded her. In the darkness and quietness of night, their situation seemed hopeless.

While Harry's life had hung in the balance she had thought only of him, but it had not taken long for him to begin asking for news. How she hated the prospect of telling him that his bravery and endeavours had been in vain. How all their endeavours, everything, had been in vain.

On the morning of 20 September the Earl of Essex had clashed with Rupert and Charles at Newbury. Essex had outmanoeuvred the Royalists, forcing them to engage in an enclosed terrain of narrow lanes and embanked hedgerows where Charles's troops could not employ their cavalry to best advantage. Essex's infantry had inflicted considerable losses on the Royalists. Their ammunition became so depleted they had to break off the fight. Charles and Rupert were both now on their way back to Oxford. The

Royalist advance in the south was halted while the road to London was left open for the Parliamentary Army to return. Oh, if only Charles had marched to London after Edgehill, when he had had the chance! To Henrietta, optimistic as she always tried to remain, the defeat at Newbury seemed like a turning point. It felt as if they had let their last chance slip away.

It was that which was keeping her awake at night, but her insomnia was compounded by the fact that since caring for Harry she had got out of the habit of sleeping at proper times. She hated lying in the dark with only her dark thoughts for company. Think happy thoughts, she told herself. But what might they be? If she turned her mind to what had once made her happy, to masques and dancing and music, that only made her sad. Her children made her sadder still, and more fearful. The younger ones who were still held by Parliament and the older boys who had already been caught up in the fighting. It was hours still until dawn. She could not lie there any longer.

Rising from her bed, she lit a candle in the embers of the fire. There was no doubt or question in her mind where she was going. Holding the candle before her, she made her way to Harry's room. Since he had been brought back from the battlefield she had spent so many long watchful hours there, so many nights, that it felt perfectly natural and right to go there now. The only place she wanted to be.

She set the candle on the table and took up her usual place by his bed.

He had been sleeping only lightly himself. Hearing a sound and sensing her presence, he languidly opened his eyes. When he saw her tired and tragic face he made a movement with his hand, searching for hers. She slid it across the bed covers and they found each other's fingers. As she looked down at his hand enfolding her own, she was shaken with an overwhelming sense that if only she could lie down beside Harry and could wrap her arms round him, have him put his arms around her and hold her, then she could sleep at last and she would be strong enough to go on and all might still be well.

She also realised suddenly that beneath the sheet he was entirely naked and it made her tremble inside.

'Is it so very bad?' he asked.

In her fuddled mind Henrietta was not sure what he was talking about. The losses at Newbury and the loss of London? Or what she wanted him to do? The disaster of the first seemed to make the second insignificant. What did it matter? What did anything matter now? Charles would return any day, weary and distraught. No matter that he had Jane Whorwood, he would look to Henrietta to shore him up again. She would need to find the strength to console him, to encourage him to go on with the fight, tell him what he should do. She had faced impeachment, exile, shipwreck, execution for treason . . . and all for nothing, because the king had hesitated and did not march to London when he could. She was so very tired, tired of having to be strong for them both. She said: 'I have not the the strength to be strong any longer.'

Harry moved away slightly on the bed, enough to make room for her. Without further words or hesitation, she lay down beside him. He turned on to his right, she on her left, so that they were facing one another. She was still afraid of hurting him but they moved closer, curled up together, his wounded arm lying gently over her waist.

And then what she had longed for and dreamed of so often was happening. Only it felt like a dream still. When the intensity of unfulfilled desire had driven her mad with longing, Henrietta's imagination had run wild with fantasies of passionate embraces and ardent kisses. She had imagined that lovemaking born of years of frustration, of close proximity and thwarted yearning and denial, must when finally unleashed be far wilder even than the playful, passionate fondlings of their youth. That it would be rampant and abandoned, laces and buttons ripped away in lust-fuelled haste. Sweat and a tangle of limbs. Grappling and clasping then release.

It was nothing like that. Instead they moved together with a gentleness made sweetly and profoundly intense by the intimacies they had once enjoyed, by the depth of their feelings for each other, by all they had shared and by the length of time they had waited.

They knew each other so well.

For years she had watched his beautiful long-fingered hands perform a variety of humble day-to-day tasks: crack nuts, hold a pen, guide the reins of his horse. The simple tasks were charged with significance because of the way she had always wanted those hands to touch her, caress her, again. She had watched his mouth, too. Laughing, speaking French words and English, eating bread and fruit, drinking ale . . . all the time longing to feel it upon her mouth, to kiss him once more.

Now he was kissing her, touching her, with a passion that was devastating in its simplicity. They lay together, very close and still, looking into each other's eyes, breathing each other's breath. He ran his hands lightly up her shift, over the swell of her hips, her buttocks, her breasts, making her shiver and tingle all over, inside and out. Her own fingers slid over his thighs, wandered through the forest of curly hairs on his chest. She touched one of his nipples and he shuddered, arched his hips closer to hers.

She slipped her hand down between their bodies and wrapped her fingers around the silkiness of him, and he moaned as he had from pain. In the quietness and stillness she felt the thrusting hardness of him in her hand, a pulsing power that seemed to her at that moment the answer to all her needs and prayers. More than anything else in the world, more than food to eat or air to breathe, more than rest or sleep, she needed not just to hold that power but to have it inside her. She had the sense that if she could only have him, just once, it would renew her. A man's seed was thought to be immensely powerful. She believed that the spurt of it inside her would fill up what was empty. That once again she would have the strength she needed to go on.

She opened her legs and he closed his eyes. His whole body shivered again and she knew then that he lacked the strength to resist her. He drew her closer, seeming to forget the pain in his arm, wrapping her so tight to him that he almost crushed her. He kissed her lips, her eyes, her neck and brow, and his hand moved lower, between her legs, pushing up her nightgown. She removed it and pressed herself against him, feeling his skin against hers, the hot taut shaft of his erection pushing and flexing insistently against the gentle curve of her belly. While they were still lying side-by-side he slid between her thighs and entered her. But that was all. For a moment, he was entirely still inside her. She could not remain still for long. It had been beautiful and satisfying what they had done before, but it was nothing to this sense of connection, of feeling him moving deep within her, touching her from the inside, their bodies joined.

She tightened her muscles around him to draw him deeper, as he had once taught her to do with his finger, clutching him inside as if she was sucking him with her mouth. The feeling was so intense that she began to thrust against him, feeling her muscles pulse around him, a pleasure so acute that she was almost ravished by it. When he gave a gushing leap, she yielded to the tugging waves of bliss that flooded her own body.

Now I know, she thought. Now I know what it feels like.

Now I know that some things are worth waiting a lifetime for.

Charles returned deeply demoralised as autumn fogs began to settle and severe floods made the roads so waterlogged that soldiers marching to their garrisons sank right up to their thighs. The bad weather was killing more than had died on the battlefields. There was a virulent outbreak of typhus amongst the troops that spread to the families packed tightly into lodgings in the narrow Oxford streets. The enforced inactivity and air of despondency across the camp led to rivalries and backstabbing, which proved just as unhealthy as the garrison town itself. It culminated in Rupert trying to persuade Charles to dismiss Harry.

'His argument is sound,' Charles said to Henrietta, after summoning her to visit him in Christ Church. 'Jermyn has been identified as the most influential figure in the Army Plot. His continued presence here casts me in a bad light.'

Henrietta was so incandescent with rage that for a moment she was speechless, but she knew Charles would respond better to a reproach than a rant and that when she regained the power of speech she'd better say something that sounded eminently reasonable rather than emotional. It was such a battle, having constantly to bite her tongue, keep control of her emotions, that she wondered why she bothered. Of course, all too often she didn't. And lived to regret it. But for Harry's sake, she must do so now. For Harry's sake, she would do anything.

'It was on your orders that he led the Army Plot,' she reminded her husband. 'He did it purely to serve you. He has risked his life for you and for me. He *saved* my life. Besides which, he is the only person we can trust to cipher.'

'Parliament's propaganda sheets are all naming him as a chief aggressor in this war.'

Now Henrietta did lose her temper. 'Saints preserve us! Ignore Parliament's propaganda. Ignore Rupert. Listen to me instead. Do not be such a fool as to dismiss our most loyal friend!'

Charles had stood by George Villiers and Thomas Wentworth and herself. Why could he not do the same for Harry? She knew why, of course. He had tolerated Harry's presence but underneath had always remained suspicous, jealous. Did he know, somehow, what they had done? How could he know?

'Is that all he is?' Charles asked. 'A loyal friend?'

'Is that what Jane Whorwood is?' she asked archly in return. 'A loyal friend?'

'I think you had better go.'

'Yes, I think I had.'

Charles did not dismiss Harry, but when the time came to allot new places in his Privy Council, everyone said that Harry should by rights have been made Second Secretary of State. Instead the post went to George Digby.

Harry's physical wound was healing well. Though he showed no sign of his pride having been hurt by the king's slight, Henrietta knew that it had been. He was proud and ambitious, and he deserved recognition and status beyond titles and sinecures. She wanted to tell him so, to say something to make him feel better, but she herself was feeling so ill and nauseous she could not think how best to do it.

He was sitting, as he had taken to doing, at the scholar's desk by the west window in her rooms. It was a wintry day and the elm trees in the Fellows' Garden looked particularly dark and melancholy, backed by the glistening water meadows.

'Don't stand up,' she said as he made to do so. 'What are you so busy writing?' She rested her hand on the shoulder of his wounded arm and looked down at his neat and elegant handwriting which she had always admired, so different from her own large scrawl.

'Articles for the propaganda newsbooks,' he replied. He put down his pen and turned to her. 'Parliament has caused much damage with its pamphlets and placards. Now it is our turn. Though we can't fight on the battlefield until spring, we can still fight them on paper.'

Slighted or not, his loyalty and energy were undiminished. He never stopped working.

'Rupert is proposing a different kind of revenge altogether,' she said. 'That troops should be allowed to exact the same reprisals on those found to be assisting Parliament as Parliament does on our supporters.'

'In other words, he wants permission to burn down houses, assault men and rape their women.' Harry did not immediately condemn Rupert, even given such an ideal opportunity, but attempted to see his point of view, as he always did. 'It is unsavoury and unchivalrous and I'd want no part in it. But this is war.'

'I did not think you had it in you to be so ruthless.'

'Being feared less than Parliament is proving to be no advantage to our . . .' He broke off and sprang to his feet. 'Take my seat.'

Henrietta collapsed into the chair.

There was alarm in Harry's face. Typhus was still raging in the city. William Harvey, an eminent physician who had recently discovered how blood travelled round the body, was in attendance upon Prince Rupert's younger brother Maurice, who had contracted the disease. 'I don't have typhus,' Henrietta said. 'If that is what you are thinking.' The symptoms she was suffering from were all too familiar to her. It was just that she was not ready to acknowledge them yet. 'I am so weary. Not of the possibility of being beaten, but of hearing it constantly spoken of.'

For days the talk had all been of the Scots once more, who were just over the border. The Earl of Newcastle had sent to ask for reinforcements to repulse them, but after Newbury there were no reinforcements to be spared. The situation looked bleak as the elm trees in the garden below. It was the most inconvenient time for Henrietta to discover that she was to bear another child. Yet she could not help but feel a little surge of joy combined with her fear.

For this child, she was sure, was Harry's.

# *1644*

'I cannot stay in this country.' Henrietta had been sitting coughing by the fire with a fur-lined cloak about her shoulders all afternoon. It was a persistent, hacking cough that had left her voice weak and her throat sore. Her ribs ached too. It was made worse by a crushing tightness in her chest, symptoms she had never suffered before during pregnancy. 'There is nowhere to seek safety now. We have no strongholds.'

For the past couple of hours Harry had been joined at his desk by William Davenant and the two of them had been busy, heads bowed, composing the epic anti-Parliamentary poem which they had begun some weeks ago. Outside, the Fellows' Garden was now covered in white hoar frost. Harry had taken to wearing spectacles. Hours spent ciphering and deciphering by candlelight had taken their toll on his eyesight. Henrietta herself had suffered excruciating headaches and eyestrain before he had taken charge of her correspondence, and now he was suffering in her place. Suffering for his own kindness. But he looked very well in spectacles, very wise and scholarly. 'Since when has Your Majesty sought a place of safety?' he asked.

She laid her hand on her belly. 'I have a terror of this city coming under siege, of being captured by our enemies, of delivering my baby straight into the hands of Parliament.'

The danger had never seemed greater. At the start of the war, the Royalists had held a strong ring of outposts all around Oxford, but one by one those outposts had fallen. The name of the Parliamentarian responsible for the fall of most of them was Oliver Cromwell, a name that for Henrietta had become filled with menace. A recent Parliamentary victory in Hampshire only served to add to her growing sense of dread.

She heard every day speculation concerning Parliament's resolve to march to Oxford as soon as the season was ripe. Its narrow, teeming streets seemed impossible to defend.

'If I was captured, there is nothing His Majesty would not do, no concession he would not make, in order to secure my release.'

'But that has been the case all along.' Harry frowned. 'This is unlike you.'

'You're right. I don't know what the matter is with me.'

'You are with child again,' he said. 'It is that which is making you so apprehensive.'

They made no mention of the fact that the child might be his.

'Perhaps,' Henrietta said. Perhaps that was all it was, but she had never felt so ill before in her life. The fire was banked high, throwing out heat, but she was still shivering and her bones and muscles ached ceaselessly.

'Returning to England in the first place was far more dangerous than remaining in Oxford will be now,' Harry soothed her.

Henrietta tried to smile but it ended in another fit of coughing that was more like choking. He came over to her quickly with his own cup of ale, all that was to hand.

Henrietta took a gulp, caught her breath. 'I never realised coughing was so exhausting.' She handed the cup back to him. 'I have thought much about it and should like to go home to France. I should like you to take me there.'

'What does His Majesty say?'

'Nothing. I have yet to speak with him about it. But he will think it is sensible. As it is.' Henrietta looked into Harry's face. 'You disagree with me?'

'It is not my place to disagree.'

She smiled through her pain. 'Yes, it is. And even if it were not, when has it ever stopped you?'

'If this is really what you want, ma'am,' he said, 'I will do it willingly, of course. But I have to tell you that, given your condition, I was never more against anything in my life.'

They left in the middle of April, in a sombre procession of coaches strongly guarded by a detachment of armed horsemen from the Queen's Army and foot soldiers with pikes and muskets. Henrietta was carried in a litter, an enclosed coach slung on shafts between two oxen. It lumbered and lurched but did not jolt so fiercely as did a carriage. Even so she coughed constantly, dreading every lurch for the pain she knew even that would bring. Mall and Geoffrey sat with her and tried to distract and entertain her with chatter and singing and games, and Harry and the king rode at her side, though Charles was only accompanying her to just beyond Abingdon.

As they climbed the hills south of Oxford, Henrietta asked Harry to halt the litter so that she could look back over the city's towers and spires lit by the misty spring sunlight. She had grown to love that beautiful ancient city, to see it as her home. She could not bear to think of it being attacked, overrun by Roundheads, falling into Parliamentary hands. Nor could she help but reflect on how she had ridden into the city on horseback at the head of an army, singing marching songs, so full of energy, hope and determination. How different from the way she felt now, so ill and weak she had to be carried, her ears on constant alert for the sound of Roundheads galloping in pursuit.

If only this incessant cough would go away. If only the pain would lessen, just a little. Mayerne and Harvey had both been consulted and neither could say just what was wrong with her, though Doctor Harvey did suggest some poisoning of the blood. But blood was his life's work, preoccupied and obsessed him. Henrietta had let them bleed her once, but it had done no good and she had refused a second treatment. Her last hope now was that the air of her homeland might restore her.

The party halted in the little town of Abingdon for the night, and next morning journeyed on to the Vale of the White Horse where Charles was to leave them.

Mall climbed out of the carriage and the king climbed in. He took Henrietta into his arms. Even to be held by him hurt, but she tried not to show it. When he let go she did not want him to, despite the pain. Charles always looked sad, but never had he looked sadder than at this moment. Henrietta took his thin face between her hands. 'You know I do not want to desert you or my children again, but I mean to show you by this action that nothing is so much in my thoughts as your preservation.' She had to break off to cough. 'I know your affection would make you risk everything for my sake. By God's grace, I may recover my health in France so as to serve you further. I am hazarding my life that I may not add to your difficulties.'

He kissed her, on her lips and on her forehead. 'Your merits are such that they should save you from even the most savage Indians.'

'Yours too.' She did not want to leave him alone to face that 'hellcat', as the Cavaliers had taken to calling Oliver Cromwell. Such a man would not appreciate or even see Charles's many fine qualities. He was so proud and principled. A good man. Suddenly Henrietta was overwhelmed with a desire to turn back, to stay with him. But really what use was she when she could barely stand? She kissed him again, laid her fingers against his cheek. '*Adieu, mon cher.*'

Through the open curtains of the litter Henrietta watched him mount his horse, take up the reins and turn back dejectedly for Oxford. Just as she had contrasted her own departure with her arrival in that place, so now she compared this second farewell to her husband with the first, when she had left for Holland and he had galloped along the clifftop in the wind, chasing her ship. Now, with his horse at a slow trot, his shoulders drooping, he did not look as if he had the heart left to gallop anywhere and it broke her heart to see him so defeated. She had the strongest urge to run after him, even though she did not have the strength. To call to him, even though she could not speak without coughing.

The second leg of the journey did nothing to lift Henrietta's spirits. Everywhere they travelled the countryside bore the brutal scars of war. Pastures and meadows and arable land had been churned over by hungry troops, farms stood neglected because all the labourers had gone off to fight. Workhorses had been commandeered for cavalry and oxen were pulling cannons and wagons full of weapons instead of ploughing the furrows. Stables and once grand houses were burned out shells; towns were ringed by ugly earthwork defences that had been torn up from the ground as if by a giant's shovel. The landlord of the coaching inn where they stopped to water the horses warned them that in Bath plague and other deadly diseases were rampant, and when they entered the town, they encountered decaying corpses at the corner of every street, dead from wounds as well as from disease. Even though travelling was so painful for Henrietta, they did not stop but pressed on west, into the Somerset Fens, a landscape as different from the horrors of Bath as could be. It was like a scene from a pastoral play.

The wide flat fields around Bridgewater reminded her of Holland, but a tamer, far prettier version. In such a fertile land, nature seemed to act faster to cover the ravages of war. The water meadows were alight with golden buttercups and criss-crossed by drainage channels that formed a network of small canals, sparkling like silver ribbons in the sunshine.

Henrietta called out to Harry, up on his horse, to halt the litter. 'I should like to walk a while,' she told him.

He shouted to the men driving the oxen to bring them to a halt, waited until they had done so before he tried to dissuade Henrietta from getting out. 'The physicians have told Your Majesty you must not try to walk.'

'I never do as I am told, as well you know. Now lend me your hand and help me down, will you?'

He dismounted, leaned into the litter and slid his arm around her, lifting her out on to the road. He set her gently on her feet but kept his arm around her to support her as she leaned on him. They walked slowly together. She watched the mallards on the water and the birds of prey wheeling in the sky over the lush green meadows, and in her own sickness felt a powerful empathy with England, devastated and damaged by war, brought to its knees, hurt and bleeding but still struggling on.

She faltered and Harry tightened his hold on her. She should have been haunted by fear that her sickness was divine retribution for having lain with him. There was a sinister symmetry to events which might once have troubled her greatly. She had gone to him in a moment of weakness, seeking strength, and had afterwards been rendered weaker than she had ever felt in her life or imagined it possible to feel. She could not confess her adultery even to Father Philip, but she had confessed it in her heart and truly believed that God had forgiven her, that He understood completely. She'd had that strange sense all along that Harry had been given to her. That his love for her was the most precious gift of her life, something to sustain her through all its great trials. What else could it be? Charles said her love sustained him. He depended on her and turned to her for strength. And she in turn was sustained by Harry, depended on him and leaned on him, just as she was doing now. It was from him that her strength derived. She did not, could not ever regret what they had done. It had not felt like giving in to temptation, but rather abandoning themselves to fate, their destiny.

'You are growing so brown in the sun,' she said to him.

He looked down at her, his gaze gentle with a tender passion, and she saw the fear in his eyes. His fear of losing her was as great as her own fear of losing him. 'Your Majesty is growing very pale. I think you had better get back in the litter now.'

She did as he said, and as they journeyed on through the winding high-hedged lanes of Devon her condition worsened. She began to feel so faint she could barely sit up.

'Why does Your Majesty not lie down and sleep?' Mall said, huddling closer to Geoffrey to make more room.

Henrietta closed her eyes and did sleep a little until they reached Exeter, a large, rich and populous city with a beautiful cathedral and castle. They were met there by Harry's young cousin, Jack Berkeley, and taken to his home, Bedford House, in the centre of the town. It was a tall, airy mansion with high ceilings and vast windows. Jack was like a shorter version of Harry, with the same curly hair and blue eyes and amenable nature. But the convivial company and comfort of Bedford House barely lessened Henrietta's fears. She was due to be brought to bed in a matter of weeks and could not conceive how she would bear the pain of childbirth in addition to the cruel pains she was already suffering. How her broken body would ever find the strength to push out a baby.

'I can't feel my toes,' she said to Harry one morning in terror. 'I cannot feel them at all.' Her knees were going numb too. 'I feel like a person poisoned.'

'It is just the baby,' he said, sitting with her on the bed. 'As soon as the baby is here you will feel better.'

The loss of sensation in her legs left her barely able to stand and she had such a constriction round her heart that at times she thought she would suffocate. Newssheets were already reporting her death after the birth of a stillborn child. It seemed more like a prophecy than a lie.

'Would you write to the king for me? Now.'

Harry moved to the desk and took up his pen. 'What would you have me write?'

She felt the press of tears behind her eyes. 'Tell him that it is perhaps the last letter he will ever receive from me.' She watched him write it, wait for her to go on. 'Oh, there is so much I want to say to him! Yet I cannot be certain he will ever read it. The roads are so unsafe . . .'

'I am safe,' Harry said. 'I will tell His Majesty personally, whatever you want me to tell him. If need be.'

She took a deep breath, the air knifing through her lungs and stinging her throat.

'There is nothing you cannot say to me, ma'am,' Harry assured her. 'I hope you know that.'

She nodded. 'Tell him . . . tell him that my last and dearest wish is that I might see him regain the position which ought to be his. Tell him that . . . that I . . .'

'That you love him dearly and always will?'

'It is not that I do not . . .'

'I know that. And I am privileged to have even a small portion of your heart. It is worth more to me than the whole of anyone else's.'

She was so grateful to him for not belittling her fears, for not trying to convince her that she would be able to tell all this herself to Charles soon enough.

Madame Peronne was unable to come to England but had sent Henrietta a generous gift of money. Retaining a small amount for her own immediate needs, she forwarded the rest of it with the letter to Charles.

Not two weeks later, Thomas Mayerne arrived in Exeter. 'His Majesty wrote me an urgent letter,' he explained. '"Mayerne, for the love of God, go to my wife,"' it said. So, for the love of God, here I am! Though I am an old man now and not far from death myself, and have embarked on a journey of over three hundred and seventy miles to get here. I feared I might be too late. A Cornish Royalist gentleman I met who happened to pass you on the road here said Your Majesty was the most woeful spectacle he had ever set eyes upon. Tell me, what troubles you?'

'The pain is so bad, I am afraid I shall go mad.'

'Nay,' he replied. 'Your Majesty need not fear going mad. You have been so for some time.'

Henrietta knew this was no joke but a political jibe. Mayerne, like many others, had come to believe her religion to be one of the principal causes of the troubled state of England, and had turned against her. But even the curmudgeonly physican softened towards her when he saw that she could not move her legs.

'Mayerne may not know what is wrong with me but he believes I shall die,' she said to Harry after he had gone. 'I heard it in his voice.'

'If Mayerne does not know what is wrong with you then it does not matter what he believes.' Harry came to her and took her hand. 'You are the bravest person I know,' he said. 'And the most tenacious and determined. You must not give up. Not now. Not after all you have been through. After all that we have been through.' She saw there were tears in his eyes. 'Please do not give up. You once told me you had no strength left to be strong. But you found it.'

'You gave it to me.'

'Then I will again. I have enough for both of us.'

She almost felt it, in the warm grip of his hand. She took it and placed it on the tight mound of her belly, pressing his fingers flat. 'Feel,' she said, as the baby kicked and turned over. 'You are right. There is life inside me yet.'

On 16 June she gave birth to a living child, a daughter.

'She has enchanted you, I think,' said Henrietta. Harry did not seem able to take his eyes off the baby who was lying awake very peacefully, swaddled in her crib, looking up at him with wide blue eyes. She was exceptionally delicate and beautiful. 'She is lovely, isn't she?'

'Of course she is. She is your daughter.'

'She is your daughter too.'

Harry glanced at Henrietta. 'I did not dare even to wonder. Are you sure?'

'As sure as I can ever be.' Now the baby was safely delivered, Henrietta desperately wanted her to to be Harry's. How sick with jealousy it had made her when Eleanor had said she was carrying his child. How she had wanted him for herself. Wanted to feel his seed take root inside her. There was practically no chance this ninth baby of hers would inherit the throne. No risk of corrupting the line of heredity. Harry had given his life to her. Sacrificed any chance of a wife and family. She wanted to give him life back. To give him a child. 'In my heart, I know she is yours.'

'What will you call her?'

'Henrietta. What else? For you and for me.'

It seemed fitting to Henrietta that she should pass on her own name to this child since she feared her daughter would never know her, just as Henrietta had not known the father for whom she was named. Now Harry had some part of her to love if death took her from him as she was sure it would. The pain inside her had lessened after the birth and she had regained some sensation and movement in her legs, but she was still partially paralysed, with no feeling in one of her arms. All her limbs were colder than ice. Most frightening of all was the fact that she had lost the sight in one of her eyes. She was not afraid of dying; indeed, welcomed the prospect. She half wished that sickness would take her before Parliament surely must. The Earl of Essex had come west again with the intention of relieving a siege at Lyme, but his army was now advancing towards Exeter with the intention of bombarding the city.

'I sent to Essex to ask him to grant Your Majesty safe conduct,' Harry told her.

She could tell by his tone that the response was not what he had hoped. 'What did he say?'

'That your safety is no concern of his.'

'I cannot stay here.' She struggled to sit, was already trying to throw off the blankets. Harry moved to stop her, putting his hand over hers. ' If I die trying to leave, it will be better than to be taken alive,' she insisted. 'We have to go. Immediately. It is no better here than at Oxford. We must get to France.'

'Essex will be watching the ports. You will be exposing yourself to more danger by fleeing.

'For His Majesty's sake, I have no choice.'

Harry let go of her hand as the baby made a mewing sound. He reached down into the crib and stroked the infant's downy cheek with one finger. 'We will have to leave her behind,' he said softly. 'For her own safety and for ours. It will be too dangerous, and if we have to hide, her cries would give us away in an instant. ' His smile was so warm and yet so sad it made Henrietta's already broken heart shatter in yet another place. 'I know she is a little angel and never seems to cry,' he said, 'but we cannot take that risk.'

Henrietta's silence was enough to let him know that she acknowledged him to be right, even if she could not bring herself to tell him so. 'You have already made enquiries?'

Of course he had. He would have arranged everything as he always did, have everything meticulously planned. She need not worry. 'My cousin has a friend,' he said. 'A trusted friend. A kindly person. Lady Anne Dalkeith. She will take good care of her.'

\* \* \*

Despite her continued illness, just fifteen days after her confinement Henrietta was up and out of bed, disguising herself in a peasant's bonnet and rough woollen dress. She had regained the use of her legs and was determined that she was strong enough to make good her escape before the Roundheads arrived. The plan was to steal away from Exeter on foot. Once out of town, Henrietta could be carried in the litter again. Harry had advised that the two of them must separate, that together they would attract too much attention. They were the subject of much gossip still, and he being so tall and she so small, were hard to mistake. Henrietta was to go with Mall and Father Philip and meet up with Harry and Geoffrey at an empty cottage on the Plymouth Road.

'What about Mitte?'

'She had better come with me,' Harry said.

Henrietta, Mall and the priest slipped away first but they did not get very far. They had walked only three miles along the road that led out of Exeter when they heard ahead of them the terrifying heavy tramp of thousands upon thousands of feet and the deafening clatter of horses' hoofs. Essex's army was already advancing on the city.

Henrietta grabbed Mall's hand and pulled her into a copse of trees at the side of the road. There was a ramshackle wooden hut which they hastened towards as the footsteps grew louder, closer, accompanied by voices. Snatches of conversation were clearly distinguishable.

'Keep a look out in the bushes,' one soldier said. 'The Papist whore has left the city and there's fifty crowns reward for the man who carries her head to London.'

Shaking with terror, Henrietta looked for a way to hide herself if the soldiers should see the shed and search it. There was a heap of rubbish in the corner: moth-eaten old blankets, a three-legged chair, a broken straw pallet. She quickly pushed herself beneath them, signalling to Mall and her confessor to do likewise.

The feet and horses and cartwheels kept coming, in wave upon wave that made the ground rumble and shake. A vast army was on the move. There were breaks between battalions but never long enough for it to feel safe to come out of hiding. Fearing discovery at any minute, they lay for several hours, surrounded by rags and rubbish that stank of damp and God alone knew what else, without food or drink, knowing all the time that

Harry would be waiting further along the road, worrying and wondering what had happened to them.

At length all the Parliamentarians seemed to have passed by. As darkness fell, Henrietta and her companions crept out cautiously from their hiding place. The road was so churned up by the army's advance it was almost impassable, but Father Philip took Henrietta's arm. Twisting their ankles on the uneven earth, they hurried as best they could to the rendezvous. If only they could reach Harry, Henrietta thought, then they would be safe.

Waiting anxiously for her in the darkness outside the little wooden cabin between Exeter and Plymouth stood such an odd-looking group it made Henrietta smile despite the danger. Harry, over six foot tall, Geoffrey, half that size, and one small dog. Mitte knew Henrietta even in her strange-smelling peasant's garb and came bounding up to her, tail wagging frantically.

Guided by the moon they journeyed all night, Henrietta carried again in the litter while her small band of attendants walked or rode beside her. They skirted the southern edge of Dartmoor, a strange landscape of streams and tors topped by granite boulders. Moss and cotton grass, sedges and rushes, warned of dangerous mires and peat bogs that could swallow a man whole.

After some days they crossed into Cornwall via a wooden bridge over the Tamar, and eventually reached the tiny harbour town of Falmouth. They were to rest for the night with more of Harry's relations who lived in the granite manor house of Arwenack. It was the ancestral home of his mother and now the residence of his cousins, a gaggle of small boys and girls whose noisy, happy chatter Henrietta found soothing as she gazed out of the narrow casement windows across the Fal estuary and the deep natural harbour. The evening was serene and bright with only a little westerly breeze, the sea smooth as glass.

One of the older boys handed Harry a copy of a Parliamentary pamphlet that was circulating in the town. Henrietta watched him read it and was surprised to see him softly smiling, which was not his usual response when studying propaganda.

'What are they saying about us now?'

'It describes our journey from Oxford to Exeter.'

She frowned. 'And what do they have to say about that?'

He handed it to her to read.

*When the Queen chose not to ride in the litter but to walk on foot, she had the support of Jermyn's arm, which she conceived as mighty as the strongest pillar in this land and warranted her health more than the most skilled physicians.*

'For once Parliament tells the truth,' she said.

The queen's party moved to the stronghold of Pendennis Castle with its little round tower and curtain wall, and from there to a man-of-war, accompanied by a small fleet of Flemish vessels, that arrived in Falmouth harbour. It was under the command of a Captain Colster, a weather-beaten sailor with a face that stayed strangely immobile, as if the wind had frozen it into one expression.

As they put to sea, Henrietta's thoughts were all for her newborn baby, her namesake, whom she had left behind at but a few days old.

'She will be well cared for,' Harry said sympathetically.

'We have abandoned our daughter to the fury of those tigers.'

'She is far safer with Lady Dalkeith than with us.'

As if to prove him right, they were barely out of the harbour when Parliamentary sails appeared on the horizon. Two warships. As the crafts drew closer, in pursuit, Mall started crying and begged that they should turn back.

Henrietta's hands tightened on the rail. 'I forbid any return to shore,' she instructed Captain Colster. 'Crowd on all sail. And if capture looks unavoidable, light the powder in the hold. I would rather you blow us all to pieces than allow me to fall into the hands of my husband's enemies.'

Mall's screams grew more piercing still.

'Be quiet, Mall,' Harry told her. 'We must all be as brave as Her Majesty. There's Jersey,' he pointed out. 'Thank God I am not going back there.'

'Rather Jersey than the bottom of the sea,' Mall sobbed.

The Parliamentary ships were closing in, their cannons aimed.

'You should all go below decks, ma'am,' Captain Colster advised.

'I prefer to keep my enemy within sight, sir,' Henrietta replied.

The ships opened fire with the familiar boom and thud that she had once associated with royal celebrations. Mall screamed.

'How long ago it seems since cannons were fired in salute,' Henrietta shouted to Harry above the noise. 'They welcomed me to England and now they are trying to kill me rather than let me leave.' But though balls came whistling past, their aim was too high and they were landing with almighty splashes in the sea all around the ship. 'Lord be praised, they are missing us!'

Captain Colster ordered his sailors to employ the oars to increase speed. Their Parliamentary pursuers, being heavier, could not do likewise and began to lose ground. Then mercifully, the queen's fleet found the wind, the sails filled and the ships drew further away still. But just as they were almost at a distance to put them out of imminent danger, a shot hit the mizzenmast and with a rending of timber the ship listed wildly under the blow. Henrietta was flung against the main mast. Harry caught her in his arms as the ship righted. As Captain Colster called out to slacken the sail she and Harry both looked up and saw the broken spar, crooked against the grey sky, the rigging hanging in tatters.

'This is it then,' Henrietta said. 'We give ourselves up for lost?' She was thinking that if it were so and they were facing certain capture, she would order the powder to be fired and ask Harry to go on holding her as the ship went down.

'Look, ma'am,' he said. Instead of Parliamentary ships on the horizon half a dozen French ones were visible. 'They have come to escort their princess home.'

The enemy immediately abandoned the chase and the French ships, white sails bellying in the wind, drew alongside the queen's fleet, taking it under their protection. But the French vessels could offer no protection from the weather. Having seen off one enemy, wind and rain became their adversary yet again. Before the boats could reach the safety of Dieppe harbour, roiling black clouds gathered in the sky and a violent storm broke overhead. Sheltering below decks, Henrietta did not see the monstrous forty-foot wave that caused the French escort to disappear momentarily from view. Ahead reared a savage range of rocks. The ships, at the mercy of wind and the waves, were being driven perilously closer to them. Every violent gust and heave of water threatened to smash them against the treacherous, unyielding outcrop.

The boats took a battering for hours before at last sighting the wild Breton coast. Captain Colster ordered the long boat to be put out and Harry helped the women climb down the swaying rope ladder into it. They were rowed to shore, clinging to the sides of the boat through crashing waves which soaked them all to the skin with icy seawater. By the time they reached the cove, their clothes were saturated, Henrietta's hair hanging in bedraggled, dripping rat's tails. Harry took her hand and tried to help Mall too as they began to scramble across lethally slippery rocks in their delicate slippers. Mitte was doing the best of all, scurrying on all fours, and Father Philip followed her lead, clambering on hands and feet.

As they reached the far edge of the rocks there was yet more danger to be encountered. On the hills above the bay appeared fishermen, running towards the cove brandishing hoes and scythes.

'God's blood!' Harry cursed over the hiss and boom of the surf. 'They think we're pirates.'

'Where is your pistol?' Henrietta shouted back.

'No use. Powder's wet.'

He dragged his rapier out of its scabbard and Captain Colster brandished his cutlass. Geoffrey produced his miniature sword. Above the roar of the waves and the howl of the gale Harry shouted out his identity. 'I am Lord Jermyn, Lord Chamberlain to the Queen of England.'

The peasants shouted back in angry guttural Breton that Henrietta could make no sense of, having never been exposed to country patois.

Harry shouted louder in his perfect French. 'We are not pirates!' He pointed his rapier at the queen. 'This is the daughter of Henri le Grand of France. A French princess. Now Queen of England. Henriette Marie.'

Henrietta could not blame them for taking him for an imbecile or a prankster, for not believing even for a second that a tiny, ragged, windswept waif, dressed in peasant's clothes, could ever be a queen. But she had temporarily forgotten how convincing Harry was. The fishermen all at once put down their weapons and began doffing caps and bowing to her, right there in the surf. Of all the astonishing moments she had experienced in her life, this had to be one of the strangest.

They were led up a steep winding path to a cluster of fishermen's huts which made the ones they'd stayed in in Bridlington look palatial. These were no more than hovels, but Henrietta did not care. Her clothes were set to dry near the fire and she was given another woollen dress that was far too big. Her bed for the night was a pallet in a corner of the downstairs room, partitioned off with a curtain.

But uncomfortable as it was, Harry had considerable trouble waking her in the morning. The ordeal had made Henrietta's condition worsen once more. She was so drowsy she was barely conscious. The numbness in her limbs had returned and now her heart was beating erratically.

'I have to leave you here for a few days,' he told her gently. 'I am sorry, but I have to go to Paris to tell the queen and her new minister that you are here . . . make the necessary arrangements.' He looked at her small, pale face above the rough woollen blankets. 'I will speak to the royal physicans also. I am sure you will not lack for company while I am gone,' he added with a smile. 'There are already half a dozen folk waiting outside the door, wanting to see for themselves how the daughter of Henri le Grand has returned to France like a heroine from a romance.'

'Is that what I am?'

'To me at any rate.' He smiled and touched the back of her hand. 'I will be back as soon as I can, I promise you.'

'I know you will.'

Harry was right. The remote fishing hamlet was soon overrrun with Bretons, bearing gifts of hams and cheeses, while country gentlemen came with horses and carriages and coachmen, offering to take the queen on the rest of her journey.

But she would go nowhere without Harry.

When he returned he told her that they were to journey to the royal spa at the Château d'Amboise at Bourbon-l'Archambault, in the Loire Valley.

'We are not going to Paris?'

'Not until you are well.'

So long as he was with her, Henrietta did not mind where they went. 'I suppose the physicians told you that the thermal springs there offer the best cure for both a broken spirit and a broken body?' she commented as he carried her out to the coach in his arms.

'I do not believe your spirit is broken, ma'am. Or your body.'

Even seen through a daze of pain and exhaustion, Bourbon-l'Archambault was the most peaceful, beautiful place. Ivy covered the castle walls, which were topped with high white towers, pointed red-roofed turrets and blue slate tiles. Nearby was an ancient stone chapel and a still, deep lake, rimmed with trees and surrounded by fields of wild flowers. It was harvest time and the lanes around the little village were thronged with oxen and carts.

But for three weeks all Henrietta saw were the lime-washed walls of her bedchamber. She slept for most of the day and her heart was beating so irregularly that it made her unable to sit up without feeling dizzy. A red rash covered her body and an abscess had formed in her breast. It was lanced by the local physician who instructed her to drink ass's milk every morning and to begin taking the waters, and baths too, as soon as she was feeling strong enough to reach the bathhouse.

Meanwhile, Harry brought her the warmed milk and fed her with soup, just as she had fed him when he was ill. He sat beside her bed and talked to her and held her hand. Maybe that was what love was all about when you reached a certain age, she thought. Being with the person you wanted to hold your hand when you were ill, to hold your hand when you were dying. She had to remind herself that she was not yet thirty-five years old. She might have ten years left, twenty, or more. It did not feel like it.

She was determined at least to get to the bathhouse on her own two feet. She hobbled out of the castle, stooped and in pain, Harry's arm around her waist all that was holding her upright. 'Can you believe I used to dance?' she said with a harsh little laugh.

'You will dance again.'

She stopped walking. 'Please do not humour me, Harry. Do not insult me. I barely know I have feet!'

'You have feet, ma'am,' he replied, deadly serious. 'Please take my word for that. If you'll pardon me.' He lifted her skirts a little. 'See? Feet. Two of 'em.'

Henrietta looked at her slippers and then at him, and giggled. 'We are now arguing about whether or not I have toes!'

He laughed with her, and a gaggle of ladies who were making their way back from the baths glanced over. Seeing who it was, they smiled, curtseyed politely then continued about their business. It was the same no matter who they encountered. Bourbon was a fashionable watering place but the many visitors to the spa, like the Breton country people, treated Henrietta with the greatest kindness and courtesy, smiling and curtseying to her but otherwise letting her alone. 'I am so well treated everywhere that if my lords in London saw it, I think it would make them most displeased,' she quipped.

'Or perhaps it is that they are all certain I have returned to the land of my birth only to die.' She caught a glimpse of herself in the waters of the lake and was shocked by what a pitiful sight she made, walking along like an old lady, helped by Harry, whose height and strength made her look especially tiny and frail. Her face had become so thin that her mouth, which she had always considered her worst feature, looked out of proportion. 'Dear sweet Mary, but I look ghastly.'

'You do not.' Harry looked not into the water but at her face. 'Are we to argue about this now?'

'No matter,' she dismissed his reply. 'Beauty is but a morning's bloom. Mine faded when I was about twenty-two, I think. I do not believe that the charms of other ladies continue much longer.'

Again Harry laughed. 'Your Majesty's sense of humour will never fade. Nor will your beauty. Trust me.' He smiled at her. 'There is something so sweet in your expression, and so gracious in your manner, that you will win hearts to the end of your days.'

'I think you are biased.'

He turned her gently back towards her watery reflection. 'Shall I tell you what I see?'

'Please do. I am not too old and too ill to appreciate a little flattery.'

'On the surface, I see a lady with beautiful black eyes and clear skin,' he said, looking down at her face. 'But there is something in this lady's expression that is so spiritual and delightful it commands the love of all who serve her. I see a lady of great wit, who is sweet and sincere, and who lives without form or ceremony among those who have the honour of her intimacy. A lady whose temper is gay and cheerful even in misfortune, and whose hand is generous so long as she has aught to give.'

'That is a very pretty speech. You do not regret it then?' Henrietta asked, looking into his face.

'Regret what?'

'Giving over your life to my service? It is a very different life from the one you imagined, I expect, when you first set sail with me from France. Or did you think then that being part of my court would lead you to be exiled, twice, branded a traitor, to have to pawn the crown jewels, face shipwreck and cannons and be taken for a pirate?

'I would not have missed a second of it.'

'You once said you would serve me in order to see the great queen I would be. I fear you have pinned your colours to a broken mast, sir.'

'As I have said, I do not believe you are broken.'

'I feel as if I am.'

'Then you will mend. I will mend you.'

When autumn winds from the mountains drove the other visitors home, Henrietta and her friends stayed on and slowly she began to make a recovery. But as her physical condition improved, the mental anguish returned and once again she was unable to sleep. She could think of nothing but the war in England. No news had reached their oasis but she worried constantly about baby Henrietta and Prince Charles. He would be fourteen soon and she knew he would be riding with his father's army, fighting with that army. She wrote to ask for his measurements so that she could have a French suit of armour made for him. They were much better than English ones.

Harry arranged for the payment, as he now arranged everything.

They were visited by Queen Anne's lady-of-honour, Madame de Motteville, a florid, friendly lady who, when she went with Henrietta to the steamy bathhouse, talked of nothing but the queen's relations with her lord chamberlain. Much to Madame de Motteville's astonishment, Harry had first given Henrietta strict instructions not to tire herself with too much talking.

'I am feeling much stronger today,' she had assured him.

'And you will continue to grow stronger, so long as you do as you are told.'

Which had left Madame de Motteville's mouth hanging open. 'He's so forceful,' she said, as she and Henrietta immersed themselves in the soothing, steaming waters.

Henrietta smiled. 'He is usually remarkably mild in his manners. It is not true that he governs me entirely – we pretend that he does. But I often have a will completely contrary to his, and he knows he'll have to bend to it, in the end.'

Henrietta was not actually sure he did know that at all. Or that it was true any more. During her illness she had come to rely upon Harry for everthing, was happy to let him make all the decisions. They had been due to leave for Paris two days ago but Harry had said they must wait. He would not say why, or for what, and she did not even trouble to ask. Wait they did.

Henrietta was sitting by the lake when he brought a small olive-skinned gentleman to her, with restless black eyes, an upturned moustache and tuft of beard. He was wearing a very finely cut outfit that looked to be in the height of fashion. But who was he? He smiled at Henrietta's perplexity, and his eyebrows beetled . . . and then she knew and threw her arms around him. 'Gaston! My dear, dear brother.'

'Monsier Jean-Baptiste Gaston, Duc d'Orléans,' he corrected her. 'Come to conduct Queen Henrietta Maria of England to Paris.'

They travelled through baking heat for a month, via the towns of Tours, Orléans and Nevers, where Henrietta was received in full state. Being the first major town en route, it was there that they finally heard news from England. A messenger brought letters from Charles dated nine weeks before, which assured Henrietta of the safety of all her children. Exeter had not been bombarded after all. Charles had secured a significant victory. He had advanced into Cornwall and at Lostwithiel, on the last day of August, had defeated the Earl of Essex. Charles had entered the city of Exeter himself and had made the acquaintance of little Henrietta, who had been baptised in the cathedral. Henrietta felt a pang of guilt that he should think the pretty child his own, but it was far outweighed by feelings of relief that both of them were well.

Happiness at this news gave her the strength to walk unassisted for the first time since her illness. She went down to the hall to give her personal thanks to the messenger who had brought such good tidings, and to ask him to wait for her reply. But just that short burst of activity and excitement left her so drained that she had to leave Harry to write to Charles in a new cipher. She was forced back to bed with a fever and headache which delayed her state entry to Paris for nearly a month.

It was early-November when they set off again and, the roads being miry, an enormous carpet was spread out over the mud near Montagne where Henrietta was met by Anne, now Queen Regent of France. In her gilded carriage she was attended by her dark-haired, dark-eyed son, eight-year-old King Louis XIV.

Anne and Henrietta wept and embraced and checked each other's appearance. Anne had grown plumper where Henrietta had grown thinner. She joined Anne and Louis in their golden coach, the king's guards riding before them and the French nobility following in their own coaches. Trumpets and church bells sounded, and the streets that led towards the Pont Neuf and the Louvre were decorated with bright hangings.

The palace where Henrietta was born and where she had first met Harry had been abandoned by the French court now, in favour of the Palais Royal, and though Henrietta knew her way around very well, Anne and Gaston insisted on leading her personally to the apartments that were to be hers. They were in the south wing on the ground floor, with huge rectangular windows which flooded the rooms with light and looked out over the River Seine. But Henrietta found no joy in being back once more in her former home. The splendid, richly painted rooms, filled with statues and mirrors, paintings and fine Renaissance furniture, seemed to mock her somehow. She had left here with such great hopes and plans and dreams and was returning with nothing, a sorry exile. She was surrounded by extravagance and luxury but none of it belonged to her. She had no belongings of any worth. Even her smallest jewels were in pawn.

'There was a time when I thought I would never miss England,' she said to Harry as they stood at the window looking out over the Seine. 'But I do. Walking up Greenwich Hill. Our summers in Richmond Park. The deer. The children climbing the ancient oak tree, and the meadow grass so high it reached our knees. It seems such an enchanted, gentle life.' She smiled sorrowfully. 'The trouble is that I miss England, but England does not miss me. Oh, but did I tell you?' she asked instantly brightening – there was something in her spirit which refused to let her feel downbeat or defeated for long. 'We are to be given access to St Germain-en-Laye. We will go there in the spring,' she decided. 'It is the best time to see it. We have much business to attend to before then. Thank God I begin to feel like myself again.'

He looked at her in wonder and admiration. 'You really do never give up, do you?'

'Neither do you,' she said. 'We carry on. We keep each other going and we do our best. What more can we do but that?'

Harry was installed in a grand gilded office with a great oak desk, and looked very grand and great himself, surrounded by cipher keys, letters, maps. Henrietta could see that his brain was already teeming with schemes and plans. First on the list of tasks was to find more funds. Harry secured a maintenance stipend for Henrietta from Richelieu's replacement, Cardinal

Mazarin, a polished Italian of forty plus years, with even features and animated brown eyes. He and Harry seemed to get on together particularly well. Out of this modest allowance, Harry set about feeding Henrietta's household. The French had provided the usual entourage of guards and running footmen and cooks. In addition, various Royalist exiles, including George Digby, were flocking to France and appealing to their queen for aid. Henrietta tried to help wherever she could, but her first priority was always England. She'd willingly starve and let everyone else do so with her in order to be able to send all the money she could back to Charles. She kept only what was absolutely necessary. And her view on what was absolutely necessary altered drastically as the weeks passed.

Within months of her arrival in Paris she had made great savings by dispensing with the carriages and footmen who had surrounded her all her life. She kept a cook but she and Mall took turns to help in the vast, empty kitchens, peeling vegetables, stirring the soup and kneading the bread, which was all they ate for their midday meal. Kitchen duties were such a novelty to Henrietta that she quite enjoyed them and went about singing.

Meanwhile, Harry took on the duties of private secretary, decipherer, chamberlain and steward, all in one. He recruited the young poet in exile Abraham Cowley to help with his business letters, but all the queen's personal correspondence he still took charge of himself. He worked harder than ever, often long into the night. Soon he had various ventures underway to raise money to pay for supplies for themselves and for the king's belea-guered army.

Charles had granted Henrietta a monopoly on selling tin from Royalist Cornwall and Harry quickly established a flourishing trade between the west of England and France. It was a neat system. A fleet of loyal merchant vessels, including Captain Colster's, ran to and fro across the Channel, landing tin in the French ports to be sold for fifteen shillings per hundredweight, before returning to England with military supplies purchased with that profit.

Within weeks the tin had paid for two thousand pistols, six thousand muskets, one thousand carbines, one hundred and fifty swords, four hundred shovels, four hundred barrels of gunpowder, plus matches and brimstone. Henrietta took as much pride in counting it all up as she had the first time, more even, because each and every weapon counted now more than ever. She listed all these acquisitions in letters to her husband.

But then, in May, with no warning and no explanation, except that it was George Digby's idea, a letter arrived from Charles in which he informed her that he had transferred her tin monopoly to Sir Edward Hyde, who was now Chancellor of the Exchequer and who was also head of the Royalist Government and of the Prince of Wales's household.

'I swear my husband is his own worst enemy,' Henrietta railed. She perched herself on a corner of Harry's huge desk. 'He can do as much damage to himself and his interests as can the entire Roundhead army! I have never trusted Hyde. He's always been too willing to negotiate with our enemies. In his heart he is not in favour of royalty. His counsels plainly show that he has no wish for an absolute monarch.'

'Well, he has scuppered us for sure.'

'How bad is it?'

Harry ran his hand over his face. 'I have just obtained an advance from Mazarin to enable me to send supplies to Montrose. I was planning on paying the loan back with profits from our next tin shipment, but now those profits will go straight into Hyde's pocket. I have also raised a personal loan in order to redeem one of the pawned crown jewels before it is lost forever. I have no way to repay that either.'

Henrietta slid off his desk and began pacing the room. 'My husband is not only his own worst enemy but ours too. Sometimes I think him a complete fool.'

For once Harry did not disagree with her or try to defend the king's actions.

'We will have to raise more money from sympathetic Catholics here in France. I cannot squeeze another *sou* from my pension.'

Harry took off his specacles and pinched the bridge of his nose. 'We have already sent to England thirty-six thousand crowns from the income assigned to your maintenance.'

'Which I am sure my husband regards as precious little in the way of assistance.'

'If he knew how you stinted yourself, he would think it great indeed.'

But rather than acknowledging Henrietta's sacrifices, the next letter from Charles was again highly critical, as so many others had been, warning her to let none know the particulars of his dispatches. Did he really think she would show his letters to anyone but Harry?

She feared too that he was keeping things from her. William Davenant in England had informed Harry that Charles was sending two emissaries to London with new terms for what he called a 'reasonable peace'. But her husband had made no mention of it to her.

'How can he propose to bargain with Parliament about a thing so very prejudicial to all our affairs – and to my whole future?' she protested.

Harry's head was bent, as almost perpetually now, over a ledger. How tired he looked. The loss of the tin and its repercussions on their loans was causing him a great deal of extra worry and work. He had taken to wearing his spectacles all the time now, periodically removing them to rub his strained eyes.

Henrietta was engulfed by a wave of pity and gratitude. Charles might let her down and disappoint her constantly, but Harry never had. Not once. To her, this was what love had come to mean. Loyalty, dependability, trust. Lust and desire were all very well when life was easy and smooth and happy; but when it was not, when the sea grew stormy, what mattered most, all that mattered, was having someone you could rely on, someone who would always be on your side.

She moved round to the back of Harry's chair, rested her hands on his shoulders. Through his silk doublet she felt how tense and tightly knotted were his muscles beneath her fingers. She began gently to rub them. She had thought he might tell her to stop, but he did not. He made a sigh and his head relaxed back so that the weight of it was resting lightly against her belly.

After a while, he reached back his arm and took hold of her hand, bringing her round so that he could see her. Henrietta was standing by the side of his chair, so close to him that one of his knees was half lost in the fullness of her skirt and petticoats. She wanted so much to run her fingers through his hair, to sit in his lap and put her arms around him. Dependability might count for more than desire, but she desired him still as much as ever she had. 'So what happens now?' she asked.

He smiled at the obvious ambiguity of her question. 'What do you think we should do?'

She looked into his eyes. Go to bed. 'Can't you ask Cardinal Mazarin to delay repayment of that loan? I am sure he will, if you ask him nicely.'

'I am not begging him for sweetmeats.'

'But he likes you.' She waited a moment before saying what she really wanted to say. 'You and he are very alike, you know.'

Harry cocked his brow, stroked his beard. 'Hmmm, I can see that. I have fair hair and blue eyes . . . and he is Italian through and through.'

'You are both consummate courtiers who have devoted your lives to serving queens,' she said gently. 'But more than that . . . the little French king was born to Anne after twenty barren years of marriage to my brother.'

'What are you saying?'

'What everyone knows. That Anne and Cardinal Mazarin are lovers. That Louis and Anne's marriage was loveless as well as childless. Mazarin is the father of her sons.'

Harry looked so shocked it made Henrietta smile. 'We are in France,' she said. 'Have you not noticed, everything is different here? Those acquaintances from your days in the Paris Embassy who are so pleased to see you again . . . my family . . . no one questions your constant presence at my side. What caused so much scandal in England is accepted here.'

There was an urgent knock at the door. Correspondence with Charles now depended on a few loyal messengers who ran the Parliamentary blockade, crossing and recrossing the Channel. The correspondence itself came in all shapes and sizes. Many messages came in notes measuring two inches by five. They were folded into sixteen so they were small enough to be concealed in a shoe, the finger of a glove, a crack in the panelling or sewn into the binding of a book.

It was a man named Elliot who had come now with another tiny folded note from Charles. Harry read it quickly to himself, then said: 'Cavendish has been defeated. At a place called Marston Moor. Parliament now controls two-thirds of the country.'

# 1645

For Henrietta and Harry, winter and spring were taken up with the relentless task of raising more money, more arms, more support. But apart from the sad news of the execution of Archbishop Laud, who had been locked in the Tower for years, affairs in England looked to be going well again. Charles left Oxford to begin his summer campaign and was on his way to the relief of Chester, which was vital for the planned landing of reinforcements from Ireland. He wrote from Daventry in June to say they were all very hopeful and his affairs had never been in so fair a way.

In France the summer was growing excessively hot so Henrietta and Harry left the Louvre for St Germain.

'It is just how I imagined it,' Harry said as they walked past the fountains and grottos towards the terrace in the sweltering sun. 'From the way you described it, that first time we met. You said it was a wonderland, and so it is.'

'What a good memory you have.'

'Show me the view of the Seine. I remember, too, that you told me you could see it winding all the way to Paris.'

They stood and looked out over the snaking course of the river. Though the roofs of Paris were clearly visible in the distance, the city seemed very far away, shimmering through the haze of heat. Everything and everywhere else seemed suddenly far away. England. War. Charles.

Harry took Henrietta's hand and they walked back down a sanded pathway that wound its way through trees and shrubs and flowers to one of the grottos, the one with shells and the fountain that hit the roof and automata like nightingales that sang and flew around and about it. The birds were silent now, but the sound of the water cascading and trickling into the fern-fringed stillness of the pool beneath was just as musical and very restful.

'Something else I remember,' Harry said. 'You told me also that as a child you used to stand beneath these fountains and that it was very refreshing on a hot day.'

'Do you remember every single word?' It was so hot now, even in the shade. Sweat was glistening on his brow. With a little laugh, Henrietta dipped her hand into the pool and flicked water at him, splashing his arm and face. 'See what I mean?' she asked as he ducked. 'Isn't that refreshing?'

When he put his own hand in the water she gave a screech, raising her hands to shield her face and half turning away. He splashed her hair and the bodice of her dress. She splashed him back again, with much more gusto this time, drenching the front of his shirt. When he tried to get her back, she made to run away but he gently caught hold of her hand. They stood looking at one another for a moment. Water was trickling down her temples, the bodice of her dress. His shirt was sticking to his chest.

He took her corseted waist between his hands. In the soft spray of the fountain that was like summer rain, he pulled her towards him and kissed her lips – a kiss that was sweeter even than the cool droplets of water on her hot skin.

'I love you,' she said simply. 'I. Love. You.'

'I love you too.'

Still holding her hand, he led her into the shelter of the little grotto. The walls and pillars were covered with shells, corals, rocks and fossils but for a moment, until their eyes adjusted to the darkness after the glare of the sun, they could make out nothing.

'Where are you?' she whispered. 'I can't see you.'

'I can see you every day,' he said softly. 'I want to feel you.'

She felt his mouth on her neck, just below her ear. She dragged his shirt free and put her hands up inside it. As she ran her fingers around from his back to his chest, his muscles contracted in a shudder and he pulled her closer.

She slipped her hand down to his breeches and unfastened him. He hooked his arms around her thighs and effortlessly lifted her up. She bunched her skirts out of the way and wrapped her legs around his hips, and he moved to rest her against the wall so that she might slide down on to him.

As she felt him slip inside her she tightened the grip of her legs to draw him deeper.

Above the sound of the waterfall she could hear the sounds of him sliding in and out of her as the waves of pleasure swept through her body. No sooner had he lifted her down than she began to be tickled again with the sweet itching and took his hand and put it up her skirts to show him what she wanted him to do. He put his fingers inside as he used to do and, stirring up and down, made her spend so rapturously that it wetted him again.

From the terraces of St Germain Paris might have looked to be a long way away, but it was not so far that letters did not filter through from England with the same erratic regularity. Harry had been deciphering the latest. It was an unusually long letter but even so it seemed to be taking him a particularly long time to decode. Henrietta's patience was wearing thin. 'Is it bad news or good?'

He looked up at her, quill in hand. 'His Majesty says that for the sake of your health he will trust to my judgement as to how much of this letter to impart to you.'

'If he cares so much about my wellbeing, he should not have given my tin mines to Edward Hyde.'

'It is being called the battle of all against all,' Harry said slowly. 'It was fought at Naseby, midway between Daventry and Market Harborough, on the fourteenth of June. Not a week after the king wrote that last letter to you, when he sounded so full of hope.'

Henrietta sat down. 'How heavily were we defeated this time?'

'A thousand casualties.'

'Dear God.'

'Parliament has taken five thousand prisoners, our entire artillery train with its powder and ammunition, about eight thousand other weapons and a forest of colours.' She had never seen him look so despondent. 'There are reports of slain bodies four miles in length, fallen most thickly on the hill where the king stood.'

'How? How could this happen?'

'Parliament has a new force. They are calling it the New Model Army, and it is very different from the old one, and from ours. It is made up not

of conscripted men led by landed gentry, but by rigorously drilled profes-
sional soldiers paid for by Parliament at great cost.'

'All psalm-singing Puritans who believe they are waging war against
the forces of the Pope and the devil, no doubt?'

'One of its generals is the hellcat, Oliver Cromwell.'

'There's worse, isn't there?'

'The king lost all his baggage, amongst which was his own cabinet
containing his private papers. These included letters from you that reveal
all our most desperate efforts to raise money and support from foreign
Catholics. Parliament is making full use of this, naturally. Your letters have
been published under the title *The King's Cabinet Opened*, with the claim
that they provide proof that he has been actively plotting with you to bring
Papists into the country. They are saying it merely confirms everything
your enemies have ever said and thought about you.'

The news from England grew ever more disastrous. After Naseby,
General Fairfax cut a swathe through the loyal west country. On 14 July
the New Model Army defeated George Goring at Langport. Bridgewater
fell on 23 July, Sherborne Castle three weeks later on 14 August. And then
on 10 September Rupert was forced to surrender Bristol.

Using all his skills in diplomacy and calling upon every friendly contact
he possessed, Harry secured a small force to cross the Irish Sea to Scotland
to reinforce Montrose. They were armed with weapons supplied by Harry's
privateers and won for Montrose what appeared to be a decisive victory at
Kilsyth.

Henrietta went back to Paris to order a Te Deum to be sung for this
triumph. But the celebration proved premature. Ten days later Charles and
what remained of his cavalry were beaten outside the walls of Chester.
Then, in the middle of September, Montrose's army of Highlanders and
a handful of Harry's Irish recruits were crushed at Philiphaugh in Somerset.

# 1646

It was past midnight when Henrietta found Harry asleep in the chair by his desk, holding a glass of whisky balanced precariously in his lap. She gently removed it. She did not have the heart to wake or to leave him. So she fetched two blankets from her bed, tucked one around him and the other around her own shoulders. She pulled up a chair close to his, sat down beside him. As she blew out the candle that was burning to a stub on his desk, she glanced at the latest deciphered letter.

Each missive that arrived now, and they came thick and fast, brought yet more bad news, so that Henrietta dreaded the sight of poor Elliot and his messenger comrades, weather-beaten and weary, waiting in the hall by the fire with a crumpled letter in hand bearing the red royal seal. The letters told of nothing but death and defeat and despair. Exeter had finally fallen to Thomas Fairfax, bringing the war in the west to an end. At Stow-on-the-Wold, all Royalist officers were either taken prisoner, killed or scattered, leaving the commander, Sir Jacob Astley, no choice but to surrender. It was the end. Fairfax was now advancing on Oxford.

Charles was given what seemed to be one last chance. The Scots had offered to receive him as their sovereign, and employ their armies and forces to assist him in recovering his rights.

He had written to Henrietta.

*If I should fail, you must continue with your endeavours for Prince Charles's sake, to do all that you can to assist him to regain his own.*

He had acknowledged the prospect of death before, and military defeat, but never before had he implied that the very crown was under threat, that Parliament might steal the throne from under him and rob his son of the right to be king. They had stripped Henrietta of her title, but it had never occurred to her that they could do the same to her husband and son.

She was tormented by worry for Charles and her children. Little Princess Henrietta had been trapped in Exeter when it was besieged, but her devoted governess had at least been allowed to take her to Oatlands. With the fall of the west, Prince Charles had been spirited away by Edward Hyde to the Scillies. But how long would her family be safe?

Harry wrote urgently to Hyde to inform him that the Prince of Wales's mother would not rest until he was removed from Scilly. The prince, as heir to the throne, was a prime target for the rebels. Henrietta wanted him to be sent to her immediately, but the only concession Hyde would make was to move him as far as Jersey.

Henrietta vented her frustration on Harry. 'Can they not see that there is no time to be lost? For the good of my son and of the kingdom, he must come here. There should be no dispute about it.'

'Hyde will not want to lose his influence over the young prince,' Harry explained. 'He has manoeuvred himself into a position of power and will not want to relinquish that power to anyone . . . not to you, and certainly not to me.'

The argument dragged on. But when news came that Oxford had finally fallen and that James, Elizabeth and Henry were all now in London as wards of Parliament, Henrietta could take no more.

'I feel so helpless,' she cried. 'I am their mother. I am supposed to protect them. Damn Hyde! I swear, this sitting and waiting and doing nothing is killing me.'

'I know it is,' Harry said. 'Which is why I do not intend to sit and wait and do nothing any longer. I am leaving in the morning for Jersey with William.'

Henrietta stared at him and then half laughed. 'You can't just . . . snatch my son.'

'Yes, I can,' he said wryly. 'For you I can do anything.'

'I don't know . . .' Henrietta frowned. This situation was too similar to the failed Army Plot which had seen him sent into exile and condemned to death. 'The last time you and William galloped off on a daring rescue on my behalf, I ended up losing you almost for good.'

'There is no risk this time.' He grinned. 'Hyde is no match for us.'

They left early in the morning with eighty other Royalists and servants and a great train of baggage wagons. Harry promised to return with the prince within a matter of weeks.

This summer was proving as hot as the last and Henrietta moved again to the fresher air of St Germain, where excitement over her son's expected arrival resulted in a buzz of activity and long discussions about the correct protocol. Should Prince Charles be seated in the little French king's presence when they met? Should he occupy the place of honour on Louis's right hand? Henrietta did not much care where or when he sat. She just wanted to have him with her.

And then there he was, riding into the courtyard at Harry's side. There was a time when she could scarce believe the prince was her husband's son. Now she could hardly believe he was her own. That her frail body had produced such a strapping boy. He was sixteen years old and rode a horse as big and powerful as Harry's, which he handled with ease. When he dismounted and took his mother into his arms to embrace her, he lifted her clean off her feet.

'Bonjour, Mam,' he exclaimed, in the deep tones of a man.

'Put me down this instant,' she laughingly commanded.

Just as when she had met him at Kineton, he was full of talk of his adventures. As they walked up to the château together he told her how Harry had marched on to Jersey, and marched him off it and on to a ship. How they had left Hyde behind, stupefied with rage. Prince Charles had developed a laugh as loud and merry as Harry's. 'Hyde was so furious he is spreading the most ridiculous story that Lord Jermyn is planning to sell Jersey to France in return for a dukedom. Would you believe it?'

'The wildness and craziness of rumours never surprises me,' Henrietta commented.

Over dinner Harry talked to the prince about appointing tutors for him and what they should teach him, and as Charles listened attentively and commented on the plan it made Henrietta's heart glad to see how the two of them had so quickly become fast friends.

The following week they all set out to ride to Fontainebleau in order to introduce Prince Charles to his French relations, who were staying there for the summer. 'You and my niece Princess Anne Marie are sure to like each other well,' Henrietta said to her son. 'She is very beautiful.'

Prince Charles exchanged a look with Harry that made Henrietta think: God help me, I have become my mother! I am as preoccupied with arranging matches for my children as she was.

When they arrived outside the palace it appeared to be deserted, with not a single courtier assembled at the entrance to greet them. They were told by the solitary servant Harry found tending the kitchen garden that, because it was so hot, everyone had gone into the forest. He gave directions and Harry led the way down a track that led into the vast swathe of forest surrounding the château. As they rode deeper into the shade of the oaks and pines it grew blissfully cool. The trees were ranged around great rocks and boulders that made it feel as if they were riding into a prehistoric landscape, a place from myth and legend. The forest floor was dotted all over with toadstools and mushrooms and flowers. Butterflies flickered high up in the branches. There was the distant rat-tat of woodpeckers at work, and then the sound of distant laughter.

They drew closer to its source and at last reached a glade beside a river, by which the entire royal family was lounging on the shady sloping banks or else immersed, laughing and splashing, in the clear flowing water.

Anne and all her attendants, as well as the little king and his governor and Henrietta's brother Gaston, wore long, trailing bathing costumes of grey linen. Only Henrietta's niece, Anne Marie d'Orléans, the foremost lady of the court, was formally dressed, in becoming blue silk which enhanced her full, regal figure, making her fair hair appear fairer and her white skin whiter.

When Prince Charles was presented to her it was clear from the lingering smiles on both faces that they were very taken with each other. Just as Henrietta had been hoping they might be. Though Anne Marie's smile was somewhat superior and there was a definite look of pity in the girl's eyes, which Henrietta could not understand and chose for the moment to ignore.

When everyone crammed into the royal carriage to return to the palace, Prince Charles graciously handed Anne Marie in and the girl remarked to Henrietta on how very tall he was for his age, and how big and black were his eyes. 'He's just like a pirate,' she murmured in French. 'With his curly black hair and swarthy skin.'

'Only far more graceful and dignified.' Henrietta smiled back proudly.

'He has nothing much to say for himself though, does he?'

This was true and Henrietta could not fathom it. Unless Anne Marie's charms had struck him dumb, why was Charles being so uncommunicative? It was not like him at all. He wasn't fluent in French but knew enough to hold a simple conversation. Yet so far he had said not a word.

Anne Marie asked him a question about Jersey and all he did was stare back at her mutely, like a simpleton. Whatever was the boy playing at? Henrietta tried to catch his eye and frowned at him, encouraging him to speak. He ignored her.

'No matter.' Anne Marie shrugged her pretty shoulders. 'He is just a penniless exile.'

She might just as well have stabbed Henrietta to the heart. 'He is heir to the throne of England!' She saw again that look of pity in her niece's eyes, this time for her. Above all else, Henrietta hated to be pitied. She did not want pity from this girl or from anyone else. Even when she was deathly ill, it had grated on her. Now she was quite well again, there was absolutely no cause for it. She blamed her son for giving Anne Marie reason to act so superciliously. In a fierce mood, she caught up with him as they followed the queen and her family back into the château.

'What do you think you are doing, Charles?' Henrietta challenged him.

'Nothing, Mam,' he replied sullenly, lengthening his stride and walking away from her. 'I am doing nothing.'

Harry appeared by Henrietta's side. 'The boy is only sixteen,' he said gently. 'What else do you expect?'

'A little politeness. Is that too much to ask? I have had more than enough of English rebels without my own son turning into one.'

'He is no rebel, but has a firmer grasp of politics than do you.'

She stopped walking, turning on him indignantly. 'I beg your pardon?'

'Charles is clearly attracted to the buxom beauty of the lovely Anne Marie. What man would not be? But he is wise enough to realise that to promise himself to a Catholic ally now would be disastrous to his father's cause . . . and indeed his own. Yet he has been ordered by his father to obey his mother in all things but religion, and knows you are angling for a match. He appreciates too that it is not at all wise to defy you. So he is taking the line of least resistance and keeping his silence.'

'You sound very certain of that. It's not just guesswork, is it? He's been talking to you, hasn't he? Even if to nobody else!'

Henrietta saw by Harry's smile that she was right and how happy it made him to have won her son's confidence. It made her just as happy. Harry had taken charge of Prince Charles's education and his finances like a father. This was his just reward. Prince Charles was confiding in him like a son would. 'I am glad,' she said. 'I am so glad that he trusts you as I do.'

Not a month after Prince Charles came to France another of Henrietta's children arrived totally unexpectedly. Out of the blue, like a miracle one morning, a message was brought to St Germain to say that Lady Dalkeith was in Calais with the youngest of England's princesses and needed a carriage to bring them both to Paris.

The vehicle was swiftly dispatched, but Henrietta did not dare believe or even hope that it would return bearing the child she had left behind as a newborn. There had been so many rumours, so much fear and false hope, she was sure this must be another disappointment.

It was not. Within a week the carriage was back and the tiniest child was being lifted down from it. If she were not so exquisitely pretty and delicate, Henrietta would have been sure that some cruel prank was being played upon her. That she had been sent an impostor in the from of a small boy. The child was wearing a homespun shirt, brown woollen breeches and a cap. But the cap could not quite contain the mass of golden ringlets beneath, and though the little princess had been just two weeks old when last Henrietta saw her, and now was nearly two years, her mother knew her in her heart. She had been an extraordinarily pretty baby and now she was an extraordinarily pretty child.

'This is your mother, Her Majesty the Queen,' Lady Dalkeith said, lifting her up. 'Say good day.'

'Good day, Mam,' the child replied, regarding Henrietta shyly.

Knowing that children associated tears only with hurt and sorrow, Henrietta had been determined not to cry, not wanting to frighten or confuse the little girl or make her think her mother was sad to see her. But when Lady Dalkeith placed in her arms the precious little person she had not seen for so long and had feared never to see again, she almost lost her resolve. She hugged and kissed her tiny namesake, and kissed her again, sure she would die of happiness.

The child was small as her mother had been at that age, but in every other way she was Harry's daughter, with her mass of golden-brown curls and blue eyes that sparkled with merriment. 'I am a princess and these are not my clothes,' the little girl announced, pulling at the rough brown breeches with dismay to find herself so strangely dressed.

Harry, standing behind Henrietta, laughed. 'Then why are you wearing them, might I ask?'

Henrietta turned so the child could see him better, her father. 'Lady Dalkeith made me wear them, sir,' she told him.

That lady was similarly plainly attired, in a tattered gown and cloak. 'The dear child nearly gave us away with her talk.' Lady Dalkeith smiled fondly. 'I was posing as a poor Frenchwoman with a bundle of rags stuffed into my dress, to make me look like a hunchback, and was passing off little Henrietta here as my son, Pierre. Only she would keep on saying to all and sundry that her name was not Pierre but Princess, and that usually she wore pretty dresses.'

'How did you get to France, my lady?' Harry asked her as they all made their way inside. 'And why did you feel it necessary to leave Oatlands?'

'I learned that I was to be dismissed and the little princess to be taken into the custody of Parliament in London. So I decided the only thing for it was to smuggle her to France. I carried her all the way from Surrey to Dover, where we boarded the cross-Channel packet.'

'That was very resourceful and brave of you,' Henrietta said to her. 'I shall be forever in your debt.'

She needed to give thanks to God too, for reuniting her with her youngest as well as her oldest child. She left Princess Henrietta with a tray of candied almonds, which her brother and Harry were helping her to eat, and went alone to the chapel. When she left its quiet and solitude, having said her prayers, it was to hear the cavernous corridors of the half empty palace ringing with joyous but unfamiliar gurgles and squeals of delight. Little Henrietta, still in her breeches, ran laughing down the echoing gallery pursued by her brother, who clearly found her an enchanting little playmate. Harry was following behind at a more leisurely stroll.

Henrietta caught up her daughter in her arms. 'We shall have to find you some gowns to wear.'

'My brother has a new name for me,' the little girl laughed. 'Minette. Little Puss.'

'I have a new name for you too,' Henrietta said. 'You are my *enfant de bénédiction*. Do you know what that means?'

The girl's nose wrinkled. 'I prefer Minette.'

'I too,' said Charles.

'*Enfant de bénédiction* means that you are a blessed child,' Henrietta said, kissing her curly head. 'But Minette you shall be from now on.'

The summer continued hot and sunny and Henrietta determined that her children should enjoy some pleasure and freedom after all the hardship and danger they had both faced. So they made the most of the glorious weather, playing in the grottos at St Germain, walking in the garden of the Luxembourg Palace, riding often back to the forest glade at Fontainebleau where Minette and Prince Charles splashed about in the cool clear river.

Harry had spread his cloak on the banks one day and he and Henrietta were sitting together on it watching the two children, her oldest and youngest, chattering together and throwing pebbles into the swift-running water. 'I know she likes being called Minette but she is a true *enfant de bénédiction,*' Henrietta insisted. 'She is surely blessed. When I think how she was born on the run, abandoned as a newborn, trapped in a beseiged city and escaped in disguise . . . What adventure she has already known in her little life. How much danger she has already faced. And yet God has spared her.'

'Indeed he has.'

'That is why I have resolved to have her instructed in the Catholic religion.'

'His Majesty may well disapprove of that,' Harry warned.

'His Majesty is not . . .' She was about to say that the king was not the child's father, but instead said: 'His Majesty is not here.' As she spoke the words, Henrietta asked herself a question. Did she wish her husband were here? And the answer, just for a second at least, was a definite no. It was not that she did not love Charles still, and miss him. Above all else, she wanted the alliance with the Scots to work and for him to be safe, well and happy, restored to his own. But at that moment, on the banks of the river in this sunny glade at Fontainebleau, with her children playing in the water and at her side a man she loved and who loved her, Henrietta wanted nothing more.

Charles was her husband, her king, but it was Harry with whom she had shared danger, exile, sickness, all her fears and hopes. Harry who shared her sense of humour. Harry to whom she turned for support and comfort. Harry who had nursed her when she was ill. Harry to whom she now felt closest and with whom she was most comfortable. And for now at least she was quite content.

Contentment was something she had not known for such a long time Henrietta had almost forgotten what it felt like. She had feared she might never experience it again, and for that reason she valued it infinitely. This contentment she felt now, this quiet happiness, was so rare and so precious, and therefore seemed so fragile, that she wanted to do nothing to disrupt it, for nothing to change.

Charles was still in Oxford when he wrote to Henrietta again to tell her the Scots were abominable rogues and had retracted all their promises. Their army refused to recognise the agreement made with their commissioners in London. His situation was worse than ever. He was now closed in on all sides by the Parliamentarians. In desperation, this man who cared so deeply for his dignity and the trappings of kingship, was planning to disguise himself as a servant and slip away secretly, to King's Lynn on the Norfolk coast, where he might gather forces, sail for Scotland or flee to France.

He wrote:

*There was never a man so alone as I. All the comfort that I have is in your love. My one desire is to quit for a time this wretched country for any other part of the world. I beg you to think seriously and speedily upon my proposal.*

Henrietta utterly opposed the idea. She was certain in her heart that this would be a false move, a disastrous one, that if he abandoned his kingdom he might as well give up his crown forever. She sensed that Harry did not wholly agree with her views, but was prepared to go along with them since she was so adamant.

'It would certainly be dangerous for him to attempt escape and might only provoke Parliament further if successful,' he agreed.

She wrote to tell Charles that in her opinion his leaving England was in no way advisable.

*Till the Scots shall declare that they will not even protect you, do not think of making any escape from England. Our efforts will have been in vain and all hope will be lost.*

# 1647

Almost instantly, Henrietta feared she had advised her husband wrongly. That he should never have listened to her. He had fled to Scotland but the Scots did not protect him. At the end of January they sold him to Parliament for the sum of £400,000. With a rare flash of humour he wrote to tell her that when he had the chance, he would reproach them for selling him too cheap. He was now a prisoner.

Henrietta's tears fell on to the letter, blurring his little joke. 'I never imagined the Scots would abandon him,' she told Harry.

'He has been sent to Hampton Court and says they are treating him with the greatest respect,' he consoled her.

Charles said he had the freedom to write letters whenever he chose, as well as to hunt in Richmond Park and entertain visitors, including his children. Elizabeth, Henry and James were spending the summer at nearby Syon House under the guardianship of the Earl of Northumberland and came to Hampton Court regularly to play in the gardens with their father. Henrietta, envying him their company, began to think that advising him not to flee had been the right thing to do after all. At least he was still present in his kingdom. At least he had not relinquished his claim on it and handed it over to Parliament. At least the children who were still in that country had one of their parents with them.

But Charles began drafting peace proposals. Henrietta was despairing and furious when she discovered that he had readily handed all control of the militia to Parliament.

'Perhaps I should just retreat to a nunnery and have done with it!' she fumed

She sat down with Harry at her desk and wrote as much to Charles, and more:

*With the granting of the militia to Parliament's control you have cut your own throat. For having given them this power you can no longer refuse them anything, not even my life, if they demand it from you. But I shall not place myself in their hands. I tell you again, for the last time, that if you grant more you are lost and I shall never return to England. Now I shall go and pray to God for you.*

He wrote back:

*For God's sake, leave off threatening me. I assure you, I and my children are ruined if you should retire from my business to a nunnery.*

But in fact it was too late. Radicals, who called themselves Levellers, were now demanding the king be brought to justice.

# *1648*

Having fled England to escape one civil war, Henrietta, her children and companions now found themselves caught up in another, in France, which had sinister parallels with the situation in England. As in England, there was a clash with the judicial bodies, the *parlements*. The major source of discontent was taxes and fiscal policies. As in England, the crown needed to increase revenue to recover its expenditures in recent wars. And, as in England, the *parlements* refused to approve the taxes levied.

'I cannot worry about all this,' Henrietta said to Harry impatiently. 'It is Anne and Mazarin's problem.'

But already it was hers too. Thanks to the unrest and the loss of revenue, Mazarin had stopped her allowance. Prices had doubled and trebled overnight, and try as Harry might to stretch the household's income, money was fast running out and with it food and fuel. They were living on credit which the French merchants were increasingly unwilling to provide. Henrietta began selling off what precious few personal possessions she had left, her gowns and cloaks, as well as beautiful furniture and treasures from the Louvre, in order to subsist for a few days longer. It was heartbreaking to see the gilded tables and ebony cabinets that had always graced the Louvre's grand halls be carted off by the highest bidder in exchange for bread or fish.

But it was not to discuss money or the worsening political situation in France that Harry had asked her and Prince Charles to come to his gilded study in the Louvre. It was the worsening situation in England they must talk about.

He took a deep breath. 'We have to accept that Oliver Cromwell is now the ruler of the country,' he said. 'That all decisions are made by him. That he alone holds the power to restore His Majesty to his throne.'

Henrietta said nothing. After all their efforts, all they had endured and still endured, she was prepared to accept no such thing. To accept that was to accept defeat.

Prince Charles spoke for them both. 'Go on, sir.'

'I propose that I send my cousin, Jack Berkeley, to offer Cromwell great wealth in return for the king's restoration.'

'We barely have enough food to eat,' the prince pointed out. 'If this continues, come winter we will not have enough fuel for the fires. We do not have great wealth to offer to Mr Cromwell, do we?'

'No,' Harry replied truthfully. 'But that is by the by. We will find it if it is needed.'

'Do you think Cromwell will accept the offer?'

'The bribe, you mean?' Henrietta interjected.

'I fear he is a man who values power above great wealth,' Harry admitted. 'But it is worth a try. Anything is worth a try, I believe. Short of trying to rescue His Majesty, I don't know what else to suggest.'

The unrest in France escalated. An Assembly of Courts had made a list of demands, including approval of all new taxes by the *parlements*. Anne and Mazarin arrested two outspoken members, which led to an uprising in Paris so similar to the conflicts that had caused Henrietta and Charles to flee London that it terrified her. Barricades were built in the streets and violent mobs attacked the houses of Mazarin's supporters, calling for liberty, just as they had done in London. The insurrection was being called La Fronde, after the sling used in a children's game, which the rebels were using to hurl stones and smash windows. Anne and Mazarin, having no army at their disposal, released the prisoners, promised to agree to the terms of the Assembly and fled to St Germain.

Henrietta refused to flee, and had besides nowhere to flee to. She stubbornly refused to think about anything but England and Charles. Jack Berkeley had successfully secured an audience with Cromwell, but he had refused their offer, bribe, incentive. Whatever it was, he wanted none of it.

Henrietta stood at the windows of her apartment, looking out at the grey skies and the flooded gardens, ignoring the rumbling of her belly. They were reduced to one meagre meal a day now and had already consumed this day's portion. Henrietta had given most of hers to her children. Despite all the dangers she had faced, she had never before gone to bed hungry, woken up hungry, spent the day anticipating a tiny meal she knew would take the edge off her hunger for but a few hours. Her corsets were growing loose on her, even when drawn as tight as they would go. She had always been slight, but now had so little flesh on her bones that sitting on hard wooden chairs made her hips ache. And she shivered constantly. When winter set in, what they would burn on the fires she had no idea.

Thankfully, though, it was the end of October and still mild. It had also been raining incessantly for days with no break in the clouds. She had watched the river rise against its banks until it burst them. The Seine was in full flood and Paris was more like Venice or the English Fens, the rampaging mobs going about the streets in boats.

'So what do we do now?' she asked Harry, relying on him to have a solution as he always did.

'Jack will help His Majesty escape to the Isle of Wight,' he said. 'And thence to France.'

Henrietta turned away from the rain-lashed window. Again that nagging fear that she had done wrong, made a grave and unforgivable mistake. Charles should have escaped to France before, when he'd wanted to, when it would have been so much easier. Nothing had been achieved by his remaining in England. But if all went well now, nothing would have been lost either. 'Is escape possible from Hampton Court? He is under guard,' she reminded Harry.

'There is an underground passage leading from the palace to the Banqueting House. From there he can take a boat over the Thames to Surrey. And we will have a ship waiting to take him to the Isle of Wight.'

A month later, at the end of November, Paris was still flooded but the rain had been replaced by heavy flurries of snow. The floodwater had iced over and the cold was bitter.

Waiting for news of Charles's escape attempt, Henrietta felt as if they were all prisoners too, shut up in the Louvre with no money to buy fuel for the fires. The huge rooms were so icy their breath turned to mist. She would not let little Minette rise from her bed even though it was noon, for fear she would catch her death of cold.

Wrapped in a blanket, Henrietta kept her daughter company, sitting shivering at her bedside, amusing her with stories taken from the masques and plays she had enjoyed as a girl. She was halfway through the story of

Lancelot and Guinivere when Harry came into the room. Minette's blue eyes lit up as they peeped over the top of the blankets.

'You look very warm and snug in there, little puss.' Harry smiled back at her.

'It is a sorry state of affairs,' Henrietta said, 'when a Princess of England is kept to bed for lack of a faggot.'

But Harry had sorrier affairs to report. He led Henrietta aside to tell her, out of Minette's hearing. A messenger had braved the frozen streets to bring a letter from Jack Berkeley, reporting that the king's escape from Hampton Court had been successful. Jack and a man named Ashburnham and the king had safely crossed the Solent to Cowes on the Isle of Wight. But upon arrival at Carisbrooke Castle on the island, Charles had been apprehended by its governor, Colonel Hammond.

'Apparently Hammond has connections to General Cromwell,' Harry said. 'His Majesty says they are treating him well. Governor Hammond has even turfed a bowling green for him on the castle drill ground, complete with gilded pavilion to shelter him from cloudbursts.'

'Are Jack and Ashburnham being held too?'

'They were expelled by Hammond to the mainland but are staying at Netley Abbey, home of the Marquess of Hertford. They say they are in communication with the king through a woman who brings him his clean linen.'

'Jane Whorwood?'

'Aye. It seems she is still in touch with the city as well as the Tower. While the king remained in Oxford she was acting as a link and go-between in the lobbying of Parliament, while also smuggling intelligence to His Majesty. Now she has smuggled him a silk cord to aid his escape.'

'A silk cord?'

'Easier to conceal than hempen rope. The plan is for the king to use it to lower himself by night from his bedchamber on the first floor. Carisbrooke is dry moated, so once across the courtyard and on to the south curtain wall he can again be lowered about fifteen feet to the outer bastion. Jack will have a boat waiting for him on the beach.'

But the king never reached the boat. This second escape attempt failed as had the first.

'The bars at his window would not give him passage,' Harry said, after deciphering Jack's latest letter. 'His Majesty was stuck fast between his breast and shoulders. By means of the cord tied to a bar of the window he managed to force himself back. Jack was waiting below and the king set a candle at the window to let him know the design was broken. Fortunately the guards that night had some quantity of wine in them so he was able to flee. Another attempt is already being planned.'

'By Jack?'

'By Jane. Or 715 as she appears in the cipher, or sometimes 39, or simply "N". Her brother-in-law, the Earl of Lanark, is attending His Majesty as Scots commissioner on the island and has been collaborating with him. She seems to have made the business of His Majesty's escape her sole responsibility.'

'And what does she propose?'

Harry looked down at the minutely folded letter in his hand with its neat italic script. Jane's wax seal depicted a shield and wyvern. 'She has done more than propose. She brought the king a book annotated in citrus juice with detailed instructions for the accomplishment of the escape. She has provided him with money, with nitric acid to weaken the metal of the bars, and, through an ingenious locksmith in Bow Lane, with a saw to cut the bars asunder. If that does not work, she has instructed the king to improvise a forcer with fire shovel and tongs to bend them.'

Henrietta could not help but be impressed, and very grateful. 'And then what?'

'Horses are waiting near Portsmouth to take him to Arundel and thence to Queensborough on the Medway Estuary where there is a ship at anchor, chartered by Mistress Whorwood, which will sail him to Holland.'

'And Mistress Whorwood is no doubt aboard, ready to wait upon His Majesty in person?'

'She has thought of everything,' Harry agreed. 'Even stockings to muffle his footsteps on the paved courtyard.'

'Then the plan is likely to succeed?'

'Not only does Mistress Whorwood share the same goal as you, ma'am, but the same frustrations. She has noted that the king himself is the most likely hindrance and has urged him in the strongest terms to be resolute.'

'She clearly knows him very well!'

The next communication was from Jack Berkely via the king's usher, Henry Firebrace.

The king had applied nitric acid to the base of one bar at his window, but two sentries had informed Hammond who entered the chamber at midnight when the king was working on it with the saw. The conspirators were pursued by musket fire but hid in the woods and escaped.

'Has Jane been apprehended?' Henrietta asked.

'She is still at large. Jack says that had the rest played their parts as carefully as she, the king would have been at large too.'

'What is that?' Henrietta asked, seeing a second letter that he had put behind the first.

'It is a copy of a note from His Majesty to Jane Whorwood,' Harry said heavily. 'It has been sent to us anonymously. It may be a fake.'

'I will be able to tell.' Henrietta held out her hand. 'Let me see.'

*Sweet 39,*

*Your two letters of the 19th this month I received yesterday. I cannot give you a greater compliment than to satisfy your desires. You will not get leave to speak privately with me but there is one way you may get a swiving from me. You must excuse my plain expressions. The new stool pan woman conveys all my letters and by her acquaintance and means you may be conveyed into the stool room, which is within my bedchamber, while I am at dinner. I shall have three hours to embrace and nip you for every day after dinner I shut myself up alone for so long and so will not be missed.*

*If you fear impossible the way that I have set you down for a passage to me, invite yourself to dine to Captain Mildmay's chamber which is next door to mine. I will surprise you there and get you alone to my chamber and smother you with embraces and kisses. For now this letter is the best caudle I can send you but if you would have better you must come to fetch it yourself. Your platonic way spoils the taste. I will be in much impatience until I receive your answer.*

*Your most loving 391*

It was not the words 'swiving' and 'embraces' and 'kisses' that proved the letter's veracity, but 'caudle', the Scottish version of the '*médecin*' that the king had called Henrietta's own love. It was one thing knowing of an infidelity, another having such tangible proof. 'I am glad that he has someone to love and assist him in these dark and lonely days,' was all Henrietta could bring herself to say.

She could clearly understand why their enemies would want her to read that letter, to cause a rift between herself and the king.

'I would have kept it from you,' Harry said. 'But given the circumstances . . .'

'What circumstances?'

'His Majesty has been taken to another place. Another . . . castle.' He made the word sound somehow unconvincing.

'Which castle?'

'Hurst. I did not know of it. William describes it as a fortress built on a spit of shingle overlooking the Solent. He says that at high tide it is totally cut off from the Isle of Wight and from all civilisation. His Majesty is being held there in a cell.'

'From which escape is impossible?'

'From which escape is impossible.'

Harry rested his brow against his fingertips, massaged it a little. 'There is much talk amongst the Royalists in England and here,' he said. 'I do not want you to hear it from them. But I do not want to tell you either.'

'One thing I am used to is talk.'

'This is especially cruel.'

'Having to drag it out of you is making it worse. '

They are saying . . .' He took a steadying breath, his eyes shadowed. 'They are saying how you . . . how we . . . dissuaded the king from attempting to escape when he had the opportunity. How you did not want him to come to Paris, because you were enjoying an affair here with me.'

Henrietta bit her lip, closed her eyes for a moment. 'I cannot say if that is true or not.'

'It would have been wrong for His Majesty to abandon his kingdom.'

'Yes.'

'Yes,' Henrietta agreed, her voice ringing hollow in her own ears.

# *1649*

It was Twelfth Night and Henrietta was dancing entirely alone in the Grand Salon of the Louvre. There was no music, only the music in her head, an orchestra of lutes and violas. She was wearing a tattered white gown and the salon was empty even of furniture. What had not been sold, she had ordered to be broken up to burn on the fire. Paris was under siege. The Frondeurs had taken the city and the English royal family were now barricaded inside the palace, not daring to venture out into the streets. Frost and snow and ice lay all around.

She danced partly to keep warm. Partly because she had always loved to dance and it made her forget all else. The merchants had refused to extend further credit but she would have given her last *sou* and what precious bread they had left for news from England. Apart from the occasional smuggled letter it was nearly a year since she'd heard from Charles. She kept writing to him, not knowing how many, if any, of her own letters were reaching him.

She extended her leg and pointed her toes. Her thin arms floated up in an arc, drifted down, light and graceful and pale as a falling feather. Her skirts floated around her as she glided around the vast empty marble floor, her breath against the cold air wreathing her in a fine mist.

'I told you you would dance again.' Harry had spoken only softly, but his voice in the cavernous space sounded especially rich and deep. 'When you were ill and could not feel your feet.'

'My great and glorious destiny?' she asked, in a voice tinged with bitterness and sadness. 'To dance alone in an empty palace while broken furniture burns on the fire.' She shivered, wrapping her arms around herself. 'And still I am so cold.'

He walked towards her, his footsteps echoing. Encircling her waist with one arm, he took her hand in his and lifted it. 'What melody were you dancing to?' he asked.

She rested her hand on his shoulder and tentatively began to hum the tune. As his feet moved, leading her, she laid her cheek against his chest. 'It is much warmer in bed,' he whispered into her ear, his voice as warm as any blanket or fire.

She let him lead her to his chamber, to the bed.

'Undress me first,' she said.

'Would you not rather keep your clothes on? The cold . . .'

'I would rather see and feel you.'

His chest hairs were all white now, white as the snow. But by the time they were both snuggled under the bedcovers she felt as warm and as languid as if he had already penetrated her.

'You move,' he said quietly, when he was inside her, on top of her, and she lifted her hips to meet him and wrapped her arms around his neck and pulled him closer.

For warmth, she told herself, she returned to his bed that night and every night after. He did not seem to suffer from the cold as acutely as she did, and did not mind when she warmed her cold feet between his legs and her icy fingers under his armpits.

She curled around his back or he curled around hers, and she found a quiet delight in sleeping with him; in waking in the morning with him, opening her eyes to see his head on the pillow. Sometimes, when she woke in the night, she liked to watch him sleeping, or to touch his penis and feel it spring up hard under her figners. Sometimes it woke him and sometimes not. One morning, just before dawn, when she was stroking him expertly and talking to him fluently in English, she said: 'You have taught me all that I know.'

It was the end of January when a letter finally arrived, and the news it carried struck Henrietta to the heart with despair and confusion. On New Year's Day, Oliver Cromwell had passed a decree that Charles Stuart, the man of blood, was to be brought to London to be tried on a charge of treason.

Sitting at his desk, wrapped in a cloak and blowing on his fingers to get the feeling back in them in order to hold his pen, Harry began crafting letters to Lord General Thomas Fairfax, to the House of Lords and the

House of Commons, begging them to allow the queen the consolation of going to her husband. Harry was nearly fifty now and Henrietta saw how close he had to lean over the paper in order to see what he was writing. He was nearly blind.

'I will have the letters sent to the French Ambassador in London,' he said. 'He will ensure their safe delivery.'

'I dare not promise myself that they will accord me the liberty of going,' Henrietta said. 'I wish it too much, and so little of what I wish for comes to pass.'

The letters were never answered.

Those in France were kept in complete ignorance of the trial going on in London, until, early in February, Harry brought to Henrietta horrifying news that had the smallest glimmer of hope wrapped inside it, like a nugget of gold inside a cannonball.

He made her sit, took her hands in his and held them very tightly. 'I have to inform Your Majesty that there are reports that His Majesty has now been tried and convicted as a tyrant, traitor, murderer public enemy.' He spoke in a strangely flat voice, devoid of emotion, and yet quickly, for him. She sensed that he wanted to hurry over that part because, as had always been his practice, he had found a way to temper bad news with good, even now, and wanted to skirt over the bad to reach the good and put her mind at rest. And so it was. 'His Majesty was to be put to death by the severing of his head from his body. But when he was led from prison to the scaffold, an outraged mob rose up to save him.'

Henrietta stared at him, feeling an irrational surge of anger. How could he say such preposterous words? She took her hands from his, sprang to her feet. 'Go away.'

He hesitated a moment, but when she turned her back on him she heard him leave the room.

It could not be true. Charles, sentenced to execution? They had executed Strafford, Laud, would have executed her if they could. But it had never occurred to her that it might happen to Charles. That it was even possible. To kill a king. Her own father, King Henri, had died at the hands of a madman, a lone assassin. But for Parliament and people to act in unison to such an end . . . it was unimaginable. What kind of evil world did they live in if a king, who was next to God, could lawfully be put to death?

But Charles had been saved. Oh, she could believe that part. He was dearly beloved by many who would willingly sacrifice their lives for him. Then relief gave way again to dismay and despair and she was plunged into a depth of misery such as she had never known before.

The next days passed beneath a pall of the darkest gloom. Until she heard from Charles himself, Henrietta could not rest.

Over dinner she saw that Harry's hand, reaching for bread, was shaking. She looked into his face and it was as white as death. She had never been so afraid in all her life, because she had never seen him afraid. Throughout all their troubles . . . when he was riding off to lead the Army Plot, when they were nearly shipwrecked in the storm, when they lay in the ditch under cannon fire, when he had been almost mortally wounded after riding into battle crying her name . . . he had always been strong and capable and brave. And now, sitting there pretending to eat a piece of bread, he looked terrified.

'What has happened?' she asked.

He looked at her. Looked away. 'Nothing.'

She did not believe him and that confused her. He had never lied to her or kept anything from her.

'Are you ill?'

'Maybe a cold, that's all. I shall be all right.'

The short February afternoon drew in, but at supper he looked no better. While Father Philip said grace Henrietta kept her eyes open, fixed on Harry, and his eyes were screwed up tight in a frown, as they sometimes were when he read without his spectacles. He said nothing and ate nothing, which was unlike him. Again she asked what was wrong and again he evaded answering. But when, after supper, Father Philip rose to retire, Harry placed his hand on the priest's arm and entreated him to stay.

Harry did not join the queen's circle as he usually did, but sat to one side on his own. A ghastly hour passed in uneasy conversation until at last Henrietta could stand it no more. 'Something terrible has happened, hasn't it?'

Harry slowly rose to his feet as if it took every last ounce of energy he possessed and came to stand before her. Normally so tall and upright, he was visibly sagging with despair. 'I have received . . .' He faltered and began again. 'There is bad news from England, Your Majesty. Very bad news.' He looked stricken. 'I fear this time it is no rumour but the truth.'

'This time? What do you mean?'

'This time . . . there was no mob.'

'What are you talking about? You make no sense. If it is some calamitous tiding you are to break to me and you are aiming to do it by degrees, for kindess' sake, I would rather you just came out with it.'

'His Majesty . . . the king has been executed, ma'am.'

Rather than making her collapse, the words brought Henrietta to her feet.

She was aware of sounds of weeping and extreme distress all around her but could find no voice of her own. She stood staring at Harry's anguished face, transfixed. She felt as if she had turned to marble.

In all their eleven years of frantic struggle, she had never conceived of such an end.

People were touching her arm, her hand, talking to her, as if trying to rouse her from a deep stupor. Had she fainted from the shock? Was she lying on the ground even as she felt herself to be standing?

At last the sounds died away and she looked around to see her friends all grouped together in profound silence, as if they too had all been turned to stone, as if they had died with their king.

Candles lit the room. The Duchess of Vendôme, wife of one of Henrietta's illegitimate half-brothers and a friend from childhood days, came and knelt at her feet and kissed her hand. She started to talk gently, and as she did grief and realisation broke inside Henrietta and she found she could not breathe. There was a horrible howling sound, and she realised it was she who was making it.

Horrific as those last hours of his life must have been, she needed to know everything. Every tiny detail. It was macabre. Like a form of self-torture. But she had to picture it in her mind. The tragic information came from the unlikeliest of sources. A letter from their daughter, the Princess Elizabeth.

After his trial, Charles had been taken from Westminster Hall to the Palace of St James's and had asked to see his children. James had escaped from England and was making his way even now to Holland, but Elizabeth and Henry were brought from Syon House. Immediately after leaving him, Elizabeth set down her recollections. She had titled her testimony: *What the King said to me on the 29th January 1648. The last time I had the happiness to see him.*

She said that he was very grey and his appearance looked wild and neglected. He had kissed her and Henry and given them his blessing; had afterwards turned to his daughter and told her he was glad she had come. He said he wished her not to grieve and torment herself for him for it would be a glorious death that he should die, it being for the laws and liberties of this land. He told her he had forgiven all his enemies and hoped God would forgive them also. He commanded her and the rest of her brothers and sisters to forgive them. He had taken her little brother on to his knee and said, 'Sweetheart, now they will cut off thy father's head.'

He had asked Elizabeth to deliver a last message to Henrietta, saying that his thoughts had never strayed from her and that his love should be the same to the last.

The messenger who brought Elizabeth's letter had also brought a Parliamentary newssheet which reported the King's last moments. His last words were: 'I go from corruptible to an incorruptible crown where no disturbance can be.'

*Sic transit Gloria mundi*, the newssheet gloated. Thus passes the glory of the world.

There were other reports which Harry kept to himself.

On the king's procession through St James's Park to the scaffold at Whitehall, a tall, red-haired figure stepped forward from the crowd to embrace him and kiss his hand. Sir Purbeck Temple claimed that after the execution he received a command from a lady of great honour, a servant of His Majesty, that he should find where the body of the martyred king was kept. She gave a sentry half a crown and visted the open coffin under guard in the king's lodgings in Whitehall.

The one person Henrietta had turned to in every sad, lonely or frightening moment of her life was now the one she could not bear to look upon. Harry. If there was even a grain of truth in the rumour that she had dissuaded Charles from coming to France, not because she believed it prejudicial to his cause, but because she had wanted to be alone with Harry, she could never permit herself to be alone with him again.

She longed only to be completely alone. To have to speak to no one, see no one, to be silent or to weep whenever she chose.

It was Father Philip who suggested she retreat to a Carmelite convent and made all the necessary arrangements. With a black lace veil covering her face, Henrietta left the Louvre amidst more tears, though she herself could not shed one. It was as if she too had died. Grief had made of her a ghost. She moved amongst the living feeling unconnected to them, as if the blood had stopped in her veins. She could talk, walk. But inside she was as cold as the dead.

The small, bare cell became her crypt. She took her meals with the sisters and joined them for mass and silent prayers, but otherwise remained alone. She gave herself up to silent contemplation and solitary prayer. She prayed for her late husband's soul. The girl who had once loved to dance and giggle and chatter with her friends, now spoke to no one but God and Mary for days on end. Her own life was over too, she was sure of that. All that lay ahead for her was poverty and desolation. It was not that she missed Charles as such, not his physical presence. She had grown so used to his not being with her. But he had been her purpose in life. Being a wife to him, helping him win his war, that was in a way her war. The war that was begun in hatred of her and of her faith.

Round and round in her head it went. If Charles had never married her. If he had never loved her. If he had loved less well and more wisely.

If she had never loved Harry.

Now the world had been destroyed. They had destroyed themselves, for love.

It was to her cell that a letter from Charles was delivered, written by him after sentence of death had been passed. The last letter from him she would ever receive. Father Philip brought it but Henrietta refused to see him.

She knew he and Harry had visited several times but she refused to see anyone.

For days she stared at the letter but could not bring herself to open it. For hours she just sat and looked at it, lying on the small table which was the only piece of furniture in the cell. She picked it up, ran her fingers over the wax seal, stroked the paper. It became for her like a holy relic. Just seeing his hand writing was torment to her. She could not believe he had written to her and now he was gone. She did not want the letter to give her comfort she did not believe she deserved, nor to heap more pain on her than she could bear.

She thought of how in the past Harry had always read Charles's letters before she did, and perversely wished he were here now to do so again.

In the end she made herself open it, for Charles's sake. If he had written to her, he wanted her to read what he had written. How could she not obey? It was the last thing she could do for him. And once she had read it, she could not stop reading it. Even when she had learned it off by heart she needed to read it in his writing, to touch the page that his hand had touched to write those words to her. Beautiful words.

*I am content to be tossed, weather beaten and shipwrecked so you may be in safe harbour. I perish but half if you are preserved. In your memory and in your children I may yet survive the malice of my enemies. I must leave you to the love and loyalty of my good subjects. Pity it is that so noble and peaceful a soul as yours should see such suffering. Your sympathy with my afflictions makes your virtues shine as stars in the darkest night.*

Months passed. By and by the routine of convent life and the atmosphere of holy calm restored Henrietta. She still felt detached from life yet she continued to live. It surprised her that she wanted to eat, that she could, that she drew breath, but she did. And through her prayers and contemplation she began to see that the king's death must be God's will. That everything was God's will. And she must accept it, just as it was God's will that she had not died too. Whatever his purpose for her was, he was not done with her yet. Perhaps he wished for her to live out the rest of her life as a nun as she had once threatened Charles she would become, and if that was so, so be it. She was waiting for God to speak to her.

And so when, at the end of the summer, Harry arrived at the convent with Father Philip, this time she did not turn them away, but said she would meet them in the garden.

As Harry walked towards her, she saw through her veil that he was hobbling. The bright sunshine revealed how grey his face was. The sight of him tore at her, penetrated the hard shell she had erected around herself and reminded her that she had a heart, that it was still beating.

'Are you ill?' she asked, very gently, after he had kissed her hand.

'I have gout, ma'am.'

'Does it hurt very much?'

'It feels as if I am walking on broken glass. As if my feet are filled with it.'

'Then let us sit.' She led them to a bench. 'Why did you not say immediately?'

'It is no matter. I have grown used to it.'

She asked after Minette and Prince Charles, realising that there was no longer a need to distinguish him from his father, that he was king now.

'It is on account of your son that I am here,' Harry said, twisting round to face her fully. 'I am come to remind Your Majesty that the great cause which has occupied all your thoughts and energies for the best part of eleven years still has to be served. Your work is not yet done. You have lost one king, but there is another still to fight for.'

# Epilogue

## 1662

It was only the second time Henrietta had returned to England since leaving Oxford for exile in France.

In her fifty-fourth year and still wearing mourning, she was as stylish as ever.

Her black robe had full skirts which swept the ground, and a bodice which came to a fashionable point in front. Its cuffs and high collar were of linen, edged with lace and veiled by fine muslin. Her hair was still dressed in ringlets but on her head she wore a cap with a widow's peak, bordered with black lace, from which fell a black veil.

The outfit was adorned with a single strand of pearls and one jewel in the form of a cross. In cold weather she wore over her shoulders a little mantle of ermine, lined with taffeta, and a black velvet cloak furred with sables.

Though dressed for a funeral, she had travelled to Portsmouth with Harry for a wedding: that of King Charles II to Catherine of Braganza, which was to be celebrated in Domus Dei Church. Henrietta was delighted with the new queen, her Catholic daughter-in-law. In a rose-coloured wedding gown, trimmed with knots of blue ribbons, she was very beautiful, tall and shapely, with large dark eyes and a sweet nature. She and the king were very much in love, and England was in love with them both.

It had not taken the people long to grow weary of Oliver Cromwell's Puritan rule, an austere one which banned Christmas and dancing. It did not take people long to look back with fondness to the days of monarchy, and the rule of the man they now saw as a saintly martyred king.

Henrietta had always preferred to look forward rather than back. She had done what she had thought best at the time. What was done was done. The past was unchangeable. The future was there for the taking. There was no point wondering what might have been.

If.

If Charles had escaped to France. If he had been able to bide his time until he could reclaim his throne. Had he lived, everything might have been very different. The truth is, people love a martyr. Only the dead can become saints and angels, shining paragons with whom those left alive can never compete. The dead are missed and appreciated in a way that the living can never be. England needed to miss its dead king in order to welcome its new one.

Nobody had tried harder than Harry to bring Charles to France. She could not blame or punish him.

The dead will take you with them if they can, claim you for their own. They reach with cold fingers from beyond the grave. And if you let them hold you too long, you die with them, a slow, living death.

Henrietta had lived with the threat of death for long enough. She was not yet ready to die.

You cannot mourn or grieve forever.

You cannot wrap your arms around a memory.

Henrietta had celebrated the restoration of her son at at the Château de Colombes, the gracious mansion Harry had found for them on the outskirts of Paris. She had lived with him there since leaving the convent. She had not wanted ever to return to England's capital. She could not face seeing her ransacked chapels, the ruined palaces from which all Charles's beloved treasures had been pillaged, sold by the Parliamentarians.

But after the Restoration Harry, his hair close-cropped and silver now, had longed to return to the centre of things. He had come back to King Charles II's court as Ambassador Extraordinaire and had been made Earl of St Albans. Henrietta had remained in France where she had expected to live out the rest of her days. But she would not miss her son's marriage.

She arrived in London to find that Harry had restored Somerset House to its former glory. That evening the young people of the court flocked to her elegant rooms where she sat enthroned in black robes on a black velvet chair. Madame la Mère they called her, and they sat for hours listening to the tales she told of all those heroes and villains from what now seemed a bygone age: Buckingham and Strafford, Archbishop Laud and John Pym. She kept them entertained too with stories of the various dogs she had owned. But Henrietta knew very well that these same guests who made her palace ring with their youthful laughter also thrilled to the scandalous notion that the widow of the martyr king who had secretly married her lord chamberlain. According to some, she had a child by Lord St Albans, born sometime in France.

She had come to accept that there would always be rumours about the two of them.

In the morning Harry took her by barge down-river. To Greenwich.

As they stepped ashore Henrietta saw that painters and gilders and gardeners were busy at work, just like once before, when she'd brought Harry to see this house after it was newly built. Now he was bringing her to see how it had been rebuilt, repaired, restored.

It looked as good as new. But the gardens . . .

'They had run wild,' he said. 'It was a wilderness. We have to start from scratch. I commissioned designs from France, based on the ornamental gardens at Fontainebleau and the Louvre.'

He took Henrietta's hand and led her to the front door of the Queen's House. 'All of London is looking to the Louvre for inspiration now,' he said. 'To be French is to be fashionable. Homes are filling with mirrors and French cabinets.'

'No more talk of Papist houses?'

'Plenty. But all admiring.'

Harry's sinecures now brought him an enormous income. He was Commissioner for Prizes, Commissioner for the Coronation, a Justice of the Peace for Middlesex and Surrey, and Governor of Jersey, all of which required no work save for the instruction of his lawyer to collect the fees due to him. He was also paid £1,000 a year for overseeing the Treasury, while income also came in from landholdings in East Anglia, Virginia, and County Antrim. Oatlands had become his by royal grant, together with the water meadows of Byfleet and Weybridge

And the land around St James's was also now leased to Harry. Which is where he took Henrietta next.

Her hand tucked in his arm they walked in the summer sun, stood in the shade of the palace and watched the builders and surveyors at work, digging the foundations of the houses in what would become Jermyn Street and marking with ropes the grand central squares that would become St James's

Square, the centre-piece of their new development, from which would grow the whole of the new west end of London.

'Mansions ranged round grand Parisian squares,' Harry said. 'Like subjects ranged around a throne.' He touched her face. 'The beauty of France, come to England.'

# Postscript

When Henrietta Maria died in 1669 at the age of fifty-nine Henry Jermyn suffered a collapse.

He returned to Paris to oversee her funeral arrangements personally. He followed the funeral train on its way to the ancient Cathedral of St Denis, leaning heavily on the white wand which denoted his position as the queen's lord chamberlain. His hair now close-cropped and grey, he chose to forego the slashed black silk suits he had always worn. He dressed instead in the sackcloth habit of a Capuchin monk, out of homage to the faith and piety of the woman he had loved since his youth.

'I have no tears in reserve,' he said. 'Love has cost me too much.'

# Bibliography & Acknowledgements

This novel would never have been written had it not been for Anthony Adolph's painstaking and devoted research into the life of Henry Jermyn, 1st Earl of St Albans, which formed the basis for his wonderful biography, *Full of Soup and Gold: the Life of Henry Jermyn* (Anthony Adolph, 2006, www.anthonyadolph.co.uk/jermyn.htm). Credit must also go to John Fox for unearthing and illuminating the story of Jane in *The King's Smuggler: Jane Whorwood, Secret Agent to Charles I* (The History Press, 2010).

There are many biographies of Henrietta Maria. By far the best, to my mind, and the two I relied on most heavily for this novel and would recommend to anyone with an interest in Charles I's queen, are Carola Oman's *Henrietta Maria* (Hodder and Stoughton, 1936, and reissues) and Alison Plowden's *Henrietta Maria: Charles I's Indomitable Queen* (Sutton Publishing, 2001). *Letters of Queen Henrietta Maria, Including her Private Correspondence with Charles I* (Mary Anne E. Green ed. Kessinger, 2010) helped me to find Henrietta's voice. Katie Whitaker's *A Royal Passion: The Turbulent Marriage of Charles I and Henrietta Maria* (Weidenfeld & Nicolson, 2010) was published while I was writing this book and made me revise whole sections of it. The most useful biography of King Charles I was Richard Cust's *Charles I: A Political Life* (Longman, 2005), as well as *The Sale of the Late King's Goods* by Jerry Brotton (Macmillan, 2006).

I am indebted to Diane Purkiss for bringing the sights and sounds of the Civil War to life in *The English Civil War: A People's History* (Harper Perennial, 2007). Other valuable source books were *The Art of Courtly Love* by Andreas Capellanus (Columbia University Press, 1941); *The Book of Courtly Love: The Passionate Code of the Troubadours* by Andrea Hopkins (HarperCollins, 1994); *Imagining Sex: Pornography and Bodies in*

*Seventeenth-century England* by Sarah Toulalan (Oxford University Press, 2007); Lucy Worsley's *Cavalier: A Tale of Chivalry, Passion and Great Houses* (Faber & Faber, 2007); *Birth, Marriage and Death Ritual: Religion and the Life-cycle in Tudor and Stuart England* by David Cressy (Oxford University Press, 1997).

For support and patience, thanks as always to my family: Kezia, Gabriel, James, Daniel and Tim. To my agent Broo Doherty for being Madame Peronne to this book. To Rosie de Courcy for being a wonderfully encouraging editor and for providing me with the most beautiful and peaceful place to finish writing. To the staff of the St Moritz Hotel in Trebetherick. Also to Nicola Taplin and Richard Ogle at Random House.

My thanks to Paul Blezard-Gymer, for inspiration, insulation, combobulation – warmth, wit and wisdom, and so much more.